The Pattern Of Fear

The Pattern of Fear

DREW CHAPMAN

MICHAEL JOSEPH
an imprint of
PENGUIN BOOKS

MICHAEL JOSEPH

Published by the Penguin Group
Penguin Books Ltd, 80 Strand, London WC2R 0RL, England
Penguin Group (USA) Inc., 375 Hudson Street, New York, New York 10014, USA
Penguin Group (Canada), 90 Eglinton Avenue East, Suite 700, Toronto, Ontario, Canada M4P 2Y3
(a division of Penguin Canada Books Inc.)
Penguin Ireland, 25 St Stephen's Green, Dublin 2, Ireland (a division of Penguin Books Ltd)
Penguin Group (Australia), 707 Collins Street, Melbourne, Victoria 3008, Australia
(a division of Penguin Australia Pty Ltd)
Penguin Books India Pvt Ltd, 11 Community Centre, Panchsheel Park, New Delhi – 110 017, India
Penguin Group (NZ), 67 Apollo Drive, Rosedale, Auckland 0632, New Zealand
(a division of Penguin New Zealand Pty Ltd)
Penguin Books (South Africa) (Pty) Ltd, Block D, Rosebank Office Park,
181 Jan Smuts Avenue, Parktown North, Gauteng 2193, South Africa
Penguin (Beijing) Ltd, 7F, Tower B, Jiaming Center, 27 East Third Ring Road North,
Chaoyang District, Beijing 100020, China

Penguin Books Ltd, Registered Offices: 80 Strand, London WC2R 0RL, England

First published 2014
This edition published by Penguin Group (Australia) 2014

3 5 7 9 10 8 6 4 2

Designed by Nancy Singer
Cover by Jae Song

Printed and bound in Australia by McPherson's Printing Group, Maryborough, Victoria

A CIP catalogue record for this book is available from the British Library

ISBN: 978-1-405-91726-1

penguin.com.au

MIX
Paper from
responsible sources
FSC® C001695

To the three extraordinary women in my life:
Lisa, Augusta, and Nora

The Pattern of Fear

PROLOGUE

HUAXI TOWNSHIP, SHANXI PROVINCE, CHINA, NOVEMBER 16, 6:42 AM

Hu Mei woke to the sound of firecrackers. Two sets of rattling, rapid-fire explosions cut through the quiet country night, echoed, and then abruptly died. That was the agreed-upon signal—as many packets as the sentries could light in the shortest amount of time—and it meant the police were moving down the one road that led through the narrow, twisting ravine and into Huaxi Township, probably in buses, followed by a pair of jeeps carrying party officials. The officials always stayed in back, out of the line of fire, but nearby, so they could have their pictures taken and claim credit after the police did their dirty work.

These would be prefecture-level officials, Mei thought as she rolled off the foam sleeping pad laid across her makeshift tent; minor party functionaries from Taiyuan, city of the endless steel mills, or maybe even one step up, pompous municipality magistrates from Jinan. Mei didn't care. No matter who they were or where they came from, she hated them with her entire being: mind, heart, soul.

Hu Mei sat on her knees and folded her blanket neatly—she prided herself on her attention to detail, her unhurried tranquility in the face of impending chaos—then stowed it in her backpack. She closed her brown, thirty-two-year-old eyes and took a moment to contemplate the memory of her husband, Yi, the creases of his lopsided smile, gentle lips, the funny flop of black hair that he used to brush across his forehead. Just the briefest thought of him, dead now six months, brought her comfort. The day would be troubled, she knew this, and that was exactly why she started it with a meditation on Yi's face. He was, after all, why she was here in the first place.

The grind and groan of a bus engine brought her back to the present. They were close now, out of the ravine probably, passing the marshy ponds on the edge of town. She crawled from her jury-rigged tent—a bolt of blue plastic stretched between bent sticks—and was hit with the first cold blast of a November dawn. The cold didn't bother her. She had grown up on a farm, had risen before sunrise practically every morning of her entire childhood to feed pigs and chickens and goats. She was a peasant and she knew it, and, like the cold, that didn't bother her either. On the contrary—she was proud of it.

Hu Mei cupped her hands to her mouth and bellowed as loudly as she could: *"Qi lai! Qi lai! Jǐngchá lai le!" Get up, get up! The police are coming!*

In the darkness, Mei could see the other men and women climbing out of the tents that made up their protest city on the trampled barley field, at the edge of the fence that ringed the pesticide factory. Of course no barley actually grew in the field. It was as dead as her husband, poisoned and worthless. Everything in Huaxi was poisoned and worthless, everything except the money that came out of the factory.

"Kuài, kuài," she said, clapping her hands. *Quick, quick!* Most of the protestors—there were eighty-seven in all—were already on their feet, sticks and banners at the ready. Mei knew that none of them had eaten yet, or had tea, and that all of them were cold. She also knew each was ready to lay down his life for the cause. Each had had his land rights taken, forcibly, secretly, and without warning by the party, which had transferred those rights to the factory owners—a consortium of investors from Shanghai—who had then built this monstrosity. And they had all suffered for it. Their fields had shriveled, their pigs had died, and now, worst of all, they and their loved ones were getting sick: breathing sickness, stomach sickness, skin sickness. Mei didn't know the names of the diseases, but she knew those diseases were killing them. The factory was going to kill them all, and no one was going to help them. Not the village party leader; he was fully *fŭ bài*—corrupt—not the township leader, the provincial magistrate, not even the leader of all of China's Communist Party, Xi Jinping himself. They all suffered from *dào dé dún luò*—moral decadence. They were all deaf to the villagers' pleas.

But not for much longer. Not if Hu Mei could help it.

The buses' headlights swept across the ragged protest tents. The air brakes hissed as the buses stopped and their doors folded open. Black-uniformed riot police trundled off the buses and into the field, quickly forming two straight lines, one behind the other. Mei guessed there were about two hundred of them; she could see their batons and shields flashing in the pink of the dawn, but their faces were covered by black neck scarves. Even from across the field, Mei could sense the policemen's confidence. They would sweep across the protest village, smash the tents, batter any villagers who got in their way, then arrest the remainder and haul them off to the provincial jail in Taiyuan. A routine maneuver—the protestors were nothing but peasants. They used firecrackers as warning signals. Firecrackers? That was how backward they were.

Hu Mei suppressed a smile. If the police and the party thought they were simpletons, then so much the better.

Mei slipped a cell phone from her pocket. It was shiny and new, unused, not her old phone, the one the police were tracking, and blocking. This one was a gift from a cousin who worked in Chengdu. He was a quality-assurance manager in a cell phone factory. He had stolen two crates of them, along with SIM cards and a list of anonymous phone accounts, and given them all to Mei, who then handed them out to every like-minded person she knew in the Huaxi Valley. Five hundred cell phones. Five hundred untraceable numbers. Five hundred families and their friends, all waiting for a signal from Mei. She calculated them to be about two thousand people. What the party lackeys didn't understand was that all these villagers, from Huaxi and every neighboring town, felt the same way as Mei—their hearts were bitter. They had been wronged, cheated, ignored.

And here's the other thing the party didn't understand. The villagers—these peasants—they trusted Mei. She and her husband, Yi, had spent a lifetime doing good for them, bringing their sick grandparents soup, helping in the middle of the night when a sow gave birth, clearing the milfoil from their ponds so they could have drinking water. Hu Mei loved helping her fellow villagers—it was in her blood—and they loved her for it.

Her fingers tapped quickly across the tiny keyboard: "*Tóng zhì men. Shí jiān daò le.*" *Comrades. Now is the time.*

She looked across the trampled field at the eyes of the policemen, now visible in the cold morning light. Arrogant. If she were asked, that was how she would describe them: arrogant. But they wouldn't be arrogant for long, because there were two thousand angry peasants waiting for them, awake, hiding in the darkness, gripping an armory's worth of sharpened farm tools.

Hu Mei smiled at the thought of it. And pressed send.

1

NEW YORK CITY, MARCH 24, 9:53 AM

Garrett Reilly did *not* bake that morning, which was unusual. He hadn't dipped into his bag of Hindu Skunk because it was a Tuesday, and new bond issues priced in the market on Tuesdays, usually right at 8:00 a.m., and if you were stoned when the new issues priced you would miss a step, and if you missed a step you would make mistakes, and if you made mistakes you would lose money.

Garrett Reilly hated losing money.

So he was straight, and he was happy about it, which was doubly unusual. Mostly when he was sober he was angry: angry at his parents, his brother, the government, corporations, his boss. Everybody and everything. He considered anger a constant—his equilibrium state. But when he was high, a fuzzy, contented peace settled on his brain as he watched the buy and sell numbers float across his Bloomberg terminal. Stoned, he could ignore the twenty ringing phone lines at his elbow, and he would wander to the large, noisy room's single window and watch the seagulls circle over Rockefeller Park and glide out over the Hudson River, or he would trade video-game tips and stories of botched hookups with his coworkers at the other cubicles. They were all young, horny, indifferent to the wider world if it didn't involve money. Or sex.

But today was different. He had fielded all the calls, had bid on the bonds conservatively, but well, and had made enough money for his firm—Jenkins & Altshuler—to justify his growing salary. That was all run-of-the-mill. Garrett Diego Reilly, two weeks past his twenty-sixth birthday, with a freckled, black-haired, half-Irish, half-Mexican face and the languid drawl of a kid from the slums of Long Beach, California, was a rising star at the firm, a bond trader, probably the best young talent the company had, maybe the best in all of lower Manhattan, so a day of profits was normal. What wasn't normal were the Treasury bond CUSIP numbers scrolling across his screen. T-bonds, as they were called, were long-term, government-issued debt, backed by the full faith and credit of the U.S. Treasury, and there were a lot of them out there—trillions of dollars' worth. They had, by and large, financed the deficit spending of the last two presidential administrations, and accounted for a massive amount of the country's red ink. A CUSIP number—named after the Committee on Uniform Securities Identification Procedures—was a way of tracking every bond and share of stock sold in the United States and Canada. Every T-bond had a nine-digit alphanumeric CUSIP number.

Garrett knew his CUSIP numbers. His memory for numbers was photographic. He could scan a page of new bond issues and then repeat them back, number by number, verbatim, a week later. It was part of the reason Garrett, a janitor's kid, had gotten into Yale. That, and a push from his nagging older brother. It was also part of how he'd landed a job at Jenkins & Altshuler, and then risen to the top of his department. But it wasn't the entire reason. That came from another, related skill: pattern recognition.

Garrett didn't just memorize numbers. He sorted them, ranked them, shifted them into discrete categories, until a pattern emerged. A flow. Until the numbers made sense. Garrett didn't mean to do it—he just did it. Obsessively, 24/7, 365. It was simply how he saw the world, how he interpreted information. It wasn't even that he *found* patterns.

He sensed them.

Just the barest hint of a pattern—in numbers, colors, sounds, smells—would start a tingling feeling at the base of his spine, the faintest electric shock that was somewhere between pleasure and alarm. As the pattern, whatever it happened to be, became clearer to him, the tingling dissipated, melding quickly into hard fact. It was always at that point that he knew he had a recognizable, quantifiable thing in front of him—a sine curve of equity prices, a three-to-one ratio of descending musical notes, a purple-to-green blended fade of bus transfer colors—and he would jot it down or discard it and move on to the next one. It didn't matter if there was purpose or intent behind the patterns; Garrett simply saw them, felt them, *everywhere*, and then recorded them in his brain. Just like that. Every minute of every hour of every day.

And *that* was another reason he smoked marijuana: when he was stoned, the tingling went away, patterns melted into the chaotic white noise of everyday life, and Garrett became, at least momentarily, like everybody else. Information wasn't sorted. It simply *was*. And that was a relief. Getting high was a vacation from Garrett's singular ability.

But today, he wasn't high. He was straight. And he could feel the pattern emerging from the CUSIP numbers on T-bonds being sold all around the world since yesterday, 1:04 a.m., Greenwich Mean Time. The familiar tingle had started just after his second coffee. This one was an almost sensual pulse as he read what must have been the four hundredth CUSIP on a bond selling out of the Middle East. He had read that number five times. And then he let the memory of all the other CUSIP numbers he knew wash over him like a tsunami of digits. And just like that, *boom*, a pattern emerged.

The first six places of a CUSIP were simple—they identified the issuer of the security or bond. The seventh and eighth digits identified the issue—what it was that was being sold; numbers, usually, for equities, letters for fixed income, or bonds. The ninth—and sometimes tenth—digits were what was known as checksums, automatically generated numbers that ensured the rest of the CUSIP was delivered without transmission errors.

Garrett knew the first four digits of U.S. Treasury bond issues cold: 9128. After that, the digits varied according to type of issue: inflation-protected securities were 10. Short maturing T-bills: 08.

But this pattern wasn't about inflation-protected securities or T-bills. It involved Treasury bonds maturing in twenty to thirty years, the longest of the government's debt issues. Someone, somewhere, was selling off T-bonds in small packets, in lots of different markets, all over the world. That alone wasn't so very unusual. The market for Treasury bonds was huge, and buying and selling them was a twenty-four-hour-a-day game.

But two things *were* unusual, and they both caught Garrett's attention.

The first was that all the bonds being sold had been bought at one auction, a dozen years ago, and by one, unspecified buyer.

The second was that if you added up the net worth of all those bonds that had been bought twelve years ago, by that one buyer, it totaled two hundred billion dollars. And even to Garrett, that was a fuckload of money.

2

JENKINS & ALTSHULER, NEW YORK CITY, MARCH 24, 11:02 AM

"Someone is secretly selling off U.S. Treasuries?" Avery Bernstein asked, brushing the few strands of thinning hair off his high, fifty-five-year-old forehead, a hint of annoyance seeping into his raspy, Brooklyn-inflected voice.

"Two hundred billion dollars' worth," Garrett answered. "Half that much is on the market this morning."

"And this is a hunch? Or do you have proof?" Avery rolled his shoulders with irritation under the tweed jacket he habitually wore, even though he was no longer a college professor and could afford whatever style of Italian suit he pleased. To Avery, the tweed was a fuck-you to all the big shots on Wall Street: I'll wear whatever the hell I please, and still make more money than you.

Garrett laid a stack of printed serial numbers on his boss's desk. "I know it," he said. "I checked. Absolutely positive."

"You went through the provenance of each CUSIP number?" Avery asked as he thumbed through the ream of paper. There were easily a hundred sheets there, all in all a few million separate ID numbers. He didn't have time for this.

"Yes. Well, no. I mean. I didn't have to. I scan the CUSIPs when they're issued. And if they show up again, I just . . . I can see the provenance. Not here, on the paper. But in my head. Two hundred billion dollars dumped on the market since midnight yesterday, all from the same auction more than ten years ago." Garrett's voice trailed off as he caught Avery's long, slow-burning, and very dubious stare.

"You read CUSIPs when T-bonds are issued? Why? For fun?"

Garrett shrugged. "Not fun exactly. I just do it sometimes. Especially if the *World of Warcraft* servers are slow . . ."

Avery glared at Garrett. He could still remember the first time he saw the freckled eighteen-year-old slouched in the back of the Dunham Lab lecture hall at Yale, not even bothering to take notes in Avery's advanced number theory class. Nothing pissed Avery off more than a student who thought he was too good for the course material. As a not-so-subtle warning, he made his teaching assistant give Garrett—and only Garrett—a clustering algorithms test at the end of the week, but Garrett's scores were so high as to strain credulity—no one could pick out a sequence in that many number sets. Avery made Garrett take the test again, monitored and in a locked office, but Garrett's scores were even higher the second time.

Humbled, the TA transferred into the art history program the next day. And thenceforth, instead of trying to scare Garrett into paying attention, Avery took him under his wing.

He mentored Garrett for the rest of that year, bumping him up to graduate-level classes when he seemed bored or distracted, making him do research on stock market return predictability and interest rate fluctuations, even taking him out for the occasional Sunday dinner. Avery had seen his share of genius at Yale, but he grew to have a particular fondness for Garrett. Yes, he was arrogant, often obnoxious, and sometimes completely oblivious to other people's feelings, but he was honest. Relentlessly so. And when his hardscrabble roots receded into the background, Garrett could be open, even vulnerable. Over plates of lo mein and broccoli beef they had talked about family, about expectations, about disappointment. He reminded Avery of himself at that age.

Then Garrett's brother died.

Avery still winced at the memory of that bright June morning, the cold fury etched into Garrett's face as he stood in Avery's office and told him he was dropping out of Yale. Avery tried to convince him not to, but Garrett was beyond reason. He packed up and went home to Long Beach that very afternoon, wasting all that brilliance. Avery checked in on him from time to time; he knew that Garrett had eventually gotten his degree in computer science from Long Beach State, and then been hired as a programmer for a gaming company in L.A. Still, it seemed a squandered gift.

So when Avery left Yale for the top job at Jenkins & Altshuler four years later, Garrett was one of his first phone calls. He knew what Garrett was capable of and wanted minds like his on the team. And he'd been right to hire him—Garrett was the firm's best young trader—but recognizing a bunch of CUSIPs and then claiming to see a sell-off of Treasuries on a scale like this was beyond outlandish. It was, well . . .

"And you think you know who is doing this?"

Garrett nodded confidently, arching his back lazily and then plopping his feet onto the coffee table in front of Avery's office couch. He was so bloody fucking sure of himself, thought Avery, amazed that so much arrogance could radiate from someone who had done so little—so far—to earn it. It was still what most annoyed Avery about Garrett. But then again, the older man thought, that was the trait in Garrett that most annoyed everybody. Twice in the last six months Avery had had to talk an older trader out of moving to Stern, Ferguson because Garrett kept bragging about the returns he'd made that day.

If only he weren't so right so much of the time.

"You want to tell me?"

"You don't want to guess?" Garrett asked with a smile.

"Damn it, Garrett, I'm the CEO of a multibillion-dollar international trading—"

"The Chinese," Garrett blurted out, cutting him off.

Avery sputtered to a stop. He took a deep breath. "Explain."

"The bonds were bought twelve years ago at auction through a third-party intermediary out of Dubai. Trading house called Al Samir. The People's Bank of China uses them—"

Avery cut in: "A lot of people use Al Samir. "

"Sure," Garrett continued, "but who else has two hundred billion in cash to throw down on U.S. bonds? In one shot? Maybe three sovereign wealth funds in the whole world."

"Speculative. Means nothing."

"I'm getting there." Garrett smiled, clearly relishing the fact that he knew something Avery didn't. "I'm like a lawyer building a case."

"Fine. Continue," Avery grunted.

"There's been a pattern to the trading. Sixteen different brokerage houses. But none of them are in China, or anywhere in Asia for that matter. If you were Chinese and wanted to dump bonds, but wanted to throw off suspicion . . ."

"You'd use houses anywhere else but your turf," Avery said, finishing Garrett's sentence. "Interesting, but still speculative."

"Trading started at 1:04 a.m., Greenwich Mean Time. Which is nine o'clock in the morning in Beijing. Start of their trading day. Means someone over there woke up, pushed the button, and tracked all day."

Avery nodded, listening carefully, a ball of worry beginning to grow in his stomach. He rubbed his thumb uneasily along the worn teak handrail of his old college desk chair. "You have more?"

"Oh yeah, big time," Garrett said. "The kicker was the sell times. After the CUSIP numbers, it's how I knew something was up. Sell times from every one of the brokerage houses were in a pattern. Timed to the second. I didn't see it at first, but then I just followed them for a while, and bingo, I knew."

"What was the pattern?"

"Four, fourteen, four, fourteen. A repeating loop."

"That means nothing," Avery said, oddly disappointed. Somewhere in the back of his mind he'd wanted Garrett to be onto something.

"To you. And me. But if you're Chinese . . ."

Avery squinted, the awful truth of what Garrett was saying becoming suddenly clear. Avery had spent five years teaching mathematics at the University of Hong Kong, five long years immersed in Chinese culture. He whispered: "Four means death."

"And fourteen means accident. The two most unlucky numbers in China. If you were going to attack your enemy through numbers, and you were way superstitious, you'd sell their bonds every four and fourteen minutes. And the Chinese are crazy superstitious." Garrett smiled, then he shrugged, a touch of humility seeping through. "I had to Google that whole last bit. I really don't know crap about China."

Avery tried to take in the enormity of what he was hearing. The implications of Garrett's speculation were vast.

"If this is true . . ." Avery hissed.

"It's true," Garrett interrupted, rolling up his white shirtsleeves as if to signify how much hard mental work he'd done. "Guaranteed."

"Then you know what it means?"

Garrett nodded enthusiastically. "Flooding the market with U.S. debt will make interest rates skyrocket. Economic panic. And the dollar will crater."

Avery frowned. "You seem happy about this."

"Happy? Not happy? I don't give a shit. But I know it's a way to make money. And that's what we do, right? Make money?"

"You want to bet on a falling dollar?" Avery said slowly, carefully. The ball of worry in his stomach had exploded; a wave of nausea was rising in his throat.

"Fuck *yes*!" Garrett said, popping out of his seat with excitement, arms waving. "I want to short the shit out of it. I mean, if the Chinese are dumping secretly now, that means they're going to dump openly later. Probably pretty soon. So, hell yeah, I want to bet on a falling dollar. Bet the farm."

Avery looked out the window, gazing due west. A plane was on its final descent into Newark Liberty airport. "Garrett, you realize it has the potential to destroy the American economy?"

"But we'll be stinking rich," Garrett said. "So who cares?"

Avery turned to look at the young man, whom he had taught as an eighteen-year-old, nurtured and cared for, and was suddenly overwhelmed by the desire to pack it up and head back to Yale, to give teaching another go-round, because it was clear to him that in his twenty years behind the lectern, he had fallen far short of his goal of imbuing the youth of tomorrow with even the most basic sense of morality.

3

WASHINGTON, D.C., MARCH 24, 4:14 PM

Major General Hadley Kline could barely keep still. His compact, barrel-chested body, which usually twitched and jerked in rhythmic time to his continuous train of hyperactive thoughts, was now a blur of motion. His arms whirled like windmills as his head shook, his thick tuft of black hair bobbing as he circled the long table at the center of the bland conference room in the basement of the Defense Intelligence Agency's Office of Analysis Building. A large, white, unremarkable structure tucked in a corner of suburban Washington, D.C.'s Bolling Air Force Base, the DIA building housed the American military's nexus of all spying, planning, and reconnaissance, and General Kline was the head of the Analysis Directorate. His group's job was to track all of the voluminous information that flowed into the military's intelligence machine and make sense of it. In a nutshell, General Kline was there to figure things out. And he loved doing it.

"First question," Kline barked excitedly in his thick, South Boston accent. "Is it true?"

The table was crowded with two dozen staffers, young men and women from all the different services, all in uniform, scanning laptops and open file folders. Howell, a young Air Force captain from Texas, snapped an answer: "High probability, sir."

"High? How high?" Kline focused in on Howell. "*Certainty* high?"

"Ninety percent, sir."

"How'd we find out?"

"NSA intercept of a phone call to the Treasury Department, sir," a female lieutenant called out from the back of the table. "Made from an unsecured cell phone."

"And the call came from"—Kline stopped briefly to tap on an open laptop set at one end of the table—"Avery Bernstein? I know him, don't I? How do I know him?"

The analysis staffers knew the drill. Kline used his own form of the Socratic method, holding a long, engaged, combative argument—with himself—in front of everyone who had any chance of adding information to The Pile. That's what Kline called the imaginary open box into which his team dropped useful intelligence: The Pile.

A young black Army captain, Caulk, projected a corporate PR photo of Avery Bernstein onto a flat screen. "CEO of Jenkins & Altshuler, a New York trading firm, sir. Was a professor of advanced mathematics at Yale before that. Served on the previous president's Council of Economic Advisers . . ."

"Yes. Right. That's how I know him. We did a deep background on him, didn't we?" The conversation came quickly now.

"We did, sir."

"He was clean?"

"He was, sir."

Kline wheeled again, hands scratching at his neck, as if digging out an unseen mosquito bite. "How'd they react at Treasury?"

A broad-shouldered captain shouted from the back: "No official word—"

Kline interrupted angrily: "Official word is for fucki—"

The captain didn't let his boss finish: "—but my inside source said that the advanced warning will allow them to buy up the excess supply in the market before word leaks out. Sir."

Kline smiled. He didn't mind getting interrupted. He despised the pompous regimentation of the armed services. Titles, saluting, pay grades—in Kline's experience, they were all impediments to productive, creative thinking. He was in it for one thing, and one thing alone: the thrill of the hunt.

"Okay," Kline growled, pausing to look out at his assembled team. "The big question? Why? Why'd the Chinese dump a crapload of our Treasuries in secret?"

Captain Howell spoke first: "Annual Taiwan arms sale bill comes up in

Congress in two weeks. This is a warning shot off our bow. Stop selling F-16s to their enemy."

"Not impossible, but conventional," Kline barked. "Anyone have an idea with balls on it?"

Captain Howell reddened as muffled laughter echoed in the room.

A female lieutenant colonel stood up. "Sir. Malicious mischief. To keep us off balance while they make deals with the rest of the world."

Kline shrugged. "More ballsy. But two hundred billion is a wicked lot of mischief."

The broad-shouldered captain broke in. "Sir, aren't we overlooking the most reasonable explanation? The Chinese no longer think U.S. Treasuries are a good investment, so they're getting rid of them. They're doing it in secret in order not to upset the world markets. Or make us angry. We've been waiting for the Chinese to dump our Treasuries for a while now."

Kline stopped pacing and nodded thoughtfully. "Yes, Captain Mackenzie, that is the most probable explanation." He scanned the room. "Are we in consensus?"

There was a general nodding of heads. Kline waited. And then a sly smile cracked the right side of his rugged face. A young, black-haired Army captain rose up from the back of the conference table. She stood ramrod straight, lithe, and naturally athletic, her intense blue eyes focusing in on Kline. Good Lord, she was beautiful, Kline thought, quickly reminding himself that he was happily married, and that coming on to a military subordinate was punishable with life-ruining jail time.

"Yes, Captain Truffant?" he asked. "You have an alternate theory?"

"Yes sir, I do," Alexis Truffant said quietly but surely. "It is only a theory."

"For now, everything we say is theoretical. Speak."

"Sir, I think . . ." She hesitated. "I think China just declared war on us."

The intakes of air around the room were audible. And so was the silence that followed. Kline nodded without saying anything, still staring at Alexis Truffant's sparkling blue eyes. She was physically beautiful, yes, but she was also in possession of the ability to think logically and independently, no matter what the situation, or how intense the pressure. To Kline, that was *true* beauty. It was why she was here.

She continued: "I just think it's a war we've never seen before."

• • •

Kline caught up with Alexis as she waited for the elevator back to her office on the third floor. "Captain Truffant, walk with me."

"Yes sir."

Alexis turned and quickly fell in step with General Kline. "You want to query me on my war thesis? I have reasons that I think—"

"No. I agree with you." Kline cut her off. "Selling our Treasuries in the shadow market is as close to a declaration of war as you can get these days. Even if we've been expecting it. And I also agree that it will be a war that we don't really understand."

"Oh, I, I . . ." Alexis stammered in surprise, immediately regretting it, waiting for her boss to jump all over her. She'd been with Kline long enough—two years now—to know he brooked no hesitation or indecision. He wanted the people working for him confident, determined, and forceful—even if they were wrong. But instead of chiding her, he shook his head quickly.

"Was it Bernstein who spotted this?"

"No sir, a subordinate in his office."

"We have a name?"

"Garrett Reilly. Twenty-six years old. Bond trader."

"Twenty-six? He performed a pretty spectacular feat of intuitive mathematical investigative work."

"He did, sir."

"We know anything else about him?"

"His name is on the lease on a two-bedroom apartment in lower Manhattan. He's in an impressive tax bracket for a twenty-six-year-old. Yale dropout. Graduated Long Beach State with a computer science and math degree."

"Dropped out of Yale to go to Long Beach State? Shows a distinct lack of judgment."

"Dematriculated Yale two days after his brother was killed . . . in Afghanistan."

Kline pulled up short and stared at Alexis. She continued: "Marine Lance Corporal Brandon Reilly. KIA at Camp Salerno, June 2nd, 2008. Sniper round to the neck."

Kline said nothing and, for once, didn't move. Alexis watched him, knowing exactly what gears were turning in her superior's head. After ten long seconds, Kline nodded slowly, almost imperceptibly. "Garrett Reilly? You think he could be the one?" The question hung in the air. "*For Ascendant?*"

Alexis Truffant had asked herself the same question when she first glanced at Garrett Reilly's file two hours before. She had studied the young man's picture, his handsome, boyish face, blue eyes, the sullen, almost arrogant smirk on his lips; she had run his brief work and education history through the brute logic processing of her own extremely ordered brain. They'd been looking for someone for more than a year, with no success, and the clock was ticking; funding for the project was about to run out. And so she answered her boss, couching her response as carefully as possible, because Alexis Truffant was, at heart, intensely risk averse: "A distinct possibility, sir."

Kline stared at his subordinate, and Alexis knew he was looking for some trace of doubt on her face, some hint of reservation. The Army was a quagmire of double-talk and hedged bets. So she took a deep breath and said it again: "Distinct possibility."

Kline nodded, wheeled, and started to walk away. He barked over his shoulder: "You know the drill, Captain. Get to it."

"On it, sir," she said, already running for the elevator.

4

NEW YORK CITY, MARCH 24, 9:27 PM

Garrett sat at a table in the back of McSorley's, near the bathrooms, where it smelled more like stale urine than stale beer, but he didn't care because he was with his friends, and the three of them had already plowed through four pitchers of half-and-half and six shots of tequila, and anyway, the back afforded him the best view of all the other half-wits in the crowded East Village bar, and Garrett loved casting scattershot aspersions. Like the four young, gray-suited hedgies at the window, singing an off-key rendition of that stupid Journey song they played to end *The Sopranos*—he could really hate on them.

"Fucking hedge-fund guys," Garrett growled between sips of beer. "Look at those assholes. Hedge funds are a Ponzi scheme. How can people not see that?"

Mitty Rodriguez, five foot four and two hundred pounds of squat, Puerto Rican gaming programmer, and Garrett's best friend, raised her beer in a salute. "Why don't you get off your sorry ass and hit one of them? Knock his teeth out."

"Maybe I will," Garrett said, sizing up the biggest of the hedgies: six foot two, muscled, looked like he might have been a lacrosse player.

Shane Michelson shook his head. The lanky junior currency analyst with bad skin was by no means a fighter. "Can we please not get kicked out of another bar, Gare? Please. I'm running out of happy-hour spots."

"Yeah. Sure. Fuck 'em. I'm going to make more money this week than they'll make in their entire lives."

Shane shook his head disbelievingly. "How you gonna do that?"

Garrett scanned the young women standing at the bar. One caught his attention: striking, tall, olive-skinned. "Dollar's gonna tank. And I'm going to ride it all the way to the bottom."

Shane laughed. "Garrett. I'm a currency analyst. The dollar shows no sign of tanking."

"Maybe you're not a very good currency analyst."

Mitty gave out a squeal of delight. "Ooo. Bitch slap. Catfight, catfight!"

"Fuck you, Garrett." Shane looked away, pissed. Then his curiosity got the better of him. His friends knew better than to discount Garrett's boasts entirely; they had a nasty habit of coming true. "What do you know? Tell me."

"T-bond dump. It's coming. Sovereign wealth fund. Flooding the market. Carnage on the horizon."

"I didn't see excess Treasuries on the block."

"Federal Reserve probably buying up the excess. So no one panics. Hey, see that girl at the bar?" Garrett nodded. "I think she's checking me out."

"Who would want to kill the dollar? Is it the euro zone? They're our friends."

"She's a hottie."

"Russia? They don't hold enough of our debt. An Arab state? We'd nuke them. The Japanese? It would sink their economy."

"Can we not talk about money for a change?" Mitty said. "I did a forty-man raid on Kel'Thuzad today. Almost took the Citadel, but that pissant Nefarian screwed me . . ."

Garrett smiled. He and Mitty were kindred souls—tech-obsessed gamers who lived as much online as they did in the real world. They'd met in a first-person shooter chat room and become best friends long before they ever set eyes on each other. Virtual life was what bonded them. That, and a deep-seated love of stirring up trouble. Mitty was the only person Garrett knew who could piss off as many people as he could, and do it faster as well. Some nights it seemed like there were entire neighborhoods of New York City where the two of them were no longer welcome.

Shane closed his eyes for a moment, then opened them in surprise. "China?"

Garrett stood up, straightened his loosely hung tie, and smiled. "I'm going home with her tonight."

Shane shook his head: "No way. The yuan is tied to the dollar. We sink, China sinks. Their exports to us will go in the toilet. Why would they do it?"

Garrett stared at Shane. He was drunk, and tottering, but even tottering Garrett radiated an arrogant self-assurance. "I haven't quite figured that part out yet. But the Chinese are sitting on 2.7 trillion dollars in cash, so I'm guessing they'll do just fine. See you guys tomorrow."

He waded across the crowded bar, weaving unsteadily between tables. He stopped short when he reached the girl at the bar. One of the hedgies was chatting her up. Garrett scowled—fucking hedgies—then elbowed his way between them. "Dude. Sorry. I was talking to her already. You'll have to go back and sing some more with your friends."

The hedgie—it was the lacrosse player, and he was big, for sure—shot Garrett an angry look. "You out of your mind? I was talking to her. Fuck off, buddy."

Garrett smiled at the young woman. She didn't seem particularly impressed with either of them. Garrett leaned close: "What I meant to say was, in my head I've been talking to you for the last hour. We've been having this amazing conversation. But then this joker interrupted us, and I knew I had to come to your rescue."

The young woman snorted a half laugh. The lacrosse player grabbed Garrett by the shoulder. "I'm gonna crack your fucking head in, asshole."

Garrett let himself be turned around. He looked the lacrosse player up and down. "Lemme guess. Duke. Econ major. Varsity lacrosse. Third year at Apogee Capital Group?"

The lacrosse player gaped. "How the fuck did you know that? You been stalking me?"

Garrett smiled. "Why would I bother stalking *you*? No, it was easy. Apogee Capital is four blocks away. But they're down seventy percent on the year. Your suit is a knockoff from Hong Kong, not Kiton from Italy, and your shoes are at least two years old, which, for a hedgie, is ancient. They were hiring three years ago, but not now, so you're a bottom-rung guy and you've stayed at the bottom, but you got the job because Apogee's CEO played lacrosse at Duke, which is where your accent places you, and only a hedgie loser would sing Journey at the top of his lungs in a crowded bar."

The next thirty seconds were a blur to Garrett. He knew for sure the hedgie took a swing at him, and also that he was ready, so he ducked left and drove his right fist into the hedgie's solar plexus. He'd used that move on the streets of Long Beach more times than he could count. He wasn't the strongest guy out there, but he was quick and he was an experienced street fighter. He kicked hard at the doubled-over hedgie, then raced toward his three hedgie friends, who were crossing the bar to join in. Garrett shot a kick at the first one's knee, putting him out of commission, then shoved the second one into the third, the two of them tumbling onto a table, sending pitchers of beer and glasses shattering to the ground. By this time the entire bar was in motion, some people running for the exits, others trying to get a better view. A few girls were shrieking as Mitty rumbled across the room to get a couple of licks in—she never missed a chance to throw a punch—but she was too late, because the hedgies were down for the count and Garrett was already out the door and onto the street, looking for an alley to sprint down and resigning himself to the fact that he was going to sleep alone tonight.

Garrett ran for three blocks, due east, figuring the hedgies would never find him, then slowed for half a block and vomited into a trash can. He wiped his mouth clean, still tasting the hot dog he'd had for lunch but feeling better, and was cutting across Tompkins Square Park when out of the corner of his eye he saw someone following him, about a hundred yards away. He hurried across the park without looking back, then tucked around the corner of a building on Avenue B and Tenth. He waited, thirty seconds at most, then jumped out as the person who was following him turned the corner. He grinned. "Couldn't stay away, could you?"

It was the girl from the bar.

5

LOWER EAST SIDE, MANHATTAN, MARCH 24, 11:01 PM

Garrett ordered two coffees, a plate of fries, and a bowl of avgolemono soup. "Two spoons for the soup," he told the waitress at the Greek diner. "The lady will probably want to share."

The waitress shrugged and shuffled off to the kitchen, passing a series of travel-agency posters with pictures of whitewashed houses on stark Aegean islands. The lone other customer at the diner's counter sipped his coffee and read a paperback.

The girl from the bar shook her head. "Is that your dinner?"

"Already barfed up lunch," Garrett said. "So, yes."

"I'm beginning to worry about your long-term health prospects."

"Are we planning on knowing each other long-term?"

The girl stared at him. "You always get into fights at bars?"

"I've been in a few."

"You're pretty good at it. Fighting, that is."

"I'll take that as a compliment. Why'd you follow me?"

"To see if you were okay."

"And if I wasn't, you were going to help me how, exactly? Call 9-1-1?"

"How'd you know where that guy worked? The guy in the bar?"

Garrett shrugged. "You heard my explanation. The clues were there if you pay attention."

"But most people don't pay attention?"

"That's right, most people don't. But let's talk about you, not me. For instance, I don't think you wanted me to notice you. I think you were spying on me."

"Why would I do that?"

The waitress brought two coffees. Garrett dumped sugar and cream in his. He stirred the coffee and thought about the question. He studied the girl from the bar, her face, her clothes, then went back to stirring his coffee. After about thirty seconds of thinking, he said, "Two possibilities. One, you're desperate to fuck me. But even at my most arrogant I would say that's remote. I don't get that vibe off of you, which is a shame, because I could rock your world if you gave me the chance."

"And two?"

"This morning my boss called the Treasury Department and told them I figured out the Chinese were dumping U.S. bonds in a big way. The Treasury Department told the CIA or the NSA or some such spook agency—no, wait, gotta be military, you seem military, the way you sit, your seriously out-of-style haircut—and they sent you here to figure out if I was an insane person or actually knew what I was talking about."

Captain Alexis Truffant tried not to let the surprise show on her face. Garrett had made her in less than five minutes. And with astonishing accuracy.

Garrett smiled at her. "I'll tell you what. How about we forget I ever mentioned possibility number two, we pretend number one is right, and you and I head back to my apartment, which is just around the corner?"

Alexis sipped her coffee. "How did you know?"

Garrett leaned back, shrugged. "Like you said, I pay attention. It's the only thing that makes sense. The dollar didn't sink today, so Avery must have made that phone call. The Fed bought up the T-bonds. You and whatever agency you work for caught wind of this. Or maybe you listened in. Avery doesn't have some secure phone line. And that freaked you out, 'cause what China did could be seen as an act of war, right? I mean, it's pretty aggressive. Maybe there's a million Chinese infantrymen landing at Zuma Beach right this second. All doing kung fu in the sand, like in a Tarantino movie. That would fucking rock, right? Anyway, I wouldn't have put any of it together if you hadn't followed me, but I should have guessed, because you were watching me pretty intensely at McSorley's, and, honestly, I've never, ever gotten lucky at that bar. The chicks there just want to drink. And none of them are as hot as you."

Alexis leaned forward. "The act-of-war idea. You just came up with it? Right now?"

The waitress brought a plate of fries and a bowl of avgolemono soup and set them down on the table. Garrett fork-speared a fry, dunked it in ketchup, then looked at Alexis.

"You have a name?"

"Alexis Truffant."

"Army, right? First lieutenant? Maybe captain?"

"The latter."

"Impressive. Shooting up the ranks. You save someone's life? Cap a bunch of bad guys in Fallujah?"

Alexis shook her head no. "I just show up for work on time."

"Yeah, right," Garrett snorted dubiously. "So it's the act of war you're interested in? You work for some kind of military intelligence division?"

"I'm not at liberty to say."

"Gimme a fucking break, *Captain* Truffant." Garrett spit out her rank. "You think I give a shit what bunch of monkeys you work for?"

"I'm sure you don't. But I can't tell you, all the same."

Garrett laughed. "Military people. All the same. Rules. Regulations. Just following orders. Just killing people. Launch Predator drones. Whoops. Collateral damage. Whoops. Friendly fire. Just remember, you followed me. I didn't spy on you. I didn't go knocking on your door."

Alexis watched as Garrett snarled, stabbed more french fries and chewed them angrily. His face was suddenly flushed. "Is this about your brother?"

This time it was Garrett's turn to fall silent. He stared hard at the food on the table in front of him, jaw set, lips quivering. He stood abruptly, rocking the table and spilling his cup of coffee. He glared down at Alexis, who was still seated.

"You know nothing about me. About my brother. About my life. Nothing." He threw a twenty-dollar bill on the table and marched out of the diner.

6

BETHESDA, MARYLAND, MARCH 24, 11:55 PM

General Kline's computer screen in his home office showed that the incoming call was from an unsecured cell phone. It was five minutes before midnight. He had been reading through a packet of intelligence briefs on Chinese intentions toward Taiwan, and now he couldn't fall asleep. There were 250,000 People's Liberation Army regulars sitting on the coast of mainland China, ready to make the ninety-mile boat ride to unite the two Chinas. And the U.S. Pacific Fleet was not far away. He answered on the second ring.

"Kline here."

"I'm calling from my cell phone. It's a personal line." It was Alexis. Kline could hear the street sounds of New York City in the background. She was using no armed services formalities—no *yes sirs* or *no sirs*—as he had taught them to do when in the field.

"Understood."

"I met him."

"You talked to him?" Kline was surprised. "Your directive was to not make contact . . ."

"I had no choice. He figured out who I was pretty quickly."

"Okay. So be it. Give me the rundown."

"Angry. Very. Aggressive. Confrontational. Unafraid."

Kline pulled out a notebook and scribbled down what she told him. She would be insightful—Alexis Truffant could read people. It was part of what made her so valuable to Kline. "Unafraid how?"

"He got into a bar fight with four guys. All bigger than him."

"Who won?"

"He did. Handily."

"Okay. I guess I like that."

"He's also smart. Observant. He pegged who I was almost immediately. And who I worked for. And how I knew about him. With a minimum of clues."

"No shit?" Kline said, a smile creasing his face. "He knew our company name?"

"No. Generalities. But he was close. Very close. About me. About how the information was transferred. And why. He even guessed at the thesis you and I talked about in the hallway. About why this was happening."

"He knew the country and why they might be doing it?"

"Yes. And he clearly had just come up with the idea on the spot. His ability to detect underlying patterns is off the charts."

"What else?"

"Arrogant. Emotional. Volatile. He likes to drink. And he likes women. A lot."

Kline chuckled. He could only imagine how Garrett Reilly must have come on to Alexis. He would have paid to see that. "I like to drink. And I like women."

"Then the two of you will get along great." Kline could hear an edge in her voice. He ignored the attitude—he deserved that one.

"Okay. He could be a match. Any drawbacks?"

There was a brief silence on the line. Kline could hear an ambulance somewhere in the New York night. "Yes," Alexis said, "and it's a big one."

"Lay it on me."

"He hates the United States military. With a passion."

7

MOFFAT COUNTY, COLORADO, MARCH 25, 8:55 AM

Matt Sawyer downshifted his Ford F-150 pickup truck into second gear to climb around the last switchback of Colorado County Road 55 before he approached the mine. To his right was a thousand-foot drop down Henderson Canyon, lined with pine trees. To his left was the jagged flank of Tanks Peak, still snowcapped, clouds breaking against its summit on their journey east across the country. It was beautiful, but Sawyer didn't care. He took a deep breath, gunned the engine, and passed the last stand of trees before the fenced-in parking lot.

The first thing he saw were the half dozen men holding homemade signs standing in a knot by the edge of the lot. They'd been there three weeks ago, when Sawyer started the job, and they were still there today. They wore hard hats and lined denim jackets. They turned toward the sound as his truck rumbled past, and Sawyer could see the lifeless despair in their eyes. They were protesting, but their hearts were no longer in it. One man shook a sign, and Sawyer read it briefly: "Save Our Mine. Save Our Jobs." Yeah, Sawyer thought, good luck with that.

The next thing he saw as he parked near the mine's cyclone fence were the armed guards watching the protestors. There were about forty of them, some with rifles, others with handguns tucked into their holsters, all wearing visible Kevlar vests. They wore sunglasses and baseball caps, each man buff and anonymous-looking. That's a bit of overkill, thought Sawyer. Who the hell would mess with *one* of those guys? But *forty*? Good Lord.

Sawyer grabbed his wallet and work box and jumped out of the truck. He flashed his contractor ID to a particularly hostile-looking guard at the gate, and was halfway to the main mine building when McAfee, in his tailored gray suit, strode out to meet him. Sawyer couldn't remember if McAfee had ever told him his first name—probably not—and hell, Sawyer didn't really care to know it, anyway.

"Sawyer, good morning, how are you?" McAfee said, shaking his hand. As usual, McAfee wore nothing over his suit jacket despite the high-altitude cold. Sawyer thought he might actually be a robot.

"I'm okay, I guess," Sawyer said, lying.

He opened his mouth to say more but McAfee cut him off. "Good. Let's get this over with." He walked quickly to the mine-shaft elevator entrance, a small concrete blockhouse with a single, rusting iron door. Sawyer frowned, then followed. He had maybe two minutes to give McAfee one last pitch—somehow, he'd hoped to do it aboveground. The iron door was open, and the elevator was waiting for Sawyer. He stepped inside. McAfee stepped in with him. "I'll inspect with you, if you don't mind?"

That wasn't really a question, Sawyer thought, was it? He said, "No. Please do."

Sawyer closed the gate, keyed the winch engine, and started the elevator's descent into the mine. The moment the car slipped below the surface the two men were surrounded by darkness and by sound: the mechanical grind of the cables straining overhead, and the wind being displaced below them, as they dropped three thousand feet into the earth. Dim yellow light illuminated their faces and not much else.

Five minutes later the elevator stopped with a low crunch as they reached the main shaft of the mine. Sawyer opened the gate and stepped out. He loved being inside mines. It was still a thrill for him, one he'd probably never get over: dark, strange, the smell of earth, the heat that grew as you descended. Other people got claustrophobic, but not him. He paused, took a breath, and turned to McAfee. It was now or never.

"A lot of molybdenum left in these seams," he said.

"I'm sure there is, Mr. Sawyer."

"Worth a lot of money. Maybe a billion dollars."

McAfee squinted in the dim lamplight. Sawyer could tell he didn't like being underground. He was trying to control his breathing, control his panic. "I wouldn't know," McAfee said.

"The U.S. used to produce a quarter of the world's supply of molybdenum. Now maybe ten percent. Without this mine that will drop to five. We'll become a net importer of the stuff."

McAfee fixed Sawyer with his most lawyerly stare. Sawyer bit his lip and continued: "It's a rare element. It's vital. We use it in heat-resistant alloys—you know, for fighter planes, rocket engines. All kinds of high-tech stuff. It's damn valuable."

"Mr. Sawyer," McAfee said curtly. "Please check the detonators now."

Sawyer winced, then nodded. The conversation was officially over. He walked the length of the shaft. There were five separate branches, tributary seams that led off from the main one. Sawyer carefully checked the detonators, explosives, and cables at each spot in the mine. Everything was secure. As usual, he'd done an excellent job, even if it broke his heart to do it. He returned to McAfee, standing by the elevator, twenty minutes later.

"Good to go," Sawyer said.

"Then let's get the fuck out of here," McAfee said. It was the first time Sawyer had ever heard him use a profanity.

They rode up the elevator in silence. Sawyer stopped the car halfway up and primed the explosive he'd rigged in the elevator shaft. When it blew, the only channel into the mine would be destroyed. It would take a new owner many years and many millions of dollars to get back in here. In fact, it might just be impossible. That's what McAfee had told him the new owners wanted when they hired him: Make it impossible to get back down here. Sawyer shook his head at the memory. Why had he agreed to this?

McAfee bolted from the elevator the moment it reached the surface. Sawyer lingered a moment, then shut the door and walked to the outer edge of the farthest mine building, a low-slung brick building where he had rigged the blasting control panel yesterday. McAfee joined him, this time accompanied by two bulky, gun-toting guards. Sawyer asked one of the guards to put out the first warning. The guard barked into a walkie-talkie. Sawyer armed the control panel.

"Put out the second warning, please," he instructed the guard, who broadcast it into the walkie-talkie.

Sawyer glanced over his shoulder. The protestors were inching closer to the fence that surrounded the mine, knowing what was about to happen. A phalanx of guards inside the fence moved to block their view. Sawyer turned one last time to McAfee.

"I just don't understand," he said, emotion creeping into his voice. "Why would a new owner buy a mine for a hundred million dollars and then destroy it? Can someone, somewhere, explain that to me?"

McAfee looked serenely unperturbed. "Mr. Sawyer. You and I, we are employees. We are hired once, and if we want to be hired again, we do our jobs without question. The owners of this mine have their reasons. I do not care what they are, and neither should you. My records indicate you are being paid $213,000 for your demolition services. That is twice your initial bid. If you want the remainder of your fee, then you should push that button. And push it now. I have a flight to catch."

Sawyer put his thumb on the red button that would send an electric pulse down the blasting wire to the detonator caps, heating the explosive to charge level and destroying the Henderson Canyon Molybdenum Mine. He thought he heard someone yell "Don't do it!" from the parking lot. But maybe not. He pressed the detonate button. There was a faint rumble, like distant thunder. The ground under his feet shook, pebbles dancing on the dirt. Pine trees above him swayed, and then were still.

And that was it. The mine was obliterated.

The protestors in the parking lot turned despondently away from the fence and climbed into their cars. Sawyer watched them go.

McAfee handed him a piece of paper and smiled. "So, Mr. Sawyer, I trust we'll meet again on the next one. If there is a next one."

Sawyer looked down at the piece of paper. It was a check, made out to Matt Sawyer, for $58,500.

Sawyer grimaced and thought: *What the hell have I done?*

8

NEW YORK CITY, MARCH 25, 5:48 AM

Garrett woke up alone in his airy, fourth-floor walkup apartment Wednesday morning, hungover and annoyed; first and foremost at Avery, for calling the Treasury Department and spilling the beans about the bonds. To Garrett's mind, Avery had broken the first rule of the finance game—don't leave money on the table. But Garrett knew Avery well, knew that he was by nature conservative, and he could forgive his old professor his weakness on that front. After all, Garrett reasoned as he made a cup of instant coffee, pulled on a new pair of slacks, and took a quick, satisfying bong hit, if he'd really wanted to make the big score he should have kept the news to himself and shorted the dollar on his own. With the leveraging power of a new currency derivative he'd been toying with, Garrett could have easily parlayed his guess about the Chinese into a profit of $40 million for the firm in less than a week.

But he hadn't done it, and Garrett knew part of the reason he hadn't was vanity. Deep down inside he wanted to tell someone—someone of importance—that he'd figured it out, that he'd caught a sovereign wealth fund manipulating the global markets before anybody else had. He was proud of himself, and he wanted the world to know, and to celebrate him. Which brought him to the second person he was annoyed with: Captain Alexis Truffant.

Here again he was of two minds. On the one hand, he was furious that she had brought up his brother, used a cheap psychological trick to get a rise out of him. Why she would want to get a rise out of him he hadn't figured out yet. But he would. And how dare she—and her nameless bureaucratic spy agency—go digging around in his past? In his life? What business was it of theirs? The idiocy of not telling him things, the pompous secrecy, their air of importance, all of it drove him to distraction. It was everything that was wrong with the armed forces in this country. It was the same shroud of secrecy that he had encountered when he tried to find out about his brother's death in Afghanistan. The same stonewalling, the same cheap use of the national security card. The memory of the hours he spent on the phone with the Armed Services Bureau of Records, trying to get a clear story as to who had actually shot the bullet that cut through his brother's neck, made his stomach churn. Why hadn't they done an analysis of the slug? Couldn't it have been friendly fire? There had been Army Rangers in the vicinity at the time of the shooting.

He could feel the acid pooling in his gut. He hated them. All of them, even the cute, young ones like Truffant.

And yet, he was also secretly proud. Proud that they—whoever they might actually be—had thought enough of his analysis to investigate him. The big bad federal government had come after him, Garrett Reilly, a junior bond trader working out of a cubicle in lower Manhattan. He liked that. He liked that he could throw stones that caused ripples in the giant lake that was the nation's intelligence-gathering bureaucracy.

Garrett walked the twenty blocks south and west to Jenkins & Altshuler and still got there by 6:30, half an hour earlier than anyone else in the office. He checked the overnight London Interbank Offered Rate (the LIBOR, the rate used by banks when they loaned each other money) and the values of the euro, yen, and yuan. He scanned the prices on intermediate-grade corporate bonds that had been issued overnight. Mostly he eyed the price of the dollar, keeping a tracking window open on his Bloomberg terminal, looking for even the slightest hint of a move. But none came. The dollar held steady across the board, against all other currencies. Garrett swilled more coffee. At 7:30 he jogged up one flight of stairs to the twenty-third floor and sat in the chair outside of Avery Bernstein's office. Liz, his redheaded, middle-aged secretary, was already there, answering the phone. Garrett smiled at her, but she ignored him; then he checked the time on his cell phone, and waited. Avery Bernstein, tweed jacket draped over his shoulder and a *Wall Street Journal* tucked under his arm, walked in two minutes later. Garrett popped out of his seat.

"I don't understand why you called the Treasury Department . . ."

"Garrett—"

"You destroyed any chance we had of riding a down trend. If the dollar—"

"Garrett!"

"—crashes now we'll have no advance warning and we'll be—"

"Shut up!"

Garrett fell silent. Normally, when people told him to shut up, Garrett hit them. But he couldn't hit his boss. And, anyway, he liked Avery. A lot. Thought of him—sometimes—as the father he'd never had.

"Come into my office." Avery disappeared into his office. Garrett followed and Avery shut the door behind him, then sat at his desk. Garrett could see lower Manhattan out the window behind Avery, a writhing landscape of miniatures: people, cars, and helicopters, all specks in the distance.

"Sit down. Say nothing."

They sat in silence for what felt, to Garrett, like five minutes, but in reality was more like thirty seconds. Avery booted up his computer and tucked away his briefcase.

"You have stumbled upon something very serious . . ."

"I didn't stumble on it. I did the resear—"

"Shut. *The fuck.* Up." The tension in Avery's voice made the words crackle. Garrett pressed his teeth together. Avery's eyes scanned the walls and desktops of the office, as if searching for uninvited guests. Or, Garrett suddenly realized, listening devices. A chill ran down Garrett's neck.

Finally, Avery looked at him. "This is what I will say to you. And it is *all* I can say to you." Avery fixed Garrett with a long, unhappy stare. "Are you listening?"

"Yes."

"This is not you buying a Texas muni bond on the cheap. Or me trying to talk you out of quitting Yale. This is big. This is scary. *Bigger and scarier than you can imagine.*"

There was silence in the room. Then Avery said, "What did I just say to you?"

"That this is big. And scary. Bigger and scarier than I can imagine."

"You have learned how to listen. Good. So. I have been contacted by people. People I cannot name. And they have told me, in no uncertain terms, that you are to keep the information you have gleaned to yourself. You are to say nothing. To no one. Now. And forever. Is that also clear?"

Garrett started to reply, to argue that he didn't give a shit what the military or the government wanted him to do, but then he caught a glimpse of the flat, worried expression on Avery's face, and thought better of it. He nodded a yes.

"It's clear," Garrett said.

"Okay. Go back to work."

Garrett stood, went to the door. Avery called after him. "Garrett, one other thing." Garrett turned, and watched his boss. Avery was wincing slightly, as if pain were suddenly radiating through his body. Garrett had known Avery for eight years, and understood that he was a worrier, through and through, but he'd never seen his old professor look quite so afraid.

"Please," Avery said, swallowing hard. "Be careful."

9

JENKINS & ALTSHULER, NEW YORK CITY, MARCH 25, 8:32 AM

The bond trading room was abuzz with chatter and ringing phones. Garrett sat at his desk and tried to focus on his work. The phone rang, he answered, and tried to give coherent responses, but his mind was elsewhere.

Be careful. Say nothing.

Why was this so big? Were the Chinese really at war with the United States? He had made that claim to Captain Truffant almost as a dare. He checked online sites—the *New York Times,* the AP wire, Google News—and then foreign sites as well—the BBC and *Times* of London. There was no mention of hostilities between the U.S. and China. Anywhere. Not even some minor diplomatic incident, a trade dispute or a political prisoner jailing that threatened to escalate into something more serious.

He forced himself not to think about it. He bought and sold bond futures for the next four hours, but he wasn't sharp. He was hungover, a little stoned, and now tense and disoriented. He ended the morning session down $43,000.

At twelve-thirty he took his usual fifteen-minute lunch break and went downstairs to grab a falafel from Abu Hasheem's street cart, which was always parked a block north of his office. Garrett liked Hasheem. The falafel vendor was from Lebanon but was a fast convert to all things American. He was a diehard Knicks fan. Garrett teased him about this. Garrett was a Long Beach boy—he had spent his life following the Lakers.

Garrett paused as he stepped out of the lobby of his building, on the corner of John and William streets, and stood for a moment to take in the sounds and smells of lower Manhattan. A taxi honked. A truck rumbled past. The March light couldn't reach the street down here, blocked by the looming skyscrapers of the financial district. Garrett watched the stock traders and bond salesmen hurry to their lunches, jackets pulled tight against the wind. He stepped out of the shelter of his building and joined the flow of pedestrians moving east on John Street.

And that was when he felt it. That tingle of unease at the base of his spine. It felt like a chill almost, like a single drop of ice water trickling, very fast, from the base of his brain to the middle of his spine, and then radiating out like a faint, cold shock through his arms and legs. It was familiar to Garrett, how he felt when he discovered a pattern in a seemingly random swirl of chaos. And yet this was slightly different—it was a break in the usual. Something, somewhere near him, was wrong, deviating from the norm. Adrenaline flowed through him. He walked quickly, spooked, Avery's warning—*Be careful*—echoing through his thoughts.

Out of the corner of his eye he saw a young man in a gray sweatshirt watching him from across the street, slouching against a beat-up, white, windowless Chevy van. And then a second man, in a leather jacket, halfway down the block, cell phone to his ear, also watching him, eyes locked onto Garrett. The man in the leather jacket turned away quickly, still on his phone. Garrett felt another jolt of adrenaline course through his body. Were they watching him? Or just watching the street, as Garrett himself was doing? Was he being paranoid? Had Avery thrown off his delicate sense of what was normal, and what was a ripple in the normal?

He kept walking, cursing under his breath. The idiots in the military, spreading fear and paranoia. They played their stupid games and now he was playing along with them. But he wouldn't. Men in sweatshirts were men in sweatshirts, and New York City was full of them, whether they watched him or the pretty girls going the opposite way. He marched east another twenty steps, and then he stopped abruptly, for no reason that he could clearly state, except that every nerve in his body seemed to be telling him to do just that: stop.

A young woman carrying a salad bumped into him, muttered an "Excuse me," and walked past. Garrett's eyes flickered back and forth between the two men he had noticed, one ahead of him, the other moving parallel to him. Looking closer, he could see that one of them was Asian, but the other had turned away from him. Garrett pivoted 180 degrees, as if on an internal autopilot, and started to walk back toward his office. His mind was suddenly, inexplicably blank. He seemed to know one thing, and one thing alone: *Get back to your building.*

Behind him, he heard a sharp, staccato shout, and then an engine revving. He shot a look back over his shoulder and saw the slouching man running in the opposite direction down the street, away from Garrett, while the white van he had been leaning against pulled into the street and raced toward him. Garrett watched as the van picked up speed, and then suddenly, the driver's-side door opened and a small, dark man in a T-shirt and jeans leapt out, hitting the pavement at a sprint in the opposite direction, leaving the van to drift down the street, unguided, by itself. The small dark man ran east on John Street as Garrett watched, frozen. The van ricocheted off the side of a parked Hyundai, then barreled down the street, out of control. A taxicab honked angrily. The other pedestrians on the street—businessmen and delivery boys, secretaries and tourists—began to run. Everyone now seemed to have sensed the impending trouble that Garrett had felt in his bones. He shook himself from his frozen reverie, pivoted on his left foot, and broke into a run. He managed five steps down the street before he was suddenly tackled by someone emerging from a doorway and thrown to the ground. He landed hard on his shoulder, slamming into the pavement, then rolled, and caught a quick glimpse of the face of Captain Alexis Truffant.

She was yelling at him: "Head down! Head down!"

Those were the last words he heard, because a millisecond later there was a flash of white light, a wave of sound that battered his ears, and a cloud of dust and debris that rocketed across his field of vision. Garrett could feel the pulse of an explosion. It thrust his body across the pavement, into Alexis's, and rolled them over each other twice, maybe three or four times—he lost count—then deposited them both at the marble base of a building.

Garrett lay there for a moment. He blinked. He felt for his arms and chest, and then his face. He seemed to be all in one piece. Around him there was smoke and chaos. People staggered past, covered in dirt, one older lady with blood smeared across her face. Garrett got to his knees, but he was dizzy. He put his hand out for support, and it hit the shoulder of Alexis, squatting next to him. She seemed to be talking to him, her lips moving, but Garrett could hear nothing, and he realized the explosion had deafened him. Alexis grabbed his hand. She was yelling at him, but he could make out the words only by reading her lips—"Are you okay?"

He nodded his head yes, and then tried to speak the words "I can't hear you," but he had the strange sensation of speaking without hearing himself, as if he were wearing noise-canceling headphones. He tried to yell, but the effect was the same, worse even, because his throat was rasping and filled with dust and smoke. He wanted to retch.

Alexis tapped her own ears, then shook her head sideways, indicating no, she couldn't hear either.

"Come with me," she said, or at least Garrett assumed she had said that, because he could see her lips moving. The two of them rose, unsteadily, to their feet. Alexis held on to Garrett's hand and led him quickly down the street, past the lobby to his building. The plate-glass windows were shattered, laid about in tiny fragments across the marble floor. Garrett recognized the building's security guard wandering from his desk. He looked dazed, lost.

Alexis dragged Garrett around the corner. There, on William Street, parked in front of a fire hydrant, was a gray SUV. The back door was open, and a stocky, crew-cut man in a black suit was holding it open and signaling for them both to get in. Garrett had a moment's hesitation, but it was overridden by his dizziness and confusion. He and Alexis dove into the backseat, the door closed behind them, the SUV swerved out into the street, and Garrett had the instantaneous and very powerful thought that his life, in that one brief flash, had changed forever.

10

NEW YORK CITY, MARCH 25, 12:47 PM

The SUV sped through the narrow streets of lower Manhattan, heading south. Police cruisers flew past them in the opposite direction, blasting down one-way streets the wrong way and jumping onto the curb. Garrett fought to slow down his breathing. He closed his eyes as he was jostled in the backseat, trying to focus on his hearing. He could begin to make out passing street sounds, and then the groan of the SUV engine. This calmed Garrett—at least he wasn't permanently deaf.

He looked over at Alexis. Her face was covered in dust. She had traces of blood on her cheek and chin. She wore a brown suede jacket, which was now scraped and torn around the shoulders. Her mouth was moving—she seemed to be muttering to herself, and Garrett suspected that she too was testing her hearing.

"Can you hear?" he asked.

She nodded. "A little. You?"

"It's coming back," he said.

"Are you hurt?"

Garrett rolled his right shoulder. It was stiff, but not too bad. Nothing worse than he'd experienced playing high school football. "I'm okay. You?"

"I'm fine."

"What happened?"

"Car bomb."

"Who did it?"

"Don't know."

The SUV pulled under the East River Drive and onto the side street that bordered the water. They stopped at the edge of a dock that jutted out into the river. The whole drive had taken less than five minutes.

Alexis opened the door. "Come on. Let's go."

Garrett scanned the dock, the street around it. "This is the helipad."

"Yes. We need to go. You need to see a doctor."

"There are doctors in New York. Quite a few."

"Someone just tried to blow you up. Do you really want to stay here?"

The stocky man who had held the door open was standing next to Alexis now, and Garrett could see a black pistol showing under the vents of his suit jacket.

"How do you know it was meant for me?"

"If it wasn't meant for you, why did you run? You knew they were after you, so you ran."

"You were watching me?"

"We had you under surveillance."

"Why?"

"This is not the time. You're in danger."

Garrett shook his head, settling his body back into the seat. "I'm not moving until you tell me what the fuck is going on."

Alexis wiped the dust and blood from her face. She took a deep breath. "There are people who would like to talk to you. They've been watching you. And they're impressed. If you come with me now, I will introduce them to you. And they will explain everything."

Garrett stared at her. Alexis nodded over her shoulder. "That helicopter is waiting to take us to Washington."

11

IN TRANSIT—DISTRICT OF COLUMBIA, MARCH 25, 1:15 PM

The powder-blue Sikorsky Executive helicopter lifted vertically off the South Street helipad, dipped left briefly, then climbed to a thousand feet under a southwest compass heading. Within minutes, they were flying low and fast over the coastline of New Jersey.

Garrett lay back in the plush leather seat. Alexis made a series of cell-phone calls, talking quietly but forcefully into a Bluetooth headset. She seemed to alternate between anger and surprise. Garrett tried to hear her over the rotor and engine noise, trying all the time to regain control of his hearing, but gave up after a few minutes. He pulled out his own cell phone and tried to call Avery Bernstein, just to tell him he was okay, but Garrett couldn't get any reception—Alexis Truffant's military technology was clearly better than his. He closed his eyes, exhausted, the shock of the explosion having worn off, leaving him drained. His hands were trembling slightly. Just as he was on the verge of sleep, Alexis tapped him on the shoulder.

"You shouldn't sleep. You might have a concussion."

Garrett kept his eyes open after that. He watched the coastline rush past, then the inland scrub of South Jersey, then the yawning blue of the Delaware Bay. It was beautiful, whitecaps and sailboats and rusting freighters, all splayed out just below him. He had never flown in a helicopter before. As they sped over the Delaware peninsula, then across Chesapeake Bay and over the suburban sprawl that clustered between Baltimore and Washington, he ran over what had happened on the street in his head. He tried to focus on the face of the slouching man, and then the second man on his cell phone. Was that bomb meant to kill him? His memory told Garrett that they had been watching him. Okay, he thought, if so, then Captain Truffant was correct, and the bomb was aimed at him. But why blow him up? Was this about the Treasury bonds? And Avery's warning? But Garrett had already passed on what he knew. It made no sense. Given that it was a singular occurrence, it fit no pattern, and Garrett was not good at one-offs. His head still hurt from the explosion, so he decided to stop thinking about it.

He turned to Alexis when she was between calls.

"Where are we going? Exactly?" he asked.

"Bolling Air Force Base. It's where my agency is headquartered. The Defense Intelligence Agency." She smiled at him. "So now you know who I work for."

"Woo-hoo," Garrett answered, wagging his finger in the air.

The Sikorsky swung south to avoid the restricted air space over D.C., then approached Bolling by going up along the Potomac. From the air, the base seemed not unlike any other corporate mall or planned community, with tract homes, baseball fields, and a small marina on the river. It didn't even have a runway. The Sikorsky set down on a helipad near a parking lot, and Garrett and Alexis climbed into a waiting black sedan. They were driven to the east edge of the base, where there was a small hospital.

Garrett was waved through an admitting room, past a triage nurse and into a green examination room. A young doctor was waiting for him. She cleaned the cuts on his face and shoulder, then ran him through a series of concussion tests, all of which he passed. The doctor handed him a card and asked him to call if he felt dizzy or nauseous. Alexis seemed to have disappeared—the doctor said she was going to examine her next—and in her stead a pair of military policemen escorted Garrett out of the hospital to a single-story, windowless office-park building. They brought him to a fluorescent-lit conference room, asked him if he'd like a sandwich—he asked for a turkey and Swiss—and then returned with the food and a soda ten minutes later.

Garrett ate hurriedly, and considered whom he might call. The truth was, there were only a few people who cared about his welfare, Mitty and Avery being top of the list. It occurred to Garrett that he might finally have managed to alienate everyone else he'd ever known. That thought made him grimace involuntarily, and he quickly put his phone away.

The moment he finished eating, a pair of black-suited men entered the conference room, and Garrett realized they had been watching him the entire time. He spotted the surveillance camera in the ceiling corner, and reminded himself to check for that kind of thing from now on. The men introduced themselves as Agents Cannel and Stoddard. They said they worked for Homeland Security. Garrett asked for ID, and they dutifully let him inspect their badges.

"We just want to ask you a few questions," Stoddard, the older and larger of the two, said. Garrett assumed they would ask about the explosion, and what he'd seen, but instead they launched into questions about his family. How long had his father worked for the Long Beach Unified School District? How old had Garrett been when his father died? Had his mother ever held a job? What did she do now? Had Garrett ever been arrested? Within two minutes Garrett was growing angry.

"What do you care if I've ever been arrested?"

"These are just standard questions, Mr. Reilly."

"Have you ever been arrested?" Garrett asked them.

"I have not," Agent Stoddard said.

"Well, why not? You don't party? You never have any fun?"

"I do have fun. Just law-abiding fun."

Garrett grunted. "I just remembered. I did get arrested once. For multiple homicides. But I got a good lawyer and was acquitted."

The Homeland Security agents simply pressed on with their questions. "How about your mother—"

"How about *your* mother?"

"—was she ever arrested?"

Somewhere into the fifth minute Garrett simply stopped talking. The agents asked a few more questions, then asked if Garrett would be answering any of them, and when he said nothing, they thanked him, folded up their notebooks, and left.

In a small observation room adjacent to the conference room, the two agents ducked their heads in and nodded to Alexis Truffant and General Kline, who were watching Garrett on a color monitor.

"One thing we could ascertain, General," Agent Stoddard said, pointing to the video feed of Garrett. "He is definitely an asshole."

Alexis smirked. "He's off the charts on that."

General Kline scowled as the Homeland Security agents walked away. He was no fan of that organization; they had no real jurisdiction on an Air Force base, and yet they strutted through the place like they owned it. Theirs was an ever-growing bureaucracy, and its steady encroachment made him uneasy. He took a deep breath and turned to Alexis. "Captain, if I bring him in front of who I'd like to bring him in front of . . ."

". . . would he make you look like a fool?" Alexis finished his sentence.

"A terrible, stupid fool?"

"From what I've seen, sir, if there is even a slight possibility of his causing a disruption, then he almost certainly will."

Kline studied Garrett on the closed-circuit feed. The young man was handsome, there was no denying that, but Kline thought he had a dangerous, almost feral look about him, as if he were a man-child raised by wolves and they'd just rescued him from the wilds of some vast northern forest. He was tapping his fingers repeatedly on the desk. He seemed impatient, twitchy, angry.

Kline rubbed his temples softly, fighting off a growing tension migraine. "I'll make the phone calls. You find him some clothes and get him ready for dinner."

12

BOLLING AIR FORCE BASE, WASHINGTON, D.C., MARCH 25, 4:49 PM

The one-bedroom condo sat in the center of Bolling Air Force Base. MPs patrolled the front and back of the condo building. Inside, a pair of dark slacks and a clean button-down shirt, in Garrett's size, were laid out on a bed; a blue blazer hung from the door.

"You pick these out?" Garrett asked Alexis.

"If I say yes, are you going to refuse to wear them?" she answered.

Garrett laughed. "I'm getting predictable." He pulled off his shirt in front of her. She walked out of the bedroom and closed the door, but he nudged it back open so she could hear him. And see him. He wanted her to see him naked. Anything to make her uncomfortable. He pulled off his pants as well.

"Why didn't the Homeland guys ask me about the bomb?"

"I don't know," Alexis said, studiously avoiding looking at the open door. "Look. We're going to a dinner tonight. There will be important people there. People who are responsible for the future of this country."

"I mean, I was a witness. And maybe even the target. It's got to be the biggest news story in the country right now. That's just weird."

"If you could simply listen to what they have to say to you, that would be much appreciated. What they have to say is far more important than the bombing."

"More important than whether I live or die?"

"Considerably more important than that."

"To me, whether I live or die is surprisingly important."

"I'm sure it is," Alexis countered with undisguised disdain.

Garrett shoved the bedroom door closed and took a shower. When he came out, Alexis was gone and the front door was locked from the outside. He kicked the door once, and was pretty sure he could bust open its thin plywood frame with a little more effort, but he decided against it—what was the point? He didn't have anywhere particular to go. He looked for a TV in the condo, but there was none, so he checked the news feed on his cell phone. CNN and *The New York Times* were reporting it as a terror attack, a car bomb, with multiple injuries but no fatalities; no group or person had claimed responsibility, and the city authorities had no suspects. Garrett was not mentioned in any of the news stories, but on thinking about this, he didn't see why he would be. No one knew he had been downstairs or anywhere near the explosion. But then he realized that Avery Bernstein hadn't called him. No one from Jenkins & Altshuler had, which was strange, given that he had essentially become a missing person. Perhaps Alexis Truffant had called his boss? She seemed like the type—no loose ends.

He called Avery's office, but it went right to voice mail. They were closed for the day. He didn't really have anything to tell Avery, except maybe that he was okay, had survived the bombing, but something told him that Avery already knew this. Avery was more connected to this whole thing than Garrett had realized. He was the nexus from which all subsequent actions had radiated out. Avery, Garrett decided, was up to speed.

Next he called Mitty Rodriguez, but she didn't answer either. He left her a message, in case she was worried, but Garrett doubted she was; she was probably deep in the bowels of an online game and hadn't even noticed the bombing. Mitty often gamed for days on end without coming up for air. Or for news of the world. It was understood that either of them could disappear for long stretches of time and the other wouldn't freak out.

Alexis returned at six-thirty, as the sun was setting over eastern Virginia. She knocked on the condo door, unlocked it, and let herself in. Garrett did a double take as she stood there in the foyer in a short black dress and sheer nylons, with her hair flowing down around her shoulders and her lips bright red with lipstick. She looked stunning.

"We must be meeting some really, really important people," Garrett said, nodding to her. "Because you look fantastic."

"We are. And thank you for the compliment."

Garrett followed her down the steps of the condo and into a waiting unmarked Ford. A uniformed Air Force lieutenant drove, and Alexis and Garrett sat in back. Garrett felt a little like he was going to his high school prom—which he had not gone to, opting instead to get stoned on the beach and night-surf—and enjoyed the sensation. At least his prom date was pretty. They crossed the Frederick Douglass Bridge into Washington, D.C., proper. It was the first time Garrett had ever been in the nation's capital. He stared out the window, and it seemed to him, even though he didn't know the geography of the city, that the driver was taking them past every patriotic sight he could find. They circled the Capitol, lit up by spotlights, crossed the Mall, where he eyed the Smithsonian and the National Archives, then took a series of roundabout turns that brought them directly past the White House. It may have been a ploy, but Garrett enjoyed it nonetheless.

They drove past Foggy Bottom and the State Department, then crossed into Georgetown and maneuvered down a series of narrow, tree-lined streets filled with upscale town houses. They double-parked in front of a three-story brick brownstone on Dumbarton Street. Pairs of uniformed D.C. policemen stood guard halfway down the block on both sides, and a pair of dark-suited men that Garrett assumed were Secret Service agents blocked the door to the building. The agents stepped aside for Alexis, and Garrett trailed in her path.

The foyer of the town house was bathed in soft yellow light. Colonial-era furniture lined the hallway, and a pair of lush Hudson River School oil paintings hung opposite each other on the walls. The floors were veined slats of polished wood, topped with intricately woven rugs. To Garrett, the place reeked of money. And power.

"Nice," Garrett laughed, examining an antique pewter teapot on a mahogany table.

A young, well-dressed African-American woman entered the hallway and smiled pleasantly at Alexis. "Captain Truffant. Good to see you." The young woman turned to Garrett and took him in for a moment. "And you must be Garrett Reilly."

"Yeah. That's me."

"A pleasure. I've heard a lot about you. I'm Mackenzie Fox. Assistant to the secretary. Come this way. Everyone's here. They're all waiting for you." She opened a door at the end of the hallway and held it for them. Alexis entered, disappearing from Garrett's view, but Garrett paused a moment by Ms. Fox.

"Secretary of what?" he whispered to her.

"Defense."

"Holy fuck," Garrett gasped, before he could stop himself.

"Yes, holy fuck," she said with a smile.

13

GEORGETOWN, WASHINGTON, D.C., MARCH 25, 8:02 PM

Secretary of Defense Duke Frye, Jr., spoke first, and Garrett recognized him immediately. He was a large man, with a head of thick, bright-white hair, broad shoulders, and blue eyes. His Texas accent was barely noticeable; he'd clearly worked to rid himself of it and now spoke more like the polished global businessman that he had been before being named secretary.

"Something to drink, Mr. Reilly? We're pouring scotch tonight. Eighteen-year-old Highland Park. You know it?"

"Sure," Garrett answered, tongue-tied, leaving his host uncertain as to whether he meant "sure" he knew the scotch or "sure" he'd have some.

Secretary Frye poured him a glass anyway. He handed it to Garrett, then shook his hand. "Duke Frye. I am the secretary of defense." He fixed his eyes on Garrett, and Garrett felt a rare flash of fear and anxiety race through him. Frye was the first truly powerful man Garrett had ever met in person, and he scared Garrett. Not a lot, but just enough to throw him slightly off balance.

"Pleased to meet you," Garrett said, and then quickly added "sir," but hated himself immediately for doing it. He glanced at the dozen or so other people gathered in the large, sumptuous living room. A few were standing, two of them in front of a dark, windswept oil painting of George Washington on horseback that Garrett swore he'd seen before in an art history book. The rest of the guests were seated. Garrett quickly made out five or six men and women in uniform—generals by the looks of them. He thought he saw four actual stars on the lapel of the oldest of them, a lean, wiry African-American man in his sixties. The other men and women were a mixed bunch, most in their forties, all wearing dark suits. Garrett could feel the buzz of power in the room. And they were all staring at him.

"I'm sure you are wondering why you are here, Mr. Reilly," the secretary said. "So I think I'll let this gentleman start things off. General Kline, would you do the honors?"

General Kline stepped to the front of the group. He was one of the few there without a drink. He thrust out his hand to shake Garrett's, and spoke quickly in his clipped Boston accent. "I'm Hadley Kline. Head of the Analysis Directorate at the Defense Intelligence Agency. I'm also Alexis's boss." He nodded to Alexis, who had moved away from Garrett to stand unobtrusively in a corner. In the pecking order of the room she clearly did not rank.

Kline cleared his throat. "So, how do I start this?" Kline twitched, as was his habit, then launched in. "I'm sure you've heard the old cliché—generals are always preparing to fight the last war. Well, unfortunately, there's truth in it. The armed services spend a lot of time and money grooming the next generation of leaders—West Point, Annapolis, the Air Force Academy. Bright men and women. We explain to them how the last war was fought. And then we tell them to think about how to fight the next one. But in the process we make them like us. We make them military people. That's the whole point—we want them to be soldiers. But that . . ." And here Kline hesitated, carefully choosing his words, not for effect, but, Garrett guessed, to avoid insulting anyone else in the room. "That approach can have its drawbacks," he finished.

Kline shot a quick glance around the room, as if scanning for objections. He found none.

"We are susceptible to groupthink, no matter how hard we try to stay independent. It is human nature to be influenced by others. It's that ability that allowed the human race to evolve from being solitary hunters on the African savannah to standing around drinking scotch in a million-dollar town house in Georgetown."

"Bought it for a couple million dollars," the secretary broke in. "God only knows what it's worth now. Damn real estate market." There were chuckles across the room.

"Groupthink is especially prevalent in larger organizations," Kline continued. "And the military is the largest of them all. I think I can say, without impugning anyone here, that the military is not the world's most outside-the-box group. We value discipline, bravery, integrity. Poets and entrepreneurs need not apply." Again there was laughter.

"At least not until now." Kline turned to a young woman sitting in the corner. She rose, smiling politely. She was Hispanic, no more than thirty, and wore a tailored black skirt suit. She offered Garrett her hand. They shook.

"Garrett, my name is Julia Hernandez. I work in the Treasury Department. I'm the undersecretary for terrorism and financial intelligence. I'm the person Avery Bernstein called the other day. With your news."

"Oh." Garrett looked her up and down. She was pretty, if you liked the librarian/dominatrix archetype, which Garrett did, on occasion. "So it was you that cost me forty million bucks."

"You mean by propping up the dollar?"

"That's exactly what I mean."

"You were planning to profit from the sell-off in Treasuries?"

"Sure."

"You weren't troubled by that? Morally?"

"Not really. That's my business." He looked at the assembled generals. "We all have a business. You guys kill people. I short bad bond issues."

Out of the corner of his eye Garrett saw Alexis Truffant flinch. She looked ready to body-tackle him. Garrett guessed she had a lot of skin in this game, but none of the generals had so much as twitched at his remark. Either they were a lot tougher than she was, Garrett thought, or they didn't give a shit what he said. Probably both.

Julia Hernandez continued: "We believe that this is more than simply a bad bond issue, Garrett. We believe the Chinese are selling off Treasuries as a way to weaken the economy of the United States. To undermine the dollar and destroy our standing in the global marketplace. We believe—"

An older, deeper voice interrupted her: "We believe that this is an act of war."

Garrett turned to the voice. It came from the four-star general. His crew-cut Afro was awash in gray, and his deeply lined face seemed almost sculptural. "A new kind of war," the four-star said. "One we really haven't seen before." Garrett couldn't place his accent exactly, but he guessed it was Chicago. South Side. The general stood up, and the secretary of defense nodded to him.

"Mr. Reilly," the secretary said. "This is General Aldous Wilkerson. Decorated Vietnam War veteran and chairman of the Joint Chiefs of Staff."

General Wilkerson waved the secretary off, then walked slowly up to Garrett. "The most dangerous attack, the one a general fears most, is the one he doesn't understand, the one he never saw coming because it was deemed outside the realm of possibility. The attack that catches you completely by surprise: Hannibal's elephants crossing the Alps, the Nazi blitzkrieg, two planes crashing into the World Trade Center. Those moments change the course of history. And they can destroy entire nations."

The general's words hung in the air. Garrett looked at the older man, the deep lines on his face. "And we're at one of those moments?"

The general shrugged, as if unsure. Garrett liked that. He liked that this four-star general wasn't so arrogant as to lecture Garrett on uncertainty. Uncertainty was one of Garrett's specialties.

"My nine-year-old granddaughter understands more about computers and the Internet than I ever will," Wilkerson said. "Send. Delete. Twitter. Facebook. Good Lord. I miss writing an old-fashioned letter. But people who know these things are telling me that our enemies could swamp us in a millisecond if they wanted to. If we were not on guard." The general got up close to Garrett. "You concur with that assessment?"

"Isn't that what the National Security Agency does? Protect us against attacks like that?"

"We've got agencies protecting us from threats all over the place," the general said. "But none of them caught the massive, coordinated sell-off of U.S. Treasuries. Only you did."

Garrett smiled as the realization dawned on him. He was surprised at himself for not seeing it earlier. "So you want me to help you find more of these in the future? Because I'm good at finding patterns. And I'm outside of the groupthink of the military?"

General Kline took over: "We've been looking for someone like you, Garrett, for quite some time now, and the likes of you are not easy to find. Someone of a new generation. Raised on computers and the Web. Mathematically inclined. From a family of patriots like your brother, but himself outside of the military's sphere of influence. Intelligent, unafraid of risk, aggressive, confident. Arrogant."

Garrett snorted a laugh. "I feel so loved."

"We speak plainly and directly, Garrett," General Wilkerson said. "You might find that refreshing."

Kline continued: "I could list all the characteristics that you possess, but it would take some time, and, frankly, I think you already know them. You know what you can do, and how you can do it. So here is what we are proposing. Let us train you in our defensive and offensive capabilities, but keep you physically and mentally separate from our war machine. Captain Truffant here will be your guide. She'll bring you up to speed on what we can do, and what we can't. Meanwhile, you'll be free to track the very things that allowed you to predict what was happening in the bond market."

"You want me to be your early warning system?"

"In a way, yes."

Garrett thought about this. "What about my old job?"

"You'll be put on leave from that job. It will still be there when you get back. Alexis has already cleared this with your boss, Mr. Bernstein."

Garrett cracked a smile—he'd been right about Avery as well. The old man was in on the secret. At least part of it. "And I get paid for this?"

"You'll have a base salary. It won't be huge, but it will be something. Your responsibilities will far outweigh your pay grade."

General Wilkerson cut in: "Money is not the point here, Garrett. This is part of a larger civic responsibility. You will be protecting our nation. So what do you say?"

The room fell silent. Again, Garrett felt all eyes on him. He waited a moment, as if considering, but he had known what his answer would be for a while. He shook his head.

"I'll pass," he said.

There were muted whispers among the gathering. Secretary of Defense Frye stepped up, a look of anger and concern on his face. "What we're asking you to do is a great honor, Garrett. Don't you love your country?"

"I do, absolutely," Garrett said, with a smile. "I love my country. I just hate the fucking morons who run it."

Captain Alexis Truffant shot a look over to her boss, General Kline, and grimaced. Kline just shook his head and shrugged his shoulders, as if to say, What can I do? The quiet tension that had built in the room was gone, replaced by a low chatter of angry conversation. Garrett stood in the middle of the room, smiling pleasantly.

"Hey, someone want to tell me where the bathroom is?" he said. "I gotta go pee."

Mackenzie Fox, the assistant to the secretary of defense, led Garrett angrily—and silently—out of the room, while Alexis and General Kline huddled in a corner.

"You called it, Captain," General Kline said with a hint of resignation in his voice. "He has a deep-seated antipathy toward the armed services."

"It's more than that, sir," Alexis said. "He hates everybody. It's part of what made him a good candidate."

"So what now, General Kline?" the secretary asked, as he and General Wilkerson joined them. "Because that was a bit of a disaster, and we've still got a problem on our hands. And, quite honestly, your program's not helping much."

Alexis could see General Kline stiffen. She knew the secretary and her boss were not good friends—on the contrary, Frye worked consistently to marginalize any new DIA initiatives. Alexis guessed he was a man who hoarded power.

"We could push harder with Reilly," Kline said. "But I'm not sure it's worth our time or effort. There are other candidates out there. We'll keep looking. We'll find someone."

"Sir," Alexis cut in, "I hope I'm not being too forward, but I believe we can still recruit Mr. Reilly. Bring him onto the team."

"That seems awfully optimistic," General Wilkerson said.

"Sir, I agree. It is," Alexis continued. "But I think there is something in him that wants to help. We just need to connect with that."

"You gonna connect with it, Captain? With that hidden part of him?" the secretary asked with a sly, almost lewd smile on his face.

Alexis started to answer but was cut off by Mackenzie Fox's urgent bark. "He's climbed out the bathroom window."

"Shit!" General Kline said. "Don't we have Secret Service around the house?"

"They're out front. They didn't see him," Fox said. "They think he jumped a neighbor's fence and left via O Street. They're radioing D.C. police right now."

The secretary of defense laughed. "He's free to go, Mackenzie. He's not under house arrest. He's not a prisoner."

"We could charge him," Alexis said.

"With what?" Frye said. "Pissing us off?" The secretary snorted as he walked away. "Didn't like him anyway. Thought he was an ass."

• • •

After Garrett climbed over a wrought iron fence and then tiptoed across a carefully tended backyard garden, he jogged east on O Street, then turned south and walked until he found a cab. He didn't know D.C., but told the driver—a Sikh with a beige turban—to take him to the nearest Greyhound station. The Sikh, Indian dance music blasting from his radio, got him there in ten minutes. At the station, Garrett bought a ticket for the next bus leaving D.C., which happened to be a 10:35 p.m. express to Greensboro, North Carolina. He made the bus two minutes before it left, found a pair of seats in the back all to himself, pulled the battery and memory card out of his cell phone, and then curled up to sleep until they reached the tobacco state. The last thought he had before he drifted off was a lingering image in his brain of Secretary of Defense Frye's face as he told those military half-wits to go fuck themselves. God, he loved sticking it to people.

Especially people who deserved it.

14

LUOXIATOU, CHINA, MARCH 26, 8:07 AM

Hu Mei stepped out of the deserted alley, past the slatted wooden gate and into the small, circular garden that lay tucked behind a cinder-block shack. She closed the gate to the alley and locked it from the inside with a sliding length of wood, finally pausing to catch her breath and let the late winter sun warm her face for a moment or two. She had been on the move for the past fourteen hours, walking through the night with just a pocketful of stale *mantou* buns and a plastic bottle of water to keep her going. It had been bitterly cold out—the temperature near freezing—but now the sun was up and its faint rays warmed her hands and face.

Hu Mei rolled her stiff shoulders to get the blood flowing in her body. Around her, lining the hillside, were row upon row of concrete and cinder-block homes, each of them one room, the better ones with wood smoke curling up from their rudimentary chimneys, the less good with layers of plastic sheeting tacked inside their windows. It was a tough life here, in Luoxiatou, in central China. So many people had already left for better jobs in the coastal cities: the young people had cleared out; the able-bodied who were middle-aged worked in the mines; the old folks simply scratched out a living doing whatever they could.

Hu Mei checked the scrap of paper the old man had given her in the last town. On it were directions, and a name, Bao. Bao was an old woman—so Mei had been told—but she was a sympathizer, and had promised to give Hu Mei a meal and a bed for a few hours. That's all Mei needed. A few hours' rest, some food, and the chance to meet another person who believed in her cause.

Was this the place? Mei asked herself silently as she looked around the yard. If she made a mistake, she would be caught. And if she were caught, she would be jailed, beaten, and executed. Probably all within a few days.

So a mistake was out of the question.

But where was the old woman whose house this was? Why hadn't she come out to meet her? Hu Mei's heart raced. She forced herself to remain calm, but a prudent amount of anxiety would keep her alert. And alert meant free. Alert meant alive.

Hu Mei could feel the authorities, like the Chinese winter, forcing themselves down upon her since the rebellion in Huaxi Township four months ago. Rebellion. That was what she was calling it. The government called it a criminal provocation. But that is what they called anything they did not like. And they did not like what had happened: the humiliation of two hundred of their officers; disarmed, forced to flee, eighty of them beaten, twenty-five badly enough to be sent to the district hospital. Word had spread through the valley like a brush fire, leaping from village to village. Word of mouth was still Hu Mei's best ally. There had been postings on the Internet, but those were scrubbed by government censors almost as fast as they appeared. But the government could not monitor chitchat between villagers, men riding on buses, women at the market, or schoolchildren walking home at the end of lessons. These people were spreading the word, and the word was potent: Hu Mei was the tip of a very sharp sword, and that sword was swinging at the neck of the government.

She laughed mirthlessly at her own far-fetched metaphor. Swords? Necks? How ridiculous. The Communist Party was massive and vastly powerful. Her minuscule rebellion was a mere irritant, not a potential death blow. And yet, the reaction she felt all around her—the squadrons of police officers searching for her and her followers day and night, the wanted posters with her name on them, the preposterous stories of her numerous lovers and vast wealth—all were signs of a government that feared her. Or at least feared what she represented. And that, along with the weak March sun, warmed her.

An old woman shuffled into the garden from her home. Hu Mei sighed deeply—this would be Bao. She had not made a mistake. She would be safe, at least for another twelve hours. The old woman's face was deeply wrinkled, her white hair pulled back under a scarf. Her gray eyes were mere slits in the morning sun. She bowed immediately before Mei, as if approaching a dignitary. Mei hated that. Groveling. It was unbecoming in anyone, but especially a wise old woman.

"*Shīfu,*" the old woman said. *Master.*

"Do not call me that," Mei said quickly. "Please, do not."

The old woman straightened herself with barely a nod. Her eyes darted around the garden, and immediately Hu Mei's anxiety shot back to the surface. What was the old woman looking for?

"What is it?" Mei asked.

The old woman hesitated. She clenched her gnarled hands briefly. "I tried to send him away . . ."

"Send who away?"

"I said I had never heard of Hu Mei. But he did not believe me."

Mei scanned the garden. She tried to see back into the alley behind her, but the wooden fence was too high. "Who did not believe you? Who!" she hissed.

"The man," the old woman said. "From the party." Bao looked back down at the hard-packed dirt. "He has been waiting in my house all morning."

Hu Mei's blood froze. How could this have happened? She had followers in every local township. She had a network of sympathizers and spies. They tracked policemen and bureaucrats everywhere she went, keeping Hu Mei safe, keeping the movement alive, and now this old woman was saying that it had somehow all gone wrong? Here in this tiny out-of-the-way village?

She took a deep breath and managed to gasp: "Is he alone?" Her chest was tight.

"I am, comrade." A potbellied man in a worn suit stepped out of the shack and into the frosty garden. His feet splayed apart like a duck's, and his large bald forehead was shiny in the weak sun. He pushed importantly past Bao, elbowing the old woman to one side. "I am alone, but I am not alone. A party member is never alone in China. I have policemen—fifty of them—all over this town. So no, I am not exactly alone."

Hu Mei spun around, reaching behind her, into the folds of her winter jacket. She had a short shiv of a knife tucked into her belt, just above her hip. Now would be the moment, she thought, to stab this man and run from this place. She could overpower him before he understood what she was doing—just run the knife quickly into his chest, then flee the village. Hu Mei was sure this fat, soft, party flunky would not be quick or strong enough to stop her. He spent all his time behind a desk, eating candy and signing meaningless proclamation papers. She should end his pitiful life, here and now.

And yet, she didn't. She hesitated. Perhaps he was not here to arrest her. Perhaps he did not even know who she was. He did not seem ready to grab her, no matter the self-importance that wafted off him like the smell of rotting meat. And if she did stab him, it would be Bao, the old woman, who would take the blame. Hu Mei could not do that to her. That was not her nature.

"You are," the party official said, "who I believe you to be, are you not?"

"Who are you?" she answered, trying to give herself a few more moments to think this through, to consider her options.

"I am Party Township Director Chen Fei. A humble and obscure provincial official with little real power. Around me and above me are the powerful and the wealthy. But what do I have?"

Hu Mei frowned. This was the usual bureaucratic prelude: after professions of powerlessness and poverty came the subtle—or not so subtle—requests for a bribe. Perhaps he was simply out for himself, looking for a handout? That would be a relief, Mei thought. She had a few yuan. She could pay off this man. And then move on.

She released her grip on the knife in her belt and mentally started to count the money in her pocket. Mei was about to claim poverty herself—the customary retort—but she waited. There was something about this Chen Fei. His approach did not make sense. He could make far more money turning Hu Mei in than extorting a few yuan from her.

"I can see by the look on your face," he continued, "that you are confused. Allow me to sit, will you?" Without waiting for a reply he squatted on a piece of wood covering a patch of frozen mud in the garden. "Yes, I know you are the bandit Hu Mei. I know you have stolen money from poor shopkeepers, have personally slit the throats of many policemen, and have many husbands, from whom you demand constant sexual satisfaction."

Hu Mei started to respond, but the party man cut her off. "And I know all these things to be untrue as well." He smiled up at her, as she was now standing above him, and he was drumming on the frozen ground with his fingers. "But still, they are amusing to repeat."

Hu Mei pushed a weak smile to her lips. "Party Township Director Chen, if you know these things to be lies, then why are you here?"

Chen Fei looked up at Hu Mei. His wispy black hair lay motionless on his half-bald scalp. His eyes were flat and dull; Hu Mei had seen many men like him before. They were dead inside, from years of kowtowing to other soul-dead men just above them, and now they took simple pleasure in extracting pain from those below them. But then, as she stared at him, the most unexpected thing happened. Tears welled up in the party township director's eyes and trickled down his cheeks, tiny drops of water that steamed in the winter air. His once stolid, lifeless face suddenly broke into a shattered picture of pain.

"I, too," he said, stammering, and then regaining his breath, "I too have lost someone I dearly loved. My son, in the mines, two years ago. An explosion that should never have happened. So many boys killed. My Yao was one of them. No safety measures, no escape routes. Just dig, dig, dig, make money for someone else." He stared up at Hu Mei. "The world means so little to me since." Now tears were freely coursing down his face. "And then I heard your story. About your fight. About what happened in Huaxi Township." He gasped for breath, emotion bubbling out of him. He stopped, wiping the freezing snot from his nose, took a breath, and continued.

"They want us to find you. Us, the provincial officials. To hunt you down. To kill you. And this morning, when I suspected that it was you my villagers were hiding, I considered it. I knew I would receive a reward. And influence as well. And yet . . ." Again, he broke down in tears. "Forgive me."

Chen Fei struggled to his feet, and turned away from Hu Mei, hiding his grief. And then, in one swift motion, he turned to her again, a small wooden, lacquered box in his hand. The trim was painted black, and the Chinese symbol for peace, *Hé*, was written on its top. "Take it. For you."

Hu Mei took the box, confused. She opened it, slowly, carefully. Inside were sheets of folded paper. She opened the first sheet, the edges of the paper crackling in the cold, crisp air. In cramped, artless calligraphy was a list of names. She thumbed quickly through the other sheets. By each name was an address. By some were phone numbers. A few had e-mail addresses. There were hundreds of names. Maybe thousands.

The party township director smiled through his pain. "They are suspected of provocation. Of being enemies of the party. But they are not. I know that they are not. They are just citizens. Unhappy citizens."

"But why?" Mei asked. "Why give this to me?"

"So that you may talk to them. So that they may become followers." The party director dropped to his knees and bowed deeply, his face touching the hard, cold ground at Hu Mei's feet, only inches from her worn, ragged shoes.

"Followers of the great Hu Mei."

15

BOLLING AIR FORCE BASE, WASHINGTON, D.C., MARCH 26, 3:11 AM

It was three in the morning and Alexis Truffant was tired. The three cups of coffee weren't helping. They were just making her jumpy and short-tempered. Not that she wasn't used to sleepless nights—they were, in her experience, one of the defining conditions of military life. That, and bad food.

Well, she thought as she worked the phone at her desk in her windowless room at Bolling AFB, at least she had warned General Kline about Garrett, telling him that he was hardwired for aggression, contrariness, and arrogance and was an odds-on favorite to cause trouble. She hadn't held anything back—quite the opposite.

Still, she was angry at herself for allowing it to get that far, angry for letting a glimmer of hope and expectation sway her judgment. She couldn't help taking some responsibility for what had happened at the defense secretary's brownstone. It was just part of who Alexis Truffant was: a leader. And leaders took responsibility.

It was a portion of what made her a great Army officer. It was why she had graduated third in her class from West Point, and why she was a captain at age twenty-eight, and would soon make the jump to major. When Alexis was given a task, she took it personally; she followed through, took pride not just in her work but in the larger mission. She had guided forty-two consecutive resupply convoys down the most hazardous highways of central Iraq without losing a single soldier. It was why she had wanted to enlist in the Army in the first place—a deep-seated sense of being responsible for the safety of the nation, as crazy and overblown as that sounded. She was a caretaker. To Alexis, it felt completely natural to want to protect other people, whether you were related to them—or even knew them—or not. It was a roundabout way of coming to patriotism, but to Alexis it made sense. It felt true.

But Alexis suspected that this wasn't why General Kline had recruited her into the Defense Intelligence Agency. The military was full of bright young leaders-to-be. No, it was something else. It was, Alexis guessed, that she didn't quite belong. She was a woman in what was still a man's business, a thinker in a world full of warriors, and a skeptic in an organization where it was the true believers who often shot to the top. Those things kept Alexis slightly off balance, made her wary of conventional wisdom, and General Kline seemed to want that. He had said as much when he first interviewed her, two years ago, in the Bolling AFB cafeteria.

"People who think they know exactly what's going on are dangerous," he had said as they had sipped sodas. "Nobody ever knows what's really going on. Nobody."

Alexis had written that down on a notepad later that night, and reminded herself of it every day that followed. *Nobody ever knows what's really going on. Nobody.*

So, she thought as she glanced at the wall clock that read 3:20 a.m., the only thing that she was reasonably sure of was that Garrett Reilly was out there, and she needed to find him. He had clearly been the target of an assassination attempt and was now in the open and vulnerable. But, additionally, Alexis felt she needed to give him one more chance, because despite what had happened, and all appearances to the contrary, she thought there was some part of Garrett that wanted to be led down a different path. She believed she could sense who needed saving and who was beyond help, and one thing was clear to her—Garrett Reilly was not beyond help.

Earlier in the evening she had tried to cajole the D.C. police into taking Garrett's escape seriously, but when she couldn't provide specific charges against him, they had said they would issue an alert at the beginning of the next shift, though she doubted they actually had. In any case, no sightings came in from officers on patrol. Next she called the TSA chiefs at Reagan and Dulles airports, but Garrett hadn't boarded a plane at either location. She tried a few car rental companies, but none of their offices were open, so she figured he hadn't fled D.C. by that mode of transportation. That left trains and buses, and she knew both would be a nightmare to track. She checked the Greyhound schedule online, and narrowed the number of buses he could have taken that night to seventeen. Amtrak was a bit better: only four trains had left Union Station since nine that evening. But, all told, those trains had stopped fourteen different times since leaving the D.C. metropolitan area.

There was another alternative, and that one seemed reasonable to Alexis: Garrett had simply stayed in Washington, maybe taking a motel room or sleeping in a park. Either way, she finally decided, there wasn't much point in looking for him as he traveled. If she couldn't find him, then whoever had tried to blow him up in New York probably wouldn't be able to either. Instead, she thought, she would try to find him once he arrived. She went home to her Arlington condo at 4:00 a.m. and slept for five hours. She woke at nine, called General Kline, told him her plans, and caught an 11:30 US Airways shuttle to New York City.

She had never liked New York. Alexis was a country girl at heart; she had spent her entire childhood on a farm in rural Virginia, surrounded by rolling hills thick with flowering dogwoods. She could ride a horse almost before she could walk; she could fish, hunt, and tell you every species of warbler in the woods around her home. Virginia made her happy. It was more than home. It was where her soul lived. Still, she respected New York's energy, its life, even if she hated its concrete and glass. To Alexis, New York was an animal that you treated with a wary caution: dangerous if you let your guard down, but a bounteous prize if you could manage to tame it.

She rented a car at LaGuardia and drove into Manhattan, then parked near Wall Street so she could pay a visit to Jenkins & Altshuler. She wasn't looking forward to it. She had called Avery Bernstein the day before, from the helicopter, and told him that Garrett was fine, but more than that she couldn't say.

Avery's response had crackled in her ear over the spotty cell phone connection: "If anything happens to Garrett Reilly I will bring all my connections and all my money down on your head in a shitstorm. And I have a lot of fucking money."

Now, a day later, walking through the bond-trading room, Alexis could see that everyone at the firm was on tenterhooks—the building lobby was still a crime scene and a dust-strewn wreck. Only half the trading employees had made it to work that day. And Avery Bernstein was apoplectic.

He hissed at her as they stood toe-to-toe in his office, the blinds pulled down so no one else in the firm could see their argument. "What the fuck do you mean you don't know where Garrett is?" Spit flew from his lips as he waved a stubby finger in Alexis's face. "Yesterday you told me he was with you in some freaking helicopter? And now he's missing? How the fuck did that happen?"

Alexis remained calm. Staying cool under fire was another one of her leadership qualities. Her voice barely above a whisper, she said a search for Garrett was under way, and if he called Avery, could Avery please alert her immediately. Avery continued to growl curses at her, and the Army, as she walked out of his office. Not that she blamed him. He had done what he thought was a good deed by calling the Treasury Department. But events had overtaken him, his firm, and one of his best employees.

No good deed goes unpunished.

Alexis grabbed a salad from a downtown deli, then drove her car thirty blocks to Garrett's apartment, at the corner of Twelfth and Avenue B. She found a parking spot in front of an ice-cream shop and went up to ring his buzzer. There was no answer. She tried his cell, but it went right to voice mail, so she settled back into her rental car and waited for Garrett to return, watching the tourists and the street people, the fabulous mothers dressed in clothes Alexis could never hope to afford, the immigrants yelling into their cell phones in a dozen different languages, the businessmen marching purposefully to their next appointments. She told herself stories about the lives of some of the more eccentric passersby; she listened to AM radio; she booked herself a room in a hotel two blocks away and slept four hours that night before getting back into her car to keep the vigil going.

She waited and watched for two days, on and off, before deciding it would be more profitable to look elsewhere.

Garrett thought Greensboro, North Carolina, was quaint. He was only there for four hours, and that was between midnight and 4:00 a.m., so he really had no idea how quaint it was, but he thought he'd give the place the benefit of the doubt. He caught the first bus out of Greensboro, and that was a local to Nashville. Exhausted, he found a motel in Nashville, paid cash, and slept for twelve hours, then caught another bus to Oklahoma City. It was on that bus that he realized he was heading west, toward home, even though he hadn't planned on it. He hadn't planned on anything, not consciously, anyway—he just wanted to keep moving. In Oklahoma City he decided to finish what he'd started, and bought a ticket on a Greyhound direct to downtown Los Angeles. By then more than seventy-two hours had passed since he had climbed out of the secretary of defense's bathroom window in Georgetown. He was wrung out, hungry, and his clothes stank. He used the last of his cash—he thought he might get tracked if he used a credit card—to buy jeans and a T-shirt in a Mexican clothing store near Pershing Square and a Subway sandwich with no drink, and then caught the Blue Line to Long Beach. Sitting in the sleek light-rail car with a host of Mexican immigrants and rowdy schoolkids, Garrett felt his stomach tighten. He hadn't been home in four years.

He walked from the Long Beach transit mall to his mother's house. It took him an hour, but he was glad for the exercise and the time to collect his thoughts. He stood for ten minutes outside the house he had grown up in, in the rough working-class neighborhood called Drake Park, letting the Southern California sun warm his skin. A few gangbangers drove by in their lowriders, music thumping from bass speakers set just below their rear windshields. Nobody stared. Nobody really gave a shit. Garrett knocked on the front door, hard and repeatedly, until he could hear his mother turning off the television. She peeked through the iron-grated screen door. Garrett watched her face. It had grown more creased in the time he'd been gone: there were scabby red streaks on her cheek, as if a cat had scratched her, and her black hair was flecked with gray. Never a tall woman, Inez Reilly seemed even shorter to her son now. An unlit Newport hung from her mouth. Garrett knew she was only forty-five, but she looked sixty-five, and not a day younger.

"Garrett?" Inez blinked over and over again. "What the fuck are you doing here?"

16

LONG BEACH, CALIFORNIA, MARCH 30, 1:28 PM

Garrett sipped the Budweiser his mother had given him. It was cold, which he expected—the one thing his mother knew how to do was store alcohol. She sat opposite him on a threadbare purple couch. She had turned the TV back on in the other room, full volume; an infomercial blared. Inez Reilly looked at her son, tugged on her cigarette, then sipped her own beer.

"You living in New York now?" Her accent had singsong traces of Mexico in it, that slightest of California-Sinaloa lineage, the weird in-between of the Mexican-American born in California and raised speaking Spanish. Garrett had to admit he loved hearing that accent. It reminded him of the good things of his childhood: handmade corn tortillas, ranchera music at backyard weddings, his childhood dog, Ponzo. That was about it, though. Everything else about his childhood sucked.

He nodded a yes to his mother.

"That's a cool city, right? I never been there."

"It's okay. You know. A lot of people. Stuff."

Silence enveloped the room.

"Your brother went there. To work. Some kind of money thing. I haven't heard from him in a while, though."

Garrett sighed. "No. That's me, Mom. Garrett."

She stared at him. "Yeah. Right." She relit her cigarette and drew deeply on it. Garrett sniffed the air. It didn't smell entirely of tobacco, but Garrett couldn't place the odor: it was faintly chemical, almost like burning plastic.

"So how you like it?"

"New York? It's okay. I like my work."

"A money thing, right? Like finances?"

He nodded and his mother stared off into space for a minute. Her eyes were unfocused. Garrett knew she was drunk, but then it occurred to him that she was high as well, and then he placed the odor: she was smoking methamphetamine, which was full of additives. That explained the scratches on her face. She'd become a tweaker: an addict who couldn't stop scratching herself. Garrett grimaced at the realization. It disgusted him. She had been so lively, so smart once. She had been top of her class at Long Beach Poly High School, could have gone to a UC school on scholarship, but got married instead. Had kids. And drank. The waste of it made Garrett want to run from the house.

His mother looked up at him, smiled. "It's good to have you home."

"Thanks, Mom."

"I miss you. All alone in this house. No one comes to visit. Nobody from the family. Nothing." She waved at the dilapidated wall. "You get a week's leave? You can sleep in your old room."

"No, Mom, I'm—"

"I'm proud of you, fighting for the country, you know? Makes me feel good. You're a hero. My son. A hero."

Garrett was too wrung out to correct his mother; it was hard enough just being home. He sunk lower in the beat-up La-Z-Boy, willing himself to disappear into the furniture. It was a familiar feeling. The memories came flooding back: his mother berating him for being lazy and selfish, for smoking pot and getting into fights; Brandon stepping between them, defending Garrett to little effect; his mother eventually relenting, then stomping off to the backyard to smoke another cigarette. He had wished, over and over again, to be dead.

The springs creaked. He was still there. And so was his mother.

"Not like your brother. All he thinks about is himself. How I raised him wrong I do not know."

Garrett winced. Bile collected in his stomach. His mother took another drag on her cigarette. She shook her head. "What the fuck is his problem? Huh? I ask you?"

"Mom, I'm Garrett. Brandon is dead."

Inez stared at her son, blank confusion on her face. To Garrett she looked like she was trying hard to process what he had just said, a flicker of the real world that she had seen but was quickly vanishing. She closed her eyes and sat motionless for a minute. Garrett watched her, then stood up and waved his hands in front of her face.

"Mom?" he whispered. Nothing. She didn't stir.

Garrett gave his childhood home one last cursory inspection, glancing in at the tiny, cluttered bedroom he'd shared with his brother for seventeen years, then walked out the front door, promising himself never to return.

17

LONG BEACH, CALIFORNIA, MARCH 30, 4:37 PM

If someone wants to kill me, fine, Garrett thought as he watched the surfers off Long Beach ride the shoulders, dive right with the break of the waves, and then ease into the shallow water. Blow me up. Just get it over with, and fast.

But no one came to kill him. So he simply sat in the sand.

The waves weren't that good here—the beaches in Long Beach faced the wrong way for the winter surf, and the port breakwater did the rest. But Garrett had still ridden them his entire life. He and Brandon had ruled this stretch of beach for a good five years. Well, Brandon had. He had been bigger, faster, three years older than Garrett, and he'd been ready to tangle with any outsiders who dropped in on them. L.B. locals only. That was their war cry. Brandon had taught Garrett every fighting move he knew. They'd lost a few dustups, sure, but mostly they'd been kings.

In his mind's eye he could see his brother's suntanned face, his long, tangled black hair, his pumped arms windmilling as he rode a wave into shore.

Garrett felt hollowed out inside. He hated coming back here, hated seeing his mother, their home, the baby pictures, the empty beer bottles, the squalor, all of it. And then the way she mistook him for Brandon. Or did she, really? She never said Brandon's name. Only Garrett's. Maybe she was doing it on purpose? It didn't matter. She was a drug addict, and trying to figure out the motives of a drug addict was putting yourself on a direct road to insanity. And yet, they still stung—her complaints about his selfishness, her casual taunts about Brandon's heroism. Coherent or not, she had gotten under his skin. It was an old wound, the comparison with Brandon; a wound that was easily reopened. It ate him up inside. Garrett didn't want to care, but he did.

He sat on the beach like that for two hours, feet and hands dug into the sand, and watched the surfers as, one by one, they called it a day and the sun slipped down over the Pacific. The sunset glowed orange and then purple, and it was just before night fell for real that Garrett saw the man watching him from the beach parking lot. He was sitting inside a large, dark sedan, American, with the lights out. Garrett had seen him when he first went to the beach, and thought nothing of it, but now that it was almost night, and he and his watcher were the only ones out, he knew who the man was. Garrett put his shoes back on and trudged across the sand to the parking lot. He walked to the sedan and knocked on the driver's-side window.

The man, dark-haired, broad-shouldered, no beard or mustache, wearing a bland, dark suit, rolled down his window.

Garrett said, "Tell Captain Truffant that I'll do it."

The man in the car said nothing, rolled his window back up, and made a phone call. He rolled the window down again and said, "She says to wait here."

Garrett shrugged and leaned against the car, watching the last of the light disappear. Dusk came on fast in Southern California, and left just as quickly. Five minutes later another car pulled up, and Alexis got out of the passenger seat.

"You're making the right decision," she said.

"I'm tired."

"I'll get you a hotel room. Get a good night's sleep. Tomorrow we'll start over."

18

ORANGE COUNTY, CALIFORNIA, MARCH 31, 7:45 AM

Garrett spent the night at the Hilton just off the I-5 freeway, south of Long Beach in Orange County. He had lain down at nine in the evening, fully dressed, just to rest for a moment before getting some dinner, and the next thing he knew Alexis Truffant was knocking on his door and it was six-thirty in the morning. He showered, ate a quick breakfast in the hotel restaurant, then got back into the unmarked car with the man in the dark suit at the wheel. Alexis sat next to him, a folder full of papers on her lap. She seemed chipper and all business. Garrett had the sense that his agreeing to work with her was a feather in her cap—whatever battle she had been fighting, she had clearly just won it.

"Is the Army okay with you?" she asked.

"Excuse me?"

"You have to be a member of an armed service. For all the clearances and information I'm going to give you. So I thought Army. I know your brother was a Marine. I figured you might want something different."

Garrett had to laugh. Garrett Reilly? In the Army? How ridiculous was that?

"I won't wear a uniform. No fucking way."

"Think of it as paperwork. A document you've got to sign."

"Army will work fine," he said.

They stopped at an Army recruiting station at a ratty strip mall on the border between Long Beach and Lakewood. A broad-shouldered Hispanic lieutenant saluted Alexis as she entered. They'd clearly been expecting her. He took a few lines of personal information, then had Garrett raise his right hand and repeat the oath of enlistment.

"I, Garrett Reilly, do solemnly swear that I will support and defend the Constitution of the United States against all enemies, foreign and domestic; that I will bear true faith and allegiance to the same; and that I will obey the orders of the President of the United States and the orders of the officers appointed over me, according to regulations and the Uniform Code of Military Justice. So help me God."

Garrett felt a rush of contradictory feelings as he said those words. He'd never pledged to any group, never sworn to protect anyone or anything, and wasn't comfortable doing it now. On the other hand, it made him think of his brother, and that made him smile. Brandon would have laughed to see his little brother in the service. Brandon would have laughed and laughed. And then probably punched him.

"Congratulations," the lieutenant said, shaking Garrett's hand.

"Yeah, thanks."

"I'd remind you that you need to address me as sir," the lieutenant said, "but the captain here says it's not going to work like that with you." He gave Garrett a dubious stare. "Which I'd like someone to explain to me sometime."

"Maybe next time, Lieutenant," Alexis interrupted. "And he doesn't need a physical, either."

Back in the car Garrett asked about his rank, and Alexis told him he was a private first class, but that wasn't important either. "All we ask is that you pass a urine test sometime in the next month. You think you can do that?"

Garrett shrugged. "Depends how much pot I smoke."

19

LAS VEGAS, NEVADA, MARCH 31, 11:57 AM

Denny Constantine paced through the empty rooms of his two-bedroom condo. The midday Las Vegas sun glared through the bedroom windows. The sunlight had already faded half the room's carpet, and Constantine had only installed the high-pile wall-to-wall six months ago. The elements in the desert were brutal to a condo. Then again, everything in Las Vegas was brutal to condos these days.

Constantine had thought of himself as a smart, conservative real estate entrepreneur. But even the smartest people in the real estate game had been burned lately. Constantine owned ten properties. That was down from twenty-three, two years ago. He'd sold off two at break even, seven at a loss, and four he'd simply walked away from. But the ten he still owned were killing him: the loans, the upkeep, the building fees. He was drained. Completely broke. And *broken*. Physically. Mentally.

He ran his thumb along the outer edge of his cell phone, rubbing the device for luck as if it were a talisman. If he massaged it long and hard enough, perhaps it would bring him the news he wanted: an offer. He had had a couple walk in here yesterday, and they seemed to like the place. The guy worked as a pit boss at the Mirage; his wife was a hairdresser. The price was right—$195,000—the building was in a prime Strip-adjacent location, and the apartment was in excellent shape. Yes, this would be another almost zero-profit sale for Constantine, but it would provide him with the trickle of cash flow he needed to cover his expenses for another month. It would give him breathing room, something he'd had precious little of lately. And yet still the phone didn't ring.

He stepped out onto the balcony to get better phone reception. Maybe the buyer's agent had been trying him but couldn't get through? The spring desert heat hit Constantine like a body blow. He immediately began to sweat into his black suit. He didn't care. He would wait right here, ten stories above the Vegas sidewalks, until his goddamned phone rang, even if his suit ended up a wet rag. And then, just as he had that determined thought, a miracle happened. His phone rang. It was the buyer's agent. He snapped open the flip phone in a fluid, practiced blur: "Denny speaking."

"Hey, buddy. How you doing?"

"I'm good, I'm good." Constantine tried to keep his nervousness in check. Deep breath. Talk slow. "Trying to stay out of the heat."

"Little hot. Little hot. But I can never get too much sun."

"Yeah." Constantine could feel rivulets of sweat running down his cheek. "So talk to me. Tell me some good news."

"Well actually . . ."

Constantine winced. Fuck. Fuck. Fuckety-fuck. The blood drained out of his face.

". . . my clients are not going to put in an offer."

Constantine grabbed the railing for support. He felt like he might faint. "I can go a little lower on this one. I mean, I know they liked the property. It's a great building. Did I show them the pool in back? And the workout room?"

"You did, man. Absolutely. And those were great, and they were really considering putting in an offer. But then, you know, all those other places came on."

"Other places? What other places?"

"You didn't hear?"

"No. Hear what?"

"Dude. Seven hundred separate condo units all came on the market this morning."

Constantine shook his head. "*What?* That's not possible. Seven hundred units?"

"Seven hundred and four actually. All over the city. Different buildings, different neighborhoods. But here's the really fucked-up thing. They all came on at half assessment. Like fire sale, half price. Or less."

Constantine's head swam. "Were they all owned by the same person?"

"Nobody knows. All kinds of guesses. Some distressed corp. Or maybe a hedge fund that's going under. People are digging through the titles like crazy, but it's weird complicated. Frigging mortgage mess, right?"

Constantine blinked in the heat. Sweat dripped into his eyes. "I . . . you sure your clients won't . . . ? I mean I could drop the . . ."

"I don't wanna ruin your day, but my clients can buy two other units in your building, same layout, for less than a hundred grand. Half what you're asking. I'm real sorry, dude. But that's the way the market goes, right?"

"I guess. Yeah."

"I gotta go. Stay strong, man. Later." The agent hung up.

Constantine was stunned. Seven hundred condo units all put up for sale, all at the same time, at half price? Or less? The market, already in steep decline, would drop dead. Prices would plummet, like a stone dropped off a building. All of Vegas would crash by this afternoon, if it hadn't already. Maybe all of Nevada.

He tried to grasp the enormity of what had just happened. Who the hell would do that? They were setting themselves up for gigantic losses. The only explanation he could think of was that they, like him, were completely desperate. Well, he hoped they were happy, because now everyone in all of Las Vegas was going to be desperate with them. They would all go down the sinkhole together. And wouldn't that be fun? One big fucking toilet.

No, Denny Constantine thought, still running his no-longer-magic cell phone in between his thumb and forefinger. He would not go down the sinkhole with them. He would blaze his own path. No one, and no market, would push him around.

Fuck that. I am still a free man, with free will, and I make my own decisions. And this is my decision . . .

He straightened his tie, tucked in his white shirt, and in one swift motion flung himself over the railing of the condo balcony. The last thought he had as he spun down toward the blistering hot pavement was that maybe he was wrong. Maybe the owners of those seven hundred units weren't desperate.

Maybe they did it on purpose.

20

CAMP PENDLETON, CALIFORNIA, MARCH 31, 2:31 PM

Garrett sat in a large, airy room in one of the low, wooden Marine barracks on the south end of Camp Pendleton Marine Base, just off Vandergrift Boulevard. The room was beat up, the paint peeling, the slatted ceiling rickety. There were half a dozen computers and monitors set up on school desks around the room, and a large projection screen hung on one wall. The other three walls were lined with charts and world maps, and they rattled when Marine helicopters took off and landed at the airstrip half a mile away, or when Humvees rumbled past on the rutted dirt tracks that crisscrossed the dry hills that surrounded the base.

Garrett was slightly disappointed. The computers were relatively new, but there wasn't any James Bond– or *Mission Impossible*–style fancy technology—no holograms or live feeds from covert NSA satellites. Instead there were a lot of file folders and dog-eared books stacked in corners. He had just started inspecting a map of South China when Alexis entered the room with three people in tow: two men and a woman, all young, late twenties at most. One of the men wore green Army fatigues; the other two were civilians—at least they appeared to be, judging by their clothes.

"Fancy digs," Garrett said, gesturing to the cracks in the walls.

"They won't attract attention," Alexis said. "Secrecy is the goal."

"Why Camp Pendleton? Isn't that Marines? I thought I was Army now?"

"It is Marines, but all the services occasionally use the base. It's a secure location. We won't have to spend extra resources protecting you. And, quite honestly, we don't have all the money in the world for this right now. It's low-rent, but it works."

"Low-rent is an understatement."

Alexis ignored Garrett's jibe and motioned to the people she'd brought with her. "We've assembled a team to help you. Together, we'll run you through the basics of what you need to know. About the world situation, about the military, about intelligence any of our services gather in the short and long term."

"*All* the intelligence your services gather?"

"Whatever intelligence is deemed vital for you to know."

Garrett laughed—the backpedaling had already begun. That was okay, though; he'd made his decision. He would see it through. At least for a while.

Alexis pointed to the young man in fatigues. He was about Garrett's height—six feet tall—and lean, with black buzz-cut hair and tortoiseshell glasses that were clearly not Army issue. "This is Lieutenant Jimmy Lefebvre."

Lefebvre stepped up and shook Garrett's hand. "Very pleased to meet you." He had a slight southern accent, and his gaze was cool and steady. Garrett thought he sensed a reserve in him, as if the lieutenant wasn't entirely happy to be there. He also thought he smelled money.

"Lieutenant Lefebvre is an assistant professor at the U.S. Army War College in Pennsylvania," Alexis said. "His specialty is developing-nation politics. Intercountry relationships, media dissemination of propaganda. He has a Ph.D. in political philosophy, and his knowledge of the world scene is vast. Consider him your political Wikipedia."

Lefebvre dipped his head and smiled uneasily, almost as if annoyed by Alexis's introduction. "Captain Truffant exaggerates," Lefebvre said. "But I hope to be useful to the team, regardless."

Alexis pointed to the young woman next. "This is Celeste Chen." Celeste was thin, with short black hair and bright-red lips. She wore a tight Decemberists T-shirt and ripped jeans, and she looked fantastic. At least Garrett thought so. He caught a brief glimpse of a snake tattoo coiled around her bicep, just below the sleeve of her shirt. Garrett loved a nicely placed tat—they were the epitome of sexy for him.

Celeste nodded coolly to Garrett. "Hey."

"Lemme guess," Garrett said. "You're the indie rock expert? Festivals, concert dates, band member bios?"

"Wow. You are good." She scowled at Garrett and sat down.

"Ms. Chen is a language analyst," Alexis said. "She is fluent in Chinese, all three major dialects, Mandarin, Cantonese, and Wu, as well as Japanese and Tagalog. She also does contract work in cryptology, for the military and the State Department. She's on loan from UCLA, and we're lucky to have her. She's also an experienced code breaker."

"Awesome," Garrett said. "I don't do any of that stuff." He liked Celeste immediately: she had attitude to burn, and Garrett held a special place in his heart for women with attitude.

Alexis turned to the last member of the trio. He was the oddest-looking of the three: young, no more than twenty-five, African-American, and huge—six foot three at least, with an extra fifty pounds around his midsection. He wore chinos and a blue button-down shirt that was a size too small, and which made him seem all the larger.

"This is Bingo Clemens," Alexis said. "He's our advisor on all things military and military hardware."

Garrett blinked in surprise. Of all the people in the room, Bingo appeared the least likely to have been in the military—or to have had anything to do with the military. If he could do five push-ups without collapsing, Garrett would have been astonished. Garrett was surprised they let him on the base.

"Nice to meet you, Bingo," Garrett said, sticking out his hand.

"Yep," Bingo mumbled, quickly shaking Garrett's hand. Bingo's fingers engulfed Garrett's. His hand was the size of a baseball glove.

"He can be shy," Alexis said, almost maternally. "But he has an encyclopedic knowledge of the armed services. Ours, the Russians', the Chinese. Anyone's. And he's up-to-date on capabilities, deployments, and materiel."

"But he's not part of the military, so he has no prejudices, and won't engage in the dreaded groupthink," Garrett said.

"Exactly," Alexis replied.

"I'm not shy," Bingo grunted, staring at the ground.

"Okay. I apologize for saying that, Bingo," Alexis said. "He does research for the Rand Corporation out of their Santa Monica offices. They specialize in national defense matters. Bingo actually has the highest security clearance of any of us."

Garrett gave Bingo another look. If he was who the military was entrusting high-level secrets to, then this country was doomed.

"I'm really not shy," Bingo muttered, clearly having trouble moving on.

"Hey, I believe you," Garrett said, smiling. He thought Bingo was amusing—if a little out there. "So," Garrett said, dropping into a rolling desk chair. "Nice to meet you all. When do we start?"

"Right now," Alexis said, booting up a laptop and opening an Excel spreadsheet. "Because we figure we have about a week."

"A week until what?" Garrett asked.

"Until a full-blown war."

21

BEIJING, APRIL 2, 3:08 PM

Xu Jin, director of the Ministry of State Security, walked quickly, purposefully, through the crowds that clogged the streets of Dashengzhuang Village, the sprawling suburban section of South Beijing. New immigrants to the Chinese capital—farmers and peasants just off the bus, mothers with babies wrapped in soiled clothes—elbowed the director as if he were just another citizen looking for a bargain in the stores and open-air stalls of this crowded, bustling community. They could not have known he was a member of the Politburo Standing Committee of the Communist Party, the most powerful ruling body in the entire People's Republic. But why should they know him, Xu Jin thought, as he sidestepped a hulking man carrying a sofa-sized load of cardboard on his back. Practically nobody in China knew the faces of their leaders. The premier, yes, and the president and vice president, of course. But below those esteemed men? Faceless technocrats. And that was just the way they liked it.

And it wasn't like Xu Jin was alone. There were two bodyguards—soldiers from the Beijing garrison, in plainclothes—following a few steps behind him. And behind them, four more soldiers, likewise dressed in slacks and black coats, but with pistols in their belts, on the lookout for subversives, anarchists, and Muslim extremists from the northwest. Or maybe followers of that insurrectionist bandit woman roaming the villages of central China. But he wouldn't be thinking of her—there were any number of enemies of the state wandering the streets of Beijing's immigrant villages; they blended in with the hordes looking for work, staying out of sight of the government's vast security apparatus while recruiting miscreants and criminals for their acts of subversion and destruction. They were nihilists, misguided zealots who sowed chaos, thinking that it would get them what they wanted. At least that was the way Xu Jin saw it. But they were mistaken. All acts of resistance to the state security forces would be met with unhesitating force.

They would be crushed.

Xu Jin ducked down an alley, his bodyguards following at a discreet distance, then shoved open the glass door of an Internet café. Inside, he was met with the low hum of a hundred computers, and the incessant click-clack of a hundred sets of fingers tapping on a hundred keyboards. There was little or no conversation, except for the bored cackle of the pair of teenaged girls behind the counter. Nobody looked up when Xu Jin entered the long, narrow, smoke-filled café, nobody noticed as he strode past the crammed-in desks lined with monitors and desktop computers. Kids, Xu Jin thought dismissively, playing their idiotic video games, posting their opinions on sports teams or girls—or whatever those people did online. He despised them all.

Xu Jin, fifty-six years old, trim and fastidious, from a sophisticated, urban family, had almost no experience using computers. He didn't have to. He had people on the committee—secretaries and assistants and endless functionaries—who did that for him. But it bothered him, the way people threw all their time and attention to the Internet. Didn't they realize that real life was out there, on the streets, waiting for them, not in here, in dingy, smelly Internet cafés? They let their hair grow long; they didn't shave or bathe, simply played and played all day long. *To what end?* It didn't matter. He knew what he wanted, and who would make it happen for him.

Xu Jin navigated the computer stations as they bunched even closer together toward the back of the café. There, in the last booth, before a chain-locked exit door, sat the man he was looking for. Or, rather, the boy. He pulled up a chair beside the gangly, pimpled programmer hunched over his keyboard. God, he was horrible to look at, pale and strung-out, vacant eyes staring at some idiotic video game. Were those dragons on his computer monitor? Is that what he does? Play dragon games?

"Gong Zhen," the ministry director hissed quietly. "It is me, Xu Jin. Look at me. Gong Zhen!" He let his voice rise over the hum of hard drives and whirring fans.

Gong Zhen, twenty-three years old, brushed his greasy black bangs from his forehead and turned slowly to look at the bureaucrat. He blinked twice, as if to reorient his thoughts, then frowned slightly. "What time is it?"

"'Director Xu, could you please tell me the time?' That is how you address me, Gong Zhen. That is how you address your elders. Your superiors."

Gong Zhen said nothing. Instead, he scratched lazily at his nose.

Xu Jin's whole body tightened with the impudence of this man-child: he should have him dragged from this horrible place and shot. That is what he should do, Xu Jin thought, and he should do it now. He started to stand up, and then caught himself, and sat back down. He could not have this boy shot. That was a ridiculous notion. Such things were no longer done in modern China. And for what? Not addressing a minister of state with proper respect? He calmed himself and looked the boy in the eye.

"We talked before. You remember?"

"Uh-huh."

"About some work you would do for me."

"I remember."

"How you would put a team together? Of computer people? Like yourself? Friends from the university? Loyal and trustworthy people? With some who had worked in the United States, maybe as interns for Microsoft or Apple, but had come home?"

"Uh-huh."

"I gave you money for this. Enough to hire two dozen people. Maybe more."

"Yeah."

"So you would write something, and then set that thing in motion? This thing I asked for. Like a train. A great runaway train?"

"Uh-huh. Sure."

Xu Jin collected himself. All that grunting would put him over the edge again. He rubbed the tops of his fingers, a soothing motion that never failed to bring him a moment's inner peace. "Have you done what I asked you for? You and your team?"

This time, Gong Zhen didn't answer, but instead turned to his keyboard and tapped out a series of rapid-fire commands. He pivoted the computer monitor so the director of state security could see the readout. Thousands of lines of computer code scrolled down the screen, black and red and blue fonts dancing over the white background. Xu Jin stared at it for a moment, but it was meaningless to him, a foreign language he neither understood nor had any interest in understanding.

"Are you saying this is the work?"

Gong Zhen nodded, then sipped at a can of energy drink.

"And you are ready to send it out into the world?"

Gong Zhen shrugged noncommittally. Xu Jin sighed; he was an infuriating, idiot child.

"And no one will be able to trace it back to here? To China?"

"Finland. And Ukraine," the boy said. "Multiple anonymous proxy servers."

"Yes, of course," Xu Jin said, baffled by the whole thing. "And in the writing of it. The writing of this code you did. There are the things I asked for?"

Again Gong Zhen shrugged.

Ahhrr! Xu Jin wanted to throttle the boy. Did he not realize that lives depended on this? More than that, the fate of nations was hanging in the balance? No, Xu Jin thought to himself, he does not realize this. No one does. Except for myself, a few members of the Standing Council, and some equally high-placed enemies in the United States of America. And that was the whole point, wasn't it? Attack and defend so that no one ever knew what was going on.

"So. How long would it take you to implement our plan? To get the process rolling? If we wanted to start soon, today, for instance? Can your people do it?"

Gong Zhen swung back to his monitor, tapped out a few keystrokes. The screen blinked, and without another word, Gong Zhen went back to playing that damned dragon-slaying game again. Director Xu watched in astonishment. Had this boy no sense whatsoever? He grabbed Gong Zhen by his shoulder and shook him roughly. "I asked you a question!" His voice rose above the clack of keyboards and the hiss of lips sucking on dozens of individual cigarettes. "When can you do this?"

Gong Zhen blinked rapidly again, as if he were already on another planet with his dragons and chain-mailed warriors.

"When?" Xu Jin barked again. "When can you start it?"

Gong Zhen frowned at the director. "I just did."

22

CAMP PENDLETON, APRIL 3, 7:12 PM

Garrett's head was swimming.

He was exhausted, hungry, his legs ached, and he was having trouble keeping his eyes focused. They had been at it for three days straight—not that he could really separate the days from the nights anymore. The streak of red sunlight that washed through the open barracks window and across his computer screen wasn't helping. Was that the sunrise or the sunset? It was all a blur.

The process had started the moment Alexis had booted up her laptop, three days ago. She had explained that Garrett would be working with each member of the team individually, for four hours at a time. After four hours, they would break for food, and then he would be passed on to the next member; another four hours, more food, then the next handoff. Alexis said they should work for as long as Garrett could endure. Then they would sleep—never more than a few hours—and get right back to it.

Lieutenant Lefebvre was Garrett's first instructor. Alexis sat them in a corner of the main barracks room, opened the windows to allow in a breeze, brought hot coffee, and let them have at it.

It wasn't at all what Garrett expected: Lefebvre didn't lecture Garrett, so much as he engaged him in a fast-paced, carefully structured conversation. It was all politics, all the time—most of it concerning China.

Lefebvre pulled up jpegs on a computer screen. These, he said, were the highest ranking members of the Chinese Communist Party Politburo. These were their names, and this was where they came from. This was each one's philosophical point of view. Lefebvre urged Garrett to ask questions, and he did. Why were they all men? (The party hierarchy was overwhelmingly male and extremely sexist.) Why were they all old? (It was a slow-moving, conservative bureaucracy.) How come Chinese exchange students got so much acne when they came to the United States?

At the last question, Lefebvre pressed his lips together in a tight, uncomfortable smile. He looked at Garrett like he could barely stand his company . . . and pushed on.

These were the Spratly Islands, claimed by China, Japan, and Vietnam. Vast oil reserves lay within their territorial waters. It was a burgeoning hot spot. Fine, now, this was the difference between a princeling—the offspring of a high-ranking party member—and a Chinese bureaucrat who had worked his way up the ranks. This was China's most recent GDP, its primary imports, exports, a brief history of its conflict with Korea, India, Russia. These were the world's primary trade routes; these were the Strait of Malacca. The U.S. Navy patrolled here. And here. And here.

Garrett doubted he'd remember any of it. When he stared out the window, watching the helicopters bank left over the beach and south toward San Diego, the lieutenant snapped at him: "Focus please, Mr. Reilly. We don't have a lot of time."

Garrett started to say fuck you, but caught himself. Lefebvre was goading him, for sure, but Garrett couldn't figure out why. On the Garrett Reilly scale of How Big of an Asshole Had I Been, he'd barely even gotten started with Lefebvre. Still, Lefebvre clearly didn't like him. When Garrett asked Alexis about this, she just shrugged.

"Maybe you offended him. You seem good at that."

During a five-minute break, Garrett did an online background check on Lefebvre. He'd been right about the money—the lieutenant was the heir to an old, and dwindling, Georgia timber fortune. Huh, Garrett thought, that's interesting, because now he was a low-level researcher at the Army War College. He liked that little bit of family rebellion. Garrett tried to see his Army records, but those were on a secure Human Resources server, and he didn't have time to hack it. He'd get to that later.

Lefebvre ended their session by giving Garrett a stack of books, three feet high, on Mao, the party, and the current state of the Chinese economy.

"You really expect me to read all this?"

"I don't expect anything of you," Lefebvre said with that same distasteful look.

Next it was Celeste Chen's turn. Much to Garrett's relief, Celeste didn't lecture him. Instead, they read Asian papers together. She called them up online and then translated the gist of any article he pointed out, steering him away from pieces that seemed completely off topic. They read the *Gōngrén Rìbào* (the Workers' Daily), the *Guanming Rìbào* (the organ of the Communist Party), the *Nongmin Rìbào* (agricultural news), and the *Jiefangjun Bao* (the mouthpiece for the People's Liberation Army). They sampled papers from Japan (*Asahi Shimbun* and *Mainichi Shimbun*), from Malaysia (the *Star*), and from Hong Kong (*Sing Tao Daily*). They read economic news, cultural news, and political news, but mostly they looked for any mention of the United States, for any reason: diplomacy, trade, movies, conflict, criticism . . . *war*.

At first, Garrett wasn't entirely sure what she was trying to teach him, but reading through the papers had a calming effect on him. He closed his eyes and began to imagine that Celeste's voice was actually the voices of Chinese citizens. They were talking to him. Telling him how they felt about the world. He let their opinions wash over him, drinking them in.

That's when he realized that they—Alexis and the DIA and whoever else was behind this—were treating him as if he were a computer. They were feeding him massive amounts of data and expecting him to sort it, filter it, process it, and then spit out answers—answers that would come in the form of pattern recognition. This revelation cheered him considerably: this he could do, and do well. Hell, he could mine patterns out of chaos in his sleep.

Celeste stayed cool to Garrett, clearly not interested in him in any way sexual or romantic, which disappointed Garrett, given that he viewed pretty much any good-looking woman as a possible hookup. He asked her if she had a boyfriend.

"Don't even go there," she said, barely pausing as she read through an article about hackers in the *China Public Security Daily*. "I'll kick your fucking teeth in."

Garrett laughed. He thought she might be a lesbian, which was okay with him, especially given how hot she was. But Celeste knew her stuff, that much was evident, and Garrett marveled at her grasp of languages. She was able to slip from Mandarin (her immigrant parents spoke it at home) to Japanese (learned it at school) to Cantonese (picked it up in her spare time) in quick succession, and all with equal fluency. She even spoke passable Arabic. Her linguistic skills seemed to be on a par with his ability to sort data—she mastered languages on an unconscious level, and that, to Garrett at least, was way fucking cool.

In the evening Alexis had food brought in. It was nasty cafeteria slop, obviously from the nearby Marine mess hall—beans and wilted salad and a mystery meat—but Garrett was starving, so he didn't care. He drank three cups of coffee and a Diet Coke. The moment he finished eating he was moved on to the next session, which belonged to Bingo Clemens.

Bingo talked in a steady, low whisper, barely audible, his face hunched over a computer keyboard. Garrett had to lean close to hear him, and also to see the screen past Bingo's large, fleshy head. Images flashed past—missiles and warships and planes and more missiles and maps and soldiers—while Bingo's voice rambled on without interruption: ". . . the tactical range of an AGM-84 Harpoon antiship missile is 278 kilometers . . . the Chinese have six Jianghu V–class frigates in service in the South China Sea . . . the Russian Federation has four armies headquartered in its Eastern Military Command, guarding its border with China . . ." Garrett interrupted him occasionally, asking him to slow down or explain an acronym, and Bingo would stop on a dime and go into even more excruciating detail.

Then Garrett, jonesing to get high, asked Bingo if he knew where Garrett could score some weed. Bingo fell silent for almost a minute, and then said, flatly, "You should not smoke pot. It's bad for you."

That was the sum total of the conversation.

It was clear to Garrett that Bingo was a seriously odd bird, but in a way that he kind of liked. He seemed incapable of harming a living thing—he scooped up stray spiders in coffee cups and released them in the brush outside—but when Garrett caught him playing *Call of Duty* on a laptop late that night, he saw the burning intensity of a killer in Bingo's eyes. Bingo was slaughtering Soviet agents with abandon, grunting in pleasure whenever a soldier bit the dust. That was when Garrett decided that the two of them were connected, however tangentially. Like Garrett, Bingo was a hard-core geek. Like Garrett, he had rage issues. He even had crappy social skills, a problem with which Garrett could sympathize.

By three in the morning Garrett was wrung out and asked to go to sleep. He sacked out in a small bunk room with a thin mattress and a window that was painted shut. An American flag hung on one wall, along with a Marine Corps recruiting poster. A square-jawed Marine in a white dress cap held a gleaming silver sword in front of his face. Brandon had brought home a poster just like it after he had signed up for the Corps. The few, the proud, the Marines, he had said over and over again, half taunt for his little brother and half catechism for himself.

Garrett ripped the poster off the wall and stuffed it into a garbage can, then curled up and passed out without taking off his clothes.

Day two had started at 6:00 a.m., with Alexis pounding on his door.

"Get up," she said. "We're going for a run."

"*We're* not doing anything," Garrett said, a pillow over his head. "You go for a fucking run."

Alexis opened the door anyway and shook Garrett roughly. "You need exercise. Good for the brain."

"My brain is fine," he said. "Fuck off and die."

She put a portable radio next to the bed and turned it on. Kesha screeched through the tinny speaker. She turned on the lights and pulled back the curtain on the window, flooding the room with sunlight.

"Ah, *shit*," Garrett said. "Have a fucking heart."

Garrett staggered out of bed and pulled on a pair of sweatpants and a T-shirt that she had left on a chair for him. He stumbled out of the barracks into the early-morning light and blearily put one foot in front of the other, following Alexis down a dirt path, working his way up to a reluctant, if steady, shuffle.

It was awful: the dust, the rocks, the dry wind, the sweat, the thirst, the pain in his muscles. He had never liked exercise of any kind, always thought it a waste of his time—after all, he was in perfectly good shape, and could push an elevator button as well as the next guy—and running seemed the ultimate in pointlessness. The fact that Alexis was able to lope effortlessly up and down hills like some kind of African springbok only furthered his humiliation. When she waited for him to catch up every quarter mile he had to restrain himself from smashing in her kneecaps with a rock.

After twenty minutes he dropped to his knees and began to dry-heave. Alexis relented, and walked him back to the barracks for the next set of sessions.

The rest of day two was more of the same: politics with Lefebvre, Chinese culture with Celeste, military briefings with Bingo. Four hours, then food, four hours, then food, and on and on into the night.

Alexis oversaw every session, sitting nearby, taking notes and asking questions. She didn't seem to tire, ever, or get distracted when her cell rang, which it did regularly. As far as Garrett could tell it was mostly General Kline badgering her for progress reports. If she was standing close enough he could hear the general barking at her about schedules and funding, and sometimes about the military, and once even about the president. Alexis would answer in flat, even tones—yes sir, no sir—never letting Kline's hyperbolic emotions ruffle her. That impressed Garrett, because keeping his cool was one of the things he was truly terrible at.

The other thing that impressed him was her flexibility. She was clearly running the show, but Garrett had to admit that she did it without ever throwing her weight around or restricting the conversation to subjects deemed "on topic." That surprised Garrett. His first impression of her had been that she was a rigid thinker, and he despised rigid thinking. Fluidity and change were the intellectual seas in which he swam. But Alexis was not so easy to pin down. She let the flow of information swing from place to place, arena to arena, and she showed no irritation when Garrett wanted to explore with Celeste—conversationally, of course—the differences between male and female masturbation, or when, exhausted and cranky, he finally told Lefebvre that diplomacy was a waste of time, and that the U.S. should just nuke China off the face of the earth.

At the end of day two, Garrett stopped studying Alexis's behavior and just thought of her as another member of the team. Well, almost. He had to admit that he still found her extremely attractive. He even found, in moments of distraction, that he had begun to have feelings for her, beyond just wanting to bed her. He wasn't exactly sure what those feelings were, but he did know that was new territory for him. Very new.

On the morning of day three Garrett and Alexis had run again, predawn. It still hurt, but Garrett only gagged twice and managed to make it a full three miles down the dirt jogging path, albeit very slowly. Alexis didn't break a sweat. That just killed him.

When they returned to the barracks, ten file-folder boxes full of intelligence briefings—with the providing agencies' names and officers redacted—had been delivered along with breakfast. The team—and Alexis had started calling them that somewhere in the middle of day two—broke from instruction sessions and instead dug through the briefings, each of them taking two boxes. It was a fascinating trove of global information that was often prosaic (the Brazilian wheat harvest was up seven percent for the first quarter, leading to an increase of 20,000 hectares of the grain being planted for the coming year), sometimes titillating (the prime minister of Cameroon was having an affair with a young Thai prostitute, which wasn't that unusual, but the prostitute was thought to have had a sex change, and that could prove embarrassing), and occasionally fraught with peril (Ukraine was believed to be shipping two hundred North Korean antiaircraft missiles to Iran, and the Israelis were contemplating intercepting the freighter, which American officials feared might set off a new Middle Eastern conflagration).

Halfway through his first briefing box, still covered in a fine layer of dirt from his run, eye sockets still sore from lack of sleep, Garrett had another revelation. He realized that he liked it. He had always loved learning esoteric things, especially if they had to do with numbers and economics, but he could not have guessed that amassing all this information at once would be so—he had hunted for the word while sipping a coffee and studying a map of the Sea of Japan—*thrilling*. It filled him with excitement. It was like being back at Yale, when Avery would push him not just to find the answer to a problem, but to figure out why the problem existed in the first place. But it was more than that now. He felt, for the first time, like he was doing something worthwhile. And useful. And those two concepts were strange bedfellows for Garrett Reilly.

It was as if all that privileged information was being funneled *only to him*, because someone out there believed that he could make sense of it all. He could sort the information, recognize the latent patterns, see through the random nature of the Chinese actions and bring coherency to them.

He was embarrassed to admit it, but he loved the feeling of being needed. He knew, consciously, that Alexis and her cronies at the DIA had planned it this way—that he was supposed to well up with a sense of purpose, and that in fact this was information that had already been vetted by some junior analyst in Washington. He knew that he wasn't *that* special. And yet, it worked. He felt a juvenile inner glow, no matter how much he hated himself for feeling it.

What he decided he really felt—head swimming, exhausted, waiting half-starved at the end of day three for more inedible mess-hall food to arrive at the barracks—was, well . . . *proud*.

23

QUEENS, NEW YORK, APRIL 4, 1:42 AM

Mitty Rodriguez was glad no one could hear her. She'd laughed so hard that Mountain Dew had come spraying out of her nose. And if anyone had seen that, well—major humiliation. But it was almost two in the morning and she was in an alley behind Thirty-fifth Avenue in Astoria, Queens, hunting through a Dumpster that belonged to an auto parts store, so no one was listening, and absolutely no one was watching.

She was looking for servomotors. Big ones, not the little pieces of shit that you bought at hobby stores. She needed them to control a pair of forward-reaching arms on the battle robot she was entering into the Destroy All Robots competition in Yonkers next week. Her plan was to attach a thin section of sharpened aluminum tubing to the right arm, and a circular Plexiglas shield to the left, which would make Morloc—that was her name for the as yet unfinished, two-foot-tall mechanical man—a seriously gangsta piece of machinery. Morloc was going to drive that aluminum spear right into the motherboard of all her challengers, frying out their circuits and rendering them electronically brain-dead.

In her mind's eye, Mitty could see the jig she would dance when Morloc won, and how she would pour beer on the heads of those semi-Asperger's Orenstein twins who beat her last year. But this was in the future. First she needed to find those servomotors, but it was dark, and she was having no luck.

The Dumpster was full of plastic bubble wrap and half-empty 10W-40 oil cans, which was making it stink like an old car engine. Also, Garrett kept calling, which was why she was laughing in the first place. He was talking some hilariously crazy shit. She would listen briefly, phone tucked to her ear, flashlight in her left hand, right hand digging through the crap, then hang up on him when his story started sounding too much like he was blowing crank up his nose.

Garrett was telling her that he was on a military base on the other side of the country. That he was working on some top-secret Defense Department shit—he couldn't tell her what because that would be illegal and they were probably listening in on this phone call—and that they had recruited him after the bombing at his office.

That's when Mitty started laughing.

"You're a lying sack of shit," she had said, and hung up.

He called back thirty seconds later and continued his tale. He was reading top-secret intelligence briefings and being tutored on all this classified junk by experts.

Doubt it. Laugh in face. End call.

Okay, maybe he wasn't a hundred percent trippin'. Yes, she had gotten his voice mail a couple of days ago: there had been that bombing downtown, he had been close to it, but he was fine, and he was leaving the city. She hadn't known anything about the bombing when she heard his message—she had been fighting with the Horde to conquer Azeroth in the Mists of Pandaria and had missed out on a couple of days' news—so she wasn't that relieved when she found out he was okay. That didn't make her insensitive—it was like someone telling you they had survived a car crash when you didn't even know they'd been in a car. Okay, maybe she was a little oblivious. Whatever. She had her priorities. Garrett understood that. That's why they were friends.

It did seem a little weird, though, that Garrett had left town and not told her why. And when she had listened to the voice mail again, she could hear strain in his voice. But Garrett was always getting into situations that put strain in his voice—buying stocks on loan or selling stocks on loan or trading contracts on loans. She didn't understand half of what he did, and didn't care.

But she did understand one thing: there was no way in the world Garrett Reilly was working for the U.S. military. For a lot of reasons.

First off, he hated the military. Those assholes had killed his brother. And then they had lied about it. Hell, she'd been with Garrett the night he took a drunken swing at the Marine sergeant at the recruiting center in Times Square, which had been hella funny, btw.

Second, what military in the world would want Garrett Reilly on their team? He had an unfixable attitude problem. She loved him and all, and he was her best friend, but you have to call a spade a spade—Garrett Reilly was just as likely to punch a coworker in the face as he was to scrap with our country's enemies. The dude was a 24/7 liability.

Mitty banged down a gulp of Mountain Dew (she brought a can with her everywhere she went) as her phone rang again. It was Garrett.

"You gotta cut it out," she said. "I'm a busy woman. If you're on the inside, prove it. *Muéstrame.*"

She hung up again. It was time to give up on the AutoZone Dumpsters. There were no servos down there, which was disappointing, but not surprising. It was hard to build a killer robot on the cheap, but it was a labor of love, and Mitty would not be denied. She climbed out of the Dumpster and walked the ten blocks back to her building on Thirty-first Avenue, trying to brush the dirt and grease off her pants as she went, then slogged up the three flights of stairs to her apartment and sat on her couch, gazing mournfully at the pieces of Morloc spread out on her living room floor. She had had such big plans for him . . .

Her phone chimed. It was a text. From Garrett. It read: Preguntas. *Questions.* That was their code. It meant that he had something to share with her, but that it was a secret, and he was sending it on their own virtual private network. They used the VPN mostly for passing game cheats and ripped movies.

She sighed, tired of the charade with Garrett, but booted up one of her laptops anyway. It was the computer she kept offline ninety-nine percent of the time, and only connected to the Web on an isolated dial-up that she had hacked from the phone company. No one was going to be snooping on *that* line. There was one unread e-mail on the account, and it was from Garrett, and of course it was encrypted, but she had the encryption key. Hell, she had written it.

She opened it. There was a link. And a password. She clicked it and waited, tired and stinking of motor oil and ready for bed, but then what loaded on-screen made her heart race . . . and forget all about Morloc's pitiful, lifeless arms.

Destroy All Robots could wait, she thought, gazing at the scroll of military enlistment records, because her homeboy Garrett had just struck the mother lode.

24

CAMP PENDLETON, APRIL 4, 12:39 AM

Garrett lay in his slatted bunk bed and smiled. He smiled because he knew that across the country, Mitty Rodriguez was staring at his e-mail and hyperventilating.

He hadn't sent her anything important—just a backdoor portal into a Camp Pendleton HR account. He'd hacked it himself, after Alexis had broken them off for the evening and he had a few minutes to lurk in the base's secured intranet. Of course it was secured from outside of Pendleton, but not from sniffers *inside* the military's firewall. He hadn't done any real damage; the HR server was a dead end, and Mitty would find that out pretty soon. But it proved where he was, and that he wasn't just bullshitting her.

It also allowed Garrett to see Jimmy Lefebvre's Army records, and reading them had been an eye-opener. Lefebvre had graduated with top honors from Officer Candidate School, and had been about to ship out to Iraq when doctors discovered he had a heart arrhythmia. Those were grounds for an immediate medical discharge, but someone, somewhere, had pulled strings and Lefebvre was offered a desk job instead—poli-sci research at the War College. It saved his career, but Garrett guessed that not seeing combat must have been crushing to a proud southern aristocrat like Lefebvre. It helped explain his attitude: Lefebvre probably saw Garrett as an able-bodied freeloader. That must eat him up.

Garrett decided to cut him some slack.

He eyed the stack of books Lefebvre had given him. They were beginning to pile up all around his tiny bunk room. Maybe the first part of cutting the lieutenant slack was actually doing what he asked.

Garrett leafed through them. They were all about China: biographies of its leaders, histories of its culture, the revolution, its wars, essays on Chinese painting, poetry, literature. Name an aspect of modern Chinese life and Garrett was pretty sure that in the last five years there had been a book published about it. Probably two. Or a dozen.

Some were more interesting than others, but Garrett didn't mind that. He had come to terms with his role on the team, that of human database. By definition, a database needed as much information as it could hold. And Garrett could hold a lot.

One book caught his attention: a biography of Mao Zedong. The son of a peasant who had grown rich selling grain, Mao had grown up not poor—as Garrett had assumed—but in fact relatively well off. He had been well educated, going to secondary school—a rarity in that age in China—and eventually attending Peking University, where he met and married the daughter of a college professor. It was there, at university, that he had discovered Marxism and promptly joined the Chinese Communist Party. And it was in the party that Mao discovered his true calling.

What struck Garrett most about Mao was his intellect. He was brilliant. He was also a futurist of the highest order. He understood the logistics of political organizing, and he implemented those logistics by placing loyal commissars in all local party cells. He also understood the future of warfare in a way that no one else at the time did; he knew that the modern armies facing his ragtag revolutionaries could only be beaten by what would now be termed asymmetric warfare—sporadic, surprise guerrilla attacks meant to disrupt and demoralize. And so that was exactly the military strategy he employed. He knew, instinctively, that he had to win the hearts and minds of the local peasantry in order to change a country as vast and populous as China, and that once those hearts and minds were won, they had to be kept in line through iron-fisted control.

Mao had struck fear in all those who opposed him, whether in the ruling class of China's corrupt government, or in the lackeys who worked for him once the Communists seized power. Mao was tough when he had to be, and then brutal later on when being humane would have sufficed. He was a committed partisan, and he never showed weakness. It was Mao who had single-handedly shaped what was now modern China, and no matter what reforms had been implemented since his death, no matter how much growth and capitalism had been allowed to flourish in the country, it was Mao's shadow that blanketed the country. It was his steely personality that ruled the Communist Party. And it was the party that ran China.

Only Garrett wasn't so sure that Mao, were he alive today, would be so happy with the state of modern China: the wild disparity between rich and poor, the population drain from interior farms to coastal cities, the growing power of the party and the disenfranchisement of the peasants. Everything that Mao had fought so hard against was now the norm in modern China. The bureaucrats and princelings in the party today more resembled the corrupt aristocrats of prerevolutionary China than they did the reformers of Mao's heyday. And things were clearly getting worse—the locomotive that was Chinese modernization was barreling down the tracks, unchecked.

Everything they had studied in the past week painted a picture of a country deep in the wilds of change, a change so profound and all-encompassing as to render the nation unrecognizable, even to people who had visited it as recently as ten years ago. And if the last time you'd visited China was in 1976, when Mao died, then you'd feel like a space traveler visiting an entirely new planet. China had completely remade itself.

All of which led Garrett to the realization, finally, at 3:30 in the morning, lying on his bunk, that the leaders of modern China might revere Mao, but if he were to miraculously walk into a party Politburo meeting tomorrow morning . . . *he'd probably have them all shot.*

25

CAMP PENDLETON, APRIL 4, 6:17 AM

On the morning of day four Garrett began to get his wind back.

He'd gotten up before Alexis and started a run on his own. Something about being on a military base and seeing all the other young men and women working at being fit made him want to give it a try. He ran hard, sweating, grunting, straining, even sprinting up and down a few hills. Garrett thought this wasn't just progress but a minor miracle. His legs still ached with each stride, but his gag reflex lessened, and his toes didn't chafe horribly into the front of his running shoes. He even found he wasn't longing for a bong hit quite so desperately.

"Good pace on those hills," Alexis said as she caught up with him at the base of the last incline before their barracks. She wasn't even panting. "Didn't think you had it in you."

"Is that supposed to make me feel better or worse?"

Alexis shrugged, then sprinted past him up the dirt path. Garrett didn't bother trying to match her speed up the hill; he was happy just to finish without doubling over.

He paused at the top of the bluff and watched the Marines as they practiced and maneuvered on Camp Pendleton's seemingly endless expanse of scrub brush and beach. Each morning he had observed them as he shuffled past—watched as motorized assault vehicles splashed off landing boats and onto smooth beaches, listened as lieutenants urged their platoons over crumbling concrete walls, and studied silently as swarms of new recruits fired, ducked, advanced, and then fired again at the myriad shooting ranges scattered across the base.

It was on this hillside that Garrett began to glimpse the dread groupthink that the general had mentioned; the bravery, the physical fitness, but also the mindless obedience and grinding repetition. He began to think that to be a soldier was to be worn down, stripped of one's distinct and original thoughts, and then remade into a killing machine, an automaton that did what it was told.

There was something distinctly wrong about that—all those men and women, doing what they were told without question, never stopping to probe at the efficacy of the commands being barked at them. He didn't even have to go so far as to think about lives being at stake, grieving families being left behind—he knew all about that—no, what was wrong with what he was observing was much simpler: it seemed like a waste of brain power.

And that, to Garrett, was inexcusable.

When he returned to the barracks, Alexis, Bingo, Celeste, and Lefebvre were already sifting through a new batch of intelligence briefs. Garrett grabbed a stack and thumbed through them. Half an hour in, a small dispatch buried deep in a natural-resources report caught his attention. A demolition expert named Sawyer had called an FBI field office in Denver a week ago to report a job he'd done for an undisclosed client: destroying the Henderson Canyon Molybdenum Mine. The FBI had tried to contact the DIA, but the message hit detours within the interagency bureaucracy. And, anyway, it was too late—the mine had already been blown; the molybdenum inside it was unrecoverable.

"Hey, Bingo," Garrett asked, still in his sweatpants and T-shirt. "Molybdenum. We use that for military stuff, right?"

"Transition metal," Bingo answered. "Used in alloys in fighters, tanks, satellites, missiles."

Garrett looked up the mine's ownership online. An international consortium had bought the mine, and the House Energy and Commerce Committee had rubber-stamped the sale. Rare earth metal mining was a high-cost, low-margin pursuit. An Australian businessman had been the figurehead for the consortium, and had promised to keep the mine open, but he resigned two weeks after the purchase and was nowhere to be found.

"We need to do a chain-of-title search," Garrett told Alexis. "I think this is important."

Alexis called the DIA, and within an hour an analyst called back. He had worked up a paper trail for the buying consortium—loans, stock guarantees, and voting-rights certificates—that led east, across the Pacific, and ended on the shores of Victoria Harbor, in the glittering office buildings of downtown Hong Kong. It was circumstantial evidence, but Garrett thought it damning.

"The Chinese government was behind this," Garrett said.

"All that money just to destroy a mine? Seems like a waste," Celeste said.

"Not really," Garrett replied. "Now we're at their mercy. They've cornered a rare earth metal market. They'll make back their investment by raising prices at Chinese mines in a year. Maybe less. And we're screwed."

"That's if it really was the Chinese that did it," Lefebvre countered.

"It was them. Guaranteed."

Lefebvre shot Garrett a skeptical look. "And why are you so sure, Mr. Reilly? Maybe it was just international businessmen making a cost–benefit decision."

Garrett leaned back in his chair and thought about this. Why was he so sure? It wasn't a full-blown pattern, but something about it ran a shiver through the base of his spine in a familiar way. Mines. Money. Destruction. Rare earth metals. They were linked, that much was obvious, but there was also an organizing principle at work here. What was it?

"Mao," Garrett said, the answer coming to him in a flash.

"Excuse me?" Lefebvre said.

"Mao would have destroyed that mine. Asymmetric warfare. Destabilize a more powerful enemy through targeted hit-and-run attacks on his materiel infrastructure. Mao did it all the time during the revolution. The party reveres Mao. They're just doing what he would have done." Garrett looked over to the lieutenant. "I'm sure . . . *because it fits.*"

Lefebvre stared at Garrett in amazement: "You read the books I gave you?"

"Yep," Garrett said. "Mao's books in particular: *On Guerrilla Warfare*. *Political Democracy*. Also two biographies." Garrett shrugged. "Truth is, I skimmed the bios."

Garrett thought he saw a trace of a smile forming at the corners of Lefebvre's face. "Well, since you put it that way," Lefebvre said, adjusting his glasses and leaning back in his chair. "I have to concur with Mr. Reilly. It was the Chinese government."

Garrett beamed: he suspected he'd just broken through to the lieutenant.

Alexis looked over at Lefebvre in surprise, but before she could say anything, Celeste nodded vigorously from the other side of the table: "I'm with them. China."

Bingo ducked his head. "Me too."

Garrett grinned as Alexis let out a short breath, pushed back her chair, and stood up. She was still dressed in her running shorts and a fitted Lycra top.

"All right, then," she said. "I'll call Washington." She paused and shot each of the four of them a quick look, almost, Garrett thought, as if to give them another chance to tell her that they considered Garrett a lunatic. But nobody said anything, and Alexis strode quickly out of the room, pulling out her cell phone as she left.

When she returned a minute later she stared right at Garrett, a look of what he could only describe as satisfaction on her face, as if she were thinking, Son of a bitch, we might have something here after all. But she didn't say that. What she said was: "Shower up. We need to keep going."

"Yes ma'am," Garrett said, and headed back to his room.

Bingo Clemens caught the real estate sell-off in Las Vegas later that morning. Celeste was running Garrett through a primer on Confucian ethics on the other side of the room, and Bingo was using his free time to trawl military blogs. Someone had posted a comment on a blog out of Nellis AFB outside of Vegas about all the condos that had come on the market, and how no one knew who had done it.

Rumors were spreading about a precipitous drop in prices and two real estate brokers who had committed suicide. Someone else wrote that he'd heard the *New York Times* had been calling around, but their reporters couldn't find the original owners of the seven hundred properties. They'd all been sold through multiple limited-liability corporations from around the country, with dummy names and fake addresses. In Nevada, all it took was ten minutes and seventy-five dollars to create your own LLC online. In other states it was even easier.

Bingo took the news to Alexis.

"Interesting," she said. "How'd you find it?"

"Well," Bingo said, "I was trying to think in patterns. Like Garrett." He scratched at the scruff on his chin, then gave her a crooked smile. "He's badass."

Alexis almost spit out her coffee. "Okay," she said, recovering. "Go tell the group."

Bingo called the team together and told them about the mystery he had discovered.

"Not a mystery," Garrett said. "We all know exactly who did it. It dovetails perfectly with the mine destruction and the Treasuries sell-off. A high-value asset sold suddenly and without warning at a considerable loss. Owners who go to great lengths to stay hidden. And no obvious purpose to the transactions other than to freak people out. They're sowing chaos in the American economy."

"Well, we'll need to prove that," Alexis said. "So—any ideas?"

There was momentary silence, until Bingo raised a hand from the corner. "The DIA has supercomputers, right?"

Alexis nodded.

"We could ask them to drill down into online incorporation records. There's gotta be state databases that their computers could sort through pretty fast."

"Worth a try," she said and handed Bingo her cell phone. "Call Kline. Have him hook you up with Analytics."

"I'm really not so good on the phone asking people for—" Bingo started to say.

"Badasses know how to work the phones," Alexis said, cutting him off.

Bingo frowned and took the phone. He called General Kline and told him, with Garrett at his side, coaching him, what they wanted without mentioning any specifics, and Kline forwarded him to an information officer. Bingo gave the guy a couple dozen search parameters—Las Vegas, condominiums, thirty-year-fixed mortgages, LLC, real estate corps, among others—and a five-year time frame, and asked, politely, if he could please expedite the search.

The results came back in half an hour. Most of it was white noise, but one name did surface a few too many times to be completely random: an offshore shell company in the Bahamas called Fifty-Four MT. The owners were listed as local Bahamians, but when Alexis called, they knew nothing about the business, claimed to have been paid five hundred bucks to sign the ownership documents, and generally sounded very, very drunk.

It seemed like a dead end. They couldn't exactly blame the Bahamas. But Garrett wouldn't let it go. "The name is a clue," he said, scowling. "Somebody out there wants us to figure it out."

That was all the prodding it took for Celeste Chen. "It's not just a clue, it's code," she said. "Fifty-Four MT? MT might stand for, what? Mount? Mountain? Montana? The fifty-fourth mountain in Montana?"

She spoke to herself quietly and quickly, pacing, while everyone else watched her, then let out a guttural grunt of surprise and revelation.

"No, not fifty-four—you idiot!" she blurted out. "Five. Four. Fifth month, fourth day. May fourth. MT stands for movement, not mountain. The May Fourth Movement. It's a historic anti-imperialism protest from the 1920s. It's considered the birth moment of Chinese communism."

Bingo, Alexis, and Lefebvre broke out in spontaneous applause. Garrett just nodded his head. "Good code breaking," he said. "Seriously cool."

"Well done," Alexis said to Celeste. Then she turned to the rest of the team. "All of you. Well done."

Alexis typed up a report and sent it in an e-mail to General Kline, who dutifully relayed the information to the Treasury Department and the president. That afternoon, a dozen unnamed real estate speculators flew into Vegas's McCarran airport and started snapping up condos for 25 percent over listing price, no questions asked. The Las Vegas real estate market wobbled, but it didn't collapse.

Just before nightfall, Kline cc'ed the entire team on a one-word e-mail. It said, simply: *Nice.* Garrett laughed when he read it, but he couldn't deny that he enjoyed the praise, however bare-bones.

26

THE DALLES, OREGON, APRIL 4, 7:09 PM

Lillian Pradesh knew computers. She had grown up with them, practically having one thrust into her crib when she was a baby. Her father, an Indian immigrant and Microsoft engineer, had made sure of it. "The computer is the future," he had said. "Make it a part of your body." And so she had. She could code with the best of them. She could debug any piece of software. She could network a hundred computers together in less than two hours. She could build her own laptop, work station, even a mainframe. And she had, more times than she could remember—the first one at the tender age of nine. All of these skills had gotten her a free ride at MIT, a postgraduate degree from Carnegie Mellon, and a sweet job at Google. At thirty-one, she was the youngest director of regional network operations the company had ever had.

Her fiefdom was two football field–sized buildings on the banks of the Columbia River in The Dalles. Their code name was 02, and inside the massive, bland, white buildings were 150,000 clustered computers, housed in semi-truck-sized containers, with massive fans blowing cool air up into them twenty-four hours a day, 365 days a year.

Lillian monitored the servers night and day. She was familiar with all the specs—top secret of course—and every piece of hardware and software in the place. Routers, switches, hard drives, DNS servers, filters, firewalls. Everything. You might even say that she loved the servers, all 150,000 of them. Loved their humming efficiency, loved the way they spat out answers in milliseconds, directing search results to every conceivable corner of the globe. She felt, as her father had told her, that they were an extension of herself. A part of her body.

So on a late Monday afternoon, when her screen flickered a warning about a malware intrusion on one of their servers, she took it personally. It happened every day, all the time, and yet it still made her skin crawl. These were her servers, damn it. They were as much a part of her personality as her sense of humor. How dare anyone attack them?

It was a small piece of code, buried deep in the operating instructions of a quad core 2.5 GHz Pentium class, Linux-based squid server. It was currently up and running, so she couldn't look at the code until she had isolated it and killed it. She wasn't too worried, because the Google security software was written to automatically block malicious code on infected servers from the rest of the farm. And it did that, all in the bat of an eye. But then that same piece of malware showed up in another container's worth of servers, this one in building two, unconnected to the first infected container.

Immediately, the security software isolated that container as well. Lillian breathed a sigh of relief. She would have to call her superior, the director of all networking operations in Silicon Valley. She did a quick scan of the malware. It was self-replicating, as all malware was, and well hidden. Lillian checked the access requests buried in the server logs. They were essentially a road map of what the malware had been doing. What jumped out at Lillian right away was the access request in the data head of the code. It was asking to get into the programmable logic controller data bloc—or PLC—in the original server software. This was seriously treacherous code, aimed at shutting down servers in a big way. She still couldn't read it, but she could see what it was up to. It seemed to be trying to rewrite code in the brain stem of her beloved servers. That wasn't hard in and of itself—many cyber attacks tried to do just that. What was surprising was that it had gotten past the initial Google intrusion prevention software. The company had some of the best computer security code in the world. In Lillian's opinion, it *was* the best in the world.

She had helped write it.

She sipped her coffee and fantasized about how she would rip the malware to pieces, imagining it as a burglar in the night, breaking into her house, who she would personally blow to bits with her own 12-gauge digital shotgun. She laughed at the metaphor, but then came up short. Another container was registering the malware. What the hell? That made three separate sections of the server farm that were infected. This was highly unusual. It occurred to Lillian that the malware might have self-replicated long ago, well before detection by her security software. If that was the case, then there might be many, many more computers infected. In fact, she thought, as a horrifying chill ran down her spine, the malware might have infected the entire . . .

But Lillian Pradesh did not even have time to finish the thought. At that very moment, her computer screen began to register a massive shutdown of server CPUs across the server farm. One, then two, then twenty, two hundred, a thousand, ten thousand, then . . .

. . . *All of them.*

Every single server in the two buildings, all 150,000 of them, all at once, turned off, the digital equivalent of going from the speed of light to zero in an instant. Lillian stared, openmouthed. Her computer screen showed her the completely unimaginable: they had been breached, compromised, and basically destroyed. Her entire server farm was offline. The attack had been swift and unrelenting. She was too stunned to even move. The only sound she heard was the blowing of the massive cooling fans on the floor of the cavernous server farm. They whirred and whirred, relentless, as the very thing the fans were meant to cool died.

Then her computer shut itself down as well. The entire building was dead.

27

CAMP PENDLETON, APRIL 4, 8:17 PM

Garrett dipped his feet in the cold Pacific Ocean. He had tossed his shoes into the sand behind him, rolled up his jeans, then waded up to his knees in the frigid water. He didn't mind the cold—it felt good on his skin. He needed to clear his head. It had been more than four days of uninterrupted work and his brain was fried. Behind him, he could make out a Marine sentry standing thirty yards back from the water, night-vision goggles flipped down, silhouette lit up by the full moon that hung low over the black horizon.

"Nice night, huh?"

Garrett turned. Alexis walked out of the darkness and stood at the edge of the water. Her face was bathed in silver luminescence, her body outlined by the white sand. She had changed out of her Army dress slacks and into jeans and an old Adidas T-shirt.

"Good night to be back in California," she said.

"I always missed the beach in New York." He stepped out of the waves and back onto the beach. "I missed swimming in it. Surfing in it. The Atlantic just doesn't cut it."

"Take a walk for a few minutes?" she asked.

"Sure."

She turned, and they walked side by side on the beach, right along the invisible line where the waves broke and the water dissolved into the sand.

"Tell me about yourself," she said. "About your life."

"Nothing to tell."

"Did you like your job at Jenkins & Altshuler?"

"I liked the money. And bond trading was easy. For me at least." A wave rolled up to his feet.

"But?"

"But nothing. I didn't give it too much thought. I just did it." He looked at her, half her face in darkness, the other half illuminated by the rising moon. She was beautiful, her smooth olive skin glimmering in the dim light. "Now you tell me something. You like your job?"

"Love it," she said, without hesitation.

"You ever had another job? Before the military?"

"Waitressing. In college. Which I hated. But I guess everyone should wait tables once in their lives."

"You saw combat?"

"Waiting tables? Constantly."

He laughed. She smiled briefly, then shook her head no. "Two tours of duty in Iraq. But logistics mostly. I never fired my gun."

"Not once?"

"Nope."

"You sad about that? Not shooting anyone?"

"Hardly. I didn't join the Army to kill people. I would have, if I'd had to. But the occasion never presented itself."

"So why did you join? I mean, if you weren't looking to kill anyone?"

"To serve my country. To give back. To find purpose in my life."

"Whoa. That's a lot of sincerity. I was looking for something more cynical."

Alexis smiled and shrugged. "I don't do cynical well."

"I've noticed."

They walked for a moment in silence. The waves thudded against the shore, broke, and bubbled onto the sand. A thin line of foam zigzagged ahead of them into the night. Garrett looked at her. "So? Have you? Found purpose?"

"Absolutely. I'm the front line of defense. Keeping my country safe. Every morning I get up knowing exactly what I am doing and why I'm doing it. I love that feeling. To me, that's purpose."

Garrett tried to think of something cutting to say, but nothing came to mind. He let out a long breath instead. At his side, Alexis stopped walking, and her feet sunk into the sand. Her shoulder accidentally rubbed up against his.

"I've been meaning to ask you this question," she said, "and I don't want you to take it the wrong way. But if you're so cynical, why'd you agree to help out? I thought you hated the military?"

"I hate what the military does."

"What do we do?"

"Destroy lives. Lots of lives. Lives of enemies. The lives of its own soldiers."

"Your brother's life."

"My brother's life for sure."

"And yet you're here?"

"Yeah. I am here." Garrett looked out at the black sea. He had been asking himself the same question, but found the answer to be elusive. Why the hell was he here, on a Marine base, aiding and abetting the one organization in the world that he absolutely detested, hands down, above any other?

"I can't explain that one . . ." His voice drifted off. He watched the rhythmic waves rolling onto the sand. "I look for patterns. But my own life, it wasn't falling into a pattern. It was just . . . random. Making some money. Losing some money. Drinking. Partying. Sleeping with a girl, not seeing her again. Back at work. Not that it was bad. It just wasn't . . . *anything*. I can't accept that. There are always answers."

"You can't live without patterns." She seemed to say this more as a statement than a question, and Garrett nodded in the affirmative. It was a truth about him that he had known for a long time—since childhood, really—but it wasn't a truth he volunteered readily. Alexis had sensed it intuitively. Garrett suspected she understood him a lot better than she let on.

"I try not to," he said. "Without patterns, the world is too . . . chaotic. Truth is, chaos scares the shit out of me."

"Chaos scares everyone."

"Does it?" He smiled. "I guess I'm glad to hear that. What I mean is—nice to have company."

Alexis watched his face carefully. "Are you happy with the decision? To join us?"

Garrett laughed. "Happy? Let's not go overboard. I'm here, doing the job. That's about as far as I'm willing to go."

Alexis smiled at him. "Well, I'm happy with your decision. Very happy."

Garrett cocked his head sideways. What had he just heard in her voice? A softness, a quiet affection? It gave him chills. He turned to her—she had never looked quite so pretty as she did now. He thought about stepping forward to kiss her—it seemed like the right thing to do, even with Marine sentries staring at them through their night-vision goggles—when a voice rang out.

"Guys! We have a problem!" Lefebvre was sprinting down the beach. "Google is crashing!"

28

NEW YORK CITY, APRIL 4, 11:23 PM

Avery Bernstein ducked into the White Horse Tavern on the corner of Eleventh and Hudson. The day had been slow, unproductive for most of the team, and tediously long for himself. The truth was, no one at Jenkins & Altshuler had recovered fully from the bombing. None of them had been hurt in the blast, but everyone had heard it, had their desks rattled by it, had seen the debris scattered across the pockmarked lobby and the shattered street. And rumors about Garrett Reilly had been flying around the office for days now.

At first all the other brokers had bought the story Avery had been told to spread—Garrett had been hurt, but was recovering, and had decided to take some time off by visiting his family in California. But coworkers who knew Garrett had trouble believing he would go anywhere near his family, especially if rest and relaxation were what was called for.

Now, ten days later, new stories were surfacing: Garrett had been the target of the bomb. He had happened onto some kind of top-secret financial scandal. He had been abducted by a foreign government and was being held for ransom. Avery tried to beat back the rumors, but that only stoked more speculation. This morning he had found an online bulletin board on the company servers dedicated to half-cocked theories as to who had detonated the bomb—Armenian extremists, irate Goldman Sachs directors—and where Garrett Reilly really was—in jail, a mental institution, two floors below the Jenkins & Altshuler offices, trading highly speculative derivatives. Avery shut the bulletin board down, but not before reading that he himself was suspected in Garrett's disappearance. "AB is complicit and not to be trusted," read one post. "Watch your back around him."

Well, they're sort of right, Avery thought as he ordered a shot of Basil Hayden's bourbon with one ice cube. He was complicit. But complicit was different from responsible. He was not *responsible* for what had happened, he had merely been a conduit for information. And still, he sighed as the bourbon's hint of sweetness trickled down his throat; he worried about Garrett and what would happen to him. The government was a soulless machine. Its bureaucrats did not care a whit for who was ground up in its cogs. And as big a pain in the ass as Garrett was, Avery loved him. As corny as it sounded, Garrett really was the son he had never had. Avery would be devastated if anything happened to Garrett—utterly devastated.

"But what can I do now?" he muttered as he downed his drink, disgusted at the catty workers in his office, disgusted at the gossips in other financial firms across lower Manhattan, and disgusted mostly at himself for allowing the military to cajole and bully him. Why did he play along with their games, their secrets? He knew the answer—he played along because he was scared of them. He was scared of their power, their ability to ferret out nasty intelligence about his business, about his personal life, and he was even slightly afraid for his personal safety. He wasn't one of those people who believed the United States government went around killing its internal enemies, but he wasn't ready to put that theory to the test, either.

The truth about Avery was that he was a coward. He'd been picked on as a child, beaten up more times than he could remember for being short, geeky, and then, when he was a little older, for being gay. Avery had been out of the closet for years now, but he still recoiled at the memory of the savage pounding he'd gotten in high school when he'd dared to kiss another boy. The boy had panicked, desperate to hide who he really was, and told everyone at the school what had happened, and then Avery knew it would only be a matter of time before the starting nine of the baseball team trapped him in the men's bathroom, which they did, and punched him and kicked him until he blacked out. Which they also did.

The incident didn't make him tough. Or brave. It made him cautious. He didn't kiss a boy again until he was twenty-seven, and even then he was sure his world would come crashing down around him. But it didn't, and slowly Avery gained his dignity as a scholar, later a businessman, and eventually a gay scholar and businessman. But he still stayed away from gay bars, and kept his sexual identity mostly to himself.

He dropped a twenty-dollar bill on the bar and hurried out into the cold. Lower Manhattan was dark and quiet, for a change. The tourists were gone for the day; it was too cold and wet for anyone to stay outside for very long. Avery pulled his coat collar tight around his neck and put his head down against the relentless wind blowing off the Hudson River. His brownstone was three blocks away, due west, and Avery needed to get home. He needed to curl up in bed with a good book—he was a voracious reader of historical fiction—and wait for the sunrise and promise of a new day.

He was dreaming of falling into the intricate plot of the thriller of Imperial Rome he'd been reading when he noticed a short, thick-set man in a down jacket appear out of the shadows and walk directly toward him. Avery was crossing Washington Street, a block from home, and he got the distinct sense that this man was heading for him—that he was aiming to intercept him.

Avery's shoulders tightened and he quickened his pace. The short man did the same. Avery looked up and down the street, and now he cursed the street's emptiness, which only seconds ago he'd enjoyed. Where were the packs of Irish tourists when you needed them? He was on the verge of breaking into a run when the man caught up with him and asked quietly: "Avery Bernstein?"

Avery kept walking—he was in the middle of the street—and decided not to slow down. If this man knew him, or had business with him, he could do it as they walked.

"Who are you?" Avery said.

"My name is Hans," the short man said as he jogged to catch up with Avery. "Hans Metternich." He had a thick accent that Avery pegged as Dutch probably, or maybe Danish. His face was square and clean-shaven, and he was noticeably good-looking. But Avery was still not going to slow down.

"I don't know you," Avery said.

"No reason you should," the man said, falling into a quick walk alongside Avery. "But I know you. At least I know about you."

Avery gave him a worried look. And now that he heard the man speak more, Avery thought his accent wasn't Dutch or Danish, but actually a put-on. What kind of name was Hans Metternich? The guy could have been from Bensonhurst for all Avery knew.

"I need to have a word with you," Metternich said.

"Well, it's late, and I don't talk to strangers on the street, so why don't you call me tomorrow at the office?" Avery walked a little faster. Only half a block until his home. He clutched at his cell phone in his pocket. He would call the police in a heartbeat if this man came at him.

"I would call you at your office, yes, for sure, but, I don't know if you are aware of this—people are listening to your phone calls."

Avery pulled up short. He stared at the man in the down coat, trying hard to memorize the particulars of his face. "Who are you?"

"I am an investigative journalist."

"Journalists call on the phone," Avery said.

"As I said . . ."

"People are listening to my calls. Who?"

"Hard to say. Government. Police maybe. There are a host of suspects."

"How do you know this?"

"I have investigated," Metternich said brightly, amused by what he seemed to consider a joke. "That's why I use *investigative* in front of the *journalist* part."

Avery shivered in the cold April wind. The two of them had stopped walking. Avery's brownstone was in sight now, just a quick sprint from where they stood. "Bullshit. You're a journalist like I'm a UPS driver. What do you want?"

"I need to get in touch with Garrett Reilly."

Avery thought he felt his heart skipping a beat. Shit, he thought. *What the hell is going on?*

"I know all about his discovery of the Treasuries sell-off by the Chinese," Metternich continued. "And that the government took him away."

Avery took a moment to collect his thoughts. "Why do you need to get in touch with him?"

"I have things to tell him."

"Such as?"

"Who set off the bomb in front of your offices. And why they did it. It was not terrorists, as the police and media have suggested."

Avery stared at this man. Was he a lunatic? A crank come to discuss crank theories, like so many other people who seemed to have sprung up lately around the Jenkins & Altshuler offices? "I don't know where Garrett is."

"I know you don't. He has been taken off the grid. But I have reason to believe he is being kept at a Marine base in California."

"If you know so much about him, then why are you talking to me?"

"Because at some point in the next few days, or weeks, he will call you. Or the people who are keeping him will call you. They will put you in touch. Maybe ask you to see him? Or talk to him? I don't know for sure. But I believe this will happen. And when you do see him, I would like you to pass him my name. Hans."

"That's it? Just your name?"

"No, no," Metternich said, eyes twinkling with amusement and, Avery thought, mischief. "Tell him to make himself known to me. So that I can make contact with him. But tell him to be clever about it. Very clever."

The man named Hans Metternich reached into his pocket and Avery flinched, afraid of what was about to happen. Metternich smiled. "Don't worry, Mr. Bernstein. Just a piece of paper. On it I have written my e-mail address. If you could give it to Garrett when you see him?"

The man handed the paper to Avery, and Avery, out of habit—and he immediately wished he hadn't—took it. Metternich bowed slightly, then backed away from Avery, lips still curled into a smile. "Sorry to have startled you, Mr. Bernstein. And I am most sorry for the odd circumstances surrounding our meeting." With that, he turned and hurried down the street.

Avery watched him go a moment, then shouted after him. "Hey! You! Hans!"

Metternich pirouetted in a pool of orange lamplight. Leaves and plastic bags swirled at his feet. "Yes?" he said.

"Why do you need to tell Garrett anything? What fucking business is it of yours?"

Again, Metternich smiled—a mischievous, knowing, slightly cynical smile that Avery, had he been in a more comfortable place and a better mood, would have found charming.

"Because Garrett Reilly is at the center of something very new, and very important. Important not just to you and to me, but to millions of people in this country. Billions more people on the planet. Garrett thinks he is doing one thing, but in fact he is doing something else altogether. He should know this, because everything is not as it seems and, at the risk of sounding melodramatic, very much hangs in the balance."

Metternich bowed again, then broke into a run and within seconds cut around the corner of Washington Street and disappeared into the New York City night.

29

CAMP PENDLETON, APRIL 4, 9:15 PM

"It's loading super slow," Bingo said as he stared at his computer screen, waiting for his response page to load. "Molasses slow."

Celeste and Jimmy Lefebvre stood over his shoulder, waiting for the ever-present blue, red, orange, and green Google logo to appear. Garrett and Alexis were hunched over a second screen. Alexis counted to herself as the logo on her page appeared in bits, faltered, then finally assembled itself on the screen.

"Eleven seconds," she said. "That's miserable. Something's up. Google's load time is usually measured in milliseconds."

The team went into overdrive, each of them searching the Web for something anomalous, something that would explain a crash at Google. They checked the wire news services, which had nothing—it was midnight on the East Coast—but a few online bulletin boards were already buzzing with complaints, most of which were aimed at Internet service providers. The slowdown seemed to be confined to one company—Google—and they weren't commenting, at least not publicly.

Alexis tried calling Google headquarters in Mountain View, California, but no one was answering the phone at ten o'clock at night. Then, around midnight, Garrett found a bulletin, just issued, from the Oregon Department of Energy. It was composed of one terse paragraph, which said, without explanation, that there had been a sudden drop in electricity usage in the Pacific Northwest. It wasn't a huge decrease, compared to the overall burn rate in the Washington-Oregon-Idaho area, just five percent, but it was enough to necessitate a rapid redistribution of power to keep the electricity flowing efficiently in the region's grid. But what caught Garrett's eye was where the drop had originated: along the Columbia River, on the border between Washington and Oregon, in a tiny town that Garrett had heard of for only one reason.

Alexis had Lefebvre call the Oregon Department of Energy. They confirmed the drop-off, and said, as Garrett suspected, that it was entirely from one generating station: The Dalles hydroelectric dam on the Columbia River. They had gone from thirty megawatts of power usage to almost zero in under a minute.

Bingo did a double take when he heard the name: "The Dalles? Isn't that where they built . . . ?

Garrett nodded. "Google server farm."

"Good Lord," Lefebvre said.

"The only way they get a shutdown of power that fast is if that farm went completely offline," Garrett said.

Alexis stared at her screen, grimacing. "And the only way Google goes offline all at once . . ."

Garrett finished her sentence: ". . . is if they've been hacked. Massively hacked."

The room went quiet. Garrett let out a long breath, then broke the silence: "I don't know about you guys, but me, I think that if they're hacking Google at the same time as they're selling Treasuries, blowing up mines, and crashing the real estate market . . . *then we're at war.*"

30

DEFENSE MESSAGING SYSTEM

TO: MAJ. GEN. HADLEY KLINE, DEFENSE INTELLIGENCE AGENCY
FROM: CPT. ALEXIS TRUFFANT, US ARMY
TRANSCRIPT OF CONVERSATION, RE: CHINESE GOALS/MOTIVES FOR RECENT CYBER/ECONOMIC ATTACKS
PARTICIPANTS: TRUFFANT, CPT. ALEXIS; CHEN, CELESTE; LEFEBVRE, LT. JIMMY; CLEMENS, ROBERT (BINGO); (NAME REDACTED)
LOCATION: EDSON RANGE MESS HALL, CAMP PENDLETON

CONVERSATION WAS RECORDED, APRIL 5, 2:47 AM,
THEN TRANSCRIBED VERBATIM.

TRUFFANT: Look, I know you guys are tired and want to go to bed, but we need to figure out why this is happening. I get that we're being attacked, but without a reason behind the attacks I'm not sure we can figure out how to stop them. So anyone want to posit a theory?

LEFEBVRE: I think they're showing us that they have the ability. A show of strength. Politically, it would fit with a rising Chinese nationalism. Pride in their success and place in the world. Pride in their ability to hack.

TRUFFANT: You're saying they're just showing off?

LEFEBVRE: I suppose. A shot across our bow.

(**NAME REDACTED**): Yeah, but they're doing it all in secret. Black market attacks and hacking. Who the hell are they showing off to?

LEFEBVRE: Our intelligence services.

(NAME REDACTED): So it's a spy game, and we've got nothing to worry about, because it's not going anywhere? It's peacock feathers?

LEFEBVRE: I might not use exactly those words . . .

TRUFFANT: I have a problem with that. I mean, maybe you're right—but maybe you're not. If we buy into that idea and we're wrong, then we'll be facing a disaster. And we will have missed it. Like General Wilkerson said—the war the generals didn't see coming ends up swamping them.

CHEN: What if it's not exactly showing off, but more malicious mischief. They're trying to weaken our economy, our infrastructure, you know, be disruptive, but avoiding out-and-out conflict. Inflict damage that can be denied and move on.

TRUFFANT: Industrial espionage?

CHEN: Sure.

(NAME REDACTED): But they've tossed a lot of money away in the process. Selling Treasuries and condos. There's no profit in that, and industrial espionage is specifically built around profit. So they'd be losing money to profit, which makes no sense. I think this is bigger. I think this is war. And wars always start for a reason. All wars are about something, right, Bingo?

CLEMENS: Well. Um. Yeah. Sorta. Land or money. Sometimes revenge, but that's less common.

CHEN: If it's land, then the motive is Taiwan. China has never recognized the island's claim to independence. They believe everyone who lives there is actually a part of the People's Republic. It's an obsession with them.

TRUFFANT: But why attack us? And why now?

CHEN: Distract us. Panic us about something else. While we're preoccupied with our own problems, they invade Taiwan.

CLEMENS: It would take a million soldiers from the People's Army to do that. But they've got a million soldiers to spare.

CHEN: And I hate to say this about my ancestral people, but they'd sacrifice a million soldiers in the blink of an eye. The soldiers would die proud. As a nation, they're extremely nationalistic. And growing more militaristic by the minute.

(NAME REDACTED): They're animals and we're not. That what you're saying?

CHEN: No. All nations go through phases of intense nationalism. Not every nation has the resources to act on those feelings. China does now, and maybe they're doing it. So (EXPLETIVE DELETED), (NAME REDACTED).

(NAME REDACTED): Sensitive much?

LEFEBVRE: Hate to interrupt your love fest, but how about raw materials? They import almost all their petroleum. That produces a lot of anxiety in the party leadership.

TRUFFANT: But they've got coal.

LEFEBVRE: Three billion tons a year. Largest producer in the world. But they have massive consumption rates as well. And it's polluting their country. In the winter people burn so much coal in Beijing they can barely breathe. The government's making a push for other energy sources—oil being the most obvious.

(NAME REDACTED): Yeah, but why fight us over that? We don't provide energy, or keep them from it. What's the connection between oil and attacking us?

CLEMENS: Maybe they're weakening us first, so we won't be able to stop them. Once we're on the defensive, they invade Saudi Arabia.

LEFEBVRE: You cannot be serious? China invades Saudi Arabia? The obstacles would be monumental. The world would have to end first. Zero percent probability.

CLEMENS: I was joking.

(NAME REDACTED): I got your back, Bing. I think invading Saudi Arabia would be damn cool.

CLEMENS: It was a joke. It was.

CHEN: How about they invade Brunei? They're sitting on a ton of oil. Or cordon off the South China Sea. Declare it an exclusion zone.

TRUFFANT: Makes a little more sense.

(NAME REDACTED): But why go to war for oil when you can just buy it on the open market? Hell of a lot safer just spending cash. And they've got plenty of cash.

LEFEBVRE: Security. You conquer, you own it. Nobody can raise prices on you.

CHEN: Yeah, we invaded Iraq for oil. And we've got plenty of our own.

TRUFFANT: Celeste, this is not the time for conspiracy theories.

CHEN: It's not a (EXPLETIVE DELETED) conspiracy theory. Even you don't believe Saddam had weapons of (EXPLETIVE DELETED) mass destruction.

(NAME REDACTED): Hey, ladies. We're getting off topic.

CLEMENS: I get uncomfortable when you fight.

CHEN: Sorry, Alexis. (UNINTELLIGIBLE). I'm just tired.

LEFEBVRE: What about a clash of cultures or political systems? Communism versus capitalism. Wars have been fought over that.

CHEN: But what ideology does China represent today? They're hardly a bastion of Communist thought anymore. The government's too pragmatic. If we've learned anything from their leadership in the past twenty years, it's that they'll discard an ideology pronto if it doesn't work for them.

(NAME REDACTED): Attacks point to forethought. A strategic plan. We need to look at the pattern. Somebody in China is thinking this through, twisting the rope, and we've caught them in the middle of it. Maybe they weren't expecting to be caught yet—I don't know. But I do know that you don't spend all that time and energy—hiding your tracks, but still leaving clues—without a reason. It's all leading to something, something we don't understand yet. There's a point to this.

TRUFFANT: But we have no idea what that point is, so we're still at square one. Everything we've come up with either has a flaw, or flies in the face of basic logic. No sleep until we solve this, people. To go to war with the United States of America, you need a reason.

LEFEBRVE: You've got to be a dog with a bone. Ballsy as hell.

CHEN: Or desperate.

CLEMENS: Or crazy.

(NAME REDACTED): Wait. What did you say?

CLEMENS: They would have to be crazy.

(NAME REDACTED): No, Celeste . . . ?

CHEN: Desperate.

(NAME REDACTED): That's it. That's the answer right there.

LEFEBVRE: You lost me.

(NAME REDACTED): They're ballsy, sure, but to what end? None that we can see. We know they're not crazy. Celeste just told us they're incredibly pragmatic. So that leaves desperate. That's where the answer lies—the Chinese are starting a war against us because they are desperate. Now we just have to figure out what they're desperate about.

END OF CONVERSATION.

END OF DMS TRANSMISSION.

31

CHONGQING, CHINA, APRIL 5, 2:15 AM

Before, when Xi Ling had been a poor factory worker, he never worried. He planned. He spent every waking moment scheming, plotting, saving, and strategizing. Wealth was his dream, his destiny. He would achieve it, or die trying.

But now, twenty-five years later—and finally wealthy—Xi Ling worried constantly. This was the paradox of his life, he thought. You get what you want, and then you worry about keeping it.

He was worried about his health (he was too fat, his doctor said, and was risking a heart attack), about his mistress (and his wife, come to think of it), about his reputation in Chongqing (he had thrown too many lavish parties), about his relationship with the local party leaders (he had bribed each of them separately, but were they now comparing amounts, preparing to ask for more?), even about who had been driving his brand-new Mercedes CL550 coupe without his permission (he would strangle the bastard when he caught him). And now, on top of all the rest, he was worried about his factory. Very worried.

His plant manager, Quan with the craggy face, had called him fifteen minutes ago, panicked, breathlessly babbling about the stitching machines and the workers fleeing the factory floor. Xi Ling had been fast asleep—a rare pleasure for him in his middle age—and was furious to be woken. He had given strict orders not to be disturbed on Tuesday and Thursday nights—his evenings with his mistress at the small apartment he had bought her on Songshi Avenue. He treasured his mistress nights. At least he had until last month, when she had started badgering him to buy her diamonds. Didn't she understand that he was not made of money?

Well, that was not entirely true either. He *was* made of money. At least it seemed that way. Xi Ling had gotten rich making backpacks and tents and nylon bags for the European and American markets. He made fancy backpacks and not-so-fancy ones. His workers stitched together high-end brand-name bags, low-end generic bags, and illegal knockoffs of both the high-end and the low-end bags. He had all the bases covered. Some people might call that amoral, but they could go to hell. Xi Ling was nothing if not practical. At least in business. Come to think of it, he was that way in everything.

None of that mattered now, as Xi Ling swerved wildly down the four-lane highway leading west from Chongqing out into the hilly industrial suburbs at two-thirty in the morning. All of his money, all of his striving and planning could be washed away in an instant if his factory ran into production troubles. He had orders from seventeen different Western companies. Xi Ling's factory ran twenty-four hours a day, every single day of the year. It even ran through Chinese New Year. He was in the middle of constructing dormitories so that his employees could walk a few yards to their beds at the end of their shifts, get a little sleep, and then go right back to work. Some people said that was ruthless and inhuman—damned reporter from that Italian newspaper—but Xi Ling knew that was the only way he could stay ahead of the product orders. And what was wrong with the Italians anyway? It was a company out of Milan that accounted for forty-two percent of his orders. They sold his goods to other Italians, for far cheaper than if a European worker had made them, and yet people from that same country came here and wrote that Xi Ling was a barbarian? Did they not enjoy his tents and backpacks? What did they care how he treated his employees?

And who were the Italians to lecture the Chinese on business? Their country was on the verge of bankruptcy. They were a disaster. A joke. The hypocrisy of the Europeans drove him to distraction.

He swung his Mercedes off the smooth gray highway and down a series of blackened side streets, between massive warehouses glowing in yellow halogen light and fenced-off construction sites. Even with the global economic downturn, people were still building new factories in Chongqing. That inspired him as he gripped the steering wheel and stomped hard on the gas pedal. He could always start over again. And the first thought he had as he saw workers streaming out of his factory gate was—he might have to do just that.

It was as his floor manager had said on the phone: women—all his stitchers and sewers were women—were abandoning his factory, pushing their way onto the street, falling all over each other and yelling. Xi Ling slammed on the brakes and jumped out of his car, screaming at them even before he opened the door: "What are you doing! Get back to work! You cannot leave the factory! I will fire you! I will fire every one of you!"

And then Xi Ling noticed something peculiar. These workers weren't actually fleeing the factory. They were running about in the yard between the steel cyclone fence and the factory building. Some were throwing their hands in the air, shouting. Others seemed to be dancing and singing. Had they all gone completely mad? He grabbed a young woman by the arm as she stumbled past. "What are you doing? Your shift is not over until the sun rises!"

"We are celebrating! Celebrate with us!" The young woman smiled ecstatically.

"I do not pay you to celebrate!" he shouted above the din.

The young woman stopped smiling and stared into Xi Ling's face. The corners of her mouth drooped into a frown.

"It's him!" she yelled. "The owner! The criminal! He's here!"

And suddenly she was grabbing his arm, tugging at the fabric of his silk suit jacket.

"Let go of me," Xi Ling barked. "How dare you assault me! I am your employer!" But it was too late. Scores of women were crowding around him, pushing in on him, clutching at his arms and at the hair on his head.

"Let go of me!" he screamed, but the women weren't listening.

One of them, a grizzled older woman, yelled at the others: "Take him inside! Let's feed him to the Tiger!"

A tiger? Xi Ling's blood went cold. Had some lunatic brought a tiger into his factory? Was that why his workers had become hysterical? Xi Ling did not like animals—they scared him, always had, from the time he had been a child and his mother told him bedtime stories about snow tigers and black panthers. Big cats scared him more than anything else.

The women surrounding Xi Ling cheered in agreement, and all of a sudden Xi Ling found himself moving, inexorably, toward the front door of the factory, a helpless corked bottle floating on a sea of female factory workers. The women were four or five deep around him now, fifty or sixty of them in total, many holding fast to his clothes, shoving him through the factory door and into the cavernous entryway.

"I will have you all killed! I know everyone on the party Directorate!" he screamed. Blood was flowing freely from scratches on his forehead now, and his suit was in tatters. "Do you realize what you are doing?"

But they seemed to know exactly what they were doing. The mob forced Xi Ling across the entry room and through the large doorway that led to the factory floor; the doorway where Xi Ling's enforcers body-searched every woman, head-to-toe, every day, twice a day, for contraband coming in and stolen product going out. And now Xi Ling was getting a version of the same treatment, as the mass of women groped and prodded him, one hand digging into his crotch while another set of nails drew more blood from his wrists. Xi Ling screamed in pain.

And then suddenly they set him free. The crowd parted and Xi Ling stumbled to his feet. The women had fallen silent, even as their screams echoed in Xi Ling's ears. He wiped the blood from his eyes, expecting to see a giant jungle cat prowling his beloved factory floor, ready to pounce.

What he saw instead was a woman.

She was young, plain-looking, dressed in jeans and a T-shirt, her black hair cut in a mop top, like a farmer or a country bumpkin. She was surrounded by more of his workers, and some men too—men Xi Ling did not recognize. The young woman was clearly in charge, but she did not radiate force or hostility. She smiled pleasantly, as if this were a chat among friends about how to plan a birthday party. She was gesturing calmly to the machinery that crowded the factory floor. Around her, scores of other men and women—of all ages, and in all types of clothing—were methodically dismantling his sewing and stitching machines. There didn't seem to be anger in what they were doing, but they were destroying his beloved machines nonetheless, unscrewing phalanges, tearing out cranks and gears, piling yards of unsewn leather and plastic into heaps and then pouring some kind of acid on the materials. The materials hissed and steamed under the corrosive effects of the acid.

Xi Ling gathered himself and marched toward the woman. "Who are you? What are you doing!" he barked. "Are you the Tiger?"

The young woman nodded, casting her eyes downward, in a sign of humility and respect. "I am Hu Mei. They call me the Tiger. But I do not encourage that name."

"Well, Tiger," Xi Ling raged, "this is my factory! You're breaking the law! I will have the police in here in five minutes if you don't stop immediately!"

Hu Mei smiled again, very politely, and pointed to the catwalks that surrounded the floor. "Those police?" she asked.

Standing above them, on the metal walkways that stretched the length and breadth of the factory, were scores of policemen, all dressed neatly in their blue-and-white uniforms, silently watching the proceedings below them.

Xi Ling gasped. "How much did you pay them?"

Hu Mei laughed quietly, shaking her head. "I don't pay anyone. Not policemen, not factory workers, not big bosses like you, either. I talk to people. I show them what is wrong in China today, and I suggest ways we might fix things. Together."

"By destroying my factory? How is that fixing anything?" Xi Ling shouted. He started to move toward the young woman, but a line of young men stepped between them, protecting her.

"I am very sorry about your factory. But I have been told by people in town, by your workers and your managers alike, that you force people to work twenty-four hours at a stretch. Without breaks. For weeks on end. That you withhold wages. That you lie about hours worked, and deduct salary for food that is never eaten. They pointed out to me closed rooms where fumes accumulate and make people sick, but you do not vent those rooms. You treat your workers like slaves. Like they have no rights. But they are not slaves. And everybody has rights."

Xi Ling sputtered in anger. Who was this woman to lecture him about rights? Was she like the Italians, full of righteous indignation? Was all of China going soft around the edges? Xi Ling tried to control his temper—his doctor had also warned him about his rising blood pressure—and spoke calmly to Hu Mei. "These women here, before they came to me, they had nothing. They were peasants. Farmers. Scraping food from the dirt. I gave them jobs. I gave them work. They can live in the city. With their friends, not on farms with disgusting pigs and chickens. What more do they want?"

The young woman, this Tiger woman, took her time in answering, as if gathering her thoughts. She looked around the thrashed factory floor, at the women and men who had stopped dismantling the machines to listen to their conversation, and nodded serenely, proudly, at all of them, as if she were their mother, and they were playing on the nursery floor, and she was amused by her children's growing abilities with blocks and toys. Then she turned her gaze back to Xi Ling, smiled warmly at him, bowing her head again in respect.

She said: "What we want is fairness."

32

CAMP PENDLETON, APRIL 5, 6:30 AM

When Alexis Truffant walked into their barracks offices early the next morning—day five of their time at Camp Pendleton—she found Garrett already planted at the largest of the work stations. He had cabled three monitors to his computer, and all three were alive with charts and graphs and scrolling numbers. She watched over his shoulder, trying to focus on the waves of information that seemed to be cascading across the screens, but it only came across as blurred lines of figures and letters. Coffee cups were scattered at Garrett's feet.

He spoke without looking at her. "Something's up with the markets."

"The stock market?"

"The major exchanges. All of them, but mostly New York. There's selective selling of blue chips. Synchronized with sneaky selling in short-term bonds."

Alexis looked at the Dow Jones Industrial Average. The markets had just opened, but it was up ten points for the day. "But the Dow is up."

"Now. It's up now. But there's tension building. The indexes are fragile. Everything's trading to the downside of its Bollinger Band. The stochastic oscillator on my core equities is batshit crazy. Signs of a reversal. The high-speed traders are having a field day. Their spreads are insane."

"So what does it all mean?"

Garrett looked at the three synched monitors. "It's the next attack," he said. "Been building in the last few hours. Started in Asia. Spreading."

"How do you know?"

"I can feel it."

"You can *feel* a pattern forming?"

"It's why you hired me, remember?" he snapped.

Alexis flinched. Only last night she had convinced herself that the asshole act was just that—an act. She took a breath, remembered whom she was dealing with, and tried again. "So what does it mean?"

"It means something's going to break."

"I'll call the Treasury Department..."

"Too late. Wouldn't matter. This one's bigger than them. Really big. But maybe not permanent. Another shock to the system."

Alexis leaned over his shoulder and caught a glimpse of his face. He was unshaven, his eyes were ringed and bloodshot. His head snapped back and forth between the three computer screens.

"Have you slept?" she asked him.

"In my life? Yes. Last night? No."

His fingers danced across the keyboard, and all three screens began to change, graphs flipping, readouts blinking on and off.

Alexis went into the other room and dialed Bolling AFB on a secure line. General Kline picked up on the first ring.

"Captain Truffant," he said. "You have news?"

"Sir. Reilly thinks something big is going to happen in the stock market today."

"Hold on." Alexis could hear General Kline fumbling for something, then the low-level chatter of television talking heads on the other end of the line. Kline muttered into the receiver: "CNBC says nothing unusual. A little trading on the downside. Fox Business is SOP. Reilly give you any facts or figures? Examples?"

"No sir. He said he could just feel it. He was up all night. I think he might be manic."

"Maybe he should take a pill," Kline said, and then stuttered: "W-whoa. The Dow is dropping. A hundred points. No, two hundred, three hundred... holy *shit*!"

Alexis blinked her eyes. "In twenty seconds?"

"Hold on. They're talking about it on CNBC. Five hundred points down. No, wait. Seven hundred!" Alexis could hear the instant strain in her boss's voice. "Did Reilly say he thought there was anything we could do?"

She flicked on a television in the corner of the room and cycled through channels until she found CNN. The anchors on-screen were just cutting away to the breaking news on the floor of the New York Stock Exchange. She turned the sound up to a low murmur. "No," she said. "He said it was too big. I guess we're just along for the ride."

On CNN the DJIA ticker was off 1,000 points. Then 1,500. Trading curbs were triggered, and the NYSE shut down for a sixty-minute cooling-off period, but the live feed from the floor showed brokers looking shell-shocked. And scared.

"Crap. There's going to be mass panic," Kline said over the phone.

"Reilly said it might be temporary. A shock to the system."

"I hope to God he's right," Kline said.

Alexis pursed her lips. She watched the incredulity grow on the faces of the two CNN anchors. One of them was comparing it to the Flash Crash of May 2010, when the Dow lost 600 points in seven minutes. But this was worse. The Industrial Average was down nearly 1,600 points. It had taken five minutes.

"Fucked up, huh?" Alexis turned to see Garrett standing in the doorway. He was smiling from ear to ear, pointing at the television. "Sometimes I'm so good I even freak *myself* out."

Kline hissed through the telephone: "Is that him? Is he with you?"

"Yes. On both counts."

"Ask him if it'll turn around."

"Garrett. General Kline wants to know if the stock market will—"

"Come back up?" he said, cutting her off. "Sure. First, it'll drop another two thousand points when trading curbs are lifted. Maybe more. Then it'll swing back. Not all the way, though. There's going to be blood in the streets." He shook his head ruefully. "I could have made serious coin off this one."

Kline said, "Ask him how they did it."

"He wants to know how they did it."

Garrett shrugged. "Probably hyperleveraged a crapload of market shorts. Massive bets that trigger panicked computer selling. If you can make prices fall fast enough, then buyers will flee the market, and then there's no floor for stocks. If you're willing to lose enough cash—and we're talking billions—then anyone could conceivably do it. Anyone who had billions in the first place. The SEC will sort it out in a week or two. But it won't stick. The fundamentals aren't there. That's why I think it will come back." Garrett stared at the TV. "I don't think they want it to stick. They have something else in mind." With that, he walked out of the room.

"Captain Truffant?" Kline snapped.

"Yes sir?"

"He's good, isn't he?"

"He is. Very."

"Is he ready?"

"He has no idea of the plan, sir. Absolutely none. He is completely in the dark."

There was silence on the line, interrupted only by the alarmed squawks of the TV newscasters.

"We've run out of time," General Kline said. "All hell is breaking loose. We need Garrett. And we need him now."

33

CAMP PENDLETON, APRIL 5, 7:03 PM

Two hours later the Dow bottomed out at 9,682, which was a hair more than 4,000 points off the day's high. It came back up 2,500 points, but that still left a 1,500-point drop for the day; and that meant nearly two trillion dollars in capital had been wiped out, fifteen percent of the United States's gross domestic product, in a single morning. The markets remained skittish all day, despite the secretary of the treasury's reassuring press conference and the chairman of the Federal Reserve's news release claiming that this was all part of the normal course of a free market economy. When the exchanges closed at 4:00 p.m., two smaller, specialty Wall Street brokerage houses couldn't cover their margin calls and went under. Their losses had been spectacular. The air of rising panic on Wall Street was palpable.

It was palpable 2,500 miles away, on the coast of California, where Alexis lay in her bunk, wrung out. She had pushed the team hard that afternoon; they had spent the rest of the day digging into the motives of the Chinese, following Garrett's lead.

"We're looking for hints of Chinese desperation," she had said. "Anything at all. A weakness in their military preparedness. A drought. A decline in productivity. A rise in unemployment. A battle for control of the party leadership. Potential famine. Environmental disaster. A corruption epidemic. Even if it's just a whiff of fear—flag it, and let's discuss."

Alexis had them cast a wide net: CIA briefings, NSA intercepts, State Department briefings, embassy wires, think-tank papers, blogs from inside China, blogs from outside China, blogs from Japan on China, blogs from Vietnam about how the Japanese felt about China. Everything and anything. Most of it was translated, first by Celeste, or if she was busy—and they were desperate—by Google Translate, but that was still running at half speed. The trouble at The Dalles had hit Google hard—the news was all over the cable networks—but still no one from inside the company had commented.

As backup, Alexis had Celeste call in two trusted friends from the Chinese Studies Department at UCLA; they translated on the fly, helping the rest of them get the gist of any documents in Mandarin. By seven that evening they had still found nothing of significance—they had plowed through mountains of data, but no answers had revealed themselves, and they were worn out. She thought she saw Bingo start to cry, but he ran off to the bathroom before she could ask him if he was okay.

Alexis told them to take two hours off, and she retreated to her room with a mountain of intelligence briefs. Most theorized on why the sell-off had occurred, what had started it, and why the market had bounced back. Intellectually, they all seemed sound to Alexis, but none of them had hard-and-fast answers—and none of them had blamed the Chinese. She felt Garrett had a firmer hold on what was going on than all the economic analysts in Washington combined. He was a pain in the ass, arrogant, and hard to deal with, but when he plugged into a problem, he seemed to understand it on a root level; he grasped issues at their core. She hated to admit it, but his abilities, at times, were jaw-dropping. It reminded her of when she had gone to an NBA basketball game and seen Kobe Bryant slice effortlessly past three defenders and then dunk the basketball—ferociously—over a fourth. You could only marvel at an ability that you would never possess.

The other thing that impressed Alexis about Garrett was that he seemed to have courage. It often came across as arrogance or narcissism, but she thought it was actually bravery; a willingness to put forward seemingly insane ideas and then stick to them. And more often than not, he had been right. That, more than anything else, made her forgive him his flaws.

Which, it had to be said, were equally spectacular. When they had watched the Dow rebound later in the day, a look of true regret seemed etched onto Garrett's face. When Alexis asked him what was wrong, he shook his head and muttered about "money left on the table." Celeste whispered to Alexis later that she thought he must be a sociopath, and Alexis couldn't entirely disagree. However, from the interviews she'd seen on TV, she suspected that Kobe Bryant was something of a sociopath as well. Maybe when you possessed that much talent, it was hard to take the troubles of those around you seriously.

A knock on the door interrupted her train of thought. She was lying on her bunk, wearing sweatpants and a T-shirt. She was hungry, distracted, unkempt.

"Come in."

The door swung open, and Garrett stepped into her room. It amused Alexis that she had been thinking of him, at that very moment, and now here he was. He carried two trays: one loaded with white, takeout Chinese food cartons, the other holding two bottles of Corona, glasses, and a pair of lit candles. He was smiling from ear to ear.

"I thought you might be hungry."

"Wow," Alexis said, sitting up on the bed. "Candles. And beer."

"Chinese from Oceanside. Recommended by a staff sergeant. Beer from the officers' lounge. The candles I stole from an earthquake kit."

She laughed. Garrett set the food on a desk, scooping out garlic beef and white rice onto paper plates from the cafeteria. "You're not a vegetarian, are you?"

"I'm from the South. There are no vegetarians in the South."

"And Corona will do, yes?"

"Any alcohol will do." She pulled two chairs up to the desk and sat in front of the meal. "It's lovely. And very thoughtful."

"Nobody ate all afternoon."

"We were running on fumes."

"So I took it upon myself . . ."

He poured the beers and gave one to her.

"Cheers," she said.

"To the end of the world," he said.

"That's quite a toast. You think it's imminent?"

"Unless we stop it."

They drank, then ate hungrily, and wordlessly, for a few minutes.

"God, I was starving," he said.

"You're doing a good job," she said.

"Wolfing down my food?"

"Stopping the end of the world."

Garrett looked at her. She nodded. "I mean it. You're the right person for the job. Maybe the only person. And I'm impressed."

"Thanks. You're not so bad yourself."

"I facilitate. Group leader. Not anyone can do it, but a lot of people can. Only a couple of people can do what you do. A couple of people in the whole damn world. Maybe not even a couple. Maybe only you."

Garrett stopped eating. He seemed, for the first time that she had noticed, off balance. He smiled crookedly, as if hiding something, covering some uncomfortable emotion. "So," he said, still smiling. "If the world is ending, what are your plans?"

"Post-apocalypse? I'm going to roam the planet like Mad Max. In my Ford Falcon GT. Lots of leather. "

"One of my favorite movies."

"Back when Mel Gibson was cute. And sane."

"*Thunderdome* sucked."

"Embarrassingly bad."

They ate, and talked about movies. The apocalypse seemed further away to Alexis than it had in days. Garrett might live a life that was out of control, and he might indeed turn out to be a sociopath, but around him she felt oddly protected. He was so sure of himself, so fierce in his confidence, that she felt it rub off on her. It surprised her, but she felt stronger in his presence. Together, she thought, we might actually stop whatever it is that's happening, and possibly save the country.

She drank her beer, and Garrett stepped outside the bunk room and came back with two more. "An endless supply," he said, laughing. They drank a little more and Garrett cleared away the plates.

"Do you think it's traitorous that we ate Chinese food?" she said.

"The people who made this food are as American as we are. The delivery boy said he just graduated from San Diego State. Name was Chang. Said he wanted to be a computer programmer. He talked like a surfer."

"I was kind of joking," she said.

"I know," Garrett said. "It's just that I'm not even sure the country is our enemy. Maybe the party leadership is. Or some generals. The Chinese people? No way. But can we talk about something else?" He pulled his chair a little closer to hers.

"Like what?"

"Like us."

"Us? Is there an us?"

"I'd like there to be."

He leaned close to her. Alexis was suddenly flustered. He stared at her with his intense blue eyes. He kissed her. She let him, not resisting, even liking it. Her head spun. Being kissed hadn't made her feel this way in years. He shifted his body in his chair, moving closer to her. His arms wrapped around her back. She could feel his warmth, and it made her go weak in the knees. He kissed her harder, more passionately. She got a grip on herself and pushed him away.

"No," she said.

"No? Why?"

"Because." She was at a loss for words. She was breathing hard. Her own lust for him was a revelation to her. But she fought it. Now was not the time.

Garrett moved close to her again. "I don't believe you." He kissed her clumsily, hands brushing her chest. He was perched on the edge of his chair.

She shoved him backward. "Stop!" It was a little harder than she meant to, and his chair rocked backward. Garrett lost his balance and fell hard to the floor, sprawling out onto the wood. Alexis gasped. "Are you okay?"

Garrett struggled to his feet, flustered, angry. "Why did you do that?"

"I said no, you didn't listen." He got to his feet and brushed himself off. His face was tight, hurt. "Shit. I thought you were into me. We were close. You—"

"No," Alexis cut him off, "you were mistaken." She sat up straight in her chair, pushed her hair back. "Look, it's just that . . ." She fumbled for the right words, stopping, then trying again. She didn't want to tell him, but she felt she had to. Morally, it was wrong not to. But if she did, she would be going off script, endangering everything.

"Garrett, we can't because . . ."

"Because what?" Garrett spit out.

"Because I'm married."

Garrett stared at her, stunned. "Married?" He blinked. It made no sense. "But you don't wear a ring. You never mentioned a husband. In all this time."

"I," she started, the words dying on her lips. "I took the ring off."

Garrett tried to concentrate. She had seemed so open to him, so interested, so engaged, and now . . . And suddenly he realized.

"On purpose. You took the ring off on purpose."

She said nothing. She looked down.

"To lure me in. So I would like you. Think I had a chance with you. So I would commit to your stupid project." He grimaced, pacing. "Give back to your country. Find a purpose. All bullshit." He spit it out. "A big fucking con."

"No," she said. "All true. Giving back is important. There is nothing more important."

"Then why lead me on? Why not tell me you were married? Why not wear the ring?"

She had no answers for him. She looked away. He leaned close to her, got right in her face. "I should have fucking known. All that military bullshit. Liars. You are all liars. God, I hate you people." He started toward the door.

"Garrett . . ."

"What?"

She started to say something, hesitated, then shook her head. Garrett laughed and walked out, slamming the door behind him.

He stalked out of the barracks, angry, a little buzzed from the beer, his head spinning, and walked out into the cool desert night. What a fool he had been. They had played him, completely duped him. And he was Garrett Reilly, the guy who read all the patterns, who could feel inconsistencies in his gut. But they had nailed him with his weakness—women. He was a sucker for a pretty face, a sexy body, a little flattery, someone who told him he was great. And Alexis had done exactly that. "Only a couple of people in the world can do what you do," he muttered angrily to himself. "*You dumbass.*"

He dialed a cab service on his cell phone, and jogged down to the main base entrance. By the time he reached the guard house there was a cab waiting for him. He rode it to downtown Oceanside. There were bars up and down Mission Avenue. He got out at the first one—he didn't even look at the name of the place—and ordered beer and vodka. By his third shot he was feeling much better. His mind was clearer, his anger more focused. His cell phone rang twice—it was Alexis—but he ignored it. Fuck Mao and the Chinese, he thought. And fuck saving the world.

He bought a pair of joints off a stringy kid hanging out by the pool tables and smoked them one after the other, in quick succession, in the alley behind the bar, then went back in for more booze. He lost all sense of time—and place—but he was still angry. He couldn't get Alexis's face out of his head. Her voice. Her lies. Fuck, he had really fallen for her. How could he have been so stupid? And who the fuck was shoving up against him at the bar? Through his drunken, stoned haze he saw a trio of jarheads, slamming down beers, laughing.

Garrett thumped his chest into the biggest one. The Marine said something to Garrett, but Garrett couldn't hear him over the jukebox and the chatter in the bar, and anyway, he wasn't listening and didn't give a shit what the jarhead said. "You're a fucking asshole," is what Garrett spit into his face.

"Do you have an attitude problem, douche wad?" the Marine growled.

Garrett brought the beer bottle down on the Marine's head with one swift motion of his right arm, shattering the glass on his temple. The Marine fell backwards, and time slowed down for Garrett, as it always did when he got into a fight. He stomped the fallen Marine hard with his left foot, then drove his fist into the neck of the second Marine, who was just turning to help his buddy. Marine number two staggered into his friend, the third Marine at the bar, and Garrett threw himself onto both of them, fists flashing in a rapid-fire sequence of punches. It was a scrum, but a scrum that he was on top of, and a bar brawl that he was winning. He kept his fists pistoning—pleased with himself, knowing this was how to win bar fights—when suddenly he began to fly backwards into the air. It was the strangest sensation, as if he were magically levitating, and then reality came rushing in on him in the form of a fourth Marine, twice as large as the others, wrenching Garrett backwards off his comrades, and Garrett cursed himself for being so stupid. *It was a jarhead bar.* The place was full of them. And they were all coming to their jarhead comrades' aid. No one left behind, and all that grunt bullshit. He turned in time to see a meaty fist land squarely on his cheek and then everything else became a blur.

The bar turned sideways and pain exploded in Garrett's head, and in his chest, and then his arms were wrenched behind his back and he could feel his left shoulder pop. That hurt more than all the other punches, and it was at that moment that Garrett became sure of two things: (1) that he had lost this fight, and (2) that he might die because of it. Then everything went black.

34

CAMP PENDLETON NAVAL HOSPITAL, APRIL 6, 3:36 AM

Alexis paced the antiseptic fifth-floor hallway of the Naval Hospital as the ghostly white fluorescent lights flickered over her head, making the pale walls seem even more sickly and uninviting. She'd gotten the call from the ER doctors half an hour earlier: white male, bar fight, multiple injuries, Army private, recorded as under her supervision. She'd shaken off her cobwebs, thrown on her fatigues, taken the team Humvee, and raced to the hospital, trying hard not to run off the paved road that traversed the base.

She hadn't slept well. All night she had replayed the conversation with Garrett. She thought about the dinner, the kiss, his reaction, her pushing him away. And then telling him she was married, and the look on his face. All that deception. And all that raw emotion in Garrett. She hadn't realized how hard he had fallen for her. But he had—that much had been obvious. And that, of course, was exactly as they had planned it.

The acid rose in her throat. She had been a willing participant. Hell, she had even come up with the strategy herself. Garrett liked women. She knew that, had seen him in action. And she had used it to her—and the Army's—advantage. How, she thought to herself, am I any better than Garrett? I am deceptive. I am as amoral as he is.

We are a pair.

A young doctor walked quickly through the trauma doors and introduced himself as Colonel Booker Rogers. He was the surgeon on call.

"How bad is he?"

Rogers shrugged, noncommittal. "This is a military hospital. We see some pretty bad cases, so he's not the worst of the worst. That said, he took a pounding. Oceanside Police said it was ten against one. Your man was the one."

She sighed. Garrett might be good at detecting patterns, but he also seemed to have an aptitude for fitting into them. "I'm not surprised."

"He has two broken ribs, a dislocated shoulder, a few cracked teeth, but he didn't lose any. He's got multiple bruises and cuts. He lost about a pint of blood. He probably has a concussion, but it's hard to tell because he's still unconscious. Most seriously, however, he has a linear transverse skull fracture."

"Is that bad?"

"They're the least bad of a bad thing. It will heal by itself. But he can't ever again get into a bar fight. Or play tackle football."

"I'd actually call that a good thing."

"I'm serious. He does and he *will* die."

Alexis nodded. "He's not in a coma, is he?"

"He's sedated for pain. That's part of what is keeping him asleep. But I have to tell you, Captain, he is very lucky not to have a more serious skull fracture. He was hit many times on the head. We're keeping his cranium iced right now to prevent swelling."

Alexis frowned. Well, at least he would survive. Then a thought occurred to her: "Is he going to be mentally intact? I mean, the same as he was before?"

"You can't guarantee anything with a head injury. But probably yes."

Alexis breathed a sigh of relief, and hated herself for it. She was still worrying about Garrett Reilly's usefulness to the Army. She tried to change the direction of her thinking: "Did he hurt anybody?"

"A Marine checked himself in a few hours ago with a broken nose and scalp lacerations. I suspect he was part of the fight. I think your boy hit him with a bottle."

"But he'll recover? The Marine?"

"He already has—he's a Marine. He walked out of here an hour ago."

"Can I see Reilly now?"

"Follow me." Rogers led her through the trauma unit to a room at the end of the hall. Alexis had to keep herself from gasping when she saw Garrett. He was laid up on a hospital bed, head wrapped in gauze, a plastic ice sleeve laid across his forehead. A pair of tubes ran into his nose, and there was an IV drip jabbed into his arm. EKG machines and oxygen sensors beeped and trilled at his side. But it was Garrett's face that shocked Alexis the most; there were ragged purple and orange bruises on his cheeks, and stitched cuts on his nose and chin. Alexis thought he resembled a distant cousin to Frankenstein's monster.

The doctor muttered at her side, "Why anyone would pick a fight with ten Marines is beyond me."

Alexis knew the answer to that question, but she decided it really wasn't any of the colonel's business. "When will he wake up?"

"Could be any time. But my guess is a few hours."

"I'll wait here until he does."

"There's one other thing, Captain." Alexis snapped her head around. She didn't like the tone of the doctor's voice. "We ran a blood test. Beyond a very high blood alcohol level, he tested positive for THC. I'll have to report that. It's grounds for immediate discharge."

"Have you noted it on his chart yet?"

"No. Not yet. I just got the blood workup."

"Destroy it."

"Excuse me?"

"Rip it up. Delete the digital test results. It never happened."

"I can't do that."

"Yes you can."

Colonel Rogers started to protest but Alexis cut him off: "I'll have the secretary of defense call you personally."

The doctor looked like he wanted to reply to her, then thought better of it, and stomped angrily from the room. Alexis, exhausted, grabbed a chair, pulled it next to Garrett's bed, and sat down to wait for him to wake up.

35

CAMP PENDLETON, APRIL 7, 11:15 AM

"I'm sorry," Alexis Truffant said, for the thousandth time.

Garrett said nothing. He sniffed at the breeze coming off the Pacific. It smelled clean and fresh and pure. He loved that smell. Alexis pushed his wheelchair down the ramp from the entrance to the Naval Hospital toward the waiting Humvee.

"I'm sorry for lying to you. But it wasn't a complete lie. I'm married, but separated. I haven't seen my husband in three months. We're trying to work out our differences. Not that it makes it any better."

She craned her head to catch his reaction. There was none. "You were right. I didn't tell you because I wanted you to think you had a chance with me. That was wrong."

Celeste and Bingo were waiting by the Humvee. Celeste held the rear passenger door open. Bingo stood beside her. Jimmy Lefebvre was leaning on the hood.

"Hi, Garrett. How you feeling?" Bingo asked. He tried to look at Garrett's face, but winced and quickly turned away. "You look good. Really."

"Thanks. Never felt better."

Celeste leaned close and stared at his bruises. "I dig the swollen, lumpy thing," she said. "Very fuckable."

Garrett snorted a laugh. Even that hurt. Hurt his lungs, his broken ribs, sent an electric pulse of pain through his head. It had been twenty-four hours since he'd woken up. But still the pain was intense. He would have to ask for more meds. Soon.

"Easy, big fella," Lefebvre said as he helped Garrett out of the wheelchair. "Later, you and I should talk about what happens when you break a bottle over a Marine's head. Statistically, it rarely turns out in your favor."

"Ha. Ha," Garrett said. "Fucking hilarious."

"Enough, guys," Alexis said, strapping him into the backseat. "Leave him be."

Lefebvre chuckled, then got behind the wheel and drove the stretch of road back toward their barracks headquarters. Every bump in the road sent more pain through Garrett's head. All he wanted to do was sleep. They rolled him into the barracks, where Bingo and Jimmy laid him out on the cot in his room. He closed his eyes and was instantly asleep—a deep, dreamless sleep. When he woke again, it was dark out, and he was hungry.

He hauled himself off the cot and shuffled into the kitchen, a fleece blanket wrapped around his shoulders. Alexis was standing over the stove, heating a pot of soup.

"You're up. Good. We were beginning to worry." She smiled broadly at him. He opened the refrigerator silently. "Still mad at me?" she asked.

"Not mad," Garrett muttered as he struggled to open a plastic-wrapped block of orange cheese. Even moving his fingers seemed to shoot pain up his arms. "Hate you. Completely different animal."

Alexis slumped into a chair. "Fine. Hate me. I don't blame you. But you're still going to work with us, right?"

Garrett grabbed a handful of Triscuits from an open box. It was an easier meal. "Can't decide. Head hurts too much." He turned and shuffled back into his room. He lay down on the cot, but Alexis appeared over him, her face tight with emotion.

"This is serious, Garrett. Lives are at stake. That is bigger than how we feel."

"Not sure I agree," Garrett said as he closed his eyes. "Nothing bigger than how I feel." In seconds, he was asleep. When he woke again, it was the sound of a voice he recognized that brought him to his senses. Older, authoritative, menacing; Garrett couldn't place it exactly, but he knew he didn't like it. He blinked his eyes just as the door to his room swung open. The voice preceded the body.

"A waste of time and money. It's over, you're shut down, and he's discharged." Secretary of Defense Frye marched into the room. He wore a dark gray suit and a burgundy power tie. Alexis trailed him, followed by Lefebvre. Bingo and Celeste hovered by the door, looking spooked. "Dishonorably, by the way," the secretary said.

"In all fairness, we haven't even started, sir," Alexis said, trying to step in front of the secretary and get Garrett to his feet. But Frye brushed her aside and walked up to Garrett's cot. Garrett was wrapped in a blanket and wearing a pair of gym shorts.

"There is no such thing as fairness, Captain. Not in this world. And certainly not in this Army." Frye turned his glare to Garrett, who rubbed his eyes and sat up in bed. "What do you have to say for yourself, son? Drinking. Getting stoned. Fighting with Marines. Didn't even have the good sense to win the fight."

Garrett's head hurt less. He could take deep breaths without too much pain in his ribs. He could see, from the rays of sun streaming through the drawn curtains, that it was morning, and that he had slept through the night. "I had the first three, no problem. Their friend got me from behind. Which is sneaky-ass bullshit."

Frye bent low over the bed. Garrett could smell the coffee on his breath. "Is that supposed to be funny? Because it's not." He turned to Alexis, waving his hand in the air. "Close up this office." He pointed to Celeste and Bingo. "Send the civilians home. The lieutenant goes to the War College. And you get yourself back to Bolling, where you can do some good, ASAP. "

Frye marched toward the door. Lefebvre stepped forward. "Sir, if you could see your way to giving us one more chance. I believe we are beginning to do some good—"

The secretary cut him off. "You can do good other places. And speak out of turn to me again and I will bust you to private. I don't care how rich your daddy is."

Lefebvre's face reddened. He saluted stiffly. "Sir, yes sir."

"The U.S. military can fight any war, any time," the secretary said, leaving the room. "We train our own just fine, thank you very much."

"Your officers are morons."

The secretary froze. He turned slowly and reentered the room. "What did you just say?"

Garrett staggered to his feet and fumbled for his bottle of Vicodin. He stuffed a pair in his mouth and dry-swallowed them. "I said, I can outthink any Army officer, outmaneuver any Marine commandant, on any field of battle, any time you want."

"All of a sudden you think you're a field commander? Spend a few days at a Marine base and you think you can fight a war?"

"Not me, personally. But I can lead troops. And I'll make sure they take down your best."

"Garrett," Alexis said, edging toward the bed, "the secretary is—"

"You suggesting we put you in charge of a field exercise? A battle simulation?"

"You can stack the odds. Five to one. Ten to one. I don't care. But I've seen how these Marines are trained to fight. And I can take them to pieces."

"That's preposterous. But even if it weren't, why should I give you a second chance?"

"Because you know—deep down inside, you know—that you don't really have any idea of what you're dealing with. And you suspect that I just might."

Silence enveloped the room. Secretary of Defense Frye stared at Garrett, blue eyes level and focused, for a good quarter of a minute. Then he said, "Tomorrow morning. Oh-five hundred. I'll get a Marine colonel to set the sides. Win and you get to keep going. Lose and you get a court-martial. Drug use, assault and battery. You'll spend the next ten years in a military prison."

Frye pushed past Alexis and Bingo and marched out of the room. Celeste, Bingo, and Jimmy Lefebvre stared, wide-eyed, at Garrett.

"Have you lost your mind?" Alexis asked.

"Guess so," Garrett said, feeling at his ribs. "But I figured it was worth a shot."

36

CAMP PENDLETON, APRIL 9, 5:42 AM

The sun lay just below the San Jacinto Mountains. The air was still. The yelp of a coyote broke the predawn quiet in a shallow ravine that wound its way down from the peaks of the scrubby Peninsula Range. Marine Corporal Jonathan Miller peered through the night-vision scope on his M4 carbine, scanning the low brush that ran off into the distance. He picked up the distinct green heat signature of a deer, then another one, but that was all. Nobody was moving up the arroyo toward Miller or his fire team. The enemy was not on the move. Which left an opening for Miller, and he told his squad leader as much.

"Clear below us to two clicks." Miller keyed his walkie-talkie and waited for the response.

"Roll down to the next way station and hold for my command."

Corporal Miller waved his arm and made his way down the slope of the canyon. Behind him, twelve Marines rose up out of the scrub and followed silently. Miller checked the flanks of the canyon around him, and sure enough, two more squads of Marines, all part of the 1st Marine Regiment—Inchon, they were called, after the regiment's heroics in the Korean War—appeared like ghosts out of the brush and moved toward lower ground. They were a rifle platoon, ground combat elements of the 1st Marines, headquartered at Camp Pendleton. Grunts. The shock team of the U.S. military. And they were about to inflict some serious shock on their fellow Marines, Miller thought to himself. On the poor suckers who had to fight for that asshole with the attitude. The jerk-off who had sucker-punched a Marine at Tio's in Oceanside, and then got his butt beat by all the other grunts in the bar. Put his sorry ass in the hospital.

Who picks a fight with a Marine in a Marine bar? A retard first class, that's who.

Miller's team, back from its third tour of duty in Afghanistan, had jumped at the chance to participate in this morning's field exercise. They were battle-tested hard-core shit-kickers, and they were more than happy to prove that to anyone who doubted them. And to make it even sweeter, rumor had it that the secretary of defense himself was monitoring the simulation back at field HQ. That would be some shit—winning a field exercise with the SecDef watching. Miller would tell his grandkids about that.

And they would win this field exercise pronto. They had two rifle companies, a weapons platoon, two Super Cobra helicopter gunships, and a fleet of Humvees, all matched up against one puny rifle platoon. Thirty-six Marines. Led by the asshole bar fighter. Who were trying to hold a bunkered encampment between Miller's position and the highway that ran through the middle of the camp. Good luck to them. It would be over by dawn.

"Flanking maneuver. Coordinate GPS systems," came the word from the company captain. The captain was in a field tent, on a hilltop, five kilometers behind them, supervising the exercise. Maybe, Miller thought, the SecDef is with him. Hot damn.

Miller squatted in a dry riverbed. The three other men in his fire team settled in next to him. Miller broke out his GPS and plotted the course. The enemy's bunkered encampment was three kilometers due south of his position. They could follow the dry riverbed, unseen, right to the edge of the encampment. Then the platoon would split into threes, encircle the encampment, and take the place with overwhelming force. The captain would call in air support when they were within 500 yards, effective firing distance for the M4 carbines his team carried. Standard procedure. Nothing fancy. Corner and kill.

Corporal Miller radioed the other team leaders. "Everybody have the objective on GPS? Latitude 33.315037. Longitude minus 117.409859."

"Roger that."

"On it."

Miller turned to his team. "We're point. Expect ambushes. That's their only chance."

A young private squinted toward the faint light that was gathering over the mountains to his left. "They ambush us, we die."

Corporal Miller stashed his handheld GPS. "No. That's the beauty. We got a whole 'nother company shadowing us. Alpha Company. They ambush us, Alpha ambushes them. Game over."

"No shit," the private said. "I thought we only had two companies. I read that in the exercise parameters."

"Well, the parameters lied." Miller smiled. "You can't trust the planners. Overwhelming force is a bitch. And war is hell."

Corporal Miller's team jogged quickly down the riverbed, stopping every hundred yards or so to check the GPS and reorient. Two platoons followed, tramping wordlessly in the dust. In twenty minutes they had closed to within 500 yards of the target. The sky to the east was fully orange now. In another twenty minutes it would be light out. The time to strike was now.

Corporal Miller hissed into his microphone: "Captain, sir, we have not encountered any bogies. No ambushes. No sign of them."

The captain's disembodied voice crackled over the walkie: "They're waiting for a frontal assault. Proceed as discussed. Over."

Miller walked back along the line of Marines stretched out a hundred yards behind him, and tapped the fire team corporals, telling them each the same command: "You know the drill. Flank the objective. Wait for gunship fire suppression. Then take the position." He walked back to the head of his team.

"Let's go."

Corporal Miller broke his men into a full run as they circled the encampment along the bottom of the dry riverbed. Using his GPS as a guide, he spread his men out around the objective, one man every twenty yards or so. When he reached the far edge of the bed, 180 degrees opposite the rest of the company, with the encampment between them, he dropped down and called in to his captain. "We're in place and ready for air support."

"Roger that. Three minutes."

Miller settled down to wait. He'd barely had time to sip his water and check the night scope on his carbine when he heard the telltale thudding of the helicopter rotors. The Cobras, two of them, roared up from the ocean, and hovered, thirty feet off the ground, just beyond Miller's view. Miller popped up from the riverbed, raised his binoculars, and took his first real look at the objective.

It was a pair of cinder-block structures, both one story high, with corrugated tin roofs, meant to simulate a peasant home in Iraq or Afghanistan. A ring of razor wire encircled the huts. The captain's voice rang out on the radio: "Corporal. Air support in place. On your mark to destroy."

Miller scanned the encampment. No movement. They had to be in there. Or maybe they had scattered out into the brush first thing? The exercise had started at 0500, so they would have had time to disappear into the wilderness. Didn't matter. He was about to give the go-ahead to simulate destruction of the shacks when he saw movement in a doorway. A man stepped out of the shack and into the open. Immediately, Miller raised his rifle and sighted him. Dead. Recorded in the chip in his scope. A corresponding device in the killed soldier's rifle should have chirped, alerting the Marine that he was now officially a casualty of the exercise.

But the Marine outside of the hut kept walking. Miller lowered his rifle and took up his binoculars again. The man was waving his hands. And he wasn't in uniform. In fact, Miller found it hard to believe that he was a Marine at all. He was dark-skinned, wearing a sweatshirt, and potbellied, as wide around the middle as he was tall. And he was not a tall man. Five foot two, Miller guessed.

"Corporal Miller? Your word?"

"Uh. Hold off, sir. Something's up."

"Come again, Corporal?"

"There's a noncombatant at the objective."

"Not possible, Corporal. The objective was swept by MPs right before the exercise. Only Marines in there. You are mistaken."

"Well," Miller said, looking through the binoculars. "I don't think this guy is a Marine." Behind the squat, fat man, another man stepped out of the shack. And then another, and another, a dozen in all, one after the other, all with their hands above their heads. A few of them were women, and Miller could have sworn two were kids.

"Sir, are you watching on the Cobra cameras?"

"I am now, Corporal. Halt the exercise and find out who the hell those people are!"

"Will do."

Corporal Miller signaled the rest of his platoon to move onto the mesa surrounding the shacks. The Marine regiment moved slowly, guns drawn, across the open ground and to the edge of the razor wire. The Cobra gunships moved off another two hundred yards, kicking up dust farther from the encampment.

When Miller got within twenty yards of the shacks, he blinked twice, trying to register the reality of what he saw in front of him. There were a dozen people, all Asian, ranging in age from elderly to maybe ten years old, wrapped up in sweatshirts and down vests. One of them was sipping coffee. A young woman was cradling a baby in an over-the-shoulder snuggly. A teenager was filming the whole thing on his cell phone.

"Who are you?" Miller shouted at them.

The portly man smiled and waved Miller closer. He yelled, "Can't hear you!"

Miller moved closer, as did the ring of Marines—fifty in all—who surrounded the shack. "I said who are you and what the hell are you doing here?"

The portly man bowed slightly. "I'm Leonard Chang. We are the Chang family. We own the King Fu Chinese restaurant in Oceanside."

Miller recognized the man immediately. He'd seen him at King Fu any number of times, wandering the tables, smiling, seeing if the food and service were up to snuff. King Fu was his favorite Chinese restaurant outside of New York City.

"We have coffee for you," Leonard Chang said. He motioned to a pair of men, who darted into the shacks and came out with platters crammed with styrofoam cups filled with steaming coffee. "For all of you," Leonard said. He waved the Marines closer. A dozen moved closer and grabbed cups of java.

"But how did you get here?" Miller asked.

"Garrett Reilly asked us to come. He paid us one hundred dollars per person. He said this was a war game. Is he right?"

A chill ran down Corporal Miller's spine. Garrett Reilly was the douche nozzle from the bar. He fumbled for his walkie-talkie. Leonard Chang flashed a cell phone at him. "This is a war game, right? Garrett told me to tell you that this cell phone is a pretend detonator."

Corporal Miller winced. Oh shit. He keyed his microphone, but he knew it was too late. They'd been tricked. He yelled, "Sir, we got hosed! We're at the wrong place!"

Leonard Chang smiled at the Marine Corporal: "He told me to tell you that I am a suicide bomber. And I just blew you up. You're all dead. That was fun, huh?"

37

FORWARD OPERATING HQ, CAMP PENDLETON, APRIL 9, 6:58 AM

Captain Anthony Marsden screamed into his microphone: "Cobras, lift off! Get the fuck out of there this instant!" The flaps of the field tent practically vibrated with the intensity of the captain's rage. His support staff, a dozen lieutenants and sergeants, winced at his profanity. The secretary of defense was standing in a corner, behind them, watching silently. He would not be happy. A second lieutenant peeked at the SecDef over his shoulder. Even in the gloomy darkness, the lieutenant could see that his blue eyes were radiating deep, deep disappointment.

Alexis Truffant, on the other hand, wanted to laugh out loud. She had been standing at the secretary's side for the past hour, listening to him mutter about the stupidity of the project, about how there was no place for a character like Garrett Reilly in the armed forces, about how he would cut General Kline's funding at the DIA to zero after this. And now, Garrett Reilly had tricked them. They'd challenged him to a duel, and he didn't show up. And he still won. She had to admit it, as much as she was loath to: the guy was fun to watch. He did not think like an Army officer. She wasn't sure how he thought, but it confused the hell out of the military lifers.

"Cobras backing off."

"Look for those bastards anywhere on the battlefield! This is not over. Search and destroy. They're out there someplace."

"Yes sir. Cobra One, over."

Captain Marsden wheeled on his staff. "How the hell did those people get on the base? They all work at a fucking *restaurant*?"

A young lieutenant edged forward. "Sir, yes sir. Everybody knows the

Chang family. They deliver to base all the time. Everybody loves their food, sir. They probably drove on last night with deliveries and just stayed."

Alexis must have let out a tiny snort of amusement, because Duke Frye turned to her immediately. "Do you think this is funny, Captain? Are you amused by this?"

"No sir," Alexis said, spine straightening.

"Because I thought I heard you laughing."

"I coughed, sir."

The secretary gave her a long look.

Captain Marsden pointed at the laptop on the nearest table. "That GPS program right there says the objective is five kilometers away. Due south. But they went one click west. How the fuck did our GPS systems not coordinate? How the hell did my men get led to the wrong shack? Someone needs to answer that question for me."

"He hacked the system," a sergeant ventured. "He scrambled all the coordinates."

"There's no way it could be hacked, sir," a lieutenant answered quickly. "It's on a secure network. Nobody can get in."

"They can if they have the access codes."

Heads in the tent snapped around as Garrett, dressed in jeans, sweatshirt, and a Yankees baseball cap, sauntered into the tent. He looked windswept and slightly out of breath; his right cheek was still bruised eggplant purple. A few of the support staff reached for their sidearms, but nobody drew a weapon. Garrett smiled, waved. "Hey, all. Good morning. You're all dead, by the way. My team has already surrounded the tent. We blasted it full of bullets. You know, virtual bullets. I think it would be cool if you all, like, lay down and acted dead or something."

Captain Marsden started toward Garrett. "This field tent was not part of the exercise!"

"Not part of *your* exercise, but it was part of *mine*." Garrett stepped over to the lieutenant at the GPS laptop. "Anyway, the answer to your question is that I collected the access codes from the base server and sent them to a friend of mine. She went in and reprogrammed your GPS servers so they collected data off a false download signal, full of fake topographical data. It wasn't easy, but she's good. Really good."

Duke Frye stepped past Alexis into the center of the tent. "You gave out military access codes to a civilian hacker?"

"She's not really a hacker. She's a game programmer in New York. I mean, she has hacked. But long ago. And she never got caught, she's not black hat, so no criminal record or anything."

The secretary fumed at Garrett: "Do you realize how many laws you broke?"

"I won. Wasn't that the point?"

"You cheated. That's not winning."

"You guys doubled the number of battalions against me without telling me. Isn't that cheating too?"

"Arrest him, now," Frye barked. He waved to a pair of master sergeants at the edge of the group. The sergeants, surprised by the order, hesitated. The bigger of the two looked to his captain, who nodded vigorously: Do it.

Alexis stepped into the path of the oncoming sergeants, blocking them both. "He changed the parameters of the game. That's not cheating. It's why we chose him in the first place."

Secretary Frye lowered his voice threateningly. "You really want to take his side in this, Captain? Because if you knew he was giving out access codes, then you will be court-martialed just as quickly."

"She didn't know anything about it," Garrett said. "I did it on my own. And if you want to send me to jail for it, fine." He put out his hands as if ready to be cuffed. "But I think it'd be kind of ironic to arrest me for behaving like the enemy you're looking to defeat."

The two sergeants looked to the secretary for further orders. Duke Frye scowled and waved them forward. "Take him away."

"No!" Alexis shouted, sidestepping the first sergeant. She grabbed his wrist and had started to put him into an armlock when a voice rang out, gruff and unhappy.

"He's not going anywhere." General Wilkerson, the chairman of the Joint Chiefs of Staff, stepped into the tent, flanked by a pair of aides, navy commanders in white dress uniforms and blue windbreakers. Captain Marsden, his entire support staff, and Alexis all snapped to attention.

Secretary Frye blinked in surprise. "General. When did you . . . ?"

"Last night. I was in San Diego." He walked up to Secretary Frye and lowered his voice to a whisper. "I don't want to make you look bad in front of these men, but you're going to have to let him go."

Frye stiffened. "You don't have the authority."

"The president wants him in Washington by nightfall."

Frye's face tightened. He jammed his hands into his coat pockets. "Of course I won't contradict the president," he hissed.

Wilkerson put his arm around Frye's shoulder. "There are no more rules anymore, Duke. No more rules anywhere. "

Frye let out an angry breath as HQ radio blared to life. It was the pilot of the lead Cobra gunship: "Sir, we picked up their tracking GPS signal. Enemy is hiding in Mess Hall Seven, off Basilone Road. Should we engage?"

Everyone in the room looked to Garrett, who turned his hands palms up, in a gesture of sly amusement. "We figured you guys would stash tracking devices in our gear, so we left it all in the mess hall this morning. Not really fair if you'd followed us from the get-go." Garrett smiled. "But my guys have no coats, so they're kinda cold outside. Can we call it a day?"

Captain Marsden grabbed the microphone. "Negative, Cobra One. Field exercise is terminated. Return to base."

38

CAMP PENDLETON, APRIL 9, 8:01 AM

The Marine Humvee spun gravel as it roared down from the hilltop HQ tent. Garrett sat in back, next to Alexis. General Wilkerson sat in front with the driver. His two aides rode in a follow vehicle. The sun had risen over the mountains; the California chaparral was alive in an explosion of yellows and reds.

"There's a naval transport waiting for you at Miramar," Wilkerson said. "Pack your stuff and get down there in the next hour. They'll fly you direct to Andrews. The president would like to meet you first thing tomorrow morning."

"The president of the United States?" Garrett asked.

"Yes, that president," Wilkerson grunted.

The Humvee pulled up in front of their barracks. The general craned his head back to look at Garrett. "Reilly, I'd advise you to stop pissing off the secretary of defense. He's a very powerful man. Screw with him too much and he will tear out your heart and eat it while you're still breathing. You get my meaning?"

"Yes sir," Garrett said, liking the general more and more with each moment.

"I was considering giving you another piece of counsel—which was to stop being such an asshole to everybody, all the time—but it seems to work for you, so carry on." The general stared at Reilly, then shrugged. "Now get the hell out of my Humvee."

Garrett and Alexis scrambled out of the vehicle. The moment the back door closed, the Humvee rumbled off in a cloud of dust. Alexis watched it go, shaking her head in disbelief. "The chairman of the Joint Chiefs of Staff just advised you to keep acting like an asshole. That's got to be some kind of a first."

"What can I say? I'm a trailblazer."

Garrett went to his room and stuffed what few clothes he'd accumulated into a backpack, then met Alexis in the building's open, central room. She had a duffel bag ready at her side. Celeste, Bingo, and Jimmy Lefebvre were standing across the room. None of the three was carrying bags. Garrett pointed to them. "They're not coming?"

Alexis shook her head no.

"I think they should."

"They weren't asked."

"They're part of the team."

"I don't have transit orders for them."

Garrett sat down on a rolling office chair. "They don't go, I don't go." Alexis stared at Garrett, astonished. He smiled at the team. "You do wanna come, right? Washington, D.C.? The Lincoln Memorial?"

Lefebvre laughed in amazement. "Not sure I've ever met anyone quite like you."

"That's a good thing, right?" Garrett asked.

"Never been to D.C.," Celeste said. "So, yeah, I'm in."

"I don't really love flying," Bingo said. Celeste glared at him. "But okay."

Garrett grinned at Alexis. "Just following the beloved chairman's advice."

The U.S. Navy C-37A Gulfstream roared off the tarmac at Marine Corps Air Station Miramar, gained altitude quickly over the Pacific, then banked north on its route toward the East Coast. The ten swiveling seats on the inside of the converted business jet were leather, in navy blue and aqua—not as plush as some of the corporate planes Garrett had read about, but plenty nicer than anything he'd ever been on. He laughed as Bingo and Celeste put their feet up and toggled every switch they could find, while Alexis and Lefebvre—the only true noncivilians in the passenger section—tried to play it cool, pulling out briefing folders and pretending to study them. But Garrett could tell they were just as awed as the rest of them.

Garrett drank a Coke from the onboard fridge, then booted up his laptop. He studied it for an hour, then moved to an empty seat next to Alexis and slid the computer onto a tray in front of her. On the screen was a dense scroll of computer code. Alexis glanced at it, then at Garrett.

"This supposed to mean something to me?"

"It's the malware that took down the Google server farm. Copies of it have been circulating on the Web. I had my friend Mitty in New York take a look at it."

"When did you have this done?"

"Before I got the crap beat out of me. But she e-mailed it to me before we took off from Miramar. The code is very sophisticated."

Alexis scanned the lines of code. "Would have to be if it was able to take down Google."

"Unfortunately, that's not the half of it."

"Meaning?"

"You heard of Stuxnet?"

"The virus that attacked the Iranian nuclear power plant a few years ago?"

"Actually, it attacked the Siemens-built centrifuges that worked in the Iranian power plant."

"Okay."

"It was a carefully constructed worm that hid its identity when introduced into a computer. Once inside a computer it checked to see if the computer was running a specific type of Siemens machine. If it wasn't, the worm shut itself down. But if it found a Siemens centrifuge, it replicated itself and attacked the programmable logic controller. Which was big shit, because PLCs run everything in this world. Almost anything mechanical has a PLC in it. Assembly-line machines, stoplights, airplane controls."

"The plane we're on . . . ?" Alexis asked nervously.

Garrett nodded. "Is chock-full of PLCs. Once you start attacking PLCs with computer worms and malware, the hacking genie is out of the bottle. That's why people were so upset about Stuxnet. And angry at the countries that might have created it."

"Us?"

"Maybe. Or Israel. Or both of us, together. We'll never know for sure. Once Stuxnet was inside the Siemens machines, it took over the PLCs and started issuing bogus commands. It threw the Iranian centrifuges off kilter, spun them really fast, and centrifuges are delicate things, but it also made the machines send out false readings that made the technicians monitoring them think everything was fine. The centrifuges spun themselves out of service and were destroyed."

"So the code I'm looking at on your computer did the same thing to Google's PLCs?"

"Ran their hard drives at one hundred times maximum speed. Overheated in minutes. Ruined them all. Shut the entire server farm down. Destroyed millions of dollars' worth of machinery."

"But you've isolated it. It can be stopped?"

"Isolated, yes. And stopped at Google."

"But not on other computers?"

"Mitty got about halfway through, but couldn't get any further because the code was written to self-destruct—erase itself basically—twenty-four hours after use. The copies were incomplete, but she thinks there's more to it. That it's hidden in layers under the erased level of code."

"I'm not liking the sound of that."

"She thinks the Google attack was a test run. To see if it would work on a heavily fortified network."

"So there's another target?"

"The code is complex, and the commands are hidden. But there are hints. Of another worm. A companion. That's probably already in circulation. Letters strung together. Binary code that references pieces of machinery."

"What kind of machinery?"

Garrett scrolled through the code, stopping at a section dense with stop/repeat and if/then commands. "General Electric machinery. Specifically boiling-water reactors."

"Boiling-water reactors? You mean like they use in nuclear power plants?"

Garrett nodded.

"Oh shit."

"Gets worse," Garrett said. "The execute command date is today."

39

CHENGDU, CHINA, APRIL 9, 9:04 PM

Hu Mei was happy, even though she was surrounded by people she barely knew. She'd just eaten the first home-cooked meal she'd had in months, and it had been delicious, if strange. The air in the small dining room was thick with the smell of aniseed, shallots, ginger, chili peppers sautéing in sesame oil, and freshly steamed cod. She had drunk two entire glasses of *húangjǐu*, or yellow wine, which was rare for Hu Mei. She almost never drank alcohol, but the food tonight had been *lǎo là le* ("very spicy"), as hot as you could get in Sichuan cooking. She wasn't used to spicy Sichuan food. It had made her mouth and tongue numb; she had needed the wine to keep from choking.

The wine had made her tipsy—enough so that the dining room in the old masonry-block home seemed cozy instead of small, and the family that had fed her—the Lu family; a barking mother, a sullen father, two laughing uncles, a garrulous grandmother, a shy young girl, and three overly friendly dogs—seemed amusing instead of foreign and raucous. They had a modest home on a sloping hillside, fifteen miles outside of Chengdu, with a dirt yard in back, some chickens, and a pig.

One of the uncles was a loyal supporter, vetted through and through, and he had vouched for the rest of his family; they knew who Hu Mei was, and who was after her, but still she would be safe here tonight. Once a supporter brought her into their home, the rest of the family had to keep quiet out of self-preservation—there was no telling who the government would decide to arrest or prosecute. If you harbored a traitor to the state, your entire family was suspect. It was twisted logic, but it worked to Hu Mei's continuing advantage. The party, Hu Mei had learned, could be its own worst enemy.

The Lu daughter—Mei thought her name was Jia Li—cleared the dinner plates, careful not to spill any food. They were not rich; food would never be wasted. Mei guessed her to be about eleven, bony and awkward, head bowed and hair tied up in back. She shuffled in slippers across the poured-concrete floor.

That was me twenty years ago, Hu Mei thought to herself. The little girl clearing plates for her family, hurrying to heat water so she could wash dishes in the kitchen. That had been hard work for a young girl, but Hu Mei had done it without fail, her mother coming to help when the men started talking about planting or the weather. She missed her family. A wave of sadness passed over Mei. She missed her husband, Yi. It had been a long, lonely year since his death.

At the table, the two uncles started to argue about sports. Something about a man named Jeremy Lin, and was he really Chinese? He had been born in San Francisco, one of the uncles said, but his parents were Taiwanese, and that made him Chinese. Hu Mei had only the faintest idea who Jeremy Lin was—she guessed he played basketball, probably in America. One of the uncles was demanding that Lin return to China and play for the Shanghai Sharks.

"It is the only honorable thing to do," he said. "It is his blood!"

They began to shout. Everyone had an opinion. At the beginning of the meal they had treated Hu Mei with a quiet respect—she was an infamous dissident, and any notoriety was a form of status in China now—but once everyone had had their fill of wine, the real Lu family was revealed, and they were a chaotic, bickering bunch.

Hu Mei quietly excused herself from the table and slipped into the kitchen. The shouting receded into the distance. The daughter was dutifully washing dishes in the sink. Mei grabbed a small dish towel and started to dry them.

"No, no," Jia Li said, looking horrified. She stepped sideways to block Mei's path to the wet plates and cups. "You mustn't. I will clean."

"Don't be silly," Hu Mei said. "They are talking about a basketball player. I don't care about basketball. Or basketball players." Hu Mei smiled at the young girl. "I think I don't even care about people who *talk* about basketball players."

Jia Li laughed. She shot a quick look at the dining room. "If my mother comes in, then will you stop helping, please? Before she sees you?"

Mei nodded with a grin. "Of course." She understood the family code: a guest could not help clean or cook. That would be an unforgivable breach of etiquette.

Jia Li returned to scrubbing dishes, and Hu Mei dried them at her side. It gave her a quiet pleasure to return to a mindless domestic chore. All those months making decisions and leading people had taken a toll on Hu Mei. Lately, she yearned for the tranquil rhythms of her past life; if they found her drying dishes, so be it.

"May I ask you a question, please?" Jia Li said, pausing in her cleaning.

"Of course. Ask me anything."

"Why do you hate China?"

Hu Mei's breath caught in her throat.

"My mother says you want to destroy the country. That you want to tear down the government. And we will all suffer. No more jobs. No more food."

Hu Mei tried to force an easy smile to her lips. How could she explain herself to this little girl? If she were a true revolutionary, she would have a homily at the ready—something about the people, the government, with animals perhaps as the characters, frogs or foxes, to make it all easily digestible. Simple. Plainspoken.

"It is like doing the dishes," Mei said. "You don't enjoy doing it, but your parents tell you to, so you must. Everyone listens to their parents. But China is not your parent . . . China is a place." Her voice sounded thin and desperate. She stuttered to a stop. "No . . . what I mean is . . ."

Jia Li stared at her, confusion in her eyes. Hu Mei grimaced. She was no revolutionary. She was a peasant from Huaxi Township. How could she explain the death of her husband? The grief? The loss of her home, her farm? The anger of her neighbors? How could she explain to this little girl about the corruption that lived everywhere around her? That was throttling the people of the nation?

Before she could say another word, Jia Li's mother stepped into the kitchen, carrying an armful of dishes. The moment she saw Hu Mei and her daughter, face-to-face, clearly in the middle of a conversation, her face froze in a disapproving scowl. She rushed between the two of them, laying her dishes in the sink. "I will finish the cleaning," she said quickly, authoritatively. "Jia Li, go to bed. Right away. Now. Go."

Jia Li bowed and scurried toward the door. Mei quivered in frustration. She had to say something. She could not let this child—this miniature version of herself—go away thinking that everything Hu Mei had done was destructive. Was evil.

"Jia Li," Hu Mei called out, her brain suddenly clear. The little girl stopped. "You are a lovely child." The girl looked up at her. "May you have everything you desire in this life. Love. Wealth. Children . . ."

The girl brightened.

"And justice," Hu Mei continued. "Perhaps one day even . . . *power.*"

Jia Li stared at Hu Mei, brow tight in thought, then she ducked her head once more, and hurried from the room. Her mother watched her go, then stared daggers at Hu Mei, who instinctively ducked her head as well.

"Please forgive my intrusion," Mei said. "Although I am grateful for your hospitality, I will not burden you with my presence. I will collect my belongings and leave right away."

She walked for the door, newly sober and weary once more, certain only that she would not be sleeping in a cozy, warm bed tonight. Perhaps she would find a secluded field and an old blanket. And under the cold, dim stars, she would work on her revolutionary homilies.

40

45,000 FEET OVER GARY, INDIANA, APRIL 9, 5:31 PM

Bingo knew what trouble was all about.

He'd grown up in Oakland; his dad was black, a high school history teacher, but his mom was white, an ex-hippie who took great pleasure in stirring the pot—strikes, protests, civil disobedience, you name it, she signed up for it. Bingo had taken crap for his mom's antics—and her race—pretty much every day of his life. He'd been taunted, chased, beat up. As a result, Bingo tried like hell to avoid confrontation. And other people. He was happiest in his room, shades drawn, with a book or a video game, studying the specs on the latest iPhone or dissecting Hitler's mistakes at the Battle of Stalingrad.

So it kind of blew his mind that he was part of a team whose job it was to seek out trouble, confront it, and then fix it.

It took him five minutes to locate half a dozen nuclear power plants running General Electric boiling-water reactors in the states they were currently flying over.

"Closest is the Enrico Fermi Nuclear Generating Station at Point Mouillee, Michigan," he said hurriedly. "Thirty miles south of Detroit. Right on Lake Erie."

Alexis used the plane's handheld satellite phone to call the reactor office and warn them about the worm, but the plant's shift supervisor sounded skeptical, and not particularly helpful. Alexis told him to expect authorized armed services visitors within the hour. She said they would need access to the plant's computers.

He hung up on her.

The sun was already sinking low on the horizon as the Gulfstream began its descent into the Detroit Metro Airport. The pilot radioed the local National Guard office and asked to have a car waiting for them when they landed. The team argued briefly about who should go to the plant, and who should stay. Lefebvre wanted to be in on the action—it seemed to Bingo that he was itching to prove himself—but Alexis pulled rank and said that Lefebvre and Celeste would stay with the plane. She told Lefebvre to get on his cell phone and start calling the Nuclear Regulatory Commission's emergency response teams—while she, Bingo, and Garrett would go to the reactor. The plan was to warn the engineers in person, and then get a sample of the worm before it erased itself. That was fine with Celeste—the idea of being near a nuke seemed to give her the creeps.

"What if the virus hits when you get there? And the place blows up?" she asked.

"That won't happen," Bingo said, trying as much to reassure himself as Celeste. "They'll shut down the core if there's a problem. They'll go offline immediately. It's very safe."

"Tell that to the Japanese," Celeste said.

It was six o'clock when they touched down in Detroit. A green Ford Taurus was waiting for them on the tarmac. Alexis took the wheel, punching in the coordinates for Pointe Mouillee on the car's GPS, while Garrett rode shotgun, and Bingo sat in back, humming to himself. Bingo hummed when he was nervous. As they were pulling out of the airport, Lefebvre ran after them and rapped on the car's trunk; when Alexis stopped the car and rolled down the driver's-side window, Lefebvre slipped her his Beretta M9.

"Just in case," he said. "Detroit and all."

Alexis tucked the handgun under the seat and took the highway south toward the Enrico Fermi station. Traffic was light and they got there in forty-five minutes, the plant's distinctive inverted-cone water-cooling towers becoming visible through the trees and freeway billboards from nearly a mile away. Alexis presented her Army ID at the gate, and the security guard checked it quickly. He told them the NRC had called and cleared their status. To Bingo he seemed distracted, and that only made him more nervous.

"Everything okay?" Alexis asked him.

"Uh, yeah," the guard said, glancing at the computer inside his gatehouse. "I think so."

Bingo grimaced. Not a good sign. The guard gave them visitor's badges and waved them in. The plant was huge, with a hulking containment building, ponds, and a pair of cooling towers near the lake. Alexis drove to the main operating building, took a visitor's parking space, and then the three of them hurried inside.

Engineers, mechanics, managers, and radiation EMTs were scurrying through the halls, barking into walkie-talkies, cell phones, and at each other. Bingo had never been in a nuclear power plant before, but this did not seem normal. It seemed desperate. Garrett tried to ask for directions to the control room, but no one would take the time to answer him. One red-faced engineer simply pointed down the hallway as he ran in the opposite direction.

Garrett, Alexis, and Bingo walked through a pair of heavy, steel-framed double doors—and were met with chaos. The power plant's control room was alive with voices and motion: a dozen engineers were gathered around a bank of computer monitors, shouting and typing frantically on keyboards. A shift supervisor seemed to be leading them, trying to organize the fracas into something resembling a rational discussion. Phones were ringing everywhere, and high-pitched alarms were cycling on and off across the room.

The shift supervisor—a portly man in a plaid shirt—saw Alexis in her Army uniform and raced toward her, arm and finger already extended in an accusatory point. "How the hell did you know?" he yelled. His plastic-laminated badge read: "Coyle."

"What's going on?" Garrett said.

"Who the fuck are *you*?" Coyle barked. "Who the fuck are any of you?"

"You've been attacked by a computer worm," Garrett said. "You need to tell me what's happening."

"I don't need to tell you shit," Coyle said. Then he scowled, seeming to have a change of heart. He waved at the row upon row of operating consoles. "Every goddamned sensor in this room is giving us different readings. Nothing matches."

"That's the malware," Garrett said. "We need a copy of it. And you need to shut everything down right away. Manually. You cannot trust your computers. You need to go offline, you've been breached."

"We shut down, and it can take months to restart a plant."

"Your computers will give you false readings until the reactors fail. And then you'll have a meltdown on your hands."

Coyle started to respond, then gritted his teeth and turned to his band of engineers. "Start the countdown to shut down number two reactor. Now! We are going offline. Scramming in sixty seconds!"

Garrett yelled after him—"We need a copy of the worm!"—but Coyle had moved on.

"Shit," Garrett said.

Bingo took a deep breath. Well, if he really was part of a team that went looking for trouble, he might as well embrace the mission with gusto. He slid next to Garrett. "Where would we find it? The worm?"

"Not sure. Probably in whatever program regulates the cooling rods."

Bingo reached into his pocket and pulled out a purple flash drive. He waved it in the air. "I'll need five minutes."

Garrett grinned. "You da man."

"I'm not, actually," Bingo said and sat down in front of an unused computer. Garrett and Alexis hovered over him as he started scrolling through programs. "But you should get the car started."

"Why?" Alexis asked, worry leaking into her voice. "You said they can shut down the reactors safely."

"They can," Bingo said, looking up at the two of them. "But every nuclear power plant for five states is running GE water boilers. They're all going to have to shut down at the same time. Probably in the next ten minutes. And when they do"—Bingo tried to smile—"the whole grid's going to fail."

41

CASS CORRIDOR, DETROIT, APRIL 9, 9:01 PM

Clarence Othello Hawkins, precinct captain of the All Mighty Vice Lord Nation, South Detroit Division, knew one thing, and he knew it stone cold: if the Detroit PD caught him tonight, he would spend the rest of his natural-born days in jail. He already had two felony convictions on his record—one of them a violent assault in a 7-Eleven robbery—and a third meant three strikes would kick in, and Clarence would rot in the joint until he was so old he had to use a motherfucking cane to stand up.

Clarence was no fool. He'd wiped his prints off the gun he'd just tossed over a backyard fence, but he couldn't be sure he'd gotten them all off. He'd fired the gun just fifteen minutes ago at a little punk-ass bitch from the Four Corners Hustlers. He didn't think he'd hit the Four Corners bitch, but maybe he was wrong and now the cops were after him for attempted murder. Or maybe the Four Corners Hustler had died. Not that he cared. He hated Hustlers, always moving in on his territory. But if he died, then Clarence might be wanted on a murder rap. And there was no way Clarence was doing life for murder. No fucking way.

He sprinted as fast as his twenty-four-year-old legs would carry him, south on Charlotte Street in the Cass Corridor, past the burned-out buildings and the church with the caved-in roof, then right across the vacant lots on Second Avenue, tromping down weeds and kicking garbage as he ran. He peeked over his shoulder and saw that a second squad car had joined the first one. Both cars had their cherries going, lighting up the Michigan night, and now their sirens were on as well, howling like dogs and waking up the whole damn neighborhood. Not that anyone in this neighborhood went to bed early anyway.

Shit, Clarence thought to himself, now I'm caught for sure. He wished, briefly, that he hadn't thrown away his gun. He would've turned and used it on the cops when they came to get him—at least he could've taken out a couple of those fuckers before they dropped him. Suicide by cop. There were worse ways to go. And Clarence figured he didn't have that long to live anyway. Not on the streets of Detroit.

He sprinted across the vacant lot on Second and Charlotte, knowing the cop cars couldn't traverse the deeply pitted grass and dirt. He leapt over a chain-link fence on Peterboro, hung a right, and dashed as hard as he could for the apartment complex halfway down the block. Little J lived there, on the second floor. J's spot was infested with Vice Lords. The cops would have serious trouble on their hands if Clarence could haul his ass up there. That was his salvation—his chance to live one more day as a free man—and in Detroit, one day more was all you could really ask for.

He dug deep to outrace the police cruisers. The orange halogen streetlights guided his path toward the front door. Only a hundred yards now. And Clarence could dash a hundred yards in ten seconds. He'd done it in under that in high school. Sectional Champ in 2006. Goddamned gold medal. Not that he cared. Wasn't really made of gold, and nobody made any money running track, anyway.

The cops had taken the long way around the vacant lot—he was definitely going to beat them. And then he saw it. Two more PD cruisers streaking the opposite direction down Peterboro, heading right at him, cutting off his escape route.

Motherfucker, he thought, slowing. He was screwed. He jogged to a stop, bending over to catch his breath, putting his hands on his hips. The cop cars raced at him. Game over. Well, it had been a good run, some fine times, parties and girls and a little money on the side. He wasn't going to get all weepy about his life 'cause he was tough and there was a lot worse shit out there than going to prison. Some people said prison for a Vice Lord was like a country club, all set up with drugs and twinks to keep the rough boys satisfied. But still, Clarence thought, sucking in a last lungful of cool Detroit air, he did like it better on the outside. The outside was good. Inside was a heavy load. He considered his options quickly, taking in any last chance of a possible escape. And then it happened . . .

All at once. Like the hand of motherfucking God, Clarence thought. A goddamned miracle.

Boom!

Every single light, in every single building and on every single street corner, went out. All at the same time. Detroit went dark. Pitch-black like the inside of a cave, no streetlights, window lights, building lights. Nothing but the moon and stars above.

All of a sudden, Clarence thought happily to himself, the police got way bigger problems on their hands than just catching my sorry ass. He grinned. And as he took off running, he thought . . . *Tonight will be all right after all.*

42

SOUTH DETROIT, APRIL 9, 9:10 PM

They were five miles from the power plant when Detroit went dark. The streetlights just winked out, starting in the north, on the periphery of Garrett's vision, then rolling south across the flat midwestern landscape like an inky wave.

"Holy crap," Garrett said.

Alexis turned on the car radio. Half the stations were dead, but a few came back online in a matter of minutes. They had reports from across the city: the blackout was extensive, all of Detroit was out, along with a host of suburbs. Windsor, Ontario, was also dark, as well as Ann Arbor and south all the way to Toledo, Ohio.

Another radio station said that Cleveland had experienced a brownout, while Cincinnati had gone black entirely. Chicago was struggling to stay online. Power technicians across the Midwest were juggling transmission lines, trying to keep the center of the country lit. But they were losing the battle. The grid was going down.

Garrett watched this new shadow world pass by the car's windshield; it was profoundly dark out. A few emergency lights flickered in office-park windows, as well as car headlights that passed them on the street, but other than that, it was a night as black as one in the fifteenth century. Garrett marveled at how the modern world could be left so helpless so quickly, just by cutting off its electricity. It was terrifying. He fiddled with the car's GPS, but it had stopped picking up a signal.

"I thought these things worked off satellite feeds," Garrett said.

"They do," Bingo answered. "Maybe the feed gets relayed through cell towers. And those are all down."

"I'm sure there's a map in the glove compartment," Alexis said.

"A map?" Garrett said. "You mean, like, on paper?"

Alexis didn't laugh, and Garrett fished a torn city street map from a stack of license and registration documents. It was old and faded and Garrett had to use the light from his cell phone to read it. He directed them north, away from the power plant, toward the general vicinity of the airport, but almost immediately they noticed pockets of glowing orange in the distance.

"Fires," Garrett said, changing stations on the radio. "Looters. Maybe rioters."

WWJ reported the first structure fires just south of downtown. The police and fire department were responding to calls all over the city. Alexis reached down and slid Jimmy's gun under her leg, for easier access. Garrett navigated them east, away from the center of the city, trying to find the Fisher Freeway—which would get them right to the airport—but the blocks were entirely dark, the street signs unlit and obscured, and he missed the on-ramp, overshooting it by several blocks and ending up in a battle-scarred neighborhood of run-down homes and vacant lots.

Garrett had known bad neighborhoods, growing up in Long Beach, but he'd never seen anything quite like this area of South Detroit. The wreckage and the waste of it chilled him: row after row of darkened, ruined houses and buildings, punctuated by vacant lots that seemed to glow in the moonlight and the flicker of nearby fires.

"Wow," he hissed. "Insane."

Alexis gripped the wheel hard. "My thoughts exactly," she said, and as soon as she said it shots rang out from behind them, the *pop-pop-pop* of a handgun clearly audible above the engine noise. She stomped the gas, turning quickly onto a broader boulevard. There was hardly any traffic on the streets, and people were burning garbage in trash bins on the sidewalks. Many of the storefronts had smashed-in windows, and young men and women were climbing out of the stores with armfuls of food and clothing and electronics. A few men in hoodies ran into the street to try to block their route, but Alexis swerved, laying her hand on the horn and cursing them. "Idiots!"

"Easy," said Garrett. "I'll get us out of here." He checked the map again, but without knowing what the name of the boulevard was, he was basically guessing.

"Take a right," he said.

Alexis pulled the car around a corner; there was a blur of motion to their right and then *boom*, another car T-boned their Taurus on the passenger side. There were shrieks as the National Guard car was spun 180 degrees, the outside world circling wildly around them, and then the car landed with a thick crunch against a parked minivan. Garrett hadn't buckled his seat belt—it hurt his ribs—so his body was snapped forward like the end of a cracking whip.

The hiss of leaking engine fluid punctuated the sudden silence. Garrett's head exploded in pain. Bolts of electric blue light flashed across his field of vision.

"Everyone okay?" Alexis asked, checking her arms for pain or broken bones.

"Whiplash," Bingo said plaintively. "I got whiplash."

Garrett grunted wordlessly, his mind blank with pain. Four men in hoodies were climbing out of the car that had just rammed them. One had a crowbar. Another had a gun.

"Shit," Alexis said, kicking open the driver's-side door and popping out, Lefebvre's gun in hand. She shouted at the men: "U.S. Army! Stand down!"

The man with the pistol raised it and fired at Alexis, three times fast. The report of the gun was deafening, but the bullets whizzed past Alexis without hitting her, and she immediately raised her own pistol and fired back, squeezing off two quick shots. The man with the gun spun around, hit in the shoulder, then dropped to the ground. The other three men sprinted off in several directions, disappearing into the darkness.

"I think I hit him," Alexis said, ducking back into the car. She looked at Garrett, who was crawling toward the driver's-side door because his was crumpled shut. She flinched at the sight of his face: "You're bleeding."

Garrett hauled himself out of the car as Bingo did the same. "I'm okay," Garrett said, wiping a streak of blood from his forehead as pain radiated through his skull. He looked into the night for the shooter. "And you definitely hit him."

Alexis grabbed Garrett by the arm. "We need to get out of here. Come on." The three of them ran down the block, but it was pitch-black, the only light an occasional candle in a window, or the strobe of a flashlight in a yard. Behind them they could hear the wounded man yelling—"Bitch ran that way!"

Garrett couldn't see any street signs in the darkness, and even if he could, he had left the map in the car. He and Alexis ran as fast as they could, with Bingo bringing up the rear, panting hard. Garrett thought he could feel the crack where he had fractured his skull widening, but that wasn't possible, was it? Alexis was moving faster than him, taking the lead. She pointed to an alley—"This way!"—and sprinted down it. Garrett tried to keep up, but now his skull was throbbing. Bingo waddled behind them both, huffing, "Wait up, wait up!"

When Garrett came to a chain-link fence, Alexis reached out of the darkness and grabbed his arm, tugging him through a gate and into a backyard. She grabbed Bingo next and the three of them ducked low and made their way to the back door of a boarded-up house. Garrett's vision was beginning to blur. His brain was on fire. He heard wood cracking, and assumed it was Alexis kicking in a door, but he couldn't see anything. Someone grabbed his arm and led him a few steps, and then laid him down on an old mattress.

He could hear Alexis's voice: "Garrett? Can you hear me?"

Garrett nodded, speaking very quietly: "Head hurts. Pretty bad."

"Okay," Alexis whispered. "Just stay quiet."

They huddled silently in the vacant house. The place smelled of wet wood and rotting carpet, cut powerfully with the stench of urine. Garrett tried not to breathe through his nose. In the distance he thought he heard people running and shouting, but they passed by quickly, and then Garrett heard Alexis hissing urgently on her satellite phone, trying to explain to the person on the other end of the line where they had ended up. Garrett drifted into unconsciousness, and when he woke up the house was still dark and Alexis had his head cradled in her arms, her cool palm stroking his forehead.

Intense joy washed over him. He kept his eyes closed and pretended to be asleep, but Alexis leaned her face close to his. "I know you're awake."

Garrett smiled. His head still hurt, but slightly less than it had earlier. "Don't stop. I like it."

Alexis kept her hand on his forehead. "National Guard is sending someone to find us, but it may take a while."

Garrett smiled to himself, thinking, They can take as long as they want. He opened his eyes. "You used your weapon tonight. For the first time. How's that feel?"

"Didn't think it would be in my own country," she said, her voice tinged with sadness.

"Whoever did this knew exactly what our weak spots are. Hit a power generator in our most distressed city."

"They couldn't have predicted riots."

"I think they could. I think they did," Garrett said. "We've been in a recession for four straight years. Some places are on the brink. Doesn't take much to push desperate people over the edge. All they'd have to do is read the newspapers, watch the news. America is ripe for rioting. They knew that. It's our weakness, and they played on it."

Alexis sat quietly, her hand smoothing the skin on Garrett's forehead. "It's moving faster," she said. "Whatever they're planning. It's coming to a head . . . and we don't have much time, do we?"

"We don't," he said, feeling her fingers tense up. "Bingo has the flash drive?"

"I got it, boss," Bingo said from the darkness. "Don't worry."

Garrett wanted to say more, to continue talking, but he was, oddly, so happy lying on a rotten mattress in a deserted house, in a bombed-out neighborhood, in the arms of a woman that he both was attracted to and furious at, that he could not make himself form the words. Instead he said, "I'm sorry."

"For what?"

"Everything."

With that, he closed his eyes again and drifted off to sleep.

43

BEIJING, APRIL 10, 10:44 AM

Diplomacy with the Chinese was, to U.S. Ambassador Robert Smith Towson's mind, ceremonial theater. A carefully choreographed dramatic set piece, with a first act, an interlude, a second act, the occasional reversal or surprise, the reintroduction of an early plot point, a denouement, and then a neatly wrapped-up resolution. Each actor knew his or her role, what was expected, and how the drama would turn out.

But not this time.

Towson was a career China man. He had majored in Asian studies at Harvard, minored in Mandarin, spent five years in Beijing with the State Department before returning to civilian life to start a Chinese-U.S. consulting company based in Hong Kong. He'd really only lived in the United States for a year since he left college, so Towson understood the rituals of the diplomatic ceremonial theater, and he was confident that he knew when a Chinese diplomat was stonewalling, dissembling, or simply lying. But today, Xu Jin, China's director of the Ministry of State Security, was doing something else entirely.

The ceremonial theater had gone off the rails.

Yes, Xu Jin had stonewalled when Towson asked him if he had any knowledge of the cyber attack on the Google server farm, which meant to Towson that he knew something but was trying to distance himself from that knowledge.

Fair enough, Towson thought. Plausible deniability was the name of the game. Parry, thrust.

Yes, he had dissembled when Towson, shifting in his plush chair in the middle of the great red-velvet conference hall deep in the interior of the Zhongnanhai compound adjacent to the Forbidden City, said they had traced the virus back to Chinese hackers. Xu Jin, in turn shifting to match Towson in his chair, said China was a big country and he could not possibly control every young person with a computer. These young people, he had said, do strange things with their infernal computers.

Again, this was as expected: a tacit acknowledgment that the Chinese state security apparatus knew it was native hackers who had done the work, but whether that work was condoned by the government was another question altogether. Towson figured they had not only condoned but quite possibly encouraged it. Maybe even paid for it. Ultranationalist Chinese hackers were a strategic boon to the government, especially to the military, as they were happy to spend hours—weeks and months, even—attacking perceived enemies all around the globe through cyber warfare, and they had no ties to the government whatsoever. They were young, un- or underemployed computer programmers, and burning with patriotic fervor.

Of course Towson also knew that they made Xu Jin and his security minions exceedingly nervous. It was a short distance from harassing foreign enemies to attacking the Chinese government's own cyber surveillance machine. A short distance on the Internet, at least.

And Xu Jin had lied when he said the Chinese government felt that any attack on the national utility infrastructure of the United States posed a threat to the Chinese power infrastructure as well. It had been with great sorrow that the Chinese read about the riots and inner-city troubles in the U.S., Xu Jin said. That was nonsense, and Towson knew it. The Chinese were not above feeling gleeful at the sight of their enemies' troubles, perceived or real. And a riot in an American heartland city only fed the national mythology of a superior Chinese work ethic and future greatness.

And so they had moved on to the denouement of the theater piece: Towson expressed to Xu Jin some not-so-veiled warnings about Chinese interference in the domestic affairs of a sovereign nation, that nation being the United States of course. He even went so far as to say—and this had been signed off on by none other than President Mason Cross himself—that the U.S. might see an accumulation of such interferences by China as an act of aggression. Xu Jin had feigned great indignation—expected—and blustery resentment at these threats. China had nothing to do with these things. "We cannot help the economic shortcomings of your system."

Hints of war were not made lightly by one superpower toward another. But the president and the State Department must have thought this one through and predicted the bluster from the Chinese, because Xu Jin launched into his response almost without hesitation, as if he knew full well the warning was coming. He had expected it, and parried it like a true professional.

But it was at the very last step in the ritual when the theater piece went completely off script. And it took someone of Towson's experience in diplomacy to even recognize the way his counterpart had forgotten his lines, like an actor with stage fright. Towson had said, as he stood to leave the conference hall, that he hoped their two countries could come to a diplomatic resolution of their current differences, that all misunderstandings would be worked out in a matter of time.

Yes, Xu Jin had agreed.

And, Towson had added off-handedly, he hoped the Chinese government would never encounter problems in their country equal to the level of the ones currently plaguing America. "Your tiger is still in its cage," Towson said.

At which the Chinese minister had frozen, a forced smile plastered across his broad, beefy face. It was only a second—maybe two—of paralysis, but it spoke volumes. Then Xu Jin responded angrily. "What do you mean by that?"

Towson stared, a look of true surprise on his face. "I mean only that we wish you calm and prosperity."

Xu Jin flushed slightly, then regained his composure, saying, "Yes, of course, we both hope for that. Calm and prosperity is our goal. For both nations."

But the diplomatic dance had gone awry. Towson had seen it. And Xu Jin knew that Towson had seen it. He was quickly led from the room by stiff-backed minor officials, down the hall, into the courtyard to his waiting limousine. As he sat in the back of the limo, watching the crowded Beijing streets pass by, Towson had only one thought:

What the hell was that about?

44

WASHINGTON, D.C., APRIL 10, 10:23 AM

The National Guard did come to rescue Alexis, Bingo, and Garrett, but it took them four hours after the initial phone call. The lieutenant who found them excused himself by saying it had been a pretty busy night, what with half of Detroit burning and all. They took Garrett to the University of Michigan hospital in Ann Arbor for overnight observation, where the doctors found nothing wrong—except that he had a mending skull fracture—and released him on his own recognizance.

Through the ordeal, Bingo kept the flash drive securely in his pocket. When dawn broke, and they got back on their Navy Gulfstream, Bingo gave it to Alexis, and Garrett told her to have it sent—rush—to an address in Queens. Mitty would see to the rest.

Now, to Garrett, sitting in the back of yet another black SUV, rushing through midday Washington, D.C., traffic, the whole Detroit nightmare seemed like a lifetime ago. In reality, it had been less than twelve hours. The city had gone up in flames, along with large parts of Cleveland and central Toledo. Chicago had avoided the carnage largely because the Chicago PD had swarmed the entire city the moment the lights went out. The Rust Belt had lived up to its reputation as the vanguard of American decay, and now of American discontent. It was the lead story on every news channel, in every country across the globe.

America was on fire.

Alexis sat across from him in the back of the SUV. Bingo, Celeste, and Jimmy Lefebvre had stayed at the hotel, content to eat room service and watch

TV, knowing full well that no Garrett Reilly hissy fit was going to get them invited to the White House. He might have gotten them to Washington, but sitting down with the president was another matter entirely.

Garrett stared out the window at the government buildings, but he could feel Alexis watching him. The night before, what passed between the two of them had been intense. Emotionally, physically intense. Her staying with him, holding him, his head in her lap. It had linked them in a way that Garrett hadn't experienced before. He didn't feel like he was in love with her, or that he knew her any better, but rather that he had been vulnerable with her as he had never been with any other woman—or man, for that matter—and there was no taking that back now. A weird way to bond two people, Garrett thought, but now they were bonded, for better or worse.

The SUV pulled up to the visitors' entrance on the east side of the White House, past a bevy of Marine guards in blue dress uniforms and lurking Secret Service agents. Their IDs were checked, and then checked again, and then they were led, quickly, out of their SUV, up a stairway, and into the white-hot burning center of the universe.

45

THE WHITE HOUSE, APRIL 10, 11:02 AM

When he saw Garrett Reilly enter the Oval Office, Major General Kline's first thought was that the kid looked terrible. Pale, weak, a little disoriented. But coming into the White House will do that to you. Kline remembered his first visit to the big house, fifteen years and three administrations ago, and how he was damn sure he'd piss himself, right there, in front of President Bush and all his advisors. But on closer inspection, Reilly didn't seem nervous or anxious. He just looked beat up, his face still bruised, stitches on his chin, a gash healing above his eye. Kline, of course, had read all about the bar fight in Oceanside, the fractured skull, the THC blood levels, and the night in an abandoned house in Detroit. Any one of those things could make a young man look less than his best; but roll them all into one and you were truly stressing an individual.

Kline liked observing people under stress. It showed you their true character. And he needed to understand what Garrett Reilly was made of; Kline guessed that his job depended on it. He was the architect of this project, and his career would rise or fall on its success. Hell, he thought, the fate of the nation might rise or fall on it as well.

There was something else about Reilly. It wasn't that he was wearing a dark gray suit and a serious tie (which Kline had ordered for him yesterday so the kid could meet the president in something other than jeans and a T-shirt). Kline couldn't quite put his finger on it at first, but then he realized, as he reached out to shake the kid's hand, that Garrett Reilly looked older. Physically older, yes, and that was part of the injuries probably, but emotionally older too. The kid had grown up. And that made Kline feel better. It made Kline feel safer. Maybe this meeting would go better than the last one.

President Mason Cross's southern drawl snapped Kline out of his momentary reverie, and forced him to focus on matters at hand.

"Heard you had a scrape last night," President Cross said, pumping Garrett's hand and fixing him with a cool, familiar smile. The president, a tanned forty-five-year-old, was a salesman at heart: he'd made a fortune buying Tennessee medical clinics and turning them into a privately run network of HMOs, and he'd done it by talking all the doctors involved into entrusting their futures to him. It had been a good decision for the doctors—and for Cross. Major General Kline wasn't so sure it had been good for the patients, but you can't please everybody. Now, with multiple crises erupting on multiple fronts, Kline didn't think a salesman was what the country needed. But Cross was what the country had, so he guessed they'd have to muddle through somehow.

"Christ almighty, what a disaster." President Cross motioned for Garrett to sit on a couch, and the kid did, a little stiffly. Must still be hurting, Kline thought. He shot a look over to Captain Alexis Truffant, who was careful not to leave Garrett's side, but who nodded discreetly back at Kline. I wonder if something's going on with the two of them, Kline thought quickly, but then put it out of his mind. Truffant would not let anything like that happen. Would she?

"Eighteen people died in Detroit last night. Four in Toledo," the president said, shaking his head in bewilderment. "Taking apart their own city like that. I can't claim to understand it. Well, we're just thankful you weren't hurt too bad. How you feeling?"

"Pretty good, Mr. President," Garrett said, betraying no emotion that Kline could discern. "Head hurts a little. I'll survive."

"Well, that's good, because that's a precious head you got," the president said, smiling. "Lot of brains in there that have been helping the country, from what I've read. You've been passing on some good information to us. Very good information."

"Thank you, sir."

"Don't thank me. Thank the good Lord that made you that way, right?" President Cross said, looking Garrett in the eye.

Garrett stared back at the president, a hint of confusion in his face. The president's words hung there as Garrett said nothing. Kline had to keep himself from laughing—he couldn't stomach Cross's surface-level piety, and Garrett clearly was baffled by it. From what he knew about Reilly, he didn't think the kid had ever set foot in a church, much less prayed to God.

Cross covered the awkwardness with more talk, ever the salesman. "You know why I called you here today, Mr. Reilly?"

"To brief you on what we've found, sir?"

"No, son," the president said, shaking his head quickly. "I got people briefing me on stuff night and day, till it's coming out of my ears, thank you very much. No, Lord knows I do not need another briefing."

Alexis Truffant snuck a quick look over at Kline, who nodded almost imperceptibly. This was the moment, he thought to himself. But he'd let the salesman in the room do the talking.

"I love this country, Mr. Reilly. I love it very much. And I will do whatever it takes to keep it safe. I will lay down my life for the United States of America. And I assume that everyone in this room feels the same way." The president's sweeping look around the room was met by a wave of grave nods and muttered affirmations. Kline noticed that Reilly, however, said nothing. Maybe, Kline thought, the kid hasn't changed that much after all, is psychologically incapable of going with the program.

"And as you have made so abundantly clear to me, and many others in government, this great nation—that has stood independent for two hundred plus years—is under attack. From a powerful and duplicitous enemy. An enemy that doesn't seem to want to declare its intentions, and yet is going about harming us every day, faster and faster, in ways that just a few months ago we would have thought unimaginable. Isn't that right, Mr. Reilly?"

Garrett hesitated, then nodded. "Yes sir. It is. I think."

"Cities burning. The real estate market crumbling. Our currency under siege. The stock market attacked. They're hitting us hard. Body blows. And those blows are taking their toll. I don't think I am overstating the case when I say we are reeling. But they haven't launched a single actual missile, or fired a single rifle. No bullets coming at us. No real ones, anyway. And nobody knows anything about the orchestration of it. The American people are completely in the dark. Story on Fox News ten minutes ago said the power-plant failure was a software glitch. A glitch? Hah!"

President Cross shook his head, going quiet for a moment, then stood and started pacing the room. As he spoke, he turned his head repeatedly to Garrett. "Mr. Reilly, I would unleash the full might of the U.S. military on the Chinese—I would rain down hell on them—if I thought it was the best thing for the country. But the Chinese are just as capable in a nuclear sense as the Russians. Maybe more so."

President Cross took a breath, paced a moment longer, then waved his hands in the air. "I would be dishonest if I said that there aren't some in my administration who are pushing hard for a traditional military response to what's been happening. But I'm not certain we can risk that. I'm not saying we couldn't win, but good God almighty . . . what a thing it would be."

The president stopped, rubbed his chin, shook his head. "The long and the short of it is, Mr. Reilly, we cannot go the tried-and-tested route. We need to be clever. We need to be mysterious. We need to think one, two, maybe three or four steps ahead of our enemy. We need modern, outside-the-box leadership."

The president stopped his pacing right in front of Garrett's seat on the couch. He pointed a long, slender finger at the young man. "What we need is you."

Lines formed at the edges of Garrett's mouth. Kline thought he saw the young man pale slightly. "Excuse me?" Garrett said.

"I want you to prosecute a stealth war against the Chinese. You will have whatever resources you need. Money, men, technology. You name it, it will be at your fingertips. You will marshal all the power of that spectacular brain of yours and bring it down hard, like a hammer, on our enemies. I want you to smash the daylights out of them. And I want you to do it in ways that they do not see coming. And, just as important, I want you to do it without anybody noticing. No bullets, no missiles. We cannot let the public know that we are fighting a war with China. Absolutely not. Nobody outside of a few people we deem necessary can have any knowledge of this. The consequences of the public finding out would be vast and potentially disastrous. To our economy. To the world. You're going to attack our enemies, defeat them soundly, and nobody can ever be the wiser. It will be as if it all never happened."

There was silence in the room. All eyes turned to Garrett, whose jaw hung ever so slightly slack from his face. Kline shivered involuntarily as he waited for Garrett's response. It was sink or swim. For Kline. For the country.

"I thought I was being trained to spot attacks, not plan them," Garrett finally said, eyes blinking.

"You thought wrong," President Cross answered.

"I'm not sure . . . I'm not sure I know how to do that."

"You took out three companies of the best Marines money can buy. And you never had any of your boys fire a shot. You humiliated them. From what I've been told it was masterful." The president turned to Major General Kline. "Were those not your words, Major General?"

Kline nodded slowly but confidently. "Those were my words, Mr. President."

"We have very little time to waste, Mr. Reilly," President Cross said. "But if you need the rest of the day to think on it, take it. I'd like you to report for work tomorrow morning, oh-seven hundred."

Kline watched as Garrett gulped, and then repeated the president's words, as if to reassure himself that what he'd just heard was real. "You want me to lead an underground war against the Chinese?"

"Not lead it, son," the president said. "Win it."

46

ARLINGTON, VIRGINIA, APRIL 10, 2:10 PM

"You're mad that I didn't tell you?" Alexis asked from the driver's seat of the black SUV. "About the plan?" They were crossing the low, broad expanse of the Arlington National Bridge, the black Potomac River eddying lazily below them. Garrett turned away from the window. They were the only ones in the car; their previous driver had gone back to Bolling with General Kline.

"You knew the whole time," he said, not a question but a statement.

"I did."

"Bring me in, educate me, then put me in charge. A setup from the beginning."

"Not a setup, Garrett. A recruitment. We'd been looking for someone like you for more than a year. Someone young, brilliant, brave, and outside of the military."

"We?"

"It was General Kline's idea originally. But he and I put the program together. It took two years. A lot of hard work and not a lot of money."

"So I'm part of a program?"

"We're all part of a program. Every one of us. You used to be part of the Wall Street program, now you're part of the U.S. military program."

"Convenient logic."

"You saying it's not true?"

"I don't know. I don't know anything anymore." He looked at Alexis. "What's the program called?"

"It has a code name."

"Which is?"

"Ascendant."

"Ascendant?" Garrett said. "Like, China is ascendant?"

"Or, like, you are. Or, like, the program is. We developed Ascendant because the world is changing. Fast. Faster than a large, bureaucratic organization like the military—or the government—can keep up with. We saw threats out there, and we thought the only way this country could handle them was through a project like this. Nobody outside of the DIA believed Ascendant was viable. Until you came along."

It sounded to Garrett like there was a hint of pride in her voice. He shivered involuntarily. Suddenly the whole world seemed to have expectations of him. *Everyone was making plans for Garrett Reilly.*

"How did you get involved?"

"General Kline recruited me. Specifically for Ascendant. It was a long shot," she said, smiling over at Garrett. "But I've always had a weakness for long shots."

"Have there been other recruits? Before me?"

"None that fit as perfectly." Alexis hesitated. "Or made it this far . . ."

Garrett considered this: there had been others before him. Maybe a whole host of them. Brilliant young recruits. Or misfits. *Or suckers.* It made his head ache again. They rode in silence for a few minutes.

"Where are you taking me?" Garrett asked.

"The place I go every time I return to D.C. I thought you'd like to see it."

He stared at her, studying her face for clues, but she turned away to focus on the traffic. The SUV traveled straight from the bridge onto Arlington Memorial Drive, then onto the quiet roads of Arlington National Cemetery. The headstones of the soldiers were endless, row upon row of them: plain white, some faded to gray, etched with names, dates, and details of rank, flowers and wreaths laid on the occasional marker. Garrett stared at the immensity of the place, and the multitude of the dead. Alexis parked in the northwest corner of the burial ground, section 20. She got out of the vehicle, and Garrett followed her, slowly, warily.

She waited for him at the edge of a field full of headstones. "There are sixteen Truffants buried in Arlington. All related to me. First one died in the War of 1812. We've had a casualty in every American conflict since."

"Is that supposed to make me feel patriotic?"

"Being a citizen of a democracy requires sacrifice."

"Plenty of people don't sacrifice anything."

"That doesn't make it right."

"That doesn't make it wrong, either. Okay, so the Truffants have spilled a lot of blood. Maybe you guys should call it a day, become dentists. A hell of a lot safer."

Alexis gave a short laugh, then pointed toward a distant row of grave markers. "I didn't bring you here to see my family."

And suddenly Garrett knew exactly why she had taken him here—he couldn't believe he hadn't seen it earlier—and a sadness welled up in him that seemed infinite, a wave of despair that threatened to engulf his entire body. An empty place had opened up in the pit of his stomach and reached out to the tips of his fingers and toes. He felt hollow.

"Third row, seventeenth marker," Alexis said. "I'll wait here." She walked quickly back to the car.

Garrett just stood there for a moment, unable to move, either toward the grave site or away from it. Finally, after what seemed like an hour of indecision, he trudged, feet leaden, to the third row, and then to the seventeenth marker. All the soldiers in the neighboring plots had been killed in the last five years, either in Iraq or Afghanistan. Garrett stopped at the seventeenth marker and read the headstone:

BRANDON PABLO REILLY

LANCE CORPORAL

US MARINES

PURPLE HEART

AFGHANISTAN

MAY 14, 1982–JUNE 2, 2008

There were no flowers on Brandon's grave, no wreaths or teddy bears, no boxes of cookies or framed snapshots. It looked, to Garrett's eye, like no one had ever touched his brother's headstone. Maybe no one had ever visited it. He stood there, looking down at it for a full five minutes, not really thinking of anything in particular, not remembering Brandon, or fuming about the way he had died. His mind was oddly blank. It had never occurred to him to wonder where his brother was buried; he dimly remembered a letter from the Marines, but he'd torn it up without reading it carefully. He had been angry and bitter and oblivious of the details. And probably stoned as well.

He bent low and ran his fingers along his brother's first name, the letters sharply etched into stone. He did it in order to say that he had done it, that someone had purposely visited Brandon's grave, and not as some sentimental gesture. That done, he walked back to the SUV and climbed in. Alexis was already sitting behind the wheel.

"Was bringing me here part of the program as well?"

She shook her head no. "From here on in, the program is whatever you make it. *You are the program.*"

Garrett laughed briefly, bitterly, then looked away. Instantly, the laughter was replaced with pain. He winced as the darkness welled up in him again. He could feel tears building, sadness taking physical form, distorting the corners of his mouth and the muscles around his eyes. He tried desperately to get a hold of himself.

"I miss him," Garrett said. "I miss him so much."

Alexis reached out and touched his face, and Garrett could no longer control himself.

He began to weep.

He was humiliated, but there it was, the plain, naked truth—he was bawling his eyes out in front of an Army officer, a woman no less, and one whom he was deeply attracted to. He felt like a fool, but he also felt free, cleansed, strangely lighter. He cried hard, like he had meant to cry—had wanted to cry—for years. All those years of missing his brother; all those years of bitterness and rage; all those years of loneliness. When Brandon died he had left Garrett all alone in the world. The one person he could count on had abandoned him, and that had ripped a hole in Garrett's world too large to ever be repaired. It had rent the fabric of his life, distorting, in some way, every feeling he'd had since the day he learned of the killing.

And then suddenly the weeping turned into laughter, and Garrett was laughing through the tears streaming down his face, and he said to Alexis, "What the fuck is this all about?"

He really had no idea—it was all new to him, this emotional catharsis.

Every day seemed to bring another revelation. It was wearing him out. He continued to laugh, if only because that seemed to be the path he was now on, and he didn't have the strength to do something else.

Alexis laughed as well, and Garrett wiped his eyes on the sleeve of his suit jacket. And then, before Garrett could register how it had happened, he was kissing Alexis, holding her head in his hands and kissing her, his tongue in her mouth, and her hands groping the back of his neck. She was breathing hard, and holding him tightly, and he could taste the salt of his own tears, and he wondered if she could taste them as well. They moved their bodies closer to one another, and he could feel the warmth of her chest against his, through his suit and her uniform.

She pulled away from him abruptly, shoved the key in the ignition, and started the car. They drove hurriedly out of Arlington, without saying a word, and then south, out of the cemetery and into Alexandria. She parked in front of a riverfront brick building and led Garrett inside. In the elevator Garrett clawed at her uniform and she yanked off his tie, and by the time they made it to her condo half their clothes were pulled off. She slammed the door shut and they dove into bed.

Garrett loved the feel of her body—a mixture of soft and firm, muscled and yet distinctly female. She was in spectacular shape. They felt each other's bodies, exploring, teasing, before he plunged into her and she groaned in pleasure. They writhed rhythmically, on top of each other, arms and legs intertwined. Garrett wanted to stay inside of her forever, just live there, attached to each other at their cores. She came loudly, intensely, her eyes locked on to his, and he followed her shortly after, happily, contented and, for the first time in a long time, at peace.

By then night had fallen, and the two of them fell asleep in each other's arms. He was not lonely. He felt whole.

47

CHENGDU, CHINA, APRIL 11, 12:33 PM

She should have seen it coming.

Riding in the back of a truck half-stacked with wooden crates of garlic, her most trusted assistants and lieutenants at her side, Hu Mei could see how obvious it had been: one minute the plaza outside the apartment building had been filled with passersby and street vendors, and the next it was empty. How could she not have understood that this meant the police had sealed off the area and were about to move in? And how had they known? Who had tipped them off to the meeting?

She gazed at the faces of the other men and women swaying back and forth as the truck thudded over a potholed street. There was Chen Fei, the onetime party township director who was now her head of security. He had cuts and scratches along his face from where he had battled a police officer. But he could not have betrayed her now.

Why? Because he could have done it a month ago, with far less trouble.

There was Li Wei, a nurse from the south, who was dabbing at Chen Fei's cuts and trying to hide her tears. Could she have been the traitor? Hu Mei doubted it. Li Wei had little else in her life: no husband, no children, no parents. Without the movement, she would have nothing. That made her loyal.

Lin Chao, a political science student at Peking University, sat to Hu Mei's right. He had been shot in the raid—his arm was bandaged, and a dark red patch of blood had soaked through the white linen of his shirt. He would live, thanks to the incompetence of the police, and Li Wei's careful ministrations, and he did not seem overly worried about the wound. On the contrary, he seemed pleased. Lin Chao was a true believer. His only dream in life was to die on the barricades, a protest banner in his hands, a slogan on his lips. A wound only made him purer. There was no way Lin Chao had tipped off the authorities. He would rather die—literally.

Mei grimaced as the truck turned a corner, and a box of garlic pressed against her shoulder. A policeman, trying to arrest her, had swung a baton at her, connecting with her arm, just above her elbow. Chen Fei struck the policeman down a moment later, but the damage had been done. Her arm radiated pain. She could barely move it.

It was a miracle so many of them had escaped. Two of her inner circle had been shot dead as the first policemen stormed the building. Four were captured soon after that. Seven had escaped onto this truck with Mei. Eleven others had managed to scatter into the crowd of onlookers that had gathered. They would melt into the backstreets of Chengdu, and survive to fight another day.

But just barely.

This had been their fourth close call in as many weeks. The police were getting smarter, more determined. Stealthier. And there was the real possibility of a mole within the movement's leadership. She scanned the faces of the three other people riding in the truck: Huang Jie, her strategist; Gao Gang, a computer expert; Wan Chen, who wrote her pamphlets. All shell-shocked, all trying to hide their fear. Had one of them betrayed her?

No, Hu Mei thought as the sickening smell of diesel wafted up through the cracked floorboards, this had happened because the movement had grown so large. There were so many people, in so many places, working with her—working with the organization—that some of them had to be informers, or plants, or spies. And none of them needed to be within her inner circle—there were endless opportunities to overhear a meeting time or location, and then to tell state security. It seemed to be the nature of growth—the more people you brought in to help you, the fewer you could actually trust.

"How did this happen?" Lin Chao barked over the roar of the truck engine. He pointed an accusatory finger at Chen Fei. "You let it happen."

Chen Fei growled and shook his head. "You don't know what you're talking about. Go back to school."

"School? The students will save China," Lin Chao roared.

"Like they did at Tiananmen?" Chen Fei snarled, lips curled in a cruel smile.

"You and your party are killing the soul of the country!"

"Enough!" Mei said. Her head hurt, her arm hurt, her stomach was turning with the combined stench of garlic and diesel exhaust. "If there is blame to be assigned, I will take it. I should have seen the police coming. I should have examined the surrounding area more closely. It is *my* fault."

That silenced them. It always did. Take responsibility for failure; share credit for success. It was what came naturally to Hu Mei. It was what made her a leader of men. And women. But she knew, sitting in the back of that truck, roaring away from their most disastrous mistake yet, that she was actually failing, not leading.

She could not go on like this forever, running and hiding, striking glancing blows at the party behemoth. No, that was a losing game. They were mere flies buzzing around a horse. A nuisance. Soon enough they would find her, catch her, grind her to dust. They would execute her, alone, no witnesses, as they did all people they branded as traitors to the state—and they had branded her as that months ago.

When that happened, the movement would fall apart.

She needed to strike an overwhelming blow. But how? She didn't know. And the people in the truck, her closest advisors, could not help her. It wasn't that they weren't smart or committed. It wasn't that they wouldn't lay down their lives for Hu Mei—she suspected they all would do so if asked. No, it was that they were followers, marching behind her as she led the way, and what she needed most right now was an equal, a confidant who would walk at her side. Someone who could match her, idea for idea; someone she could open up to, plan with, dream with. In her mind's eye he was a handsome young man, daring and heroic, and maybe she could even love him, although she expected never to love again.

Together they would start a true reformation in China. Doing it herself—exhausted, wounded, bouncing in the back of a garlic truck—was proving to be too hard. Too complicated. There were too many details that, if overlooked, could lead to disaster, too many life-or-death decisions where her instincts had started to fail her.

But where would she find such a person? It seemed impossible. China was huge and crowded, but not huge and crowded enough. Trust—the real trust of a soul mate—was, to Hu Mei's mind, a rare commodity. Rarer than silver or gold. Rarer than love. And more valuable. But she felt that without it she would make another mistake. Then another.

And eventually one of those mistakes would kill her.

48

ALEXANDRIA, VIRGINIA, APRIL 11, 6:45 AM

Garrett woke to the sound of his cell phone ringing insistently on the bedside table. It was General Kline.

"A pair of MPs will knock on your door in ten minutes. They'll be escorting you to the Pentagon."

Garrett rubbed his eyes, scanning Alexis's condo. "I'm not at the base."

"I know," Kline said. "The MPs will have a service uniform for you. Ten minutes." He hung up.

Garrett looked for Alexis, but she wasn't in bed.

"Alexis?"

She didn't answer. Garrett pulled on his pants and searched the small apartment, but she wasn't there. He looked for a note, or any sign of communication, but there was none. He showered quickly and was drying off when Kline's military policemen arrived. The pair of them were young and stood ramrod straight in the doorway of the apartment. The younger of the two laid a plastic-wrapped Army uniform over the back of a La-Z-Boy.

"Sir," he said. "Your uniform, sir."

Garrett pulled the plastic off the blue Army service uniform and held the jacket up to the light. There was a seven-pointed gold-colored oak leaf pinned to the shoulder.

"I'm a major?" Garrett asked.

The MPs glanced at each other. "Sir, did we bring you the wrong uniform?"

Garrett took several minutes before he decided he would actually put the uniform on. He seemed to remember telling Alexis—it felt like months ago, but in reality was only a week and a half—that there was no way he would wear a uniform, Army, Navy, Marines, or sanitation worker. And yet here he was, standing in her bathroom, looking at this highly starched piece of blue fabric and contemplating getting into it. He decided to give it a try, and when it was on, he stared at himself in the mirror. It was beyond strange. Brandon had been the one to wear a uniform, not Garrett. He remembered how heroic his brother had looked when he walked in the door in his Marine jacket, broad smile plastered across his face; how his mother had cooed over him, and how secretly jealous Garrett had felt.

It didn't just feel wrong for Garrett to be dressed as a soldier, it felt almost illegal. And yet, he sort of liked it. It fit well, and he had to admit that it made him feel powerful. There was an aura to it.

"Gonna have to watch that," he muttered to himself. "Could be dangerous."

He spent another five minutes inspecting the buttons and insignia on the suit, then headed downstairs with the MPs. They drove him in a military police car north through Alexandria to the Pentagon. The gargantuan building rose up out of nowhere, a bland, modern-day fortress. They parked in one of the building's vast outdoor parking lots, and then ran him through a security checkpoint. Garrett took all this in wordlessly, figuring that these two MPs would be able to answer a sum total of zero of his questions.

The Pentagon building looked immeasurably large and imposing from the outside, but from the inside it seemed to Garrett to resemble an endless, sprawling series of hospital corridors, only these hallways were filled with soldiers, not doctors. None of the soldiers so much as gave Garrett a second look, even though he felt like his major's uniform screamed: "I'm an imposter! Arrest me now!" In the elevator down to the subbasement a young Hispanic lieutenant saluted Garrett. Garrett grunted wordlessly, unsure of how to respond.

Once in the basement, the MPs led him through another series of smaller, institutional hallways—painted green with flickering fluorescent lights—to a large steel door guarded by a pair of Marines with M16s slung over their shoulders. The sign over the door read: "National Military Command Center Complex." The Marines checked his ID, ran his name through a computer, and waved him in. More hallways, till finally Garrett was led into a large, high-ceilinged war room.

It looked, to Garrett, almost exactly how he had imagined a Pentagon war room would look. The room was dark and quiet. On the front wall hung large—ten-foot-by-twenty, at least—digital maps, each screen showing a different continent. The maps were dotted with ship, plane, and soldier icons, each with a unit name and number attached to it. They blinked and moved slowly, as if in conjunction with a satellite image, to which, Garrett guessed, they were linked. Facing the screens were two lines of desks, each desk topped by multiple computer screens, headsets, and keyboards. Behind the desks were amphitheater seats, with a phone and bank of controls on the armrests, arrayed so that an audience could watch the proceedings on the digital screens as well as the people who monitored those screens. Everything was new and state-of-the-art. Garrett smiled: finally, here was the military technology he had been waiting for.

A smattering of Air Force officers sat at the computers, a half dozen in all. A knot of what Garrett guessed were higher-ranking officers sat in the back seats of the amphitheater, but they were shrouded in darkness and Garrett couldn't make out their faces. Then General Kline rose from a seat in front and walked up to Garrett. He looked Garrett up and down. "The uniform fits?"

"You made me a major? Is that legal?"

"The president can make you anything he wants," Kline said. "Of course I could demote you if you'd like."

The Air Force officers at the computer terminals were all watching him now. Garrett felt the starched collar of the uniform: "Does being a major come with perks?"

"It does. This is *your* war room. It belongs to you. You've got six analysts from the Defense Intelligence Agency working for you on those terminals there. The ones on the left monitor all military location and readiness information in real time. Ours, NATO's, Russia's, China's. Everybody's. You want to know where a battalion of soldiers is, anywhere in the world, they can tell you. Those screens are live Global Hawk and Predator aerial intelligence feeds. The two people on the right side are civvies—GS-13s—and they track intelligence from the CIA and NSA: political news, State Department briefings, diplomatic cables, Consider them CNN on steroids."

The officers—two women and four men—nodded from their positions at the computer terminals. Garrett nodded back into the darkness.

"Liaisons from the Navy, Army, and Marines are sitting back there, in the stadium seating. You give them orders and they will relay them to their respective high command. We also have someone from the Treasury Department, as well as from the CIA. Anything you tell them will go right to the top. You'll get answers in five minutes, tops."

"Answers?" Garrett said, trying to make out the faces of the men and women sitting in the back of the amphitheater. "Answers to what?"

"Answers to your orders."

"My orders," Garrett laughed, still not sure what Kline was saying. "What the fuck am I going to order them to do?"

"Whatever you want," Kline said. "Within reason."

"You mean, like, I want us to invade"—Garrett glanced at the digital maps—"Canada? I can have us do that? Take all their women. And beer."

"As I said—within reason," Kline said, without moving—or smiling.

"I thought you brought me here to be unreasonable?"

"We brought you here to win."

"Win? Against the Chinese? So we're at war, officially?"

"Officially none of this exists. You're a bond trader on leave, and I'm more concerned with jihadists crawling on their bellies out of the Sudan. Officially, China and the United States are friends. Allies, even. But two days ago a computer worm shut down power plants in seven midwestern states. Detroit went up in flames, and you and I both know that was just the tip of the iceberg. This morning, a hundred thousand People's Liberation Army regulars staged amphibious assault exercises off the coast of Taiwan. It's chaos out there, Garrett. And it's getting worse by the minute."

Garrett looked around the dark, cavernous war room, eyed the maps on the wall, the pinpoints of U.S. fleet positions and the arrows of bomber squadrons. "So what next?" he asked.

"You tell me," Kline said.

Garrett thought for a moment: "I do like the president said—fight them without fighting them."

"Sounds like a plan." Kline nodded, turned on his heels, and headed off. Over his shoulder he barked: "Everyone here has my phone number. Call if you need me." He had got to the door when Garrett yelled after him.

"General, wait." Garrett jogged to the door. He spoke quietly so no one else in the room could hear him: "Where's Alexis?"

"Captain Truffant is busy."

"Busy? Meaning . . . ?"

"She's been reassigned."

"*What?* Why?"

"She did her job."

"Her job? What was her job?"

"I thought that had been made clear. Training you." Kline swept his hand toward the rest of the war room. "For this."

Garrett took in that information with growing tension in his back and shoulders, an ember of rage igniting in his core. "I want her here," he said. "I need her expertise."

"You have experts. The best in the business."

"They don't know what she knows."

"Don't be an ass. They know twice as much."

"I want her!" Garrett yelled. There was silence as his words echoed through the room.

"Well," Kline said slowly, quietly, "you can't have her. She's on leave. *With her husband.*"

Garrett cocked his head slowly to one side. He started to say something, stopped, reconsidered, then started again, only to have words fail him once more.

Kline put his face up next to Garrett's. "I know, I know. You slept with her. It was earthshaking. She's the woman of your dreams, your soul mate, and so on and so on. But maybe she reconsidered? Maybe she felt like she made a mistake with you? Maybe you're not the love of her life after all? I don't know, and I don't care. She's gone now. Unavailable until further notice."

Garrett grimaced. Kline watched him. "Are you going to go out and get drunk? Get into another bar brawl? Get the living crap kicked out of you? Let me know, because if you are, I'll send all these people home. Give them the day off and try to figure out some other way to save our country."

Garrett thought about hitting Kline square in the face. He thought, just for a brief moment, about stomping the arrogant bastard, laughing gleefully, and watching as the blood flowed from his nose and mouth. But he didn't. Instead, he clenched his teeth, clenched them hard and tight, until the bones in his jaw ached, and the desire to inflict pain drained from his body.

Major General Kline studied Garrett's face, then said, "We are staring down the barrel of a gun. War between the world's only remaining superpowers is a distinct possibility. This is the big time. What you do now matters. To our entire nation. To the world. What I need—no, what we all need—is a visionary to run things. To be in charge and to lead. Lead us all. I'm hoping you're that visionary."

The general turned and marched out of the war room. Garrett watched him go, and then said, to no one in particular, "Fuck me."

49

THE PENTAGON, APRIL 11, 9:07 AM

Garrett sat by himself in the dark of the war room, considering the task ahead of him. His problem was twofold.

First off, he hadn't the slightest idea how to prosecute an unseen war against the Chinese. He was a half-Mexican surfer from Long Beach, two weeks out of a Wall Street job at which he'd spent most of his time trying to squeeze a profit out of government bond issues. He had barely finished college, had never fired a gun in his life, hated the military, and wasn't particularly crazy about his own country. But the president—the motherfucking president of the United States—had asked Garrett personally to strike out at America's enemies without their seeing it coming, or anybody else noticing that it was happening. To Garrett, that was lunacy.

The second part of his problem was more complicated still: he was in love with Alexis Truffant.

He had never been in love before, so he had no particular frame of reference for the feelings involved, but the evidence was stacking up. He had suspected it as early as when he had tried to kiss Alexis that night in Camp Pendleton, but he had forced the idea from his mind. It resurfaced again in Detroit, as he lay with his head in her lap, while around them the Midwest burned. A national catastrophe was unfolding, and he was happier than he'd ever been in his life. That was a pretty strong clue. And then there was yesterday, at Arlington, in the car, kissing, then making love in her bedroom, holding her all night long. And even though she had left this morning without a word, and was, right at this moment—at least according to General Kline—with her husband, trying to work things out, Garrett didn't care.

He didn't care and he forgave her everything.

That pretty much sealed it for him, because Garrett rarely forgave anyone anything—ever. Sitting there in the dark, cavernous, subterranean Pentagon war room, he forgave Alexis for not telling him that she wanted him for the Ascendant project. He forgave her for not telling him that there even was a project in the first place. He forgave her for leading him on, for not wearing her wedding ring, for flirting with him on the beach at night, for digging into his past, for figuring out that a pretty woman turned him into a sputtering idiot and then using that character flaw against him.

Garrett didn't care. He loved her face, her voice, her hair—the fact that she had stood up to the secretary of defense on his behalf. And he was clinging to the belief that she loved him as well—she would come back from the time spent with her husband and choose Garrett. If she really *was* with her husband. Garrett might have been in love, but he was not so naïve as to take anything General Kline—or anyone else in Washington, D.C.—told him at face value. She could have been ordered back to California, or Timbuktu, to get out of Garrett's sight and wait out world events. Either way, Garrett felt pretty certain that she would eventually come back. To him.

If that made him a hopeless romantic, caught in the grip of a delusion, so be it. That, he decided, must be what love was all about.

Not that any of these revelations made him feel like a better person. He didn't feel more virtuous or more compassionate. He certainly didn't feel like talking to all the DIA analysts and service liaisons whispering to each other or staring at their computer screens. In love or not, he didn't give a shit about any of them. Were they really waiting for him to give them orders? To lead them into battle?

That might take a while. *A long while.*

CNN played on one of the screens that hung at the front of the war room. It had been playing all morning, cutting back and forth to reporters scattered across the Midwest—Detroit, Toledo, Cleveland, Chicago—as they tried to make sense of the blackouts and rioting. Most of it was sensationalistic pap: condemnations of the amoral looters, praise for the steadfast police, a search for who screwed the pooch at the downed power plants. Nowhere and at no time did anyone mention a virus, an Internet worm, or the Chinese. For the time being, the truth was not going to see the light of day.

But it might soon, and then the public would demand an explanation. And action. They would want a plan. Garrett's plan. And with that thought, he finally returned to his first problem: he didn't have a plan. Not even the beginnings of one.

It was one thing for him to seek out patterns in raw financial data, or to learn about the habits of the Chinese Communist leadership, but it was another thing altogether to launch one's own country into a covert war. He might have successfully led a battalion of Marines against some of their comrades in a combat simulation, but it was just that—a simulation. No one was going to get hurt. The only pain was going to be felt by that dickwad secretary of defense, Duke Frye. It was just play.

And that thought made Garrett pop out of his chair. *He had been playing.* He had not taken the military seriously. He had not taken their leaders seriously, or their soldiers. They were warriors, and he, at heart, was a gamer. Money games. Video games. He lived online. He played virtually. And that's exactly what he would do now.

"I want you to drive to the nearest GameStop and buy as many game consoles, controllers, and game discs as you can get your hands on," Garrett told a young Army captain sitting in the front row of the war room.

When the captain—Hodgkin, according to his nametag—looked confused, Garrett threw his hands in the air in astonishment: "You know, Xbox? PlayStation? You never gamed before?"

Hodgkin returned an hour later with bagfuls of hardware and discs: *Halo 4, Call of Duty: Modern Warfare, Battlefield 3, KillZone, Skyrim,* and half a dozen others, all of them first-person shooters or role-playing games, all of them capable of being hooked up to a worldwide network of other gamers: massively multiplayer online role-player games, or MMORPGs, in player lingo.

Garrett had everyone in the war room sign up for accounts, then jacked the game feeds to the screens hanging on the front wall. Seven screens. Seven different games. He took the controls on one, and ran the newbies through the first steps, so they wouldn't get their avatars decapitated each time they were respawned.

He called Mitty and told her he was getting her military clearance, and that he was looping her onto his assault team on the D-Day Invasion for *Medal of Honor*.

"Military clearance?" she asked excitedly. "That mean I can launch Predator drones?"

"Yeah, whatever," Garrett said. "Can we focus on the task at hand?"

The room watched as Mitty took out German pillboxes with ease. The Marine Corps liaison—Patmore—was particularly impressed when Mitty roasted a whole company of Nazis with her flamethrower. "My kind of woman," he said with barely contained lust. Patmore was an experienced gamer, as were a few of the other analysts; downtime at a Marine base meant a fair number of hours playing shooters. Patmore also seemed a little crazy. Garrett liked that.

Garrett told the men and women who had been placed under his command that he wanted them staring at their computer screens, killing Nazis and Orcs, until their eye sockets went fuzzy, until their bodies stiffened from disuse, until everything else in the world disappeared and all that was real to them existed only on a server somewhere in the Internet cloud. Because, and this he kept to himself, if they were going to be at the cutting edge of a new war—a secret, undetectable cyber/financial/psychological war against the Chinese—then they had better get comfortable living virtually. From here on in, the virtual was real. And the real was virtual. They were one and the same.

Next he had Celeste, Bingo, and Lefebvre brought from their hotel to the war room. The three of them—as awed and spooked as Garrett had been when he first walked into the Pentagon—spent a good twenty minutes staring silently at all the gleaming military intelligence paraphernalia.

"So what do we do?" Lefebvre asked him.

"Play games," Garrett said.

"Why?"

"Practice."

Celeste frowned. "That seems really stupid. Where's Alexis?"

Garrett shrugged. "No idea."

Celeste scanned the room. "They left you in charge, didn't they?" When Garrett didn't answer, her mouth twisted in disgust. "What a disaster," she muttered, and walked away.

The three of them picked up game controllers anyway and started to play.

Bingo kicked ass—he was a ringer. Garrett had never seen him quite so happy. Lefebvre held his own—he had played some before. But Celeste got slaughtered every time she entered a game. She did not look amused.

By early afternoon the war room felt more like a college frat house than a command center, replete with tortilla chips and empty cans of Red Bull. Garrett was no fan of fraternity houses, but anything was better than the Pentagon. Although, in truth, he felt he was taking a page from the military's book: just like new recruits were worn down by their drill sergeants at Camp Pendleton, then remade to be order-following killing machines, Garrett was breaking these men and women of their former ties to the physical world, and would rebuild them to live in the global data stream. This was boot camp for the next war.

The games also served a personal purpose for Garrett, which was to help him stop thinking about Alexis. It was hard, but not impossible—and getting ever so slightly easier as the hours wore on. The pain was becoming something bearable.

Next, Garrett asked for money. A million dollars. That seemed like a puny amount of cash, given what he would trade on Wall Street, and chump change compared to what the military spent every minute of every day on tanks and missiles. He went to the liaison from Treasury—a young woman named O'Brien who had her hair pulled back in a bun, wore a dark blue pantsuit, and spent most of her time talking quietly on her cell phone—and blurted out: "I need a million dollars." He did it mostly to see what he could get away with, but O'Brien didn't blink an eye, just called her superiors, and in twenty minutes Garrett had an online bank account with the money waiting for him. A million dollars, just like that.

This, Garrett thought, is something a guy could get used to.

He split the money equally between everyone in the room—there were eleven of them, so they each got $90,909—and had them open online trading accounts. The CIA rep—her name was Finley, and she seemed to anticipate exactly what Garrett wanted—supplied them with fictional names and bogus Social Security numbers for the accounts. Garrett told them to start playing in futures options, fixed-income securities, and commodities, on the fringes of the markets, and he gave them a quick tutorial on how to do it. He said he wanted them making money by the end of the next business day, and he didn't want them to stop gaming, either. Or to stop watching the cable news feeds on the

TVs at the front of the room. Monitor your games, your market positions, and world events. And don't drop the ball on any of them.

That sent the officers and liaisons into a controlled panic. A few of them managed to eke out profits by the end of the day, most broke even, but one analyst lost his entire float in twenty minutes. He did not get refunded.

General Kline walked into the war room at four that afternoon, stared at the video games on the projection screens, saw the tortilla chips scattered on the floor, and left without saying a word. Garrett thought he saw a look of horror cross the general's face, which he found gratifying.

Garrett ordered half the team to spend the night in the war room: three he allowed to sleep on cots he had placed in back, three he kept gaming and trading. The other half of the team he sent home for four hours of sleep, telling them he expected them back at dawn. He told them not to call anyone, or talk to anyone. This was going to be a deprivation chamber.

He went home at midnight as well—driven back to Bolling Air Force Base by a pair of MPs—and slept restlessly for a few hours, dreaming briefly of Alexis, and then of his mother. He woke at four in the morning, watched CNN, Fox News, and CNBC, looking for hints that something was afoot between America and China, but the news was all about riots and shootings and politicians skewering each other. If war had broken out, America didn't know it.

It was invisible.

He had his drivers pick him up at four-thirty and bring him back to the war room. Most of the shift that had gone home was back already, gaming and trading. Garrett sent the overnighters home for a few hours' rest, giving them the same orders: talk to no one, see no one, fuck no one. Live here. Not out there.

There was an e-mail waiting for him from Mitty. The power-plant worm had definitely come from China. The code contained traces of embedded Chinese Python programming language, as well as some bits of Mandarin BASIC. She'd copied as many blocks of the code as she could, just before it deleted itself, but none of it was particularly revealing; it was simply malicious—and very clever. But at least Garrett knew for sure now—the power-plant hack had been another Chinese rocket launched in the quickly escalating conflict.

When Celeste Chen arrived from the hotel at 6:00 a.m., he had her buy a domain name—Chinawar—and start a blog. He ran the blog through offshore proxy servers, so no one could trace it back to the Pentagon. He told

Celeste what to write. The blog was more of a rant, really, about how much the blogger hated the Chinese and their culture and their food and how ugly their women were—anything Garrett could think of to piss people off. They made up a pseudonym—USA Patriot Boy—then placed a long list of meta-tags in his headers—*sex, Chinese whores, God bless the USA, kill shot,* and *President Xi Jinping.* Garrett did a keyword density analysis for search engine optimization, and then linked the blog to as many articles about China as he and Celeste could find. At the end of the first set of entries he asked his readers how they would go about attacking China.

By midday he was getting 2,000 hits an hour, as well as lengthy, racist screeds about why America should invade the People's Republic. By 7:00 p.m. those numbers had doubled. And so had the clicks coming from behind China's government censorship wall. Those page views were skyrocketing. Someone over there was paying attention.

General Kline called three times on day two, each call growing increasingly tense in tone: What are you doing? Why are they playing games? Are you following what the Chinese military is doing? Did you know their air force flew sorties over the Strait of Malacca? The American Pacific Fleet is now on high alert. *Do you have a plan, Garrett?*

Each time Garrett said, "I'm kind of busy. Can I call you back?" On the third call he hung up on Kline, mid-sentence.

The afternoon of day two he relieved Celeste Chen of her gaming duties. She was proving to be comically bad at it, and not getting any better, and Garrett thought she could be better used elsewhere. He told her to take her laptop and go back to researching Chinese desperation. What were they so afraid of? Search, search, search, he told her, and don't come back until you find something. Celeste seemed quite happy to be released from the war room. She left without saying goodbye.

Garrett slept in the war room that night, uneasily, waking over and over again on his lumpy cot, feeling detached from his body, as if split in two. Part of him was lying in the Pentagon, staring off into space, while the other part was making love to Alexis, holding her face in his hands, kissing her, whispering to her. If love was a drug, as some half-witted pop song claimed, then it was an insidiously dangerous one, and he vowed never to try it again—which was weird, because Garrett enjoyed most drugs.

But on the morning of day three he found that his heart didn't ache quite as much as it had yesterday, and that was a surprise to him. How had that happened? Was it the old trope that time heals all wounds? He still wanted Alexis back, still wanted to see her face, kiss her lips, but he could live with that longing now. It wasn't all-consuming. It occurred to him, as he splashed water on his face in a sterile Pentagon bathroom, that perhaps this was what it felt like to grow up.

By midday of day three, some of the Ascendant war room staff had begun to make money in the futures market. More important, they had begun to sense the ebb and flow of data that drove prices. Bingo and Lefebvre were even getting a step ahead of that data, and betting on which way things would go, which was exactly what Garrett wanted.

"Buying and selling stocks," Lefebvre muttered with practiced irony. "Daddy would be so proud."

They had also gotten proficient at their online games. Commies and Cubans and brain-eating zombies were falling like flies. Every officer, male and female, old and young—and most of them were young—had risen tenfold in their game levels, accumulating points and fresh lives, and pocketing spells, armor, and ammunition. Garrett had a few of the best of them hook up with gamers in China, forming teams with their Asian counterparts and chatting as they played. Garrett fed them questions: Is the government watching you? Can you speak freely? How strong is their censorship software? The answers were vague or the questions were ignored entirely, but that was okay with Garrett. They were probing, digging, circling.

Meanwhile, from her apartment in Queens, Mitty Rodriguez had begun to torture the war room. She had played so many games for so long, and knew so many people on the inside of the gaming industry, that she had accumulated a massive cache of cheat codes. Cheat codes—or cheats, as gamers called them—were bits of code written into games that, once discovered, allowed hard-core gamers special advantages over the rest of the playing multitudes. Cheats gave you special powers, like the ability to jump to new locations, or new weapons that could kill faster or more broadly. And the hardest to come by allowed you to do things in games that nobody—absolutely nobody else—was allowed to do. One of those things was to kill your own team members without being penalized.

Normally only the enemy was available for slaughter. There were games that allowed for players to be hit by "friendly fire," in order to boost realism, but those were rare. If gamers could shoot anyone—even team members—without consequences, then chaos would rule. So the game manufacturers set up fail-safes to stop them: points were deducted; an on-off switch was used. But Mitty had found a same-team kill cheat for every one of the games that she—and the members of Garrett's war room—played, overriding any existing game rules. And she used it to horrifying effect.

The first Garrett heard about it was when Patmore, the square-jawed Marine liaison, came to him practically in tears. "Every time I'm about to kill a whole shitload of alien bugs, she blasts me to smithereens. And then she screams at me through the headset and calls me a faggot. There's nothing I can do about it. It's not fucking fair," Patmore said, waving his controller in the air, then adding, "Not fucking fair—*sir*."

"Well, that's life," Garrett said, amused but uninterested.

An hour later, two more of his analyst/gamers made the same complaint. Mitty had capped them in the head, in three different games, without warning and for no particular reason, essentially invalidating the hours they'd just logged trying to get their characters as far in the game as they had. It was soul crushing.

"She keeps going berserk," they said. "She's a maniac."

"I'll talk to her," Garrett told them. He popped a wireless headset on and dropped into a firefight on the coast of Cuba in a game of *Special Ops*.

"Mitty, it's Garrett," he said.

"*Cómo estás, pinche* homeboy?" Her voice crackled over the sound of gunfire.

"Stop whacking your own team members. You're ruining their morale."

"Well," she said, sounding reasonable, "tell them to suck my dick."

"That's not helping."

"Then *you* can suck my dick."

"I'm a major now, you know. The president made me one."

"Sure. And I'm a rear admiral."

Garrett grimaced and thought about how to restart the conversation. "Why are you doing this, Mitty? What is the point of you going berserk?"

"I go berserk, they die. They die, I collect more points. The more points I collect, the more they fear me. The more they fear me, the more I win. Which is why I own your pathetic ass, Sergeant Reilly."

Garrett sighed wearily. But then he considered what she had just said. Going berserk had a certain strategic quality that following the rules did not. Looked at objectively, psycho behavior made a lot of sense: you gathered points, you had fun, and nobody but nobody could predict what you'd do next. That made you feared. Wasn't striking fear into the hearts of your enemies a battle strategy as old as war itself?

"You have a point," he said into his headset. "But you're still an asshat." He shut down his console before Mitty could protest.

For the next hour, Garrett contemplated the concept of chaos in modern warfare. Unpredictability was a potent weapon when launched against an opponent that craved order. And didn't we all crave order? Wasn't entropy the enemy all humans feared? Alexis had said so. Chaos was equated with death, order with life.

Wasn't that particularly true in Chinese culture? Practically every book he'd read at Camp Pendleton had pointed that out. Maybe the Chinese government's desperation was linked to a fear of chaos. *Maybe they were one and the same.* If that were the case, he could use this information to his advantage.

So, three days, seven hours, and one million dollars into the Ascendant project, Garrett found the thing he had been searching for . . .

. . . the beginnings of a plan.

50

THE WHITE HOUSE, APRIL 13, 9:44 AM

"What is that little prick doing?" The outrage was directed broadly at the room, but Secretary of Defense Duke Frye was looking right at Major General Hadley Kline as he said it. Kline tried not to grimace, or lash out, but it wasn't easy—he knew Frye was baiting him, and he also knew he must not take the bait. *Not yet.* The rest of the meeting would be a power play between himself and the secretary, and Kline needed to pick his battles.

Frye turned quickly to the president of the United States, his voice softening. "Please excuse my language, Mr. President. But you have to understand—he's got them playing video games. Fourteen, sixteen hours a day. While we are on the verge of going to war with China. Talk about fiddling while Rome burns."

President Cross was seated opposite Frye, at the end of a long conference table in the White House Situation Room, in the basement of the West Wing. He was flanked by Joint Chiefs chairman Wilkerson, Wilkerson's aides, and representatives from the Treasury Department, the FBI, the CIA, and Homeland Security. Kline sat farther down the table, next to the national security advisor, Jane Rhys, an older woman with striking white hair and a pair of reading glasses perched on her nose.

"We brought him in to think outside the box," General Kline said, tempering his anger. "And that's exactly what he's—"

"Playing video games is not thinking outside the box." Frye cut him off. "It's not even thinking." Frye wheeled in his chair toward Julia Hernandez, the young Treasury rep. "How much money did he requisition from Treasury?"

"A million dollars, sir," Hernandez said.

"And how much does he have left?"

"Even though we have a liaison in the war room, we're not supposed to monitor his brokerage accounts," she said. "Technically, that's illegal."

"Seven hundred eighty thousand," said an older man from the CIA. His name was Tommy Duprés, and Kline had known him for decades. He was smart, political, and Kline liked him. "We *are* monitoring his accounts. Because we supplied him with the fake account names. It falls under national security parameters."

"A quarter million dollars," Frye said. "Taxpayer money. Funneled into personal accounts, and thrown away."

"I don't think they were his bets," Duprés said. "Some of the accounts were out of money within minutes. Reilly is far more sophisticated than that. He had his team do the trades. I think he's running them through a training exercise. But with real money. Live ammo, if you will." There was a hint of admiration in the CIA man's voice—as if Garrett Reilly's intelligence and cunning had left an impression on him. Kline noted that. It might be useful later.

Secretary Frye forged ahead. "And did you see this?" he asked, sliding an open laptop to the middle of the table. Its browser was open to Garrett's anti-China blog. "It's a website all about how the U.S. is at war with China. Am I crazy, or did you, Mr. President, not tell him directly that he was not to mention that? That this was a stealth operation? That nobody in the nation could know about it? And what does he do?"—Frye shook his head ruefully—"He announces the whole damn thing on the Internet."

Kline started to interject: "The blog isn't traceable back to the Pentagon, or to—"

"He's making fools of us." Frye cut in, slapping the laptop closed. "Just like he did when we brought him to D.C. in the first place. He has an ax to grind with the military because of his brother, and now that we've given him power he's grinding that ax. Hard." The secretary turned to President Cross, who had sat silently through the entire meeting, sipping his water and occasionally patting down his tie.

"Mr. President," Frye said, leaning over the edge of the mahogany conference table. The anger was suddenly gone from his voice; he spoke in a measured, even tone, a model of calm. "Garrett Reilly has given us no reports, no intelligence, no requests for troop movements. He's done absolutely nothing. Now, do I care particularly about some experimental operation run out of the basement of the Pentagon? In general, no. Could care less. But we cannot wait around for a twenty-six-year-old hacker to fight our battles for us. We no longer have that luxury, if we ever did. It is obvious to every military mind in this room that the Chinese are bent on full-scale war." He pointed to a bank of TV monitors mounted on the wall behind the commander in chief. One of the monitors showed the coast off eastern China—the South China Sea; the other showed the Sea of Japan. Both were blinking with Chinese naval and air force activity.

"They steamed five Luzhou class destroyers out of Qingdao this morning, and a Jin class nuclear-powered sub is breaking dock right now. They are heading south to the Strait of Malacca. They secure the Strait, they will be in control of all trade to Japan, Australia, and pretty much anywhere else in the Pacific. One quarter of all the world's oil goes through those straits. If we don't get out in front of this, Southeast Asia and all our allies there run the very real risk of being swamped. Overrun by the Chinese."

"We don't know that those are offensive actions," Kline said, allowing a hint of annoyance to seep into his voice. "They could be naval exercises designed to showcase their sea power."

"If they were exercises they would have warned us about them," Frye said. "Unless your people at the DIA missed something. Like they missed the Treasuries sell-off."

Kline winced. He took a long, quieting breath. He was not skilled at the political fight—it was not his passion—but Frye had Ascendant in his sights and was moving in for the kill. The secretary was set on crushing any project that drained money and power away from his office and from traditional military programs. *But now was still not the time.*

Frye turned again to the president. "Sir, I believe we are fast approaching a make-or-break moment. They have repeatedly attacked us, our economy, our infrastructure, and now they are preparing for a major military conflict. Southeast Asia could be just the beginning. What we might well be facing is total global war."

President Cross frowned and took another sip of his water. Kline watched the president as he considered the secretary's opinion. To Kline, Cross had never been a visionary—he was more of a caretaker president, pleased to have the job, and anxious not to screw it up. That pushed him toward conservative choices—which was just fine with Kline. He could use the president's hesitancy. At least he hoped he could.

"But why, Duke?" the president asked. "Why do they want to go to war with us?"

Frye drew himself up in his chair. "Sir, I don't know that it matters. They're doing it, and we need to get moving. Their motives are, at this point, secondary. This nation must be defended by strength. We let that job fall to the weak and the undisciplined and we are doomed. I may be talking out of line, but with all due respect, sir, I have to pose the question: Do we want to be the administration that lost it all to the Chinese?"

Kline blinked in surprise. He hadn't thought the secretary would lay out the issue in such stark—and personal—terms. But he had, playing his realpolitik trump card and at the same time appealing directly to the president's character flaws: his vanity and his desire for an unsullied legacy. He had to give it to Frye—he was a master of the game. Rumor was he had his eyes on the presidency. The secretary's ambition was generally acknowledged to be boundless.

Kline thought he saw the president flinch slightly in agitation. Cross waved a hand in the air. "What are you suggesting we do, Duke?"

"Scrap the Ascendant program. If we have to, jail Reilly for fraud—"

Kline barked involuntarily. "Fraud? Give me a break!"

"He took a million dollars and funneled it into personal accounts. Those are actionable grounds right there," Frye said. "Then we launch a real piece of military strategy. Steam the Pacific Fleet, battle ready, off the coast of Shanghai. Send the Fifth Fleet out of the Middle East to the Strait. Airlift troops to the eastern border of Kyrgyzstan, and double our forces in South Korea. We can do that in a matter of days. Confront the Chinese with what America does best—overwhelming force. That will put the fear of God in the party leadership and stop them dead in their tracks."

The room fell silent. President Cross took another sip of water, carefully wiping the drip of condensation from the glass. After a few moments, he turned to Kline. "General Kline, I know you dreamed up this program, but, frankly speaking—it seems to have turned into a fool's errand."

Kline nodded. This was it. *The moment.* Ascendant would live or die on what he said.

"Sir, Ascendant is a roll of the dice. We knew that going in. Yes, Reilly's lost some money. But I don't believe it was fraud, and it's minor in the grand scheme of things. If he's making anyone look like a fool, it's me, and so far I'm willing to absorb the humiliation. I still believe in the project. And I believe in Reilly's talents. But mostly, sir, I question the alternatives. Can we push the Chinese to the brink? Yes. But we haven't the faintest idea how that would play out. It could escalate out of control in a matter of minutes. Seconds even. History has shown us that wars, once started, take on a life of their own. How many people would die? And who would end up, in the long run, the victor?" He paused and scanned the faces of the other men and women in the Situation Room. "I don't have that answer, and I would posit that anyone in this room who claims to know is fooling himself.

"Sir," Kline continued, his voice low and steady, "I understand the risk. It's my head on the chopping block as much as anyone's. But I'm asking you to consider giving Ascendant more time. Not for my sake. Or yours. For the country's sake."

President Cross rubbed his temples slowly with his fingers. The fan on a computer whirred quietly in the corner. All eyes in the room turned to him.

"Duke," he said, turning to the secretary of defense, "I'd like a comprehensive written plan of attack from you. Overwhelming force, but take into account casualties. The American people can only accept so many wars in so many years. I don't want to lose Southeast Asia—but I don't want Armageddon, either. I'll expect it on my desk in twenty-four hours."

"You'll have it, sir," Frye said with an air of muted triumph.

The president turned to Kline. "Reilly's got two more days. If he gives us nothing, then I'm shutting down the program."

Kline exhaled. Two days. It wasn't a victory, but it wasn't a defeat, either. *Yet.* The president stood, signaling that the meeting was over. Everyone in the office stood with him. Cross started for the door, then stopped, turning one last time to look at General Kline.

"And Hadley, see if you can talk a little sense into the kid. At least get him to tell us what he's up to. I know he's a pain in the ass, but, good Lord—video games?"

51

THE PENTAGON, APRIL 13, 11:32 AM

There were two feeds from NSA computers that went directly into the Ascendant war room. One tracked data provenance, the other tracked phone-call patterns. Data provenance—the process of sorting massive amounts of cloud computing intel—was the future of intelligence gathering. But phone-call monitoring was the present. Garrett made sure to check them both once an hour.

Just before noon on the third day of the Ascendant project's official/unofficial existence, Garrett noticed a spike in phone calls to the help desks of five regional banks in the southeast U.S.: First Atlanta, Southern Trust, Montgomery Credit Union, Jackson People's Bank, and Alabama Federal were all receiving massive customer complaints. Unexplained credit-card charges had suddenly started showing up on client statements. Worse, numerous checking accounts in each bank had been drained. When clients looked at their accounts online, they were empty. Zeroed out.

Nine-one-one calls from fifteen counties in Georgia, Mississippi, and Alabama went through the roof. Seven people had heart attacks. Three died.

Garrett had Bingo and Jimmy Lefebvre investigate. It took them twenty minutes to find the connection. "The banks all outsourced programming of their websites to the same company in Vietnam," Lefebvre said. "Eastern Star Data Programming, out of Saigon. But they're not answering their phones."

Garrett hunted through his collection of dark net and hacker bulletin boards, and quickly found hundreds of usernames and passwords that had just come up for sale. They'd all originated out of Eastern Star. And they were all from the same five banks in the American South.

"Someone took a shitload of account info and gave it to hackers all over the world," Garrett told Bingo and Lefebvre as they stood at his shoulder, peering down at the list of asking prices for the stolen account info. "And then they let the hackers do the real damage."

"Smart," Lefebvre said. "High level of deniability."

"Find out details on Eastern Star. Just because they were hacked doesn't mean the Chinese did it."

Lefebvre and Bingo hurried to their computers. Garrett smiled: they were coalescing into a well-oiled machine. He called Kline to tell him what they'd found, but the news had already begun to go viral. Online chatter was exploding. Twitter feeds were buzzing.

"What can we do?" Kline asked.

"Well, the money's all gone already," Garrett said. "So, basically, nothing."

"That's not good enough," Kline yelled. "Do you understand the pressure we're under? I just met with the president. About you! *Do you fully understand the stakes?*"

"I guess I understand them now."

Kline barked something that Garrett thought sounded like a curse—but he couldn't be sure—and then hung up on him. Hanging up on each other seemed to have become their preferred method of signing off.

Bingo came back with more information half an hour later: the outsourced Vietnamese programming company was a wholly owned subsidiary of a Shanghai-based IT conglomerate with ties to highly placed Communist Party leaders, and had been staffed entirely with Cantonese-speaking ethnic Chinese immigrants known in Vietnam as Hoa people. That in itself meant nothing to Garrett—he wasn't going to let himself get suspicious of every Chinese citizen or company as a knee-jerk response—but Saigon police had just detained a dozen of the company's employees trying to board a 737 back to Shanghai.

"Well," Garrett said, "that's probably all we need to know."

When news of the drained accounts finally hit the *Wall Street Journal* website an hour later, lines of spooked customers began to form outside the banks' three hundred branches across the southern United States. They all wanted their money. In cash. *Now.* On the New York Stock Exchange, each bank's Class A shares lost a third to half their value in a single afternoon. Just like that. Boom.

Bingo, Lefebvre, and the rest of the Ascendant staffers watched the CNN coverage on the center digital screen. The war room was silent except for the echoing voice of a young, blond reporter doing a stand-up in front of a suburban Atlanta bank.

"There is widespread panic here, Vanessa," the reporter said. "Everyone is very scared about their money."

"Score another one for the boys and girls in Beijing," Garrett said to no one in particular. "They see an opportunity and they jump on it. And they do not fuck around."

52

THE PENTAGON, APRIL 13, 4:32 PM

"They made you a general?" Avery Bernstein said, eyeing Garrett's Army uniform scornfully as they walked across the paved pathways of the Pentagon's open central courtyard. A café building stood in the center of the enclosed area; the high, five-sided inner walls of the structure surrounded them, making the courtyard feel more like a prison than a park.

"It's a major's uniform," Garrett said. "The president promoted me himself."

"The president? Really?" Avery shook his head in wonder. "Not sure whether to congratulate you or give you my condolences. I thought you hated the military."

Garrett sighed. His former boss had called at noon, saying he was going to be in D.C. for the day and did Garrett have a few minutes to talk. Garrett had said of course, happy to hear the sound of Avery's voice, but the moment he hung up he realized that almost no part of the phone call made any sense.

"You were in D.C. on a business trip? And you knew I was in Washington? How?"

"They told me you were. A few days ago." Avery hesitated. "No, that's a lie. They called me this morning, asked me to come talk to you."

"They?"

Avery swept an arm into the air, gesturing, in one sweep, to the officers and civilians walking through the courtyard with coffee and sandwiches in their hands, but also to the mammoth walls of the Pentagon itself. "Whoever it is you work for. The military. The government. A general named Kline. Said I should tell you to fly right. Get with the program, whatever the hell that program is, and do what you're supposed to do. Of course he wanted me to be more subtle about it. Play to your patriotism. I said you had no patriotism."

"Maybe I've changed."

"Judging from your clothes, I would say you absolutely have changed." He looked at Garrett, studying his face. "Not sure it's for the better, either. Are you on board with everything that uniform represents?"

Garrett turned away from Avery, hiding the hurt on his face. "When I told you I wanted to short Treasuries because the Chinese were dumping them, you said I had no moral center. Now I'm working for our country and you still give me grief. I can't win."

They walked in silence. A dozen pigeons cooed and pecked at breadcrumbs under a wooden bench.

"You're right. I'm sorry," Avery said, sounding genuinely remorseful. "I don't always know why I say the things I do."

Garrett nodded. "Whatever."

"Look, this Kline guy didn't sound happy, Garrett. Frankly, he sounded a little desperate. What is going on?"

"Stuff," Garrett said. "Weird stuff."

"Has to do with China?"

"It might."

"The bank run in the South this afternoon?"

Garrett said nothing. Avery stared long and hard at his former protégé.

"Don't look at me like that, Avery. I can't say. Really I can't."

Avery leaned close and whispered, "Are they watching us?"

"Is who watching us? These guys?" Garrett said, nodding to an Army captain who walked past. "Maybe. Who gives a shit?"

Avery abruptly grabbed Garrett by the elbow and turned the two of them around. "Walk with me," he said, quickly moving the two of them toward the Courtyard Café at the center of the park.

"What are you doing, Avery?"

Avery pushed open a door to the café and ushered Garrett inside. "Give me two minutes." The café was mostly empty; a busboy cleared plates from a counter and a waitress emptied a coffee urn. Half a dozen Pentagon staffers read or worked on laptops at tables across the room. Avery put his hand on the small of Garrett's back and guided him toward the rear of the café. "There," Avery said. "Men's room." He shoved open the men's room door with his foot, and led Garrett inside. The bathroom gleamed white and smelled of disinfectant.

Garrett frowned. "Are we gonna have gay sex? 'Cause, weirdly, I'm not in the mood."

Avery leaned close and whispered, "Somebody's been asking for you."

Garrett blinked, surprised. "What do you mean?"

Avery spoke in hushed, clipped clusters of words. "A man. Came to me. He knew about you. About the Treasury bonds. How you'd sniffed them out. He said you'd been taken to Camp Pendleton and that the government had drafted you to work for them."

"Who was he?" Garrett asked quietly. They were inches apart.

"Called himself Hans Metternich," Avery said. "Doubt it was his real name. He was European, I think. Middle-aged. Handsome. Didn't seem like a spy. But then again, he didn't seem *not* like a spy, either. He asked me to pass you a message."

"Christ, Avery, maybe he was a terrorist. What if he wants to kill me? Did you think of that before you went talking to some asshole named Hans?"

"Then ignore him. But the car bomb at our offices? That almost killed you? He said it wasn't terrorists."

"Who'd he say it was?"

"He wouldn't tell me. Said he could only tell you."

"Fuck that," Garrett said. "I don't give a shit who he is. Or what he has to say."

"Fine," Avery said, "I'm just a messenger. If you change your mind, he said you should make yourself known to him and he'll contact you."

"How am I supposed to do that?"

There was a loud bang, and the bathroom door burst open. A pair of military policemen—young, grim-faced and large—rushed quickly into the room. "Major Reilly," the first one said in a booming voice. "You are needed back at the command center."

Garrett turned, stunned. Had they followed him into the bathroom? "What are you doing in here?"

"I can escort you there right away, sir," the military policeman said.

"Fuck you!" Garrett stepped forward to get in the MP's face, but Avery grabbed him by the hand, as if to shake it. Garrett could immediately feel a scrap of paper in his palm, and he knew that Avery had just passed him a note.

"Great to see you again," Avery said, pulling Garrett close. "Really great."

The moment the words were out of his mouth the second policeman—buzz-cut and thick-necked—grabbed Avery securely under his arm, long fingers pressing almost to the older man's bone, and pulled him away from Garrett. "Mr. Bernstein, your flight is boarding in thirty minutes," he said.

"Ouch, that hurts," Avery said.

"A driver will take you to the airport," the MP said.

Garrett balled up a fist, ready to drive it into the MP's face, but the first MP stepped between them. "Sir," he said simply and directly, clearly ready to put Garrett on the ground if he tried anything. "I'm ready to escort you back now."

"I'm fine, Garrett," Avery said, as they tugged him toward the door. "I need to get back to New York anyway."

"Avery, I want to—" Garrett said, the scrap of paper clutched tightly in his fist.

"Keep up the good work," Avery cut in. With that, he was led from the bathroom. Garrett let out a short, disbelieving laugh and stared at the remaining MP.

"Hey, asshole," he said, "why the fuck are you watching *me*?"

The MP smiled grimly and said nothing.

53

THE PENTAGON, APRIL 13, 5:00 PM

warbyothermeans@gmail.com.

Garrett peeked at the e-mail address scribbled on the scrap of paper that Avery Bernstein had pressed into his hand, then shoved the paper into his pocket and continued to pace the back of Ascendant's hushed war room. *War by other means?* At first Garrett thought it might be a reference to Malcolm X. He seemed to remember some kind of black militant quote about "any means," but when he looked it up on the Web he realized the actual quote was "By any means necessary," so Malcolm X was out of the picture.

When Garrett plugged the phrase into Google (which had recovered fully in its response time, one week out), the top result was from the early-nineteenth-century German military theorist Carl von Clausewitz: "War is the continuation of politics by other means." Was that a joke? Was someone trying to seem clever? Because that e-mail address wasn't clever, it was idiotic, clearly the work of a tech amateur. To Garrett, clever was 2,048-bit encryption. Quoting some dead German douche bag was just lame.

And Hans Metternich? Who was named *Hans*? Garrett's rational side was telling him to ignore the whole thing. But Avery was the most conservative, risk-averse person Garrett knew. For him to chance getting his neck wrung passing on a message—didn't that mean Garrett should take it seriously, or at least not totally ignore it?

Besides, truth be told, the last month of Garrett's life *had* played out like a paranoid movie script, rife with bombs and secret programs. And now he'd learned that military policemen had him under surveillance. For fuck's sake—it's not like he'd asked to work in the Pentagon. *They* wanted *him* here.

He scanned the war room. A few staffers were playing games; two were trading FOREX futures online; a few more were monitoring incoming CIA and NSA intelligence feeds. Did he trust any of them? Probably Bingo, he thought. Bingo had no particular allegiance to the military. He could count on Celeste as well, if only because she seemed to hold the armed services in as much contempt as Garrett did. And Lefebvre? Garrett was less positive about him. The two of them had settled into an edgy détente, but Garrett thought that Lefebvre's future lay inside the military machine, not outside of it.

Trust those three or not, there were a host of unresolved questions that were nagging at him, and he wasn't ready to bring them up with anyone else. Who *had* been responsible for the car bomb? If Garrett had been the target, why hadn't they tried to kill him in a more direct way, like shooting him with a gun? Why hadn't anyone claimed responsibility? And where were the suspects? Now, looking back, he realized he should have pressed for the answers to those questions sooner, but there had always been more urgent issues—like the possibility of the next global war.

And yet, even *that* had begun to trouble Garrett. He was pretty sure that all of these disparate attacks were the work of one country—and that that country was China—but the evidence was still circumstantial. Yes, there had been blackouts, riots, bank runs, and a dilution of the U.S. currency, as well as cyber attacks and manipulation in the real estate and stock markets, but all of those things had happened numerous times in the past, and no foreign power had been responsible—it was just life in the modern world, the cycles of capitalism and the citizenry's response to hard times. Garrett had no proof of centralized coordination. And while the Chinese government's desperation was a good guess as to motivation, it was still a guess. He longed for something more concrete.

Everything about this was layers of an onion: secrets and then deeper secrets. The patterns Garrett treasured weren't falling into place—and that gave him pause. What if there were puppet masters out there? Perhaps he'd been seduced so completely by Alexis, and by the Pentagon and the president—making him a major, giving him a uniform, putting officers under his command—that he had forgotten to think for himself.

With that in mind, he asked his drivers to take him back to Bolling early that evening—at 11:00 p.m.—and got a few hours' sleep. He woke up at four, predawn, threw on sweats, ate a protein bar, stuffed his laptop into a backpack, and jogged out of his Bolling AFB apartment complex an hour before his MP escorts were due to take him back to the Pentagon. They'd stopped locking his door from the outside after that first day with Alexis, but after the incident with Avery in the men's room, he was working on the assumption that someone, somewhere, would be watching him. Taking an early-morning jog seemed relatively innocuous. They wouldn't arrest him for that.

He ran hard along a dirt jogging path on the edge of the base. After ten minutes of running he found a thicket of trees that ringed the northern perimeter of Bolling, and which also hid a cyclone fence that bordered the base. He slipped off the path and into the trees. Beyond the fence—just outside of the base—Garrett could see a strip mall and a row of two-story, stucco apartments. Garrett booted up his laptop and started searching for Wi-Fi sources that weren't password protected. It took him five minutes and a walk of about a hundred yards before he found one with a sufficiently strong signal. The rest was simple.

First he signed up for a new e-mail account. He used his real name on the account, figuring this Hans guy would need to know it was he who had sent it. Next he wrote an e-mail—"I am in DC, ready to talk"—and then encrypted it with PGP encryption software. PGP—otherwise known as "pretty good privacy" software—was about as close as you could get to unbreakable coding software, especially at the 2,048-bit level. Sure, with a supercomputer big enough and weeks of time you could break the code, but Garrett figured whoever was watching him really didn't have a lot of time. Even the National Security Agency had raised a fuss about PGP encryption, arguing that it could be used as a tool for terrorists to send e-mail messages without American agencies being able to spy on them. But PGP was still out there—in fact, it was only getting stronger, with new open-source versions showing up on the Web every week.

But sending an encrypted e-mail was pointless if the receiver of the e-mail didn't have the key to decrypt it. An encryption key was like a guide to figuring out a scrambled message—without the guide, the message was meaningless. But with the key in hand, a software program could easily decipher even the densest code. However, if Garrett sent the key via e-mail, then he was back to square one—anyone who intercepted that e-mail would use the key to read his previous, encrypted e-mail. Garrett figured this was where he would have to get creative.

He downloaded a chapter of Clausewitz's book *On War* from the Web—the chapter was titled "Boldness," which Garrett thought was cute—and then copied the first 715 characters of that chapter into his computer. He chose the number 715 randomly. Next, he made an encryption key—again using his PGP software—so that whoever possessed that key could decode his earlier e-mail. For this, he took the first 715 letters from the Clausewitz "Boldness" chapter and made them the key. He decided that was too straightforward, so he repeated the last steps, only this time he found the Clausewitz text in its original German, downloaded the first 715 letters from that version, encoded them, and sent them off to the "warbyothermeans" e-mail address. Anyone who told you their name was Hans Metternich, Garrett figured, better have the language skills to back it up.

Next he signed up for an online PayPal account. PayPal was famous for their security encryption. Of course that security was used almost exclusively to protect shoppers from having their credit-card numbers stolen while making purchases online, but that didn't mean that a clever coder couldn't use it for their own purposes. Garrett then sent a seven-dollar-and-fifteen-cent payment to warbyothermeans@gmail.com, and added a message with the payment.

The message said: "Be Boldness."

Garrett figured that if Hans Metternich had half a brain he would be able to figure out to use the book chapter as a key to the encryption, and the first 715 characters as the length of that key. And if Hans didn't have half a brain, then Garrett wanted nothing to do with him.

54

MIAMI BEACH, FLORIDA, APRIL 14, 9:22 AM

Hans Metternich preferred women to men—that is, in the realm of the physical—by a slight margin. But in his line of work, where one often needed to get close to a person, and do it quickly, sex was a useful tool, and given that a percentage of his subjects were gay men, Metternich would do whatever it took.

Not that Metternich—and Hans Metternich was simply the name he had been using lately, not his real name by any stretch of the imagination—minded terribly. The truth was, Metternich was ambivalent about sex. It didn't particularly excite him, with men or with women, and never really had. To him it was a biological imperative, hardwired into the human brain to allow us all to procreate, and nothing more than that. The corporeal human form was too full of flab and smells and jagged imperfections to stir his imagination. He understood that he was unusual in this, that it set him apart from most of the rest of his species, but he accepted his own frigidity, and had learned to exploit it to accomplish more in his career. That he had figured out that other humans—of both sexes—found him attractive had been paying dividends for him for quite some time now.

Humanity's endless need to have sex was one of Metternich's greatest weapons.

Which is why he found himself enfolded between the legs of a large, buff, hairless aerospace engineer in a hotel room in Miami Beach. Metternich knew the engineer carried a set of design schematics somewhere among numerous hi-tech gadgets he traveled with, and for the past twenty-four hours Metternich had been trying to tease out the whereabouts of those schematics in any way he could. That it took half a bottle of vodka and fellatio in an expensive hotel room was all part of the job. Now Metternich knew that the schematics were in a password-protected file in a flash drive tucked into the man's socks, and he knew how he was going to get them. He was, in fact, about to finish the process of acquiring said schematics when the incoming e-mail chime sounded on his smartphone. That specific chime—from the haunting French horn solo at the start of Brahms's piano concerto in B-flat major—told him that the message was linked to a certain address, an address that only two people in the world had. One of those people Metternich wanted to speak to in the worst way.

"Nice ringtone," the engineer said, splayed out on the bed, his wilted form draped across the sheets. "Classical music, right?"

Metternich forced a half smile to his lips, nodded in the affirmative, then hurried to his phone. He would deal with the engineer in just a moment. First the e-mail. He checked the inbox on his phone. Yes. The e-mail was from the party he had hoped it would be from. But it was unreadable—encrypted.

Not that he hadn't expected this.

He had encryption software on his computer, probably five different programs he kept loaded for just such occasions. He pulled his laptop from a leather briefcase and booted it up as the engineer watched lazily from the bed.

"That PGP software?" the engineer said, squinting without his reading glasses. "You decrypting something?"

"Maybe."

"Cool. Can I help? I'm pretty good with that stuff."

"Perhaps later," Metternich said, shifting his body slightly to block the engineer's view of his computer screen. He checked the inbox on his laptop. Another e-mail had arrived, this one from PayPal. He had been sent money. Again, the sender was the person he most ardently wanted to speak to. But to collect the money—and any messages contained in the missive—he had to sign up for a PayPal account. Metternich didn't like leaving unnecessary footprints on the Web, but he would make an exception in this case. He had started to go through the steps of setting up a PayPal account when the engineer, still splayed naked on the bed, began to paw at his leg.

"Come back to bed. You can play with your computer later."

Metternich tried to ignore him. He opened the PayPal account and collected the money. Seven dollars and fifteen cents. His mind raced. Why that amount? There was a note attached to the payment. It read: "Be Boldness."

Metternich narrowed his eyes, concentrating. *Be Boldness? Seven-fifteen?* They were clues, obviously, but to what? To the encryption key, perhaps? But the message didn't say "Be Bold." It said "Be Boldness." Boldness? Wasn't that the title of a chapter in . . . ?

The engineer snaked his hand across Metternich's lap and into his crotch. That broke his focus. He snapped the hand away, annoyed.

"Ouch. That hurt." The engineer frowned. "I get it. You want rough?" He grabbed Metternich's arm, but that was his first—and last—mistake. Metternich caught him by the wrist, and in one fluid, powerful motion, spun the engineer's arm up and around, twisting his shoulder hard. The engineer cried out in pain and surprise, but because he was lying on the bed, without anything to secure himself to, he had no choice but to spin his body to keep his arm from snapping. The next thing the engineer knew he was lying facedown on the bed, his right arm twisted tight behind his back. Metternich jammed his free elbow into the engineer's back, hard and fast, directly between his ribs.

The engineer grunted, exhaling hard. Metternich knew—from years of experience—that losing a lungful of air would significantly shorten a person's fight time, so he quickly, almost effortlessly, slid his body on top of the engineer's, locking his own legs around the other man's legs and his right arm securely around the man's neck. He pressed hard on the engineer's larynx, cutting off his air flow, using his body to keep the engineer from moving, and simply held on as tightly as he could.

After a few minutes of muted, desperate thrashing, the engineer stopped moving. Metternich held him tight for another five minutes, just to make sure. It sometimes took a surprisingly long time to choke a man to death, and Metternich was nothing if not thorough.

Lying there, muscles rigid, killing another man, Metternich zeroed in on the answer—*the sender was using Clausewitz.* Yes! Very clever, using his own reference to *On War* to hide clues. Metternich liked the sender already. He liked him very much.

Metternich unwrapped his arm from the lifeless engineer's throat and settled in to the business of code busting. This was what he lived for.

Mysteries.

Now those were sexy.

55

ALEXANDRIA, VIRGINIA, APRIL 14, 11:02 AM

Celeste Chen hated online games. She hated shooting and sneaking around post-apocalyptic war zones. She also had no interest in money markets or options to buy stocks. It made no sense to her, no matter how hard she tried to focus on it. In fact, she hated everything about the war room: it was dark, gloomy, and filled with too many macho military men wearing cheap cologne and speaking in weird, abbreviated Army jargon: "POS this." "Where's the NSTCF?" "Why don't we have EMCON-4?" It was all nonsense.

So when Garrett had told her that she didn't have to play games or trade futures anymore, that she should instead keep looking for signs of the Chinese government's desperation, Celeste happily picked up her laptop and fled to a Starbucks in the Alexandria Commons strip mall. It was quiet, uncrowded, and, most important, it wasn't within earshot of Garrett Reilly.

He might be brilliant, but he could be a real prick as well.

Case in point: when she had come to him, exasperated, after two days at the Starbucks, and said she had looked everywhere, and that there was no sign of a rebellion or disturbance in China, Garrett had said, "Don't be a pussy. Look harder."

She had stormed silently out of the war room.

She spent the next day reading the online versions of the big-city daily newspapers—the *Shanghai Daily*, the *Xinmin Evening News, Dazhong Rìbào* out of Shandong, *Xiaoxiang Morning News* from Hunan—and then the party organ papers like the *China Youth Daily*, the *China Public Security Daily*, and the Ministry of Justice's *Legal Daily*. But she had already been combing through these papers for weeks now, with little to show for it.

The main problem was that she didn't know exactly what she was looking *for*. Had it been the mention of a specific person or an incident, she could have scanned whole pages quickly, and dispensed with enormous sections of the papers that were extraneous. But Garrett had been vague: he wanted evidence of something that *might* be worrying the central government, and that could be almost anything. The leaders of the Chinese Communist Party were a skittish group of old men who saw phantom enemies at almost every turn. When the Arab world erupted in protest in the spring of 2011—and was called by some the Jasmine Revolution—the party banned the selling of jasmine anywhere in the country. Jasmine farmers were wiped out, all on the potential linkage of a flower with rebellion. The party leadership was spooked by its own shadow.

On day three she went back to the war room and told Garrett that she was no good at finding patterns. "It's not what I do."

"Well, learn," he said. "It's your job."

Celeste was used to Garrett being a jackass, but it occurred to her that he had gotten noticeably more obnoxious since Alexis had disappeared. Celeste guessed that they must have had a thing; now Alexis had flown the coop and Garrett was hurting. That surprised Celeste—not the realization that they had shacked up, which seemed perfectly reasonable, but that Garrett cared if a woman left him or not. To Celeste, Garrett seemed incapable of adult emotion. She would have figured he saw Alexis Truffant as just another conquest.

Huh, she thought, you learn something new about people every day.

So she continued hunting, angry, but persistent. She read through each article that could be of interest, from beginning to end: an old woman's lawsuit over property rights in Tianjin; an artist's arrest for painting a mural deemed threatening to the state; a truck driver's sit-in on the highway that linked Beijing to the western coal mines. Even innocuous stories held the promise of a tidbit of information: a school assembly about teacher firings in a rural district outside of Wuhan hinted at parent discontent, but revealed little else; a ceremony where a medal of gratitude was given to a citizen of Xi'an after he plucked a woman from an icy river talked about the food line that the woman had been standing in, but nothing else in that day's paper mentioned it; a murder trial was shut down in a northern Yingkou courthouse after one of the witnesses had an outburst about the corrupt local provincial committee chair, but the trial—and the witness—were never mentioned again. They were promising threads, but they led nowhere.

Celeste also scoured social media sites. Unfortunately for her, Facebook, YouTube, Tumblr, and Twitter were all banned by the Chinese government; they sat behind the infamous Golden Shield—the Great Wall of Censorship—a vast array of computers filtering and blocking every byte of digital information that entered the country. The native social networking sites—Sina Weibo, RenRen, YouKu—were heavily censored, although Chinese users had become adept at slipping euphemisms past the government monitors. "Great Actor" meant the prime minister—he'd been called that in a dissident's novel. "Sixty-Four" was code for June 4, the date of the Tiananmen Square massacre. But the party censors caught on quickly, and even the code words were scrubbed, usually within hours of first appearing online.

More informative—and lively—were blogs, loaded on anonymous servers, or sometimes through machines in Hong Kong or Macau, and photo essays. The photos masqueraded as tourist albums posted for the pride of China, but if you studied them carefully you could parse out bits and pieces of useful information on local goings-on: a smattering of antigovernment graffiti, a soldier standing guard over a town that wouldn't seem to need guarding, a billboard partially defaced by a street artist before it was discovered and torn down by the authorities. But these, too, were hard to find, and required days, if not months or years, of searching. You had to be lucky, rather than good, to get hard intel from these scattered sources.

But then, on the morning of her fourth long day in the Alexandria Commons strip mall Starbucks, Celeste Chen got lucky.

She got very, very lucky.

56

THE PENTAGON, APRIL 14, 2:22 PM

Celeste found Garrett ensconced at his desk in the war room, deep into an online shooter game. She didn't recognize the game, and didn't care.

"Garrett," she said, sitting next to him. "I found something."

Maybe it was the tone of her voice—or maybe he was finally bored of so many hours of video games—but Garrett put his controller down immediately and swiveled his chair to face Celeste. "I'm all yours."

"You know how I've been looking through newspapers, social networks, but haven't found anything?"

"I'm aware."

"Well, I started searching blogs. About China. That were written by people who had been in China but had left. I figured they had the freedom to write about their experiences and post them without Chinese government interference."

"Smart," Garrett said.

"I found a travel blog written by a Chinese-American. Adopted. In her twenties. She went back to China to try to make contact with her birth parents."

"Is this unusual?"

"No. Adopted Americans pour back into China on a daily basis. But here's the thing—she had narrowed down her search to a coal-mining province in central China. Real poor area. Targeted an orphanage in Huaxi Township. Small place. Rural. Finally, she gets there, only the authorities won't let her in. She has to wait in a neighboring town. She speaks Mandarin, says everybody's on edge, but she can't figure out why. Finally, a week passes, soldiers let her into Huaxi Township, only the place is silent. No one will talk to her, a bunch of the homes are empty. Everyone in the township is scared. She doesn't know why. The orphanage is shut down, she's disappointed, goes back to the States and writes about it. She doesn't give it a whole lot of thought because it's got nothing to do with finding her parents, quits writing, goes back to her job as an administrative assistant in Cincinnati."

"Okay," Garrett said, looking carefully at Celeste. "I'll be honest. That doesn't sound like much."

"I did a search for Huaxi Township after that. Baidu search, websites, newspapers, official bulletins. There was nothing."

"Well, maybe nothing happened in—how do you pronounce it?"

"*Huwa-shee.* But almost every township, no matter how small, gets some kind of mention in some kind of official document, somewhere in China. Or mentioned on Sina Weibo. It's their social media. At least once in six months. Huaxi Township is mentioned every week or so before November 16th of last year. After that, nothing."

"Okay. Interesting. But maybe it's been slow there for a while."

"Maybe. But then I thought maybe we've been looking for the wrong thing all this time. We've been looking for an incident. A protest, a trial, a piece of political theater. Something we can grasp and say, This is the cause. But that's not how modern China works. So I started looking for the *absence of anything.* Negative space. A void."

Celeste watched Garrett's reaction. She knew him well enough by now to guess that he would pick up on her line of reasoning very quickly. Sure enough, he tilted his head ever so slightly, his eyes boring into hers. "As if there had been an incident, but someone erased it?"

Celeste nodded, hands waving excitedly now: "So then I did searches on the citizens of the township. I could only find half the residents listed in the population census. Okay, maybe they don't keep good records. Weird, but possible. They tend to keep very good records in China."

"I'm liking this," Garrett said.

"It gets better. I searched for surrounding townships, villages. In the week or so after November 16th they were all mentioned regularly online. Then, one by one, like lights going out, they disappear from view." She plugged an ethernet cable into her laptop and a map of north-central China flashed on Garrett's right-hand computer monitor. It was centered on rural Huaxi Township. Huaxi was in red. Then it went black. As Celeste clicked on a timeline, a narrow swath of rural geography turned black alongside it, bit by bit.

"Watch the black grow. Late November. Early December. Christmas. January. Late January." A widening gyre of black began to emerge in the center of the map. "All these districts and villages have disappeared from social media and the news. It's the opposite of news. Negative news. A void."

Garrett stared at her. "That," he muttered, "is a pattern. That's a fucking pattern."

"Yes," Celeste said, knowing she had just received the highest order of compliment from her newly promoted boss. "It is."

Garrett turned to her: "So what happened? I mean, what was the incident?"

"The news and background on the area has been picked pretty clean. Here's what we do know: before November 16th of last year, the biggest employer in town was a plastics-petrochemical plant. Built four years earlier. They specialize in chlorine solvent derivatives, including highly toxic pesticides, but they have a wide range of products. Shipping mostly to the Middle East and Africa. Owned by a consortium of bigwigs in Shanghai, almost all of them with strong party connections."

"Maybe there was an explosion or a gas leak, killed a bunch of people, they swept it under the rug?"

"Could be. But industrial accidents happen regularly in China, and the government might hush it up, but they aren't obsessive about it. And they eventually punish the guilty, even if they are well-connected. We'd hear about it. But whatever this is, they've clamped down on it like a vise. So I went back further, to before the plant was built. There was land appropriation involved. Land rights are an evolving issue in China. It's still, technically, a Communist state. The government owns everything. But when industrialists want land for a factory, they usually get it. As far as I can tell, that's what happened in Huaxi. There was a smattering of protests, but it went nowhere."

"So we're back to zero?" Garrett said, his voice deflating.

"No. Almost zero. But not quite." Celeste tapped onto her laptop and a new picture flashed on Garrett's screen. It was of a young woman, Asian, pretty, standing in an open-air market in a small town. She was trying to smile, surrounded by vendors hawking crates of eggplant and garlic, but her heart clearly wasn't in it, the edges of her mouth turned slightly upward in forced gaiety.

"That's the author of the travel blog. Her name is Annie Sinclair Johnston. Her traveling companion, a girlfriend, took this photo a day after they left Huaxi Township on their way to Beijing. She posted them on Facebook, and tagged Annie. That's how I found it. The name of the town is Dengxu. It's about fifty kilometers from Huaxi. And the date of the photo would put it about twenty-four hours ahead of the government news vacuum. Notice anything?"

Garrett stared at the picture. There was nothing unusual about it: just a tourist posing in a slightly exotic local marketplace. But then he saw it. "The guy. The vegetable seller. In the background."

Celeste nodded and then zoomed in on a young man standing behind and to the right of the girl in the photograph. He had turned his face from the camera, obscuring it, but in his hand he held a piece of paper with Chinese characters written on it. It looked like a price tag for the eggplant in the basket at his feet.

Garrett stared, transfixed. "He's turning away from the camera. He doesn't want his face photographed."

"But he did want the sign taken," Celeste said. "He photo-bombed them."

"What's it say? My Chinese is rusty," Garrett said.

"*Yu Hu*. It means: I'm with the *tiger*."

"The Tiger?"

"*Hu* is a Chinese surname. But with a slight change in intonation, it can also mean *tiger*."

Garrett was silent as he absorbed, and then quickly processed, this information. "You're saying it's the equivalent of flashing a gang sign? That he's telling us he backs this person Hu. That he's a supporter?"

"That's exactly what I'm saying."

Garrett shook his head skeptically. "That seems like a stretch. A major stretch."

"Clearly you've been too busy playing *Modern Killbot* to read every word of our daily briefing packets." Celeste pulled a file triumphantly from her bag and laid it on the table. "This is a cable from the U.S. ambassador to China. Sent two days ago. A brief on his meeting with the minister of state security. Most of it is the usual diplomatic drivel, but then on page three there's this."

She folded back pages and read from the file's final sheet: "At the end of the meeting Ambassador Towson told the minister . . ." Celeste looked up at Garrett with a smile. "And I quote—'*Your tiger is still in its cage.*' At this, the minister reacted with alarm and demanded to know what the ambassador meant by his statement. The ambassador apologized and said he had meant nothing. However, Ambassador Towson found the exchange odd, strained, and potentially of value. The term *tiger* seemed to have unusual, even extreme significance to the minister."

Garrett stared at her in amazement.

Celeste nodded and put the file back in her bag. "Hu—the Tiger—is a person, Garrett. He scares the shit out of the minister of state security. He's important, secret, and he attracts followers. Remember, this picture was taken just hours ahead of the government news vacuum."

"And what kind of secret, important person attracts followers?" Garrett asked, but he already knew the answer.

"An insurgent," Celeste said. "And why would the authorities clamp down on every bit of news from an area that was growing in size by the week?"

"If that insurgent was leading a true grassroots movement," Garrett said. "The news vacuum is covering up a revolution . . ."

Celeste rushed to finish his sentence: "*. . . and the Tiger is its leader.*"

57

THE PENTAGON, APRIL 14, 5:02 PM

Garrett and Celeste spent the afternoon analyzing her Chinese rebellion theory, poking holes in the facts, such as they were, but also playing out what it could mean for them—Americans trying to get a grip on China's recent actions—if it were true. The implications were enormous—a burgeoning revolution in the heartland of China unraveled the mystery they had been grappling with for weeks. With that one piece of information, all the other details fell into place: the Chinese government was terrified of the Tiger's rebellion, and a war with the U.S. was a potent, if risky, way to deflect attention from it.

It was as simple as that, and, in both their estimations, possibly the most important piece of news coming out of China in the last fifty years. It was beyond huge.

It was history-altering.

But there was also the distinct possibility that it was wrong, that there was another, more mundane explanation for everything Celeste had found—a random photo, an industrial accident, the coincidence of a common surname, a diplomat's misstatement. Happenstance. But Garrett didn't think so. He'd spent his life—literally since he could remember—picking out the patterns in the spiraling mass of humanity's chaotic information flow, and now, with this bit of news fitted carefully into the mosaic of world events—all the cyber attacks, the bluffs and boasts, the threats to the dollar and U.S. markets—all of a sudden the chaos made sense. The facts fit a pattern.

It gave Garrett hope, but he needed more: to take action, he—and, by extension, his military minders—would need proof, not just pictures and graphs and theories.

"You need to find this Tiger guy," Garrett said as he stared at the photo from the Chinese market one last time. "You need to make contact, and tell him he has friends outside of China. Friends who will support him in any way possible."

"It's a needle in a haystack," Celeste said. "If he even exists, the odds of finding him are astronomically small."

"From here, maybe. But from inside the country, I don't think so. You need to go to China."

Celeste let out a laugh. "What?"

"If you go to those provinces that have been blacked out, there's still gotta be people living there," Garrett said. "They will know what happened. And they're going to talk. They'll talk to you."

"That's insane. I'm a grad student, not a spy."

"Exactly. And that's what everyone will see you as. A student knocking around China."

Celeste shook her head vigorously. "You have no idea what you're asking for, Garrett. You have a building full of professionals to send to China—"

"A whole building full"—Garrett cut her off—"and none of them found what you did. Not a one. I don't trust them. Any of them. They're company men. They have no imagination. They don't think like we do. *Like you do.* And, anyway—I don't know whose side they're on, but I'm pretty sure it's not mine."

Celeste grimaced with indecision. They asked the State Department liaison—a young, serious woman named Tea—if Celeste could get a rush tourist visa to China without raising eyebrows, and she said yes, and that a seat on a plane would be easy to find as well.

Celeste said she had to think about it. Garrett watched her pace in the hallway outside of the war room, calling friends on her cell phone, then pacing some more. After twenty minutes she came back inside.

"You're not leaving forever," Garrett said. "This is a reconnaissance trip."

"The party won't see it that way. They do not like foreigners getting involved in domestic politics. I could get arrested. I could go to jail for a long, long time."

"Or you could change the world."

Celeste scowled at him. "Give me a fucking break, Garrett. You're the last person I'd expect that kind of bullshit from."

Garrett shook his head. "Not bullshit. It's true."

Celeste fell silent. She rubbed her hands together, squeezing at her fingers hard. They had been talking in strained whispers. Around them Garrett could hear the constant click of fingers on keyboards. Finally, Celeste nodded her head. "I'll need to call my mom. And pack."

"You won't regret this."

"I'll leave this afternoon. And I already regret it."

She collected her laptop and her bag and hustled out of the war room. As she left, Garrett had the realization that he was sending his first soldier into combat, so he ran after her and caught her by the elevator. He didn't know quite what to say, and she looked distracted and slightly confused.

"Is there something else?" she asked. "You want me to bring you back a T-shirt?"

Garrett gave her a brief hug. "Just be safe. And good luck."

Celeste gave him a baffled look, said, "Okay," and then disappeared into the elevator.

Garrett hurried back into the war room and brought Bingo and Jimmy Lefebvre to a quiet corner in the rear. He told them what Celeste had found.

"That's brilliant," Lefebvre said, eyes dancing with the news. This was the kind of thing he, as a War College researcher, lived for: political and cultural foment was happening right in front of their eyes, on one of the biggest stages in the world, and only he and a few other people in the entire country knew about it. Garrett could tell he was ready to spin out theories on the Tiger for days.

"We need to tell Kline. And the State Department," he said. "And also—"

"No," Garrett cut in. "That's exactly who we don't need to tell." If he had learned one thing since telling Avery Bernstein that the Chinese were selling off U.S. Treasuries, it was that information was a valuable commodity, and he had no intention of disseminating it to the rest of the military before he was good and ready.

"If we don't tell them, we could be in deep shit."

"And if we do, then we lose all leverage. If you're worried about getting into trouble, fine, walk away now. I'll swear I never told you anything. But don't expect any more information out of me. Ever."

Lefebvre hesitated, then agreed, reluctantly, to keep quiet. But even in his reluctance, Garrett could sense a change in the lieutenant: up until now, there had still been a formality with Lefebvre, and a reserve between him and Garrett.

But with this news, a final wall had been breached: Lefebvre was all in. He even gave Garrett a spontaneous squeeze of the arm.

"This is big," Lefebvre said. "Really big. You did good."

"Not me," Garrett said. "Celeste."

"Okay," Lefebvre said, beaming. "*We* did good."

Bingo shuffled his feet and grimaced, as if he hadn't quite made up his mind how to feel. Then he nodded in agreement. "It's pretty cool," he said. "Way cool."

Garrett didn't tell anyone else in the war room. He was beginning to like a few of the Ascendant staffers better—Patmore, the Marine liaison the most—but he still didn't trust them. He decided it would be best if they just kept their minds on video games and online trading.

It wasn't until late that night, when he stepped through the front door of his apartment in Bolling and saw his laptop on the kitchen table, that he remembered his furtive e-mails from that morning. He grabbed his laptop and jogged back out to the bushes at the edge of the Air Force Base. And there it was. An encrypted response to his account. Garrett decoded it quickly.

The subject line said, simply: "Orange Line tomorrow." And in the body of the e-mail it read: "Ride it, Hans."

Garrett immediately deleted the e-mail, then canceled the entire account. He knew that accounts and deleted e-mails often stayed on servers for months after having been erased, but it was a chance he would have to take. From what Garrett could tell of the inner workings of the military, if they caught on to what he was doing in the next twenty-four hours it would be a miracle. They were two steps behind in everything, all the time. They were like the post office, but with guns.

He considered the various options for losing his minders that night as he went to bed, and had come up with a plan by the time he was out the door at six the next morning, jogging down to the waiting military police car. It had been the same MPs driving him to and from the Pentagon every day for the past week now, so they had grown accustomed to his routine, which was what Garrett decided he would use against them. Two of the last three days he had asked them to stop at a Starbucks in northern Alexandria so he could buy a tall, nonfat latte. One of the MPs stayed in the SUV, the other stood guard at the front of the Starbucks. They never went inside with him, and they never accepted his offer to buy them each a grande drip.

Garrett had chatted up a pretty, dark-haired barista on his last visit, and had watched her carry a bag of trash out the back door. This morning, he paid for his latte and made for the bathrooms, but hung a hard right before he got there, sprinting out the back door and into an alleyway. He dumped the latte into a trash can and ran hard, a block and a half, to the elevated Braddock Road Metrorail station, where he pulled off his military jacket and shirt, tossed them into the bushes, and paid his fare. Now he was wearing a white T-shirt and blue Army dress pants, an odd look, but at least he wasn't in full uniform. He bolted upstairs to catch the train. It arrived two minutes later, and he boarded a Blue Line train into the city, checking out the window to see if the MPs had followed him. They hadn't. But they would soon, he knew that much for sure.

He changed trains four stops later, getting on a Yellow Line train into the heart of D.C., then changed again at L'Enfant Plaza for an Orange Line train. L'Enfant Plaza was packed with commuters at seven in the morning, so he had no problem blending in, but he kept his head down anyway, in case the police were looking for him already. Though he doubted they were. It had been half an hour since he had bolted from the MPs. Half an hour was barely enough time to call General Kline at the Pentagon, much less set up a search effort.

He rode the Orange Line out to the eastern edge of the city, to the last stop, New Carrollton, then walked across the platform and boarded the next train headed west. He moved from car to car, changing at stations so as not to attract attention. At the Metro Center station he found a discarded Georgetown University sweatshirt and put it on, but it smelled like vomit, so he tossed it a few stations later. He thought he saw the conductor staring at him for a few stops, maybe even studying his face, but he wasn't positive about this, so he tried to put it out of his mind.

He wasn't sure how long he could ride the same Metro line back and forth before he became too bored or too hungry, but he didn't have to wait for the answer to that question, because at the West Falls Church station, just outside of Arlington, a young blond woman sat down opposite Garrett and smiled at him. She was pretty, with platinum hair and carefully applied red lipstick. Garrett had smiled back at her, taking in her long legs, when a man took the empty seat next to him and said in a slight German accent, "It will be best for you if you don't look over at me and see my face. That way, if they ask you later, you can say, honestly, that you don't know what I look like. So maybe keep staring at her, yes?"

Garrett silently cursed himself for being taken in so crudely by a pretty face. He swore to himself that if he survived this train ride he would work hard on this character flaw, because it was beginning to get him into deep shit. He nodded his head and kept his eyes on the blonde, who was watching him carefully now, all the flirt drained from her face.

"Okay," Garrett said, bracing himself for a bullet to the head. "Fine. I like looking at her. She's cute."

"I am Hans Metternich."

"And I'm Zoltar the Magnificent," Garrett said.

Metternich chuckled. "You have a sense of humor, Mr. Reilly. I like that. Even your encryption clues were amusing."

"Are you going to shoot me?" Garrett asked, silently counting the number of people in the Metro car. Seventeen, excluding himself, Metternich, and the girl. Enough witnesses to maybe dissuade a killer from an open assassination. "Because there are a lot of people watching."

"I have no interest in killing you, Mr. Reilly. Quite the contrary," Metternich said.

"Okay, great. That's a relief. Then can we cut to the chase? Who tried to blow me up in front of my office?"

"Your own government."

Garrett turned his head in surprise, but Metternich quickly raised his arm to shield his face. "Don't. It would be a mistake to identify me. For your own safety."

"Bullshit," Garrett said. "Why would they do that?"

"To heighten a pervasive sense of fear. To feed the military-security industry that lives off taxpayer money. And to get you to come over to their side. Terrorism is a numbers game. If there's not enough terror, then there's not enough money made available to combat it. If you reduce it down to its essence, terror is money."

Garrett said nothing, but thought about this statement, while Metternich continued: "Think about it. A big, bombastic attempt on your life that puts you in little real jeopardy. And no one is actually killed. A showpiece."

"You have no idea if that's true," Garrett said.

"I have sources inside the government who have vouched for this information's veracity. Highly placed within the Defense Intelligence Agency. I believe you are working with them. No?"

"Who the fuck are you?"

"A very interested third party."

"Interested in what?" Garrett said as the train rolled to a stop at Dunn Loring-Merrifield station. "Why are you telling me all this?"

"Because I want you to know that you are being fed lies. So that you know that what you are involved in is not what it seems."

"Why do you give a shit about lies or what I do?"

"Because you are being used as an instrument of change. And you have no idea what that change actually is. But the reality of it is so enormous that it will shape the future of the world for the next hundred years. And your own government wants you to drive it."

A chill ran down Garrett's spine. A handful of commuters trudged off the train. The doors remained open.

"I don't know what you're talking about," Garrett said.

"Because you are willfully ignoring the truth," Metternich said. "Because you like the attention and the praise and the excitement. But there will come a moment when the truth will be too obvious to ignore. When you will have to make a choice. And I want to help you make the right one."

"You are completely full of shit."

A bell rang, alerting riders that the doors would close in ten seconds.

"Perhaps, Mr. Reilly," Metternich said, quietly, precisely. "Or perhaps what I'm saying is truer than you want to admit. According to some people, we are on the verge of war between two global powers. Ask yourself: Who profits most from such a war? Once you answer that question, I would urge you to decide if you want to be a part of it. If you want to lead it. Because a war between the United States and China would just be the beginning. The real war would come next, and that one would be waged against all of us."

The doors started to close, and in a flash Metternich and his blond helper were leaping through them. They slipped out of the train just as the doors slammed shut, and all Garrett could see was the backs of their heads as they hurried for the stairs out of the station. Garrett let out a long breath and realized he'd been holding his shoulders tight practically the entire conversation with Metternich. He tried to replay the conversation in his head, but in less than two minutes the train was pulling into Vienna station. The conductor announced the final stop, a bell rang, the doors opened, and into the car rushed a dozen burly men in gray suits, guns drawn, mouths open, screaming at Garrett to freeze or die.

Garrett tried to put up his hands in surrender, but they threw him off his seat and slammed him to the floor before he could raise them above his shoulders.

58

IN TRANSIT—FAIRFAX COUNTY, VIRGINIA, APRIL 15, 10:41 AM

They kept Garrett's head covered in a black canvas hood for the entire car ride, which took, as far as Garrett could tell, about thirty minutes. His hands were handcuffed behind his back. No one read him his rights or told him where he was going, no matter how many times he asked.

No one said anything.

The car stopped and two men hustled him out of the backseat, up some steps, and inside. Whether it was into a house or an office, Garrett couldn't tell. He could tell that wherever they were, it was quiet, definitely not the heart of the city. They walked him down a hallway, into a room, then shoved him onto a chair. Someone slapped another pair of handcuffs onto his right ankle, chaining him to the leg of the chair. Then they left the room. Or at least Garrett thought they did: a door had slammed, and no one replied to his questions.

"Hello? Anyone there? Anyone want to talk to me? I'm feeling kind of neglected."

Garrett waited like that for another thirty minutes or so, tugging at his handcuffs, tapping his foot restlessly, but it was very hard for him to keep track of time; the black hood let no light in, and there was not a sound to be heard. Finally, a door opened, there were footsteps, and the hood was yanked off his head. Garrett squinted in the sterile fluorescent light. The room was empty except for a small table and chair, and a digital video camera set on a tripod by the far wall. The camera was pointed at Garrett.

Two men stood between Garrett and the only door to the room. They were both white males, midthirties, both wearing gray suits, their hair closely cut. Garrett thought he recognized them.

"Remember us?" the larger of the two men said.

Garrett stared at him, and then he recognized the speaker and his sidekick: "Agents Stoddard and Cannel. Homeland Security. You asked me about my mother."

"That's right. I'm Agent Stoddard," the big man said. "And you were an asshole to me. So guess what? Now it's my turn to be an asshole back."

A shiver of fear ran down Garrett's spine. He tried to force an easy smile to his lips. "How about I apologize for that and we just call it even?"

Neither of the two agents laughed. The shorter of the two—Cannel—pulled the empty chair close to the desk and sat. Stoddard stood motionless.

"Who was he?" Stoddard asked.

"Can you be more specific?" Garrett said, trying to keep things light.

"The conductor saw you talking to a man. There was a woman with him. You had a conversation for five minutes. Who was he?"

"I have no idea," Garrett said.

Agent Stoddard made a show of sighing loudly. "Here's the deal, Garrett," he said. "Every time you lie to me, your situation will get incrementally worse. We will show less leniency. You will be stuck here longer. And then you will face lengthier and lengthier jail time."

"Whoa, whoa, whoa," Garrett said. "Jail time? For what? I didn't do anything."

"You ran away from your military police drivers."

"How is that illegal?"

"It was highly suspicious."

"I was bored. Needed to shake it up a little."

"By riding Metro trains all morning?"

"I was people watching. It calms me down."

Agent Cannel dropped a manila folder onto the table and pulled a stack of papers from it. "We employ computer experts as well," he said.

He read aloud from the top sheet: "Tuesday, 4:38 a.m., Reilly, Garrett, sent encrypted e-mail from an unsecured wireless router on perimeter of Bolling Air Force Base to recipient at warbyothermeans@gmail.com. Subject e-mail states: I am in DC, am ready to talk. Reply received 10:42 p.m., instructing Reilly, Garrett, to ride the Metro Orange Line, today, Wednesday the 15th. Reilly,

Garrett, reported to police by train conductor on Metro Orange Line, 9:30 to 10:00, a.m. Reilly, Garrett, met unknown subject—white male, forties—on the train, 10:09 a.m., and had discussion for approximately five minutes, after which unknown subject departed Metro and Reilly, Garrett, was apprehended by federal agents."

Agent Cannel closed the file and said nothing more. Agent Stoddard looked down at Garrett. "Please. Don't insult us. At least come up with a lie that's creative."

Garrett sighed. The handcuffs were digging into his wrists. "Okay, fine, how about I get a turn?" Garrett said. "Who tried to blow me up on John Street in front of the Jenkins & Altshuler offices in New York City?"

"I have no idea. That's not our jurisdiction. The NYPD are investigating that."

Garrett smiled. "Well, now we're both lying. So we're even."

Agent Cannel scribbled a note down on a legal pad.

"Is that what he told you? That he knew who planted the car bomb?" Stoddard asked. "Did he say it was the U.S. government? Standard American imperialist conspiracy rumor?"

Garrett stared at Stoddard and said flatly, "I want a lawyer."

"A lawyer? Where exactly do you think you are? We can throw you in jail and have you rot there and you will never see a lawyer again for the rest of your life."

"On what charges?"

Stoddard smiled. The smile had changed from bland to menacing. Garrett could see the veins on the agent's neck pulse.

"You were given top-level security clearance and access to military secrets. Now we have reason to believe you met with an agent of a foreign government. That classifies you as a threat to national security, and because of that you belong to me, and only me, and I will do whatever the hell I want with you. I can have you burned at the stake if I so choose. No charges, no trial, no judge, no nothing. And nobody will give a rat's ass what happened to you. Not your deadbeat mom, not Avery Bernstein, not any of your loser friends, and certainly not Alexis Truffant. Yes, Garrett, we know all about you and Captain Truffant."

Garrett fought hard to keep an emotionless smile plastered on his lips, but it was not easy—a wave of despair was rising in his chest. He felt suddenly very, very alone, and Agent Stoddard seemed to know it.

"That's right, Garrett. She works for us too. She's on our side, not yours. She debriefed us on your little fuck session. She told us all the details that only a lover would know."

"Bullshit," Garrett blurted out.

Agent Stoddard laughed. "You are nowhere, Reilly. And you are nothing. With nobody looking out for you. I control your fate, utterly and completely. Welcome to the Patriot Act, asshole, because it is your new home."

There was silence in the small room. Garrett tried to collect himself. He was a jumble of competing emotions, sudden, desolate loneliness being the strongest of them. He grimaced, looked at the two Homeland Security agents, and said, "Fuck you."

Agent Stoddard pulled the black hood from behind his back and slammed it over Garrett's head. The room went black. Garrett could feel the agent's hot breath at his ear.

"No, Garrett, fuck *you*," he said.

There were footsteps. A door slammed. Then silence.

Garrett said nothing, and was glad the hood was covering his face. Tears rolled down his cheeks. Hot, salty, painful tears. His throat was choked with silent sobs. Could it really be true? Had he been wrong about Alexis? Utterly and completely wrong? *Again?* Was she nothing more than a spy, working for the government, leading him to this place without a shred of real feeling on her part? Or was the Homeland Security agent just saying that to throw Garrett off balance?

He no longer knew. He no longer had any sense of what was real, unreal, faked, or heartfelt. Avery? Kline? Metternich? The Chinese? What the fuck was going on in his life? *In the world?* Even his own emotions seemed upside down. The love he had been so sure of a few days ago now seemed juvenile and embarrassingly misguided.

Alone with his thoughts, time passed slowly. Seconds, minutes, hours maybe? It was silent in the small room, disorienting. He found his mind going blank. A Coldplay song—"Clocks"—played over and over again in his head. He hated Coldplay, but the song wouldn't go away.

The door opened. There were footsteps and then Garrett's chair was tilted backwards about forty-five degrees. Fingers probed at his face through the canvas hood, and suddenly, without warning, cold water was sprayed into his mouth and up his nose. It flooded his throat. Garrett gasped, caught by surprise. He tried to breathe, but the torrent of water was too much, and unending. He tried to turn his head, but a pair of hands clamped onto his ears and kept his face tilted upright. The sensation was terrifying—no air, and no chance of getting any. A pure animal fear gripped him. He thrashed, desperate for air, desperate for the water to stop. But it didn't—it just kept coming, a steady deluge directed straight into his mouth and nose. His throat began to seize up, raw with water and choking. And just when he was about to lose consciousness . . . it stopped.

Garrett gasped, his lungs heaving, sucking in every last bit of oxygen they could get. But the respite lasted only a few seconds. The hands grabbed his ears again and another blast of cold water shot against his face. This time he held his breath, but the water kept coming, and he was still oxygen-deprived from the last bout. In seconds he was gasping again, and a moment after that, choking. He tried desperately to free his hands and legs to strike out at his torturers, but the handcuffs were tight around his wrists, and he could do nothing. His body was rigid with fear, his esophagus swollen and shutting down. He felt, instinctively, that he would die. And soon.

And then it stopped again. He sucked down air.

And then it started again. Water. More water.

Three more times they doused him. Three more times they gave him five seconds to recover. Then they stopped. Garrett coughed the water out of his throat and nose. He threw up briefly into the black hood, the smell of vomit trapped now at his nose. He felt Agent Stoddard's breath at his ear again.

"It doesn't have to be like this, Garrett," the agent whispered. "We just want to know who the man on the train was."

"I don't know," Garrett grunted. He could barely speak.

"How'd you get his e-mail address?"

Garrett froze. They wanted him to betray Avery Bernstein. He wanted to cry again. If he told them that Avery had given him the e-mail address, he would be utterly and completely alone in the world. Without friend or family.

He said nothing. The room was silent for a minute, maybe two. The hands let go of his head, his chair was placed upright, and the footsteps left the room. Garrett breathed deeply. Never had oxygen seemed so exotically wonderful. His heart was pounding.

After thirty minutes, Garrett regained some of his calm, but he was physically and mentally exhausted. He must have fallen asleep, because the next thing he knew his head was drooping down onto his chest, but that lasted only a moment, because the room was instantly engulfed in sound—a throbbing, pulsing electronic blast of white noise, seemingly directed right into his ears.

Garrett woke with a start. He understood right away that they were not going to let him sleep, and another wave of despair washed over him. They were going to try to break him. Garrett had no sense of whether he could withstand that, or if he even wanted to. He didn't try to sleep again.

Twenty minutes later they came back into the room and continued his water torture. After the fourth torrent Garrett was sure he was going to die. He could feel his consciousness spiraling away into a black void. And then they stopped. But they didn't let him sleep. The pulsing, pounding noise assaulted him every time he was on the verge of slumber. How did they know his eyes were closed under the black canvas hood?

By the end of the fifth water-boarding session, Garrett had lost all sense of reality. He was a mind detached completely from its body. He could not hold a single coherent thought in his head. The worst part wasn't the actual torture—it was the brief moments in between the torture sessions, when he was waiting for the pain and terror to start again. The hope that they were finished was corrosive to his willpower. He understood that this was all part of the plan. Part of the torture.

Again and again Agent Stoddard's voice whispered at his ear. "Tell us what we want to know, Garrett, and it all stops. No more water. No more noise. Food, some sleep. What do you say, Garrett? Huh? Tell me now and I'll make it stop."

Garrett cleared his throat and managed to gasp: "Kline. I'll tell Kline."

59

A HOMELAND SECURITY SAFE HOUSE, APRIL 15, 11:32 PM

"Good Lord," General Kline said as he stared at Garrett's pale face. "What did they do to you?"

Garrett tried to keep his head up, his eyes open, but it wasn't easy. His entire body was racked with pain. Every muscle felt like it was on fire. He had been stressed to his limits, and his body was paying the price. His hair was still wet; droplets ran down his face. The line of his skull fracture felt like caustic acid seeping into his brain.

"Tortured me," Garrett whispered, his throat raw. "They tortured me. They can't do that, can they?"

Kline pursed his lips. "They did. So I guess they can."

"This is America," Garrett said. "I'm a fucking citizen."

Kline nodded slightly, as if to say, True, but not much that can be done about it now.

Garrett craned his head, looking around the small room. The floor was covered with water. There was a drain in the corner. He hadn't seen that before. The camera and tripod were gone. Garrett supposed they had been smart enough not to film what they'd done. Garrett hated the two Homeland Security agents with an intensity he hadn't even known he was capable of.

"Motherfuckers," Garrett hissed. "I'll fucking kill them."

"Garrett," Kline said, leaning close, "just tell me whatever you know and I'll try to get you out of here. I'm on your side, but you gotta help me."

Garrett stared at the general. It was clear that Kline was playing the good cop, Homeland Security the bad. But at least Garrett had gotten the good cop in the room with him. At least he could breathe. Now he had to make the most of it.

"I honestly don't know who the man on the subway was. He said his name was Hans Metternich, and he said you were lying to me. Using me. That the government had set the bomb at Jenkins & Altshuler. And that I should think twice about helping you."

"How did you get in contact with him?"

Garrett breathed deep. "I can't tell you that. But it wasn't some spy or enemy agent. It was harmless."

"Nothing is harmless anymore, Garrett. Everything has consequences. How'd you get this Metternich's e-mail address?"

Garrett swallowed hard, then shook his head. "Can't tell you." There was no way he was going to give up Avery Bernstein. If they killed him for it, so be it—at least he had taken a stand in his life.

Kline pushed his chair back and stood. "Then I can't help you, Garrett. I'm going to have to leave you with Homeland Security." He turned and headed for the door.

"Good luck with the Chinese."

General Kline stopped, turned, and sat back down across from Garrett. The anger rose in his voice. "Not sure if you've noticed this, but I could get more info on the Chinese Communist Party from a waiter at Hunan Balcony. You haven't exactly been knocking it out of the park lately. Time is up on Ascendant—the president is shutting us down. Hell, I've been trying to stop Secretary Frye from putting your head on a stake all week, and you've made me look like an idiot. You've been a complete bust, so the Chinese-intel card is not going to get you much right now."

Garrett let out a breath, trying to calm himself, trying to appear in control. He said, "I know why they're attacking us."

"Bullshit," Kline said. "You're trying to save your skin."

"Yes. I am," Garrett said. "But I also understand what's happening in China, and now it all makes sense. All the attacks. All the chaos. It fits into a pattern perfectly. It's the answer we've been seeking this whole time. And if you don't know the pattern, then you can't fight back."

Kline studied Garrett's face, the lines of vomit caked around his chin. "And if this information is true, withholding it from me gives you leverage? Is that what you're thinking?"

"Make them let me go."

"I don't control Homeland Security. Anyway, why should I believe you?"

"How many times have I been wrong so far?"

Kline seemed to consider this. Then he spoke, calmly, methodically. "I can't promise you anything, Garrett. You've been digging your own grave, and doing a damn good job of it. Just tell me what you know about the Chinese and I'll do my best. That's the only offer I'm going to make you. You have ten seconds."

Garrett didn't hesitate. "An insurgent is rising in central China. A new Mao. His name is Hu. The Tiger. He's starting a rebellion. It's gaining in popularity. And the Chinese government is terrified. They're afraid that they're going to get overrun."

Kline sat motionless for thirty seconds, staring at Garrett as he took in this piece of information. Then he wiped his glasses clean and said, "Tell me everything."

And Garrett did.

After that, they let him sleep. They didn't unlock his handcuffs, but they switched the manacles so his wrists were in front of his torso instead of behind his back. They kept cuffs on his right ankle, but even so, Garrett could lay his head on the small table in front of him, hands under his forehead, and close his eyes. The first time he did, he expected a blast of white noise to wake him, but it didn't, and he fell into a deep, exhausted sleep.

Stoddard woke him later—Garrett wasn't sure how much later—with a glass of water and a chicken-salad sandwich. Garrett drank the water in one gulp, then lingered over the sandwich. The bread was stale and the chicken salad tasted like vinegar, but Garrett didn't care. It was some of the best food he'd ever eaten.

Agent Stoddard watched him eat, then took the plate and glass away. Before he left the room he said, "You're never seeing daylight again, you know that, right, Reilly?"

"They have daylight up your ass?" Garrett said. "'Cause that's where I'm gonna stick my foot." It didn't even make any sense, but it was the first thing that came into Garrett's head, and he liked saying it. Agent Stoddard just stared at him, then left.

Garrett slept some more. He was awakened by a familiar voice.

"Garrett?"

Garrett sat up and blinked. Alexis Truffant was sitting across from him. She was studying his face. "Are you okay? General Kline said they water-boarded you."

Garrett was too stunned to answer. He swallowed, then tried, instinctively, to pat his hair down and wipe the sleep from his eyes. His wrists strained against the handcuffs.

He stared at her. "Why did you leave?"

"Now is not the time."

"I'm not going anywhere," he said. "Now's as good a time as any."

Alexis shot a glance over her shoulder. Garrett saw that the video camera and tripod were back, and aimed at him.

"I needed to sort out my feelings. I needed to see if things were going to work out with my husband."

"You could have left me a note. Or called. Anything. A post on my fucking Facebook page would have worked."

"I was confused. And upset . . ."

"And working for the government," he said. "Did Kline tell you to leave?"

Alexis hesitated, then nodded her head yes. "He suggested I clear my head. Get away from you for a while. We were never supposed to have a relationship."

Garrett grimaced as he stared at her. She was as beautiful as ever, regal cheekbones slanting down her olive-colored face, black hair pushed back behind her ears.

"Never?" he said, pain welling up in his chest.

Alexis looked away for a moment, composed herself, then turned back to Garrett. "Look, we have some questions about the information you gave to General Kline. If you could answer them . . ." Her voice trailed off.

"I know, I know. You and Kline will try to get me out of here."

Alexis lowered her voice and leaned forward slightly. "You don't begin to understand the politics of the current situation. There are agencies that believe you, fully, and have faith in what you are telling them. And there are others that would like to see you sent to Guantánamo as an enemy combatant. And those agencies are not playing well together right now. You are this close to a lifetime in prison. Given what's been done to you over the past twenty-four hours, you know that I'm not being overly dramatic."

"Ask away," Garrett said.

Alexis laid a yellow legal pad on the table and began to write on it. "What you told General Kline has been disseminated to the group. About a new Mao-like figure leading a rebellion in China. But how could we not know anything about it?"

"China is a repressive government. They keep strict controls on the media. On all forms of information."

"Sure," Alexis said, scribbling notes as she spoke. "We know that. We also have spies all over that country. And none of them are telling us what you're telling us."

Garrett took a deep breath, trying to regain strength and order his thoughts. "Because the Chinese government is clamping down, full strength. This is the one thing they fear more than anything else. They don't care about foreign invaders anymore. Who'd occupy China? They've weathered economic disintegration before as well. But a popular, grassroots insurgency? That has traction with regular people? That's a nightmare. A nightmare with plenty of historical precedence—it's what Mao did to China's previous leadership. They are doing absolutely everything in their power to keep this under wraps."

Alexis wrote down his answer. "How does your theory explain why the Chinese have launched attacks against us these last few weeks?"

"It provides motive."

"Which is?"

"War as diversion. Wars promote nationalism. During times of conflict people rally around the flag, even in China—especially in China. They listen to their government. More important, they are inclined to believe their government. The Communist Party is trying to inject a dose of nationalism into the population, hoping it will cool the revolutionary fever burning in the center of the country. At the very least, war will distract people from the issues in front of their faces: corruption, land dispossession, income inequality, environmental catastrophe. Those are burning issues in China right now. And they are at the heart of the Tiger's rebellion."

Alexis countered right away: "But why *covert* attacks? Nobody in the Chinese population knows anything about this. If we're at war, it's a secret war. That doesn't promote anything."

Garrett smiled. He was reminded of the hours they had spent in the shack at Camp Pendleton, arguing points of politics and logic. It was funny how quickly they fell back into old routines, even with his hands bound by the wrist and his lungs raw from torture. Those moments were probably what he missed most about Alexis.

He smiled. "You're right. That's why what we're experiencing, in my opinion, aren't the first shots of a war. They're provocations. The attacks have been masked, but just barely. The Treasury sell-off came in coded numerical intervals. Numbers with high significance in Chinese culture. The Vegas real estate sell-off was initiated through an offshore firm called the May Fourth Movement. And they didn't really bother to hide who bought and then destroyed a molybdenum mine in Colorado. Everyone knew it was a Chinese company. They want us to know who's behind this. They want us pissed off."

"So that . . ." Alexis waved a finger in the air as the truth began to set in.

"So that we'll hit them," Garrett confirmed. "Because if we turn around and strike openly, if we are the aggressors, then they can portray themselves as the victims. Which is guaranteed to garner domestic support. And they're figuring that will siphon off support for the insurgency. My guess is that the Chinese government figures they can handle anything we can throw at them, short of a nuclear attack. And we're not crazy enough to do that. Not yet, at least. But they are scared shitless of their own people. More than a billion pissed-off Chinese citizens could wash away the ruling elite in a matter of days. And the party knows this. It's what happened when Mao took power, and they will not risk a repeat performance."

He smiled at her, but a deep exhaustion was running through him. He had barely said that many words—in total—to anyone in days. He let out a breath.

"What the Chinese government wants," Garrett said, "is for *us* to start a shooting war with *them*."

It took a few moments for Alexis to finish writing down what he had said. She paused briefly, scratched out a line, rewrote it, then finished writing. She picked up the legal pad, turned, and presented it to the camera behind them, as if for inspection and approval, then put it back down on the table and pushed it forward to Garrett.

"Is this an accurate summation of your ideas?"

Garrett scanned her notes briefly, then nodded yes. She lifted the legal pad and paused, holding it above the table. There was a small key sitting on the desk, underneath the pad, blocked from the camera's view by Alexis's body. Garrett saw it, surprised, and was about to tell her that she had forgotten it was there when she cut him off: "Thank you, Garrett," she said slowly, carefully. "This has been very helpful. I think we'll be able to help you get out of here."

Garrett glanced again at the key, momentarily bewildered, then he snapped his head up, smiled at Alexis, and covered the key with his cuffed hands. She slipped the legal pad back into her bag.

"That would be great," Garrett said, his heart suddenly pounding. "That would be awesome."

Alexis stood, nodded once, and left the room. Garrett put his hands, with the key clutched tightly in his right fist, into his lap, and started thinking about what he would do next.

60

THE PENTAGON, APRIL 16, 9:55 AM

Jimmy Lefebvre knew something was up. Garrett had been gone for nearly forty-eight hours and no one had heard a word from him. Not a sighting, an e-mail, a phone call—nothing. This was a *very* bad sign.

In the war room, only Lefebvre seemed concerned about this. The rest of the Ascendant team continued to play their online games, trade in futures contracts, and keep an eye on world events. Lefebvre knew they were military creatures of habit; they would do what they were told until they were told to do something different, and if they were told nothing, then they would sit around and wait. That's what it was to be a soldier. If you left them without orders for too long they would probably just get drunk.

Lefebvre was a soldier as well, but the fact that he'd never seen combat—and there wasn't a day in his life that he didn't regret that—meant he wasn't war-weary. He'd never grown accustomed to waiting for orders. Left to his own devices, Lefebvre figured out what he should do, and then he did it. And every bone in his body was telling him that it was time to get the hell out of the war room. Fast.

Lefebvre knew that Garrett Reilly was constantly pushing the envelope, and now he suspected that Garrett had pushed that envelope too far. Perhaps it had to do with what Garrett and Celeste had discovered about China; maybe it was about his decision to send Celeste to hunt down the Tiger. Or maybe it had to do with the fact that he hadn't told *any of this* to his superiors. Lefebvre hadn't said anything either, and that made him complicit. Whatever had happened, Lefebvre guessed that the shit was about to hit the fan.

He found Bingo at a game console and told him that he was going back to the hotel. "Storm's coming. Keep your plans to yourself," Lefebvre said. "I don't want to know what you know or what you're going to do. Your secrets are your own."

"I've never said anything bad about this country. Or the president," Bingo said, his voice rising anxiously. "You'll vouch for me, right?"

"They can't put you in jail for criticizing America," Lefebvre said.

"They can't put *you* in jail for that. They can put *me* in jail for anything."

Lefebvre sighed. He and Bingo came from radically different universes, and there wasn't time to argue that particular point of politics and fairness. He called a cab to take him back to the hotel, and was just slipping out the door of the war room when a hulking military policeman stepped into his path and told him that he was being detained for questioning. A second MP had Bingo in a corner and was rifling through his bike messenger bag.

Lefebvre tried to signal to Bingo that it was going to be okay, but he couldn't catch Bingo's eye: Bingo was holding his hands above his head like an arrested criminal.

They brought Lefebvre to a windowless conference room on the third floor of the Pentagon's D Ring. First came a duo of military policemen. They poked around in the standard places: his contact with outsiders in the past few weeks, had he revealed any classified information—knowingly or unknowingly—to anyone, anywhere?

"Absolutely not," Lefebvre said, and that was true. He'd kept his mouth shut.

Then came two Army intelligence officers, and they ran down a checklist of questions about the war room, and what he had seen. Again, Lefebvre was truthful.

"Nothing out of the ordinary," he said. "But I wasn't really looking, either." He kept his answers short and to the point, telling only what they asked him to tell them.

Lefebvre was cautious, but not scared—he had decided right away that he would reveal everything he knew about Garrett and Celeste's Chinese rebellion theory, even if he had promised Garrett that he wouldn't. Lefebvre was part of Garrett Reilly's team, but he was also a military officer, sworn to protect his country. He hadn't joined the Army solely to escape from his father's long shadow; he really was a patriot. He was prepared to tell all.

Finally, a pair of Homeland Security agents, a man named Bellamy and a woman named Garcia, grilled him. They started with Garrett: What were his political leanings, Democratic, Republican, libertarian, anarchist? Did he drink? Had he flashed around a lot of cash? Had Lefebvre ever seen him do drugs? What about his uncontrolled outbursts of anger? Did he have any odd sexual proclivities? Obsessions? Fetishes?

Again, the truth was: Lefebvre had no idea.

Then, suddenly, the questions took a personal tack, and they were directed right at Lefebvre. How much money did he have in his savings account? Why wasn't he married? Why didn't he have a girlfriend? Had he ever had sex with a man? Why not? Did he hate homosexuals?

This caught Lefebvre off guard. He understood that they were testing him, looking for him to slip up, and that answering with even the slightest hint of attitude was a quick and easy way to derail a military career. But he couldn't help thinking, Why weren't they asking about what really mattered? What about China? What about the rebellion? Lefebvre had information they could use. He was sitting on a secret, ready to reveal it, just waiting for the right question.

But that question never came.

The agents didn't seem to give a damn about the Chinese. Or a secret war. At first that was baffling to Lefebvre. He'd been in the Army long enough to know that the federal bureaucracy wasn't without flaws, but if Garrett Reilly had done something wrong, shouldn't the very people tasked with figuring that out be interested in what he'd discovered? Shouldn't they be asking what Garrett's ultimate goal was, not just whether he was ideologically suspect?

And why were they questioning Lefebvre's loyalty, of all people?

When they had told him, a month ago, that he would be babysitting a snot-nosed civilian for some half-baked DIA project, he had accepted the assignment without complaint. And when that civilian had turned out to be as arrogant as advertised, Lefebvre had swallowed his pride and gotten on with it, teaching him as best he could, for the good of the country. He might not be a combat veteran, but he could still take one for the team. He'd even come to like Garrett Reilly—sort of—and was beginning to think of Ascendant not as half-baked but as a stroke of strategic brilliance. Whatever had been asked of him, he had done it.

But now they wanted to know if he was gay? *What was that about?*

In a flash, it became clear to Lefebvre that Agents Garcia and Bellamy were living proof that most people followed convention, and did so with a grim determination. And that idea was strangely liberating for him; the internal constructs he'd followed for most of his life—about loyalty and patriotism—were suddenly, ever so slightly, loosened.

It gave him a measure of psychological breathing room. And in that breathing room, Lefebvre found himself defending Garrett, at least in his head. He could see how Garrett's refusal to be boxed in—by anyone—was a form of bravery. The group was where you found refuge. But Garrett never sought that refuge—he did the opposite. Somehow, in Lefebvre's head, pledging allegiance to something and being blindly obedient to it had gotten confused. And that bothered him.

No, worse. At that moment, it humiliated him. These people were questioning his loyalty while the United States was perched on a precipice. That was tantamount to treason.

"Where is Garrett now?" Lefebvre finally asked the agents as they studied their notes.

"We can't tell you," Agent Garcia said.

"What did he do wrong?"

Garcia and Bellamy stared at the lieutenant as if he were an unruly puppy that had just peed on their legs.

"Why don't *you* tell *us*?" Bellamy said.

"I don't know. That's why I'm asking." Lefebvre knew he should shut his mouth, but this was ridiculous. Utterly ridiculous. *The Chinese were climbing up their asses.*

"Are you giving us trouble?" Garcia asked.

"I'm just trying to get to the truth," Lefebvre said, even though he knew that he was doing just as the agent implied—giving them trouble.

Agent Bellamy squinted in the dull fluorescent light, staring daggers at Lefebvre. "Exactly whose side are you on, Lieutenant Lefebvre?"

And for the first time in a long time Lefebvre wasn't sure of the answer.

61

A HOMELAND SECURITY SAFE HOUSE, APRIL 16, 4:32 PM

On his fourth attempt, Garrett did it. He managed to cup his right hand far enough over his left so that he could slide the universal handcuff key into the cuff's lock, and twist it, once, slowly, a full 360-degree rotation. The ratchet in the cuffs clicked open, and he was able to pull out his wrist. All of this he did with his hands in his lap, under the edge of the table that sat in front of him, blocked from the view of the video camera.

After that, he simply waited.

An hour later, Agent Stoddard entered the room, holding a plate with another chicken-salad sandwich and glass of water in his hands. He set the plate and glass on the table and backed to the corner of the room, never taking his eyes off of Garrett. Garrett made a show of inspecting the sandwich, then shook his head.

"Can't I get something else?" Garrett asked. "I'm sick of chicken."

"No," Stoddard said, not moving.

"Fine. Take it away. I won't eat it," Garrett said, leaning back in his chair.

Agent Stoddard shrugged, crossed the room, and bent at the waist to pick up the plate. Garrett watched him closely, tensing his lower back and planting his feet as firmly as he could on the linoleum floor. The moment the Homeland Security agent's eyes went from Garrett to the plate—and it was only for a moment—Garrett rocketed his body forward with every ounce of strength he could muster, pushing up with his legs and snapping his head forward like a whip. He aimed the peak of his forehead directly at the intersection of Agent

Stoddard's nose and eyes, and he hit directly where he had aimed, a bull's-eye. If there was one thing Garrett knew how to do, and do well, it was head-butt another man.

The crack of skull against skull was distinct and clear, hollow-sounding, like a cardboard box being swatted by a two-by-four, and Agent Stoddard grunted in surprise, toppling over backwards as blood streamed from his nose. He fell on his haunches, hands instinctively clutching his face, as Garrett bent immediately at the waist and jammed the handcuff key into the manacle on his right ankle. In less than a second he was free, but his head screamed in pain, the fault line of his skull fracture erupting like it had been torn open with a jagged knife. Garrett had never experienced anything like it. The sensation was nearly paralyzing—every nerve ending in his body was on fire. He felt as if he were moving in slow motion, the air around him thick like water, shock waves radiating down from his head through his entire body.

Garrett willed himself to push forward through the pain and grabbed the metal chair he'd been sitting on for hours—maybe days, he no longer knew—and swung it like a tennis racket across Stoddard's body. The chair legs connected solidly with the agent's head and hands, a muffled thud of cracking bone. Stoddard didn't make a sound after that—he went down like a discarded shirt. Garrett didn't think he'd killed him, but he didn't care, either, and he turned his attention to the door, which was opening quickly, Agent Cannel charging into the room. Before the second agent could get his entire body through the door, Garrett flew at it, right leg raised, kicking it with all his might.

The door caught Agent Cannel in the midsection, knocking the air from his lungs, stunning him. In one hand he held a gun, finger on the trigger. Garrett brought the chair down hard on the agent's gun hand, snapping the weapon out of his grip and onto the floor. Garrett tossed the chair aside and hit Cannel with punches to the face, as many as he could throw without stopping, seven or eight in all, until Cannel fell backwards out of the door, and Garrett threw it open and charged after him. Cannel collapsed to the floor and Garrett stomped his chest as hard as he could.

He didn't waste any more time. If there was one thing he'd learned from years of bar brawling it was to hit your enemy hard and then run like hell. Plus, the jagged lightning bolts of blue pain were flashing before his eyes again, and Garrett was worried he might pass out. He stumbled down the hallway of what looked to be an ordinary suburban home. He came into a bare living room, with a couch and some fast food piled on a coffee table, as well as a video monitor showing a live feed of his former jail room. The camera in the room had been kicked over in the fight, and now the image was canted ninety degrees from the vertical and showed Agent Stoddard trying to crawl across the floor, dazed and disoriented, his face dark with blood.

Well, he's alive, Garrett thought. I guess that's good.

Garrett scanned the living room, assessing if there was anything there of use. He grabbed a raincoat lying on the couch, a bag of french fries, and a ring of car keys, then ran out the door.

It was twilight outside, a wash of pink still in the sky in the west. The air was cool. The neighborhood was suburban and quiet, the street lined with innocuous one-story homes with green lawns. Other than a man smoking a cigarette on his driveway down the block, there was nobody else outside. Garrett fumbled with the car keys, squinting to focus through the ache in his head and the darkening tunnel vision that was closing in on him, then hit the unlock button on the fob repeatedly. A Chevy Malibu halfway down the block beeped and he walked to it quickly, trying not to break into a panicked run. He climbed inside, started the car, and drove.

He had no idea where he was, and he didn't care. He just wanted to get as far away from his captors as possible, and in the shortest amount of time. He followed quiet suburban streets for a few minutes, then found himself on a wide boulevard—the street signs said Colesville Road. He followed Colesville for a few minutes into a neighborhood of bland low-rise buildings and corner mini-malls. A shop sign read "Silver Spring," and he guessed he was in Maryland, just north of Washington, D.C. His hands were shaking on the steering wheel; a noise had blossomed inside his skull, and was ratcheting up into an insistent, searing screech.

He passed a pair of police cars without incident, but he wasn't too worried about the local cops. At least not yet. He didn't think Homeland Security would broadcast his escape to the general public, and they certainly wouldn't do it right away. If they did, they'd have to explain why they tortured him, and that seemed like an impractical move. They would need a cover story. He considered turning himself in to the police and telling them everything that had happened, just to put the squeeze on the bastards who had water-boarded him, but he decided against it.

He wasn't sure anyone would believe a word he said.

He pulled off the main avenue and searched the suburban streets until he found an empty home with a FOR SALE sign out front. He parked in the driveway of a spotless Tudor, then went to the fenced-in backyard and washed his hands and face with a garden hose. He ate the agents' pilfered french fries and drank as much water as he could hold. Feeling stronger, he got back in the car and drove out of Silver Spring to the neighboring suburb of Bethesda. He drove slowly. His vision was faltering. He felt as if he were seeing the world from the bottom of a deep, black well. He was careful not to break the speed limit or run any red lights. In downtown Bethesda he parked the car at a meter and walked into a strip-mall Radio Shack, wrapping the agent's raincoat around his ruined shirt.

"Hey," he said to the teenaged clerk behind the counter, trying to keep his voice steady and calm. The piercing sound in his head was lower, but it hadn't gone away. Not by a long shot. "I'm in the market for a really fast laptop. You got anything I can take on a test run?"

The clerk put him in front of a no-name Chinese knock-off brand with a quad-core processor and told him to have at it. Ninety seconds later Garrett walked out of the store with a name and an address.

And murder in his heart.

62

YANGQUAN, CHINA, APRIL 17, 8:21 AM

Celeste Chen barely had a minute to catch her breath. From the moment in the Pentagon when Garrett had ordered her to go to China to when she got out of the taxicab in the middle of Shanxi Province forty-eight hours later, her life had been a blur. She'd packed a bag in twenty minutes, flagged a taxi to the Chinese embassy, wrangled her visa from a sullen bureaucrat, grabbed another taxi to Dulles, then been the last to board her flight to New York's Kennedy airport. At Kennedy she forced down a stale taco lunch, changed two thousand U.S. dollars from her online trading account into Chinese yuan at a foreign-exchange counter, then sprinted to catch her flight to China.

She flew nonstop, coach, to Beijing's Capital International Airport. She slept for maybe an hour on the plane. Mostly she pondered how she would tackle the task ahead, all the while fending off the sagging form of a snoring Chinese businessman. Walking off the plane onto Chinese soil was like being buffeted by hurricane-force winds, even though she'd been to China half a dozen times before; the language, the signs, the noise—the chaos of it all. Eighteen hours earlier she'd been in Washington, D.C., safely ensconced in the Pentagon basement, developing abstract hypotheses about geopolitical upheavals. Now she was half a world away, on her own, trying to find signs of a nascent political rebellion.

And, most important—*now she was a spy.*

That took her breath away. She sat in a stall in the airport women's restroom for ten minutes just trying to calm down.

She took a bus into the city, marveling at the myriad new buildings—huge blocks of apartments and offices—that seemed to have sprouted up everywhere in the Beijing suburbs. It had been two years since she'd last been to China, and yet in those two years absolutely everything had changed. The pace of destruction and construction was mind-blowing. She got off the bus in the touristy Dong Cheng district, figuring she could blend in with the other foreigners there (even though a native Chinese would be hard-pressed to figure out that she was American), and immediately pounded the pavement, looking for a cheap, out-of-the-way place to stay. She considered herself a seasoned traveler, but the frenetic pace and lack of personal space on the sidewalks of Beijing startled her nonetheless. Men and women slammed into her, knocking her sideways, cutting her off without so much as a sidelong glance. When she'd been a student here she'd enjoyed it, making a game of it. Bump and move on, bump and move on. Now, frazzled and exhausted, she just tried not to get hurt.

She found a hotel—drab but modern, and relatively clean—and slept for two hours. That was just enough to keep her from collapsing. With jet lag running side by side with excitement, she packed up her bag and took a cab to Beijing's gaudy, Buddhist-temple-inspired West Train Station, where she boarded a T-class train to Yangquan, the city in central China that was the heart of the country's coal-mining district. She didn't want to attract undue attention, so she bought a ticket for a hard seat, in the back of the train, where the poorer travelers rode, and ended up standing for almost the entire four-hour trip, pinched between a fat, middle-aged farmer and his chatty, pockmarked wife. The contradictory smells of modern China wafted over her: machine oil, cooked pork, the sweat of tired factory workers, the pungent tang of a freshly peeled orange. It was exhilarating. And overwhelming.

Celeste knew when they had entered Shanxi Province because the air, instead of being gray with car and truck exhaust particulate, as it was in Beijing, took on a darker, blacker hue, to match the coal that was pulled from the ground in the mines that dotted the hills. Yangquan was, like so many smaller Chinese cities, both astonishingly modern and remarkably Third World, at least to Celeste's Western eye. This was a part of China she had never experienced before. Bleary from lack of sleep, she staggered from the train and asked around for a hotel. She found a rundown one in the center of town, where a pair of Australian students were practicing their Mandarin—loudly and badly—in the next room. It didn't matter to her in her exhausted state: she jammed wads of toilet paper in her ears and slept for another two hours before venturing out for dinner, and information.

The spring night in Yangquan was warm and muggy, filled with bugs and the honking of horns. Celeste wandered downtown, hungrily, before stopping in a small restaurant that served beef noodle soup. In her jeans and no-brand track jacket, Celeste looked like any other resident of Yangquan, and when she spoke she passed for Chinese, though not a local. The waitress wondered if she was from Shanghai. Her teeth were too white and straight for a miner's daughter. Modern dentistry—at least for the affluent—had finally come to the Middle Kingdom.

Celeste did her best to chat up the waitress and the other patrons in the restaurant, but socializing with strangers was not her strength, and she got little in the way of helpful responses. Her brain was half-fried from the travel anyway, so it was just as well. She walked the streets of Yangquan later that night, but the shops and bars were closing down, and she felt like this line of inquiry wasn't going to be particularly fruitful. The truth was, Celeste was an academic researcher, not a spy, so figuring out how to extract covert information once you were already inside of a country was not something she was particularly suited for. Still, she was game and wanted to do her best.

That night she slept a deep sleep, interrupted only by dreams of countless Asian faces rushing past her in a blur, as if she were traveling through a tunnel of Chinese humanity. In the morning, after tea and sending a brief, encrypted e-mail to Garrett, Celeste stood on the street just outside her hotel and tried to orient herself. The air was hot and still. The incessant drone of construction machinery wafted through the city, rattling her bones. All of China, she marveled, was in motion, every hour of the day.

She felt just as at home here as she did in the States, maybe even more so. Perhaps it was her looks—she had never fit in with the other girls at her white, suburban Palo Alto high school. Or perhaps it was the language. Speaking Mandarin gave her a not-so-secret joy; she loved the rising and falling intonations, the subtle variations in sound.

But in the end, she suspected that it was simply that here, in China, she could shed her old skin and become someone new. It was the age-old thrill of solo travel—reinvention was always just around the corner, and that was a powerful counterpoint to her life in the States. For Celeste, ironically, China was freedom.

Back at the Pentagon she and Garrett had made a list of ways she could seek out stories of Hu, the rebel leader. Garrett had suggested she hook up with a local boy, maybe at a bar or a restaurant. She wasn't crazy about that method—it was *so* Garrett Reilly—and figured she would hip-pocket it as a last resort. She had offered up meeting halls and open-air markets as potential nexuses of information. Garrett had not been helpful on this score, though he had made one very good suggestion: behave as if you already knew all there is to know about Hu and the insurgency. Take an attitude of resigned annoyance—you were too cool for other people's political grievances.

Celeste thought that made sense. She decided to try it.

She walked a quarter mile from the hotel and found a street lined with a series of small food stalls. In each one she searched out items that were missing from the displays—vegetables that looked rotten, bread that was stale, or a shelf that was simply empty. She waited until other shoppers passed by, then clucked loudly while staring at the missing item and said, "*Yí rén dăo luàn, dà jiā shòu kŭ.*" (*One person makes trouble, everybody suffers.*)

At the first two stalls she wasn't sure the other shoppers heard her. At the third, an old lady gave her a nasty look and shuffled past, jarring Celeste with her shoulder as she did. But at the fourth stall, she got the response she was looking for: a young man, no more than twenty-five, clutching an armful of snap peas and onions, heard what she said as she stood over a bin of wilting vegetables, and made as if to spit at her. But he didn't. He simply said, "You are spoiled. Just like that eggplant. She fights for you." Then he hurried out of the market.

She? Celeste said to herself in amazement. *She* fights for you?

The Tiger is a woman?

63

BETHESDA, MARYLAND, APRIL 16, 9:42 PM

Hadley Kline kissed his daughter, Samantha, good night, then turned off the light in her second-floor bedroom. He headed down the hallway, then stopped, mid-step, as the sound of the TV wafted upward from the main floor.

"Martin." Kline hissed the name of his twelve-year-old son in mild disappointment. The kid never remembered to turn off the TV. Or to make his bed. Or clean his room. Or do anything that didn't have to do with video games or practicing for Pop Warner football. There had been a moment when Kline had thought himself brilliant for having kids so late in life. That moment had long ago passed.

Kline padded downstairs in his socks, resigned to cleaning up after his son again, figuring he would swing by the kitchen and pour himself one last bourbon before retiring. Might as well, he thought, being on the first floor and all. He stepped into the living room and froze.

CNN was on. Martin never watched the news. Or anything other than Cartoon Network. The back door was open, a soft breeze fluttering in from the backyard.

Kline started to step backward, to put his back against a wall and prevent anyone from getting behind him, when a thin strand of wire snapped down over his head and around his neck. The wire tightened in a flash, taut and painful, before he could bring his hands to his throat.

A voice whispered, "Don't move. If you do I'll twist it one more time, tie it off, and you will choke to death."

Kline took a shallow breath. The wire was already digging into his throat, constricting his breathing. He could not turn around without the wire ripping his neck to pieces.

"Reilly?"

"Did you tell them to torture me?"

"Can we sit down?" Kline rasped. "I won't hurt you."

The wire tightened around his throat.

"Did you tell them to torture me?"

"I told Alexis to give you the handcuff key," Kline managed to hiss. "I helped you."

"Did you think I'd escape or that they would kill me?"

"I wasn't sure. But I was hoping you would escape. The wire is hurting my throat, Garrett. I can't breathe."

In response the wire was pulled even tighter, forcing Kline's head back slightly. The general shuffled his feet to keep from falling.

"Why? Why did you want me to escape?"

"Because I need you. We need you."

"We? The people who water-boarded me?"

"They're trained monkeys, doing what they're told. They think you passed secrets to a foreign government. I'm going to fall over if you keep tugging on the wire, Garrett. You'll kill me."

"I didn't pass any secrets."

"I know that."

"All you know is that I have a wire around your neck, ready to choke the life out of you. That's all you know."

"Okay," Kline said, trying to suck in as much air as he could get into his lungs and stay calm at the same time. "You're right. Okay? You're absolutely right."

Kline could feel Garrett's chin next to his ear. "I want to make your death as painful as fucking possible. I want you shitting your pants as you choke. That's what I want."

Kline closed his eyes and tried to clear his head. "Garrett. The Pacific Fleet is on its way to China. The Fifth Fleet is going to join them in a day. We're moving troops into Korea and Kyrgyzstan." Kline could feel the tension on the wire around his neck tighten. "The president is falling into their trap," Kline continued, pleading now. "Preparing to strike first. Just like you said."

"What the fuck do I care?"

"You can stop it."

"No I can't. Nobody can stop the U.S. military. And even if I could, why should I?" Garrett leaned close to Kline. "Look at me. Look what they did to me."

Kline tried to crane his head to the left slightly. Out of the corner of his eye he could see Garrett's face. He had deep circles under his eyes, and a gash on his forehead just below his hairline; a trail of dried blood was visible just above his eye.

Garrett hissed: "They poured water down my throat. For hours."

"You went off the reservation. You met with a potential spy from an unknown entity or nation."

"There is a fucking Constitution in this country. I'll meet with whoever I want to meet with."

"No. Not anymore. That's your old life talking. You have a security clearance. A very high one. Access to classified data. In your new life, you don't get to do those things."

"My new life? *Is this my new life?* Because I didn't ask for this. Not any part of it."

"I understand."

"Understand? Bullshit! You lied to me, seduced me, trained me to be your attack dog, then lied some more. You never told me the whole truth, not once."

"That's the nature of the game." Kline hated saying it, but it was true. Secrecy, lies, seduction. It was what he did for a living. What all of them did. Kline felt the wire around his neck loosen slightly. He could force a little more air into his lungs.

"A game," Garrett said. "All a game. Always has been." Kline heard a sadness in Garrett's voice. A weariness.

"A game with incredibly high stakes. People's lives. The fate of nations."

Kline could see Garrett shaking his head slightly. "You people . . . you never stop. You crazy fucking people."

"Garrett. This is your moment. We need you free so you can do what you're best at. That's why I had Alexis pass you that key. We need you to do what none of the rest of us can. Take control of Ascendant again. Stop the war."

Garrett snorted in disbelief. "Why? Give me one reason why I should do anything for you assholes ever again in my life? One reason why I shouldn't leave here and never come anywhere near this place. Ever."

"Because walking away while millions of people's lives are at stake—men, women, children, all over the world—would be wrong," Kline said. "And as of this moment—and this is just my opinion—I think you need to start doing some right in your life."

64

SCOTT'S RUN NATURE PRESERVE, MCLEAN, VIRGINIA, APRIL 17, 5:58 AM

Garrett slept in the park. It wasn't comfortable, but after sleeping with his head on a desk and his ankle chained to a chair, a bed of leaves and grass was just fine. Still, he tossed and turned all night, his skull throbbing with pain. He woke up early, before the sun had come up, to the sound of birds and a car honking in the distance. It took him a while to remember where he was, and why he was there, and when he did an anger washed over him that he thought he might never be able to expel from his body. It was an anger so all-encompassing that it blotted out everything else he felt, including hunger and thirst.

He needed to do right?

Garrett still couldn't believe General Kline had said that. Since this whole thing had started, when had it ever, even for a moment, been about doing right in the world? He was dealing with the military after all, an organization that trained people to kill. And if this was about doing right, then were the Chinese wrong? Was the United States on the side of moral good? Were we so innocent? Garrett didn't buy that for a second—moral good was for suckers.

And what about what Metternich had told him on the train, about doing somebody else's bidding? What if Metternich was telling him some form of the truth? If so, who was the bad guy then? The U.S.? Then how was working for the government doing right in the world?

Contradiction layered upon contradiction, lie upon lie.

Garrett's hands shook with rage. He had, for a moment in General Kline's living room the night before, actually considered tying off the length of wire around his neck and watching the old bastard choke to death. He had wanted to, really wanted to do it, but at the last second backed off. And, again, not for moral reasons; not because it would be wrong to kill the general, but because he would eventually get caught, and then sent to jail. Garrett did not want to go to jail.

He told himself it had been more of a cost-benefit analysis than a moral judgment. But maybe even that was a lie—a lie he told himself to keep a distance from how he really felt. But how *did* he feel? Did he see himself as a patriot? Or a traitor? Or *both*?

He opened a carton of Wheat Chex and poured the cereal directly from the box into his mouth. He had grabbed the cereal from Kline's kitchen as he left, as well as a half gallon of orange juice. He washed the Wheat Chex down with the juice, and wished he had something else to eat. He was still starving, but at least he could function now without his hands trembling. The fire in his brain, however, seemed constant, a steady ache that Garrett worried might never subside.

He had something else he'd taken from Kline's home the night before: a cell phone. It was a cheap model, one the phone companies gave away when you opened an account, and Garrett suspected it belonged to one of Kline's children. He'd snapped the battery out of the phone the first chance he'd gotten, but he was hoping Kline hadn't deactivated the account. He would hold on to the phone in case he needed it. Just for one call.

The Homeland Security agent's car was parked about a half mile away, on a quiet McLean street, keys tucked on top of the right rear wheel, but Garrett didn't dare drive it anymore. Alerts would have been issued by now. Homeland Security would have gotten its story straight: Garrett was probably listed as an international terrorist, a threat to the nation, or who knows what else. They'd probably charge him with rape and murder if they could. He was undoubtedly a wanted man.

So it was decision time. Stay? Or go?

If he fled, he would need to find a route out of D.C., and then a place to hole up until he could figure out a way to clear himself, or untangle the web of people and organizations that wanted to either use him or kill him. Or both. Without his wallet, or even a single dollar in his pocket, that would be hard at best. They had confiscated everything when they pulled him off the Metro train.

He supposed he could get a message to Mitty Rodriguez, and have her wire him some cash, but Homeland Security would undoubtedly be expecting that, and they'd be waiting for him when he went to pick it up. No matter where he went.

And then there was Hans Metternich, whoever the fuck he was. Anyone who could just show up on a Metro train and then disappear again without a trace was worth worrying about. And being afraid of. Maybe it was Metternich who had tried to blow him up in New York. Maybe Metternich, despite his protestations, actually did want Garrett dead.

To Garrett, the world had become very hostile. And very dangerous.

Plus, he had Celeste Chen's fate to consider. She was in China on *his* orders. If he cut and ran she would be on her own, with no one in the States to watch over her or provide help if she got into trouble. It wasn't like he'd suddenly become a den mother, but abandoning Celeste now was a little too selfish. Even for Garrett.

So that left staying. And cooperating with Kline and the Defense Intelligence Agency. Again, he'd be in their system. Unless, of course, he was running that system, and wasn't that what Kline had dangled in front of him? Continue running the Ascendant program? Did Garrett believe him? Or trust him? Absolutely not.

But perhaps he could use him; use Kline, and Ascendant, to give himself some time and some leverage. If he was actively working for the DIA—and whatever other government agencies were supporting him at the time—then they would be invested in keeping him safe. And breathing. At least for a while.

And Ascendant did offer up the other benefit of being in opposition to the president, Secretary Frye, and the U.S. military. If he succeeded, then those people and organizations would be furious; and there was nothing Garrett wanted more than to piss those fucking bastards off.

Still, Garrett wasn't crazy about those two options. There didn't seem to be a viable long-term solution in either of them. But he was in too much pain and too hungry to come up with any others. He brushed the dirt and leaves off the raincoat he'd wrapped himself in for warmth, hid the cereal and juice under a bush in case he needed to come back for them, then walked to an empty parking lot on the edge of the park, and slotted the battery into the back of the stolen cell phone.

Garrett Reilly dialed a number . . . and hoped he was making the right choice.

65

ALEXANDRIA, VIRGINIA, APRIL 17, 11:01 AM

The military policemen who had driven Bingo and Lefebvre back to their hotel—a Ramada Inn just west of downtown Alexandria—told them to pack their bags and await further orders. Bingo tried to explain that he wasn't in the military and that they couldn't order him to do anything, but the MPs seemed unimpressed. They said he should not leave the hotel, call no one, and that additional security agents would stop by every few hours to check on them.

Bingo packed his bag in ten minutes and spent the next twenty-four hours watching the History Channel in a cold sweat. The hotel phone rang every few hours; he always answered on the first ring, and could hear someone on the other end of the line, but they never said anything, just listened as Bingo said "Hello?" and then hung up. His heart skipped a beat every time this happened.

Lefebvre knocked on his door the next morning and said they should go get a latte at a coffee shop a few blocks away. When Bingo asked how come, Lefebvre said casually, "Stretch our legs. Get the blood flowing. Just ten minutes."

Bingo went, against his better judgment, and knew he'd made a mistake the moment he entered the coffee shop: Alexis Truffant, dressed in civilian clothes, was sitting in a corner, waiting for them. Bingo hadn't seen her in a week and a half, and she looked tense.

"We don't have a lot of time," Alexis said as Lefebvre took a seat next to her. The place was mostly empty, but Bingo noticed that Alexis's eyes were constantly scanning the front door.

"I don't think we should be here," Bingo said.

"You're probably right," she said. "But we *are* here, so let's make the most of it."

"Where's Garrett?" Lefebvre asked.

"I'm not sure," she said. "And I don't want to know."

Alexis leaned close to Lefebvre and whispered in his ear. Bingo couldn't hear what she said, but when she was finished the lieutenant was silent for a full minute. He seemed troubled to Bingo, as if at a moral crossroads. Then he said, "It's a big decision. I need some time."

Alexis said he had until midnight, but no longer. Lefebvre stood, nodded curtly, and left the coffee shop.

Alexis turned her attention next to Bingo: "Do not go back to your hotel room. Do not pick up your clothes or any other personal belongings. I'm going to give you a prepaid wireless phone. You'll go to the library, use one of their public computers to log on to the Internet. Find a commercial space that's for lease for the next month. It needs to be medium-sized, at least two thousand square feet, out of the way—preferably in a bad neighborhood—and have close access to an Internet backbone line. It would be best if the space had gone unoccupied for a long time, ideally a year or longer. The owners need to be willing to take cash up front and ask no questions. Alternatively, you need to be able to break in and secure the space without arousing suspicion or tipping off the landlord."

"Break in? You mean illegally?" Bingo asked, his voice rising an octave.

"I mean that exactly," Alexis said. "Do all of this ASAP, and make sure you're not being followed. Secure the space and wait for further instructions. After you get those instructions, ditch the prepaid cell phone."

"Uh-uh, no way," Bingo said. "They told me. Homeland Security said. The war room is shut down. They said I should wait in the hotel until further orders."

"These *are* your further orders."

Bingo tried to laugh, but it came out as more of a snort. "No they're not," Bingo said. He might not have much in the way of courage, but he was no fool, and what Alexis wanted him to do seemed of dubious legality at best, and full-out treasonous at worst.

Alexis took a deep breath, then she smiled warmly at Bingo, and for a moment he thought it was all going to turn out just fine—she'd say that he should just go on home, forget about all this craziness and get on with his life.

Instead she said, "You're right, they're not. But you're in a bit of a tricky position. If you go back to your hotel now, Homeland Security will come around. They'll see that Lefebvre is gone, and they'll ask you what you know. And you'll have to tell them you met with me, and that we discussed plans. That will make you at the very least a suspect in their eyes, and at most an accomplice. You will be detained. Indefinitely. Maybe brought up on conspiracy charges. Obstruction of justice. It will not be fun. However, if you do what I'm asking, yes, it will be risky, but at least you stand a chance of living the remainder of your life as a free man."

She stood up, still smiling, pulled a cell phone out of her purse and handed it to him. "Your choice," she said, and walked out of the coffee shop.

Bingo stared at the cell phone. He was pretty sure most of what Alexis had just said about indefinite detention and obstruction of justice was a load of crap, but given the events of the past month—and the deep-down paranoia his mother had raised him with—he couldn't be one hundred percent positive, and even a small chance of jail time was enough to make him sick to his stomach.

He dropped the phone into his pocket and slunk onto the sidewalk, hands jammed miserably into his pockets, eyes looking for anyone who might be watching him in turn, and as he did this he had one overriding thought, and that was: if he survived this lunacy, he was going back to his bedroom, locking the door, and never coming out again. Ever.

66

SILVER SPRING, MARYLAND, APRIL 17, 4:13 PM

Secretary of Defense Frye sat in the backseat of an unmarked car, parked unobtrusively on a quiet suburban street in Silver Spring. He stared at the Homeland Security safe house that, until a few hours ago, had held Garrett Reilly, but was now unoccupied. A deep weariness and disappointment ran through his body.

No one ever lived up to your expectations in this town, he thought. No one.

He shifted his body slightly to face the man sitting next to him in the darkened Chrysler. Agent Paul Stoddard had his left hand and forearm in a cast; he had dark, black stitches laced into the skin on his temple, over his left eye. The eye itself was ringed with a black and purple bruise. He looked like he'd been beaten with a baseball bat.

"How did he escape?" Frye asked, his face betraying none of the emotion he felt coursing through his veins.

"We're not sure, sir," Stoddard answered. "He managed to disengage his hand restraints. That caught us by surprise."

"How's that even possible? He's a kid. With a skull fracture."

Agent Stoddard grimaced sheepishly. "We have a forensic team going over some video we had running. We think he may have had help."

Frye frowned. "Help? Who else saw him?"

"Well, sir, us," Stoddard said, pausing. "And DIA personnel."

Secretary Frye let out a short puff of breath. He knew exactly who had seen Garrett Reilly, and why. Oh, he knew. Did no one in this town have any sense of loyalty?

"General Kline?" Frye said.

"Yes sir."

"And that girl who works for him . . . ?"

"Captain Truffant, yes sir."

Frye bit down hard on his lower lip. "I want twenty-four-hour surveillance on both of them. Get a warrant if you have to."

"Already ordered, sir. We're tracking Kline, but Captain Truffant has gone off the grid. Cell phone turned off. Not at home, or her office."

"No, of course not," Frye said. "She's disappeared. And she'll remain invisible until we no longer need to find her." Frye could taste a hint of blood in his mouth. He had bitten through his lip in frustration. "What about Reilly?" he asked. "We have leads on his whereabouts?"

"The FBI has been briefed. They're putting a team on it."

"What do they know about the case?"

"That Reilly is a national security threat."

"Metro PD informed?"

"We thought that would be"—Stoddard hesitated as he searched for the right word—"imprudent."

Secretary Frye gave him a long look. "Why? What'd you do to him?"

"We interrogated him. *Aggressively.* Sir."

Frye snorted a quiet laugh. "Almost wish I'd been there for that."

There was a minute's silence in the car. Frye wiped the droplet of blood from his lips. He had built a long and illustrious career, in business and in politics, zeroing in on the sources of problems and then fixing them with a combination of intelligence and raw power. He was never indiscriminate with that power, but he believed—truly and fervently—that if you hesitated in the application of targeted force, you would be lost. Chaos would swallow you whole. That was true in business, in politics, and in national defense—particularly in national defense.

Frye turned to the Homeland Security agent. "I may be stating the obvious, Agent Stoddard, but it's not good when a high-value prisoner under your supervision escapes."

Agent Stoddard squirmed in his seat. "Sir, I will make up for it. That I promise you."

"Of course you will," Secretary Frye said quickly. "I have faith." He smiled blandly. "But Washington, D.C., is a complicated town. Lots of money at stake. Everyone wants power. Lots of competing interests."

"Sir?"

"Organizations within the current structure are not always on the same page. They can even be at odds. People within those organizations believe they know what's right for the country, and they act on those beliefs. But people can delude themselves. I believe this is the situation in which we now find ourselves."

Agent Stoddard nodded quickly. Frye could tell that he was lost. But it didn't matter. He would understand in time.

"The point is, sides are being set. Teams, if you will. And right now, there is a team working hard to thwart you. And me. And, quite honestly, the president. And no matter what your politics, you cannot work against the president. I suspect Reilly will soon be working against the interests of the president. So the question becomes, what do we do?"

"Find Reilly," Agent Stoddard answered quickly.

"That would be a start."

"And arrest him."

Frye said nothing. The car was silent. A lawnmower started somewhere down the block. Frye watched Stoddard's face as the realization of his new task dawned on him. "He might be armed," Stoddard said.

"He might be."

"We'll have to assume he is. And take appropriate precautions when we encounter him."

Secretary Frye let out a short breath. The message was sent, the course of action was clear. Men and women of commitment would do what needed to be done. "I have to get back to the Pentagon."

Stoddard nodded, then quickly fumbled with the car door handle with his cast-covered left hand. He opened the door and climbed out of the car, standing briefly on the pavement of the Silver Spring street. He bent low to be able to look into the back of the gray sedan.

"Sir, thank you for this chance," Stoddard said. "Homeland Security is on your side."

"Glad to hear it," Frye said, and shut the door.

67

SOUTHEAST WASHINGTON, D.C., APRIL 17, 8:22 PM

Murray's Meats and Cuts had clung to life for fifteen years, but it was a relic in D.C.'s gritty Southeast side—a kosher butcher in an all-black neighborhood—and it had finally succumbed a year ago, going out of business with hardly a single local noticing its demise.

That it hadn't been occupied in twelve months was good. That it was on a bad block, in a worse neighborhood, was better. That it sat across the street from a phone company switching station—an anonymous brick structure ringed with barbed wire—was perfect.

The team trickled in one by one, careful to show up after dark. Bingo was first. He'd been there already that afternoon, shown around by an eager—Bingo would say desperate—commercial real estate broker who swore he could get him the space for $1.50 per square foot. He'd even throw in the first month free.

Bingo noted to himself that there were no security sensors, not even a basic alarm, and then apologized for wasting the broker's time. "Just not right for us," he said. He returned that evening with a crowbar, a bolt cutter, and a flashlight, and cut his way into the rear entrance. The electricity was still on in the place—Bingo had noticed that, too—but he kept the lights out for security reasons.

Alexis arrived next. She'd been on the move for the last two days, never staying in one place for more than a few hours. She had spent half a day on buses, slept in a movie theater, and showered at a YWCA using a friend's ID. When she got to Murray's, she approved of it right away. It was big, and isolated, if a bit gloomy. There was a freezer in back where they could house server computers, and multiple 220 outlets on every wall. No one could see in from the street—the windows had all been smashed in, and then boarded up with plywood—and no one was looking, anyway; that was the point of the crappy neighborhood. Alexis thought the splashes of blood on the walls of the cutting room were a bit gothic, but all in all, she could live with them. She gave the place a thumbs-up. Bingo took the praise with tempered enthusiasm; he seemed, to Alexis, to be sulking. She didn't care. She didn't have time to care.

Patmore, the Marine liaison, came next. He was the only service member Garrett said he trusted, and so he was the only one that Alexis had contacted. He arrived out of uniform, in sweatpants and a hoodie, and he seemed game for the challenge. In fact, he seemed downright excited.

"I love crazy," Patmore told Alexis. "And this seems way crazy."

That his superiors in the Corps had not signed off on this adventure was not mentioned. Alexis assumed Patmore knew, and if he didn't, well, he would find out soon enough.

"People gonna shoot at us?" was all he asked, a bit too enthusiastically.

"I hope not," Alexis answered.

Patmore just laughed.

The CIA rep, Sarah Finley, had agreed to come as well—Alexis had reached her directly through the agency—and arrived next, riding her bike from her Georgetown condo, but she had official cover for the operation, and she knew it. If everything fell apart, her bosses at the agency would stand up for her. They were, unofficially at least, on Garrett Reilly's side. Everyone else was out in the cold. Finley, quiet and observant, said little and mostly watched from the shadows. To Alexis, she seemed to embody the essence of spook.

Alexis thought Jimmy Lefebvre would show last, if he showed at all. He seemed hesitant at the coffee shop that morning, and she didn't blame him. He wasn't DIA, wasn't a gung-ho Marine, and could potentially look forward to a long, safe career at the Army War College. He would be risking all. If he decided against joining their little escapade, Alexis was okay with that, but she hoped that he wouldn't turn around and report them to his superiors. He knew the address. He knew the time. And he had some sense of what they were up to. If Lefebvre talked to the Pentagon, they would be toast.

Garrett limped in at eleven that evening. Alexis thought he looked terrible—smashed up and weak, with bits of leaves and dirt in his hair. She could see that he was trying to keep pain from registering on his face. She considered calling the whole thing off and taking him straight to the hospital, but he smiled broadly and said, "Show me the place, will you?"

She toured him through the rooms and the meat locker, and he seemed pleased; he was most pleased about being able to wash up with warm water in the kitchen.

She watched silently as he scrubbed the dirt from his cheeks.

"Thanks for the key," Garrett said, "for the handcuffs."

"Sure," Alexis answered, searching for something to add, but failing.

"Came in useful."

"I figured."

They stared at each other awkwardly, then Garrett walked out without saying another word, to continue his tour.

Lefebvre rolled in at midnight, looking wary. He gave the place a once-over and seemed ready to bolt out the door. But then Garrett grabbed his hand and shook it.

"I really appreciate your coming, Lieutenant," he said. "I know this is a risk for you. And way outside of what you'd normally do."

Lefebvre still looked dubious. Garrett leaned close, and Alexis heard him whisper: "It's going to be a battle, Jimmy. And I need soldiers."

The lieutenant seemed to stiffen, and then relax. His shoulders dropped a bit. He let out a deep breath. He looked like he might stay.

Alexis shook her head in mild wonderment: Did Garrett know about Lefebvre's medical condition? How the hell had he found that out? And was he using the lure of combat to get Lefebvre's commitment? If he was, it was brilliant. *Garrett Reilly had learned how to lead.* It seemed so unlikely, given the unformed clay that Garrett had been at the start of the process, and yet the proof was in front of her: Lefebvre was on board, and it had been Garrett's words that had secured him.

The group of them—six, including Garrett—assembled in the front room of the store, gathering by a dusty display case. Garrett smiled weakly at them, and Alexis thought she could see him wince in pain.

"You're all here, which means there's no backing out now. We're in this until the end. Together. A team. And I don't have to remind any of you that we also have a team member in China, on her own. At risk. She's our responsibility as well."

There were somber nods of acknowledgment from the group.

"A friend of mine should arrive in a couple of hours with our equipment," Garrett continued. "We'll assemble it, load software, cable up and get online. After that, we're going to be housebound for the next couple of days. No going in and out. No seeing friends. We can't let anyone spot us. We are underground, off radar, and we need to stay that way. My friend's gonna bring cell phones too. A dozen for each of you. You get to make three phone calls from each one, no personal calls, then you'll have to pop out the battery and toss the phone. People will be looking for us, and they will be looking hard." Garrett fixed them each with a hard stare. "If we get compromised, we're finished, so"—he motioned to the darkened store—"I hope you guys like abandoned butcher shops."

There were chuckles from the group.

"I think Bingo should be the only one of us who can leave and come back," Garrett continued. "He'll get food, whatever else we need. But nothing exotic. I don't want him going farther than a couple of blocks. There's old mattresses in the storage room. They're nasty, but it wouldn't be a terrible idea to grab a little sleep, because once we get started, it's going to be pretty much nonstop."

Alexis watched as the others nodded in the gloom. Bingo pointed a flashlight around the room, and she could barely make out their faces. Maybe it was her own tension ratcheting up, but Alexis thought she saw a few of them stand a little straighter, their bodies ready for action.

"Any questions?"

After a moment, Patmore, the Marine, raised his hand and stepped forward with a grin. "Yeah, just one. Is this gonna work?"

"I have no idea," Garrett said, shrugging and walking out of the room.

Well, he hasn't gotten that polished at leading, Alexis thought, because he sure hasn't learned how to lie yet.

She found him, twenty minutes later, curled up on a mattress in the back corner of the dimly lit freezer. She sat down next to him, tucked her knees up to her chest, and watched him silently in the semidarkness. His breathing was ragged. He rolled over after a few minutes and peered at her.

"Can't sleep when I'm being watched," he said.

"Sorry. I'll go." She started to stand.

"No. Stay," he said. "I wasn't sleeping anyway."

Alexis sat back down. "How're you feeling?"

"I'll survive. I think." He flashed her a faint smile, still lying sideways on the mattress. "I always wondered what it would be like to be tortured. Now I know."

"And can you recommend the experience?"

"Absolutely. Big stress reliever. All your other troubles pale in comparison."

Alexis laughed. Garrett pushed himself to an upright position. Alexis gathered up her courage, then said, "Garrett, I wanted to say that—"

Garrett cut her off sharply: "No."

She stared at him, surprised, and slightly hurt.

"It's too complicated," he said, his voice softening. He stared at her, his blue eyes shimmering in the darkness. "You and me. We need simple. Right now, we need to focus on the task at hand. We need to get through this."

"Okay," she said, nodding and staring off into the darkness. "Sure."

"And we will get through this."

68

QUEENS, NEW YORK, APRIL 17, 11:31 PM

Mitty Rodriguez got the phone call from Garrett at seven-thirty on Tuesday morning and immediately went to work. First, she dropped off the grid. She had an alias from her hacker days—Sarah Beaumont, which Mitty thought was a pretty hilarious white-girl name—and a bunch of fake IDs, including a driver's license and a debit card under her Beaumont name that she could fill up with cash. She swapped out the SIM card on her cell phone, checked around her block for surveillance—she didn't see any—then bought herself a pair of movie-star sunglasses, just for stylin', and was ready for action.

Next she hit the regular computer stores in New York City—Best Buy, J&R, Radio Shack—then ransacked the spare-parts bins in the electronics specialty joints on Flushing Boulevard. All the while, she was on the phone with her underground suppliers—the geeks, tech heads, hackers, and miscreants who built their own machines, souped up their own hard drives, and soldered their own motherboards. It was with them that she spent the big bucks. Garrett had transferred two hundred grand into her debit account, so money was not much of an issue. She visited her underground suppliers only after the sun went down. It was safer that way.

By eleven-thirty that night she had filled up her rented half-ton van with a hacker's vision of paradise: monitors, keyboards, internal hard drives, external hard drives, work station shells, server boxes, routers, HDMI and SATA cables, coax cables, webcams, color printers, laser printers, digital projectors, fans, heat sinks, flash memory, card readers, phone jacks, landlines, cell phones, digital relay boxes. And then there were the chips she had bought, almost all from her black-market sources: boxes full of dual-core processors, quad-core processors, hacked military parallel processors, stolen Intel chips, experimental AMD chips, underground Chinese chips that Mitty was pretty sure were fake but that she bought anyway because, well, what the fuck, she had the money. Plus enough video cards to power every gamer's computer from Boston to Virginia.

While she was running around the city, collecting hardware, she logged her personal machine onto a hijacked server in Florida. From the Florida zombie server she downloaded every possible hacking tool she could think of: Nmap network mapping software for security auditing; a turbo-charged update of John the Ripper for password hacking; TCP port scanning software for finding network entry vulnerabilities; Kismet electronic network sniffers for sussing out intrusion bugs; Wireshark for browsing network mainframes; pOf for fingerprinting the operating software on a target network; Yersinia for hunting down weaknesses in IP protocols. All part of the basic toolkit of a network hacker. Some of these programs she knew from working with them herself, others had come recommended to her, others still she had heard rumors of but had never dared put on her own machine for fear they would prove uncontrollable, turning her own hacking fortress into a corrupted machine in thrall to some other hacker, in some other godforsaken part of the world. That scenario was to be avoided at all costs—to be hacked by a hacker was a mark of deep shame.

All told, it cost her $93,546.88, which she thought was a pretty good deal.

She made her last purchase just after midnight, meeting an acne-covered Russian teenager in front of Gray's Papaya at Seventy-second and Broadway. He said his name was Sergei, but Mitty guessed that was an alias, not that she gave a damn—the kid came highly recommended. In hacker circles he was considered King Shit, a magic man who could break into any network, anywhere, anytime. Mitty transferred $25,000 into his bank account from her mobile phone (she loved that she even had $25,000 to transfer—thank you, Garrett Reilly), and he handed her a 32-gig flash drive.

"Any instructions?" she asked him.

"Yes," he said with a trace of a Russian accent. "Don't use it to hack NORAD. They get pissed off, try to kill you."

Mitty grinned. "Fucking awesome."

Then, with her van full of goodies, and the passenger seat loaded with beef jerky and Mountain Dew, Mitty headed south on Interstate 95 toward Washington, and drove through the night. She made it to D.C. by four in the morning, easily found the address Garrett had sent her, parked in an alley, then watched delightedly as a team of grunts, geeks, and bureaucratic types hauled the bounty into a vacant storefront and warehouse.

Mitty didn't have an opinion yet about the rest of them, but she liked being around the soldiers, all that muscle and short hair. It made her weak-kneed, even though she knew she didn't have a chance with any of them. A girl could dream.

Then she saw Garrett. The boy looked like shit: pale, like he hadn't seen the sun in months, which she guessed might have been the case, and skinny, way too skinny. He was glad to see Mitty, gave her a hug, but she thought she saw him wince a couple of times, as if walking—even just talking—was painful for him. She asked him if he was okay, and he waved her off, said yeah, sure, just tired, but she didn't buy it. He reminded her of a friend who'd been in a massive car accident and spent the next two years limping around with a cane.

She hoped to God Garrett would be okay. She loved Garrett. He was a no-shit pain in the ass, but also, underneath it all, one of the very good guys.

Garrett toured her through their new home, Murray's Meats and Cuts. Mitty said she thought the place was gross, but Garrett pointed out that freezers and cutting machines had drawn a lot of power, so the wiring was adequate to run all her new toys without fear of setting off alarms at Potomac Electric. Or blowing fuses. Also, they could force the freezer air into the rest of the store, to cool off the computers. She agreed it was clever, but still kind of bogus; if she'd wanted to work at a butcher shop there was an Italian place that was always looking for help around the corner from her apartment in Queens.

They spent the early morning setting up the computers. Garrett and his military goons dealt with the off-the-shelf, prebuilt computers—they just plugged them in and loaded them up with software. Easy as pie, from Mitty's point of view. Garrett introduced Mitty to Bingo, whom she had spoken to on the phone a whole bunch, and then the two of them got down to building the fancier, more exotic machines. She liked Bingo. He was a true geek, a misfit from birth, way more interested in machines and the numbers that they spewed out than actual people. And though he was a little on the heavy side—and Mitty was not one to cast stones, anyway—she thought he was damn cute. And big. Way big. He stammered when she stared at him. She dug that.

Him, she could fuck. Mitty made it a personal goal to sleep with him within forty-eight hours. Time allowing, of course. And also if she could find something resembling a bed to do it in.

The two of them assembled a pair of paralleled machines, each running quad processors and a fucking ton of memory, then loaded Sergei's Armageddon intrusion software on the master computer, making sure to wall it off from the rest of the group's network. Mitty wasn't positive the kid hadn't written code that would simply make the computer explode and kill them all. He seemed like the type.

By noon everything was built and networked. Now they just needed to throw the switch and tap into a mainline Web artery. Alexis Truffant—Garrett's prissy West Point bitch—said she'd already arranged for an OC-3 Internet connection, paid for anonymously, without any tracking info, that would come right in off the Verizon relay station across the street, but Mitty didn't buy that for a second. First off, if this was going to be a true underground hacking operation, then they should tap directly into a hulking OC-48 and get them some of that sweet 54 gigabytes per second, without signing up for anything, anywhere. And they should do it themselves. That was hacker credo. Secondly, where did this Alexis chick get off bossing everyone around, with her tight T-shirt and perky tits? Mitty hated women like that, acting like they owned the fucking world, and all the men in it. They made her want to barf.

Mitty argued her point for a while, but Garrett overruled her, and they fired up Alexis's connection. Everything seemed to work fine, but Mitty warned them not to do anything obviously backdoor until they were sure the hookup was really invisible. For that purpose, she booted up the TCP scanner she'd downloaded the day before. It worked like a broad-spectrum radar, but in reverse, letting her know whether she was visible to other people trying to find her. Their port of entry onto a backbone connection seemed to be throwing out multiple, simultaneous IP return numbers—meaning anyone trying to trace their activity would end up staring at a list of thousands, if not millions, of randomly generated addresses. This was good, Mitty thought, but she still wanted one extra layer of protection, so she told Garrett first thing tomorrow morning she would start hunting for the link to the nearest fat cable and patch them into that on a secondary feed.

But not now. Now she needed to sleep. And to work on getting Bingo in the sack.

69

BAODING, CHINA, APRIL 18, 11:48 AM

Hu Mei rode her Flying Pigeon bicycle happily down the uncrowded streets of the old neighborhood of Baoding, a small city some ninety miles west of Beijing. "Small" being relative, of course. There were more than a million people dodging in and out of the traffic of Baoding, but to Mei, who was still getting used to the extreme urbanization of coastal China, a million wasn't so bad. It paled in comparison to the manic pace of Shanghai. Baoding, she decided, was her kind of city.

And the Flying Pigeon bicycle, provided to her by a supporter in the northern suburbs, was definitely her kind of bicycle: it was at least as old as she was, a good thirty years, if not older, rusted in parts, paint flecking off the chassis, but it was sturdy and dependable. It didn't call attention to itself like some of the gleaming mountain bikes she saw young men pedaling, and that was perfect for Mei. She absolutely could not afford to call attention to herself. Not now, after the near disaster in Chengdu, and then all the hard work she'd done in the last week to calm her followers and make sure they were safe. She had dispersed her inner circle to points around China; she had decentralized the leadership. Some had complained—they wanted constant access to her—but Hu Mei knew it was the right thing to do. The only thing to do.

Mei allowed a brief glimmer of pride to puncture her usual modesty: with her back to the wall, she had kept the movement—and herself—alive. That made her quietly proud. And happy. Of course it made others in China considerably less happy. The party was ratcheting up the pressure: rumor had it that if you as much as mentioned the word *Tiger* on the street you could land in jail. You could be beaten. You might be executed.

The thought of it made her blood boil. Innocent people, jailed and dying, and for what? Saying the wrong word? It was obscene.

Two men were following her, also riding bicycles. They rode twenty meters behind her, seemingly uninterested in the young woman pedaling ahead of them, but in fact watching every intersection, every sidewalk, for signs of the police or agents of the Ministry of State Security. There was a third rider, half a block ahead of them, scanning the streets for roadblocks or security checkpoints or the closed-circuit surveillance cameras that seemed to be springing up on every corner. If they came across a temporary barricade or a phalanx of policemen, the lead rider would make a quick hand signal to Hu Mei, telling her to veer left or right. The lead rider would then go through the checkpoint, just to throw off suspicion. Dodging a roadblock registered immediately as suspicious behavior, and the police took suspicious behavior as a tacit admission of guilt, and then proceeded accordingly. Once again—prison, beatings, death.

But the police—and the party—still did not know what she looked like. She had seen a few leaflets distributed here and there, but none of the doctored photographs on those handouts looked anything like her. It would be a miracle if someone recognized her from the government's description. So for now, the warm sun shining on her face, the spring breeze caressing her hair, Hu Mei was still safe.

But today would be a test of that safety. Today would be a radical step outside the tried-and-true path. Today could get her killed. Or today could be the opening she had been looking for. She hoped for the best—and prayed she had prepared adequately for the worst.

She turned left on Yonghua Street, past the Xiushui shopping center, with its slabs of hastily erected white concrete walls, and started looking in earnest for the restaurant where the meeting was supposed to take place. The restaurant—Ming's Family Style, it was called—was run by a middle-aged man sympathetic to the cause. His father had died in a reeducation camp during the Cultural Revolution, starved to death by a cadre of comrades overeager to prove their fidelity to the Maoist cause. The government had never apologized, had barely bothered to alert the survivors of the patriarch's death, and the family had never forgotten that. They nursed a lifelong grudge. That made them valuable to Hu Mei. That made them loyal.

She spotted the sign for Ming's Family Style halfway down the block. She slowed her Flying Pigeon, searching the cramped street for any signs of a police presence, or just simple surveillance. But there was none, at least none that Hu Mei could see, only a sign over the restaurant that boasted that they served the best *lǘ roù huǒ shāo*—baked wheat cake stuffed with minced donkey meat, a Baoding specialty—of any establishment in the city. Mei laughed: she had seen the same pronouncement on practically every sign for every restaurant for the last ten blocks. They loved their donkey meat in Baoding. Hu Mei was no fan of that supposed delicacy, but she was starving after having ridden her bicycle twenty miles into town, so even a little donkey would be a welcome prize at this point.

The hunger in her belly mixed with the low-level anxiety in her blood as she parked her bicycle and scanned the plate-glass window in the front of Ming's. A family sat eating lunch at the counter. An older couple sipped tea by the window, a bowl of steaming soup between them. They were not what Hu Mei was looking for. Besides a waiter and a cook peeking out from behind a glass-bead curtain, the restaurant was empty. Disappointment washed over Mei. Was this the wrong restaurant? Did she have the time wrong? No, it was ten minutes after noon. Or had she been tricked? Were the police about to swoop down on this tiny street and arrest her?

A young soldier stepped out of a jewelry store down the block, and Hu Mei had a moment of gut-wrenching panic, but he only picked at his gums with a toothpick, spit loudly on the sidewalk, and strolled off in the opposite direction, unconcerned with Mei or anyone else on the street. Mei exhaled loudly, then peered back into Ming's.

And that was when she saw her: a young woman stepping out of the bathroom in the back of the restaurant. She was pretty, Hu Mei's age, nicely dressed in a white blouse. Mei watched her for a moment, sizing up her face, her posture, her attitude, even the shoes on her feet. All these things Mei considered keys to understanding the intentions of another human being: a hunched-over person was slothful; a timeworn face could betray bitterness; flashy shoes might tell Mei that the person she was dealing with was a narcissist, more concerned with image than with substantive issues.

But this woman showed none of these things. She stood straight, she smiled, and her shoes were pale-blue running sneakers. Nikes, Hu Mei guessed.

Okay, Mei thought as she reached for the restaurant door, time to take another chance. Maybe the last one I'll ever take.

70

BAODING, CHINA, APRIL 18, 12:10 PM

Celeste Chen had to admit that the donkey cakes were not as bad as all that. Yes, they smelled odd, and the bread around the meat had been flecked with green, but the meat itself had been smothered in spices—she tasted fennel, cinnamon, pepper, and ginger—giving it a pungent kick that hid the fact she was eating a relative of the horse. And, anyway, it wasn't the taste that had sent her running to the bathroom.

It was her nerves.

Ever since she'd made contact with the journalist in Hebei who had promised to connect her with Hu Mei, her stomach had been tied in knots. She found it incredible that she would be taken into anybody's confidence, much less that of a Chinese journalist and follower of the now infamous Tiger, but she quickly realized that Hu's followers were everywhere. What had seemed like a random encounter with a member of the insurgency's inner circle had soon revealed itself to only be scratching the surface. After two days in Shanxi Province, it seemed to Celeste that half the people she met, no matter how random the encounter, knew who Hu Mei was, and most of them supported her. To Celeste, it quickly became clear why the government was so terrified of the Tiger.

They had every reason to be. This was more than a grassroots movement. This was a tsunami.

The journalist had told Celeste she would need to be vetted, and so she had spent a day waiting in a cinder-block shack in the coal mountains of Shanxi, being interviewed by a series of young men and women, each asking variations on the same questions: Where was she born? Was she really American? How come she spoke such flawless Mandarin? Why did she want to meet the Tiger? Had she ever worked for the Communist Party?

Celeste's answers had been consistent. She had nothing to hide, and so she hid nothing. She told them up front that she worked for a man who worked for the American military. To her questioners this was startling news—most Chinese had been led to believe that Americans who worked for the military were gruff, aggressive, and innately hostile to anything Chinese. And yet here was a young woman who blended in seamlessly in China, who was open, honest, friendly, and seemed ready to help the cause.

But there was one problem: she wanted to meet Hu Mei herself.

So it had been more waiting, in multiple locations: a factory warehouse, a hotel room, the back of a darkened movie theater. More questions. More answers. More probing about her motives. Another move, this time to a family home in the country where Celeste slept in a barn on a mattress next to a pair of dogs and a chicken that clucked all night.

And then this morning. Word of a planned meeting. An address, a restaurant, a time. A ride in the back of a rattling Toyota pickup truck, dust flying everywhere as they careened across half-paved roads. And the subsequent butterflies in Celeste's stomach. Three times on the drive she thought she would throw up; as they passed army barracks and trucks full of green-uniformed soldiers, she told herself that she had been crazy to volunteer. She was no spy, no adventurer. She was an academic, a bookworm, a shut-in. Why in God's name had she gone along with Garrett's plan?

Perhaps it had been a wave of patriotism. But that couldn't be right, because in her more reflective moments she felt just as loyal to China as she did to the United States. Perhaps that was it, then—her loyalty to China meant working for change, and Hu Mei seemed an opening to that. But even that seemed far-fetched. Except for a week-and-a-half stint asking for signatures for a gay-marriage ballot initiative in California, Celeste had not once been politically motivated. She hated politics and nationalism. They seemed to miss the point of life. Life was learning and love and relationships.

She guessed that she'd been volunteered because she'd grown close to Alexis, Garrett, and the Ascendant team, had come to see their cause as her cause, and had, psychologically at least, made their goals hers. So when Garrett proposed the mission to China to find the Tiger, Celeste had eventually said yes. Not because she wanted to, or thought it was a good idea. She had said yes because she wanted to make Garrett happy.

God, she thought, my psyche is frail. That I voluntarily agreed to put my life on the line for something I just barely agree with, for a man who I often find completely obnoxious . . .

But there she was, standing in Ming's Family Style restaurant, having just gagged in the bathroom—not from the donkey meat, she reminded herself—waiting for possibly the most wanted person in all of China to come have tea with her. So that she herself might then become wanted, hunted, jailed. Maybe for the rest of her life.

If she were smart, had any shred of self-preservation left, she would run from the restaurant right now, grab a cab to the train station, a train to Beijing, and an economy seat in a 777 back to the safety of Westwood.

Then the door opened. Celeste's eyes snapped forward. A young woman, not more than a few years older than Celeste herself, walked into the restaurant. She was pretty, with a high forehead and brown eyes, her hair tucked up under a baseball cap with an Adidas logo on it. She wore a windbreaker over a plain white T-shirt.

Celeste dismissed her at first: that couldn't be her. She was too young, had no bodyguards, no minders. She didn't seem to have a care in the world.

The young woman looked once around the restaurant, as if taking in all the customers and staff, and then, satisfied, fixed her eyes on Celeste. She walked up to her, bowed quickly, then squinted as she studied Celeste's face.

"You are from America?" she asked in Mandarin.

Celeste stammered, surprised by the directness of her question. "American. Yes." And then added, "I grew up in California."

The young woman nodded, considering this information. Then she did a remarkable thing. At least it was remarkable to Celeste. The young woman smiled. It was a wide, white smile, open and vulnerable. It made her seem even younger than her age, which wasn't very old to begin with. But more than young, her smile made her seem warm. It made her seem inviting. Celeste was captivated.

"This is embarrassing for me," the young woman said, looking down at the ground as she said it. "And please don't think ill of me for it." She looked back up at Celeste. "But I've never met anyone from America before."

Celeste started to say something, but then changed her mind. She had no idea how to respond. The young woman grinned again. "In fact, I don't think I've ever met anyone from any other country but China. I suppose that makes me a *xiāng bā lǎo*," she said. "A real country bumpkin."

The woman laughed. Her laugh was just as open and disarming as her smile, and just as infectious. Celeste, despite herself, laughed with her, and all of a sudden, in that one moment, all her anxiety drained away. Maybe it was that Celeste was far from home, scared and lonely, and looking for a place to hide her fears, but in that instant she understood exactly why this woman, the Tiger, could lead a rebellion. She was magnetic. Vibrant. Real. Celeste felt—and she suspected that everyone must feel the same way when they met her—that this woman would never betray anyone.

It was so obvious—*she didn't have it in her.*

71

SOUTHEAST WASHINGTON, D.C., APRIL 18, 6:11 AM

Garrett smiled as he read the encrypted e-mail from Celeste one more time: I met her this morning. She is on board.

She? Garrett said to himself. The Tiger was a woman?

Fascinating. Garrett liked that. It was unexpected. The Communist Party probably found it unexpected as well. Maybe that was why the Tiger's movement had been so hard to snuff out. Perhaps being a woman in China meant something that Garrett had yet to understand. He made a mental note to research that theory, then got up to find Alexis. She was sitting at a computer monitor at the far end of the main room.

"Celeste made contact. I just got the e-mail," he said, the words tumbling out. "The Tiger is in. On board with us."

Alexis lit up with the news: "Really? That's fantastic."

"Yeah. And you know what else? The Tiger"—Garrett grinned, eyes sparkling with mischief—"is a woman."

Alexis blinked. "No shit?" She let out a short laugh. "I guess we didn't see that coming. But I mean—why not a woman, right? The next Mao is female. Wow."

Garrett watched her as she thought through the implications of this information, head cocked sideways slightly. The idea seemed to please her as much as it did him. Then he thought he detected a trace of sadness flashing in her eyes.

"That means we move to the next phase," she said. "Time for me to go see Kline."

"Yeah, that's what it means." Garrett nodded. They had discussed this at length: she would have to convince Kline to give Garrett what he wanted, and she would need to do it in person. Once Alexis showed her face at the Defense Intelligence Agency building she would not be able to return to Murray's Meats and Cuts. Homeland Security would be all over the DIA. There would be surveillance teams, military police, the works.

So this was goodbye.

Garrett and Alexis stepped into the alley behind the store. The sun had risen. The temperature was climbing. A few blocks away a siren wailed and then faded out. They said very little. She asked if he was ready, and he said he was.

He asked if she knew what he needed.

"I do," she said. "And Kline is going to flip out."

"This whole thing—this whole project—is his stupid idea."

"Let's hope he remembers that when I ask him."

She took his hand, and just held it. They hadn't made actual physical contact in the eighteen hours they'd spent at the storefront. Her skin felt warm and soft. He clutched her hand tightly.

"Okay," she said. "I'm going."

She smiled. He stared into her eyes, then let go of her hand. "Stay safe."

"You too," she said, and walked down the alley and disappeared around a corner. Garrett watched her go, and waited for that hole to open up in his chest.

But it didn't. And that was another pattern.

72

USS *DECATUR*, SOUTH CHINA SEA, APRIL 18, 6:42 PM

Ensign James Hallowell stood at the rail of the USS *Decatur* and watched the sun set brilliantly, streaming tendrils of red, orange, and purple over the South China Sea. The *Decatur* was cutting swiftly through ten-foot swells, parting the water effortlessly. The big ship—an Arleigh Burke–class destroyer—was steaming due west, aimed ten degrees north of the sunset. Behind her, spread out in a line over ten kilometers, was the rest of the 11th Carrier Strike Group: an aircraft carrier, a cruiser, and four more destroyers. Somewhere around them, unseen, a Virginia-class nuclear-powered attack submarine zigzagged one hundred feet below the ocean's surface. Together, they were as potent a military machine as could be found on the planet, with enough munitions and firepower to destroy almost any foe. Even so, they were not invulnerable.

The air was warm and humid; a tropical storm had just passed over the ship, dumping rain onto its steel decks. A few sailors had been allowed above deck to feel the rain on their skin. The *Decatur* had been steaming hard and fast for the last four days, and everyone on board had been glued to stations 24/7. A ten-minute break, standing in real weather, instead of the digital glow of radar and firing systems, was a welcome diversion.

Ensign Hallowell watched the sun slip below the horizon. He figured it was still shining in China, 700 kilometers west of their position. Probably even still shining on the Chinese destroyers they knew were shadowing them, just past visual sighting distance, just over the curvature of the earth: four Jiangwei

II–class frigates, packed with antiship missiles, helicopters, torpedoes. Enough firepower to give the *Decatur* a run for its money.

Thirty years ago, Hallowell thought, the Chinese navy had been a bunch of rowboats, junks with sails and coolies. But, man, that country has been kicking ass since then. Kicking ass and building a naval force that was top-notch, second only to the U.S. Navy. The Chinese were smart, and they had money to burn. And that scared the crap out of him.

Those Chinese frigates had been keeping a parallel course with the Americans for the last thirty-six hours, just out of sight, but well within missile range, and Hallowell knew that those missiles flew fast and low: Mach .9, twenty meters above the ocean. From just over the horizon, it would take one hundred and twenty seconds for a Chinese missile to reach the *Decatur*. If hostilities broke out, Hallowell would have two minutes to say his prayers and launch a return salvo. Two minutes of breathing space, and then it was in God's hands who lived and who went up in flames.

The thought sent shivers down his spine. He had phoned his wife—back in Dallas—four days earlier, when they'd been a hell of a lot closer to Hawaii, and told her this was just another cruise—a sun tour, he called it—but he'd been lying. Rumors had been flying all week: the Chinese were mobilizing, troops gathering on the coast opposite Taiwan, air force flying sorties off Japan; the Americans were sailing extra ships to the South China Sea, and the U.S. 8th Army in South Korea was on high alert. A shooting war was a real possibility.

Not everybody believed that. But Hallowell did. He did because he had been on deck when Commander Martinez got the word from PACOM, and while Hallowell hadn't heard the Washington side of the conversation, the look on Commander Martinez's face told him everything he needed to know. This was the real shit.

Hallowell chomped hard on his Dentyne. He hated chewing gum, but smoking was banned shipboard, and what the hell else was he going to do? He wished he could send a last e-mail to Britt, just tell her that he loved her, take care of the kids, make sure to remember to clean the filter in the air conditioner every couple of weeks, but the ship was on full lockdown now. No communication with anyone, anywhere. It was radio silence.

Damn it, he thought, spitting his wad of gum into the writhing ocean fifty feet below, he did not want to die, not out here, in the middle of the ocean, five thousand miles from everything he knew and loved. Burnt to a crisp, then sunk to the bottom of the sea. But he would if he had to. He would make the ultimate sacrifice for his country, and his fellow crewmen. And he would pray to God as he died that whatever started out here didn't spread back across the Pacific to the U.S. of A., because that really would be the end of the world.

The ship's klaxon rang three bells—everyone back to battle stations. High alert once again. That meant another twelve hours of staring at his fire radar. Which was okay with Hallowell. He had a job to do, and this was it.

If the Chinese wanted to get busy with the U.S. Navy, so be it. They could accomplish a lot in two minutes.

73

DIA HEADQUARTERS, BOLLING AFB, APRIL 18, 12:02 PM

"He wants what?" General Kline said, shutting the door to his DIA office. "Is he completely out of his mind?"

Alexis smiled, relaxing her body into the black leather chair. She was ready for this, had prepared for her boss's outrage; she knew what to say, the right tone to take. "Sir, you have as accurate a take on his sanity as I do."

"Don't play coy with me, Captain. A plane? Full of people? And he wants them in the air in a few hours? That is an enormous ask. The riskiest thing we've ever done."

"I know, sir."

"Have you brought it up with the CIA?"

Alexis looked around her boss's office. She knew it was soundproof and debugged—all senior DIA offices were—and that she could say whatever she wanted here, but still . . . you could never be too safe.

"We have a liaison from the agency with us. She's been informed."

Kline sunk into his chair. The worry was written all over his face. "They'll tell State, I guess. They'll have to."

"They might," Alexis said. "Depends."

"Frye has the president in his pocket. Homeland Security as well. They'll go nuts when this hits the news. State can't go up against the president. No way. This will be intelligence agencies against everybody else."

He let out a long, anxious breath. Alexis considered trying to say something supportive—an optimistic word of encouragement. But she couldn't think of any. At best, this would be a stealth operation that was finished before anyone realized it had happened—or could object. At worst, it would be a disaster that would turn into a gunfight between powerful bureaucracies, and there would be blood in the streets. Kline's blood. And hers. Not to mention the possibility of it touching off World War Three . . .

Her boss popped out of his chair again and began to pace his office furiously. "The Chinese are bristling. Have you been following the cables?"

"Another division positioned across the strait from Taiwan. Half the fleet steaming to meet us in the South China Sea. I have, sir."

"But they haven't gone public with it yet. They're waiting."

"They want us to fire the first shot."

"Just like Reilly said," Kline said. The general stopped pacing. Alexis could see a fine layer of sweat on his forehead. He shot a long, anxious look at Alexis.

"Does he know what he's doing?"

"I believe he does," she said.

"You're not saying that because you're in love with him, are you?"

That caught Alexis short. She felt an involuntary rush of blood to her face. She watched a sparrow flit from tree branch to tree branch outside Kline's office window. "No sir, I'm not."

"Not in love with him? Or not standing up for him because you are in love with him?"

"I'm basing my answer on a considered review of his behavior and a collective appreciation of what he's accomplished and predicted so far. As to whether I'm in love with him—that's none of your fucking business, sir. Respectfully."

Kline nodded. "You're right. Sorry I asked." Beyond him, through the window, Alexis could see gentle white clouds drifting slowly over the Potomac. They were so beautiful. So peaceful.

"If this fails, we don't just lose our jobs," Kline said. "We are disgraced, discharged, will probably go to jail. For a long time."

"I've considered that, sir."

"Are you prepared for that?"

"If we fail, people die. A lot of people. Maybe millions of people. Me in jail seems like a small price to pay."

Kline shook his head ferociously, as if working himself into agreement with her. "You're right. You're absolutely right." He turned to her. "Okay," he said. "Let's make it happen."

Alexis got up, saluted him, and headed for the door. He called after her.

"One other thing, Captain."

She stopped. "Sir?"

"I'll have to make myself scarce now."

Alexis said nothing.

"You they'll follow, hoping you lead them to Reilly. Me they'll haul in front of the president. And I will be obliged to tell him what I know."

"I understand," she said.

"Do you?" He said. "It means . . ."

"I'll be in charge," Alexis said, finishing his sentence.

"That is correct."

"And if they haul *me* in front of the president?" Alexis asked.

"You have no authority."

"But I know things."

"You were following orders. Implementing the Ascendant project, which was approved at the highest levels. "

"And if they order me to tell them where Reilly is?"

This time it was Kline who said nothing. She understood his silence: if they ordered her to reveal the whereabouts of Garrett Reilly, then she was on her own, in uncharted territory. Kline obviously hoped she'd say nothing, but he wasn't going to order her to defy the president.

That would be treasonous.

Alexis shifted her gaze from the general to the wide window behind him, and the clouds that blew, scattered, in strings of cottony white, over the river, which flowed out to the Atlantic. It occurred to her that no matter how seriously humans took their problems, nature didn't care; nature just went on its merry way, resplendent, sublime, awe-inspiring. Clouds over the Potomac. Gorgeous. It gave her strength.

"I understand," she said, saluting Kline one last time and heading out the door.

"Good luck," Kline called after her. "And Godspeed."

74

SOUTHEAST WASHINGTON, D.C., APRIL 18, 4:25 PM

Murray's Meats and Cuts was silent except for the occasional tap of fingers on a keyboard, or the crack of a Red Bull being opened. Garrett, standing above his central computer terminal, watched the blink of lights on his bank of monitors: bars and graphs, rising and descending, numbers scrolling, words unrolling, left to right, videos starting, buffering, finishing. His homegrown nerve center was in full swing.

There were twenty-four computers arrayed around him, not counting the servers in the freezer. Garrett had six monitors mounted in double rows on his desk, Mitty had four of her own, while everyone else had one, maybe two. Garrett had one monitor dedicated to tracking Internet traffic, another ran search trends from the big engines—Google, Yahoo, Bing, Baidu—to track the pulse of the world's queries. Mitty had brought him a stolen Bloomberg terminal, and a hacked Goldman Sachs account. He split that feed to everyone else in the store, so they could keep current on any trends he missed. It didn't really matter if anyone else was watching the markets—using a Bloomberg terminal was akin to breathing for Garrett. He didn't need anyone backing him up on those.

He had to admit he loved being in front of a market feed once again: the Dow, the LIBOR, the euro, Chicago futures, the Hang Seng, the DAX, the VIX . . . it was comforting to watch the world of commerce rush past his eyes. T-bills, gold prices, pork belly futures, the price of Brent Crude. It was like music to Garrett. The flow of digital information calmed his nerves. It even dulled the throbbing in his head.

And that throbbing had been explosive. Black spots had begun to appear and then vanish at the periphery of his vision. If he stood too quickly, the room spun and he had to grab the nearest chair or wall to keep from toppling over. His left arm went occasionally—and alarmingly—numb, shoulder to fingers. Garrett had never felt quite so mortal. It was as if he were eighty-six, not twenty-six. Death suddenly seemed . . .

No. He forced the thought from his mind.

On his fourth computer monitor Garrett ran a scan of dark net hacker websites and bulletin boards. He wanted to know what the underground was talking about at all times. A fifth ran RSS feeds from most of the big news sites. The sixth was hacked into a Pentagon video line that showed the position and strength of American troops and naval fleets. It had been remarkably easy to hack into the military's network, the NIPRNET, or Non-classified Internet Protocol Router Network, especially since he'd spent a good part of his week in the Pentagon war room collecting stray passwords and IP addresses. Even the most paranoid people were sometimes careless inside their own fortress.

Of course it was much harder getting onto the military's SIPRNET, or Secret Internet Protocol Router Network. In fact, it was impossible, completely sealed off from the rest of the World Wide Web. But that was okay. Garrett didn't need all of the military's secrets—just some of them.

He had six flat-screen televisions hung on the opposite wall, then mainlined to European and American news services—CNN, Fox, BBC, Sky News, France 24, Al Jazeera in English. He had another half dozen TVs hung just below the first set, these dedicated to Asian channels—China Central Television's channel 13, Hong Kong's i-Cable News, Japan's NHK News 7. He had them running continuously; a few were mentioning rumors of naval maneuvers in the South China Sea, while the BBC noted that large numbers of Chinese troops had been spotted north of Guangzhou.

Garrett left one screen unsecured to patch in to random stations from a satellite dish on the roof, and the last he tuned to Nickelodeon, just so they had something different to watch during the slow periods; Garrett had a soft spot for SpongeBob.

He rubbed his weary eyes, watched the motes of dust dance in the beams of the overhead light, shafts of brilliance in the otherwise darkened room. His eyes strayed to the map of world time zones on the right-hand wall. It was four-thirty in the afternoon in Washington. Beijing was exactly twelve hours ahead, four-thirty Thursday morning. Garrett watched the seconds tick by, watched the sine curve of sunlight on the time-zone map creep steadily westward.

His eyes snapped back and forth from screen to screen, from map to map, letting the waves of data wash over him. He let go of plans and concepts, attempting to immerse himself in the chaotic sea of information, in the pulse of the digital planet. He knew all eyes were on him, everyone in the room watching him for a sign, some signal that the time to act was now. The silence was like a blanket of expectation; a soft, quiet cover that kept the room on edge, but orderly and poised. Garrett knew that everyone felt it, that everyone was as edgy as he was, but there was no pushing the timetable. The moment would come, and he would say go, and then it would start. But before that, nothing.

A few hours ago, over a lunch of ham sandwiches, Gatorade, and Sun Chips, Garrett had tried to explain that everything had to be right, that all the disparate strands of events had to line up in order for the cumulative effect to work. It had taken half a day, for instance, just to finally get the encrypted e-mail from Celeste Chen out of China, but it had been worth it, because she was the linchpin; or, really, Hu Mei was the linchpin.

Garrett wondered what she was like. He had unscrambled a highly pixelated jpeg that Celeste had sent, but it was so blurry and undefined that it described little of the woman's features. Garrett studied it for an hour. She looked young, much younger than he would have guessed. And pretty. But her character? He couldn't tell.

Six-thirty in the evening, D.C. time. He wished he had some pot—that would help with his pain. But he knew he couldn't smoke now. He needed his mind clear. He realized he hadn't smoked pot in days, maybe even weeks, he couldn't remember, and even though he wished he had a joint, his deep craving for marijuana had lessened. That was a surprise, another shift in his personal patterns; everything about his life had been upended. He told himself he'd have to investigate this further, this lack of needing weed, because it might also be a sign that he was losing his edge. But not now; now he needed to focus.

Garrett checked one of the maps on the bank of computers in front of him, the second to the left, an air traffic control map. China, Japan, and the two Koreas appeared lit up on the screen. Hundreds of tiny airplane symbols crisscrossed the airspace between the four nations, heading east out over the vast Pacific, and south toward Australia. Fewer were aiming west into Central Asia and then onward toward Russia and Europe. None were flying into North Korean territory. It was a blackened no-man's-land, enemy state to all around it, but still something of a vassal to China.

Garrett stared at the blankness that was North Korea, the Hermit Kingdom. What did all those people think of the outside world? Did they know what they were missing? Was it an entire nation in the grip of Stockholm syndrome, where victims sided with their oppressors? Then again, wasn't all nationalism just a form of Stockholm syndrome, but by another name? Garrett certainly believed so, and yet here he was, giving everything he had for the interest of his home country. So was he, too, suffering from it?

Garrett reminded himself that he was here, now, because he'd run out of other options; working for the DIA provided him the best chance of staying out of the clutches of Homeland Security. And yet . . . he wished he could talk to Alexis about it. She would have an answer. Or at least a theory. He wondered where she was right now. Back at work? Detained? In jail?

Put her out of your mind. Clarity. What you need is clarity.

Another hour passed. And another. Eight-thirty at night on the East Coast of the United States. The sun was up over Beijing. Their day had started. The agony in his skull pulsed. Black spots danced across his eyes like crazed amoebas. Garrett took 1,200 milligrams of ibuprofen. And then another 1,200. He hoped that wasn't a toxic dose.

Lefebvre and Patmore were fidgeting at their terminals. Bingo rocked back and forth in his chair like an autistic seven-year-old. Mitty kept glancing at Bingo, smiling and winking. Had something gone on between them? Had Garrett missed it? They seemed an unlikely couple. Then again, there were weirder hypothetical couples in the world—Alexis and Garrett, for instance.

Garrett shook his head. What a ragtag army: geeks and misfits and semi-psychotic jarheads. And yet, every one of the team now appeared comfortable at their computers, fully plugged in to the dissonant symphony that was the Web. That gave him a measure of confidence. He clicked on the air traffic control map, enlarging it. He studied it, searching out the right call sign, the letters and numbers by which a commercial flight identified itself to international air traffic controllers. Qantas, Air China, Singapore Airlines. No, no, and no.

And then he spotted it. One small dot, curving gently southward over the Sea of Okhotsk, having just passed through Russian airspace and past the Kamchatka peninsula.

Garrett let out a long, silent breath. His eyes ran one last time over the half dozen computer screens, all linked together, blinking in front of him.

Okay. This was it. Time to do it. Time for a brave new world, brought to you by Garrett Reilly, Long Beach State graduate, bond analyst supreme, and soon to be, for one brief moment in time, a Master of the Universe. Garrett nodded to Lefebvre.

"Make the call," he said.

Lefebvre popped the battery into his first disposable cell phone.

75

THIRTY-NINE THOUSAND FEET ABOVE

THE SEA OF JAPAN, APRIL 20, 9:42 AM

Captain Leo Peterson checked the ACARS message that had just appeared on the MCDU, or management control display unit, of the Boeing 777 wide-body aircraft he was piloting. The early-morning sun was blasting through the right-hand cockpit window; they were high above the clouds that were scattered over the Sea of Japan. Captain Peterson flipped up his sunglasses and read the message. ACARS stood for aircraft communications addressing and reporting system; it was an airliner's equivalent of e-mail, and every commercial jet around the world sent and received them.

The message simply said: 15C24A.

The 15C24 stood for nothing. Only the last letter was meaningful. It was a prearranged code, sent from a United Airlines maintenance control center in Chicago, and Captain Peterson had expected it, and knew how to decipher it. It was simple, really. A last letter of "B" meant: *Do not do it. Cancel the operation.* But a last letter of "A" meant: *Go.*

He deleted the ACARS message, turned to his copilot, a Kentucky boy named Deakins, two years out of the Air Force, and nodded. They didn't want any verbal commands to register on the plane's cockpit voice recorder. A simple movement of the head would do. Deakins put his left hand on the engine thrust control, and dialed it back to zero. In moments, the plane's right engine—a Pratt & Whitney PW4000—sputtered and went silent. The plane shook as the airflow over the wing was disrupted.

Deakins adjusted the rudder trim to stabilize the plane, then upped the power in the left engine, exactly as procedure dictated in the event of an engine loss, while Captain Peterson punched in the radio code for an emergency—121.5 MHz, the international emergency frequency for any plane in distress.

"Captain," Deakins said in his Kentucky drawl, "we have lost power in our right engine. I believe it is an engine fire."

He was talking only for the benefit of the cockpit recorder.

Captain Peterson worked up as much panic as he could in his voice, then yelled into the microphone: "Mayday, mayday, mayday. This is United heavy 895, we are reporting right-engine fire and cabin smoke. Repeat, United heavy 895, engine fire and cabin smoke. We are declaring an emergency, need immediate runway clearance. Nearest airport."

He repeated himself two more times, then throttled back on the left engine and aimed the plane down.

Toward North Korea.

76

PYONGYANG, NORTH KOREA, APRIL 19, 9:51 AM

Soo Park had been a North Korean radar operator for ten years. He knew the country's radar profile by heart, could identify every friendly and hostile plane skirting North Korea's airspace in his sleep. But two months ago he'd asked for a transfer to the main air traffic controller's desk at the Sunan International Airport outside of Pyongyang. It was closer to his tiny apartment on the south side of the North Korean capital, the job carried a touch more prestige, and Soo Park was trying to find a bride. He needed all the prestige he could muster.

He claimed he spoke excellent English—a must for an air traffic controller—and had even passed the state's rudimentary English test. But in truth he'd cheated on the English test, promising a bottle of Canadian whisky to a friend of his who'd learned English while working as a diplomat at the embassy in Beijing. His friend had taken the test for him, aced it, and Soo Park had landed the job.

Only now Soo Park wished he hadn't. The truth was, Soo Park was quite a few levels below fluency. He could read an English-language book with a dictionary in his lap, but deciphering the spoken language was another task entirely. He strained to listen as the American pilot—Soo Park knew he was American because he'd tracked the flight a hundred times before, a Hong Kong–bound United 777—squawked into the radio again, his voice surrounded by a blast of static. He understood less than half the words: "... engine fire ... emergency landing ... runway ..." That was about it. Had the pilot said he was making an emergency landing here? *In Pyongyang?* That was impossible. Completely out of the question ...

Park's phone was ringing. It was the North Sector Radar Team, the team he used to be a part of. Yes, he answered, he had heard the distress call. And yes, he thought the American jetliner was headed for Pyongyang. Well, might be. He wasn't sure.

Yes, yes, he knew that could not happen. Absolutely could not.

The military called next, before Soo Park had a chance to catch his breath. They were scrambling four MiG-21s to intercept the plane. Soo Park was ordered to tell the 777 not to land here, no matter what the emergency. Yes, he would do that. Right away.

Soo Park hung up the phone and picked up his radio. "United 8-9-5! Do not land! Do not land Pyongyang. Must not land Pyongyang!"

The American captain came back on the radio immediately. "Negative, Pyongyang. We are experiencing thick cabin smoke. Must land Pyongyang. This is a mayday. Mayday situation. Please open FNJ runway 35 Right."

"No, no, no!" Soo Park yelled. "Cannot do this! Must not! Must not!"

"We have 277 souls on board this aircraft. We need to get on the ground right away. It is imperative."

Soo Park latched on to one word he understood. "Seoul! Yes. You go Seoul! Very close. You go Seoul!"

"No sir, souls. People. Two hundred seventy-seven. All will die if we do not land at Sunan International, FNJ. We are four minutes from wheels down, coming in hard. Please have emergency personnel on hand. We may have injuries."

Now all three phones were ringing in the cramped air traffic control room. Soo Park picked them up one after the other. First was radar, screaming, second was the military, third was the Central Party boss for the southern airport sector. Everyone was saying the same thing—tell that American plane to go somewhere else!

"I have tried," Soo Park pleaded with each of them in turn. "They say they have an engine fire and a fire in the cockpit. They will not turn around. I told them, but they will not listen."

Each of the callers hung up, furious and panicked in turn. Soo Park threw down his radio headset, shoved open the door to the air traffic control room, and ran up the two flights of dingy stairs to the main deck of the airport control tower. There, hovering over the ancient command and control radios that passed for ground-to-plane radar in North Korea, two of his fellow air traffic controllers stood wide-eyed and horrified at the broad window that gave them a view of Sunan International's main runway, 35 Right.

In the distance, barely visible, was a 777, coming in low and fast, followed tightly by a squadron of North Korean People's Air Force fighters. A thin trail of white smoke seemed to be billowing from the nose of the plane.

It was coming in for a landing. Right square in the middle of *his* airport.

77

SOUTHEAST WASHINGTON, D.C., APRIL 18, 10:01 PM

Garrett watched the news feed as it appeared on the AP wire. First reports were in: United wide-body jet forced to make emergency landing, Pyongyang, North Korea. All passengers reported safe. No injuries.

Garrett let out a long, relieved breath. There had been a very real possibility the North Korean Air Force would shoot the plane down before it could land. Garrett figured they wouldn't, that they'd pull back at the last second, but he couldn't completely dismiss the risk, so they had stocked half the plane with ex-military officers, State Department contractors, and federal volunteers, all with cover stories.

Garrett scrolled quickly through the falsified passenger manifest, checking the names and their purported places of residence. He signed off on it, then forwarded it to Patmore. He waved the Marine lieutenant over.

"Call everyone on your media list, starting at the top: the *New York Times*, *Washington Post*, CNN. Blanket coverage," he said. "You are an airline employee, and you are leaking the passenger manifest. Then hang up."

"Yes sir," Patmore answered.

Garrett's eyes scanned the news screens on his computer terminals. Sites were picking up the AP release. The story would top the news cycle for the next twenty-four hours, until the next explosion of news would bump it from that perch. But twenty-four hours was plenty of time for Garrett's purposes. Asian stock markets were all open now; news of the plane incident would begin to reach traders in about ten minutes. Uncertainty was poison to an exchange;

volatility would start to climb. It would be off the charts in a few hours. And that was just the beginning.

Garrett walked out of the darkened computer room and into the meat locker. The room was cold. It smelled faintly of old food. Garrett stood over the paralleled computers that Mitty and Bingo had set up, the ones with the Russian shell intrusion software on it. They were humming quietly. He plugged an ethernet cable into a port in the back of one of the machines. It was connected to the Web now. Whatever it had on its hard drive was milliseconds away from being loosed on the world. That would be step two.

He executed the program and waited for the show to start.

78

BEIJING, APRIL 19, 10:48 AM

Xu Jin, director of the Ministry of State Security, was having trouble understanding the news. An American commercial jetliner had made an emergency landing in Pyongyang? That was the closest airport? Couldn't they have flown the extra hundred miles to Seoul? By landing in North Korea they had placed themselves squarely in an international incident. Had the pilot no sense at all? What a fool. And what a headache for the Chinese. Already the American ambassador had called twice to demand Chinese intervention with the North Korean government.

As if we control those lunatics in Pyongyang! Xu Jin scowled and lit a Zhonghua cigarette, the most expensive brand in China. They were a hundred dollars a carton. Not that Xu Jin ever bought his own cigarettes: they were given, as were a constant stream of gifts, by groveling supplicants and party underlings. As the old saying went: The people who buy Zhonghua don't smoke it, and the people who smoke Zhonghua don't buy it.

The phone rang. It had been ringing since Xu Jin had walked into his office an hour ago.

"Yes?" he barked, irritated.

"Director Xu, we have a problem." It was one of the functionaries in the Internet Subdivision. His name was Yuan Gao. Or something like that. Their offices were in a warehouse in Beijing's Haidian district, mixed in among the university students and IT workers. The place smelled of sweat and fried pork. Xu Jin avoided the computer techs whenever possible.

"What is it? You know I have other things to deal with."

"Yes, Director Xu, I know this. But there is a problem with Golden Shield."

Xu Jin exhaled a great ball of gray cigarette smoke and growled. There was always a problem with Golden Shield, the censorship wall that the ministry had erected around all of China's incoming and outgoing Internet traffic: the wall was porous; the computer servers were down; there was a virus, and it was malicious; the virus was from inside China—no, it was foreign, from Russia, or the U.S. It was constant din, and Xu Jin understood almost none of it.

Every time they tried to tighten the specifications of Golden Shield, making it harder for Chinese citizens to access subversive or antigovernment information, another crack appeared in the wall someplace else. There were too many hackers with time on their hands—like that greasy moron Gong Zhen—always sticking their adolescent fingers where they didn't belong, usually into the gears of the Chinese government. Although, Xu Jin had to admit, Gong Zhen and his hacking team had done a masterful job with the American power-plant virus. That had succeeded beyond his wildest expectations.

"So," Xu Jin growled. "What is the problem?"

"A worm has slipped through the wall," the Internet functionary bleated.

"There is always a worm or a virus," Xu Jin interrupted. "Just fix it. Deal with it. I have an incident in North Korea to deal with."

"That's just it, Director Xu. I cannot fix it."

Xu Jin stubbed out his cigarette in the Italian marble ashtray on his desk. "Why can't you fix it? And why should I care?"

"I can't fix it because it is too widespread."

Xu Jin narrowed his eyes in frustration; this was how it always went with the Internet toads. Everything was "beyond their control," "too complicated," "of major importance": as if the Internet were the only thing that mattered in the world. What about reality? What about people walking the streets? Cars, or birds, or airplanes—airplanes that for some idiotic reason landed in the middle of North Korea?

"Explain," Xu Jin said, lighting another cigarette. It was a multicigarette morning. "And fast."

"Malicious computer code has breached the firewall. Many users downloaded it. It was attached to a video of, well, sir, one of your speeches. The one you gave at the conference in Hong Kong last fall. About Internet safety."

Xu Jin blanched. Was this somebody's idea of a bad practical joke? He would personally find that person and destroy them: ruin their reputation, have them fired, kicked out of school, have their head separated from their puny body. Xu Jin didn't care. This was beyond what was acceptable.

"Who did it?"

"We think it came from America. Or Europe. We can't be sure yet."

"Well, find it, destroy it, make it better."

"That's the problem, Director Xu. We cannot. The worm has taken over computers inside the firewall. Thousands of computers. Maybe millions. We don't know for sure."

"Taken them over to do what?"

"It turned them into zombie machines. It made them attack our servers. Golden Shield's servers. Wave upon wave of attacks. It has shut them down."

Xu Jin held his breath. His office, with its broad windows looking out onto the courtyard of the party headquarters in Zhongnanhai, in central Beijing, was silent. A battery-powered clock with a picture of Mao on its face ticked from the desk. A wisp of smoke from his newly lit cigarette curled toward the ceiling. Xu Jin breathed again.

"You mean Golden Shield is not working?"

"No. More than not working. It no longer exists."

That caused Xu Jin's heart to trill alarmingly. He put a hand on his chest to calm himself. He searched for a reasonable response.

"Well, then, turn off the entire Internet. Pull the plug. On the whole thing."

"Sir, that is not possible," the toad named Yuan said. "There are too many lines of data coming in. And anyway, now the worm has taken control of the servers. That seems to be its secondary purpose: to keep the trunk lines open."

"You mean the purpose of the virus is to open up the Internet? Anyone can read anything they like on their computers? Right now?"

"Yes, Director Xu."

"But . . . how do we stop it?"

There was no answer on the phone line. Director Xu Jin barked, louder this time: "Yuan Gao! Answer me!"

"My name is Le Lin, Director Xu."

"I don't give a shit what your name is," Xu Jin roared. "I only care how we are going to stop this. Tell me now! How are you going to put Golden Shield back up?"

"Director Xu," Le Lin said, the words catching in his throat, "I have no idea."

79

SOUTHEAST WASHINGTON, D.C., APRIL 18, 11:25 PM

The room was humming with activity. Cell phones were ringing, computers were beeping, text alerts were dinging softly in the darkness. Garrett let his fingers run across the keyboard, calling up different windows on his half dozen screens, delving deeper and deeper into the data recesses of the planet's information flow.

Internet traffic was beginning to spike in and out of the Far East. That meant that users in China were discovering that they suddenly had access to a whole new world of Web content. Word would spread fast. Traffic would grow all day, peaking in the afternoon as people logged on in the office towers of Shanghai and Tianjin.

Garrett's eyes flickered over the small TV screens on his left. CNN and Fox were doing stand-ups on the North Korean plane incident, with their respective reporters posed outside the White House. It was night. Late. The TV frame was dark. The BBC was also beginning to cover the story, breathlessly, with talking heads already spinning out possible scenarios on the fate of the American passengers: jail, soft captivity, bargaining chips? Would the Chinese get involved? Could anyone sway the North Korean government?

He scoured the wires for news out of Beijing. Nothing yet about the Golden Shield hack; but, then again, Garrett hadn't expected anything. The party would do its best to cover up the whole thing. Didn't matter, because Garrett had already leaked word to the *New York Times* and the *Washington Post*. They would be all over it. That story would start to blow up in just a few minutes.

Garrett let the data wash over him. Screen upon screen, window within window. There were charts and graphs and numbers; there were faces on the TV and voices from those faces. Garrett let his mind wander over the information, let his eyes distinguish the outlier data from the median numbers, let his ears tune into the key words: *diplomacy, China, pressure.* He settled back into his chair, fingers energetically working the keyboard, eyes darting left and right, high and low, while his body sank into the soft cushion of the leather seat.

The patterns will come. Their direction will become clear. And Garrett would nudge them. Here. There. Up. Down. He raised his hand over the front edge of a computer screen and pointed to Bingo in the corner of the room.

Bingo nodded, knowing exactly what Garrett meant—time to release the next pack of hounds.

80

FOURTH STREET NE, WASHINGTON, D.C., APRIL 18, 11:54 PM

Mitty Rodriguez knew she wasn't the world's hottest bikini babe: yes, she was a few pounds overweight; and, no, she hadn't had a professional haircut in a year, but at least she showered regularly. These video-editing dudes, they smelled like homeless people. All three of them. The Motel 6 room where she met them? Management was gonna have to hire a carpet-cleaning service after their visit.

Garrett had told her to fly them down from New York to D.C., on the last shuttle of the day out of LaGuardia. He called them Moe, Curly, and Larry, said he had worked with them once, back in the day, when he was doing gaming in L.A. She flew them down on the ten-thirty flight, told them to take a cab to the motel in the District's southeast side. They were all in their twenties; one was bald, one had a Jew-fro, and the other just looked dense. But Mitty had to admit, stinky as the threesome were, those boys could edit. And compile. And Photoshop.

Mitty sipped her Mountain Dew as the one called Moe—the bald one—blathered on about the video clip. He had a Brooklyn accent and wore his Yankees cap backwards, as if he were some kind of OG badass, which he clearly wasn't.

"See, look at this bunch of dudes right there, top right corner of the frame," Moe said as he pointed to the seventeen-inch laptop he'd set up on the motel bed. The video still frame was of a city street, shot from above, from a second- or third-story balcony. It was hard to tell exactly; the camera had been shaky up until the freeze frame, and the lens was a wide-angle one. In the top right of the screen stood a mass of people—maybe two dozen or so—all with their arms raised high, as if about to throw something. A few were screaming. Many had bandanas wrapped around their faces. The ones whose faces could be made out were clearly Asian. Mitty could see that for certain.

"I see 'em," Mitty said.

"Those motherfuckers are Koreans," Moe said proudly. "I took 'em off this news footage I stole from work at Channel Five News. From the archives. Some Korean protest about some shit. I don't know. They're always protesting over there. Know what I mean?"

"Sort of."

"And these jokers down here." Curly did the pointing this time. His accent was only slightly less thick. "These guys are from all that crazy shit that went down in Egypt. You know, the Arab Spring? Those guys are Muslims, which is fucked up, right?"

"I guess," Mitty said, squinting to see if she could tell that the rear wave of protestors in the video—all the way in the back of the frame, barely recognizable as people at all, much less Arabs—were not Chinese. No, not possible. They just looked like angry protestors. "And the street? That's a street in China?"

"Guaranteed, one hundred percent Chinese street, or your money back," Moe said, smiling gleefully. "Got it off YouTube. A video about crazy Chinese drivers."

"Play it for me. From the beginning."

"Sho 'nuff, boss," Moe said, restarting the short digital video in his computer editing program. On the screen, a phalanx of black-uniformed riot police charged down a street. They wore black metal helmets with hard plastic visors, and carried baseball-bat-sized truncheons, which they waved menacingly at arm's length.

"Those are Chinese police?"

"From a riot in Tibet. A monk-ass dude filmed them. Only I doubled up the number, and changed their body movements a little, so it looks like different people."

The police were suddenly met with a hail of rocks and bottles. They hoisted shields and arms above their heads. A few of the policemen fell to their knees. But before you could see what happened to the injured policemen, the jittery camera panned down the street to the protestors. Now, not stop-frame, but live and continuous, the army of protestors seemed huge and enraged. They chanted and howled and lobbed bricks and road stones at the police.

"And that's from a bunch of different protests?" Mitty asked.

"Top-speed, high-res rendering, baby. I can make the normalist shit look totally crazy. You know how long it took me after you called? Four hours. *Four hours, bitch.*"

Mitty stared at Moe. "You call me bitch again," she said, her voice dropping an octave, "I'll tear out your rectum with my fingers."

Moe's face fell momentarily. "Sorry," he said weakly. "Just an expression."

On the screen, the protestors surged forward, breaking the ranks of the police. A few riot policemen were trampled underfoot, lost from the screen; other police fled in the face of superior numbers. And suddenly, the video stopped. Mitty looked over at Moe: "What happened?"

He shrugged. "I figured short was better than long. Keep 'em wanting more."

"Okay," Mitty said. "You have others?"

Moe shot a conspiratorial look at Curly, who tapped on the keyboard of his own laptop. On his screen, a dozen tiny tiles popped up, all in a cluster. Each one seemed to show a different freeze-frame angle on a different street, with different policemen, and different protestors. Lots and lots of protestors.

"I got a million angry Chinese," Curly said happily. "All just sitting around on my laptop. Waiting for some motherfucker to upload 'em. Right?"

Moe and Curly burst into cackling laughter, while the one dubbed Larry just sat there, staring into empty space.

Moe grinned expectantly at Mitty. "Right? Am I right?"

Mitty grimaced. She hated these morons. But they got the job done.

"You are so right. Let's roll," she said. "'Cause I gotta get back to headquarters before the fun starts."

81

NEW YORK CITY, APRIL 19, 3:26 AM

Cherise Ochs Verlander hung up the phone just as three of her other lines lit up. It had been that way for the last four hours. It seemed to Cherise, who was sitting in the middle of the now bustling *New York Times* newsroom, that she currently had four different page-one stories, all breaking at exactly the same time. It was insanity. And it was all happening at three-thirty in the morning.

She'd never seen anything like it: an American jetliner had made an emergency landing in North Korea. Half an hour later word had leaked out that the Chinese Internet wall had been massively hacked. Ten minutes after that, rumors from a military source hinted that the American and Chinese navies were facing off in the South China Sea. Apparently, both navies were on full combat alert. In between all those leads came reports—from an FBI source—that there was some kind of rogue operation blossoming in D.C., and that Homeland Security was putting a full court press on finding the source and destroying it. What kind of rogue operation, no one was really sure.

All of these stories would have been front page, above the fold, on a normal day. Today, Cherise thought, they might need to run half a dozen separate front pages.

She answered the first line. "Cherise Verlander."

"Cherise, hey. Art Saunders, State Department."

"Mr. Saunders," she said, eyes widening. Saunders was the deputy secretary of state, one rung beneath Madam Secretary herself. "You're up early."

"Lot going on. Have you checked YouTube?"

"Not since I saw that cat singing the National Anthem yesterday."

"I'll send you a link. Amazing stuff. All live. From ten different cities, all over China."

"Okay," she said, slightly baffled. "Can you tell me what it's about?"

"All hell breaking loose," Saunders said. "Check it out. Gotta run."

"Wait, I need a comment on the United flight that made that emergency la—" But Saunders had hung up. Cherise sighed. *What the fuck?*

She checked her e-mail. There were ten e-mails from the deputy secretary already waiting in her inbox. This had to be preplanned. She clicked on the link in the first e-mail. A new browser tab popped up, and a YouTube video began to load. The descriptive tags on the page were all in Mandarin. She stared, stunned.

Cherise didn't read Mandarin, but she knew a riot when she saw one. And she was looking at ten of them.

82

THE WHITE HOUSE, APRIL 19, 4:10 AM

By the time he got to the White House Situation Room at 4:10 in the morning, the president had been awake for exactly nine minutes. He was unshaven, his hair was unwashed; he wore a sweatshirt, slacks, and a pair of sneakers with no socks. He'd only gotten two hours of sleep. He hated looking disheveled, but sometimes the job required it.

The entire national security team, including Jane Rhys, his national security advisor, was already gathered in the Situation Room. Cross noticed immediately that Secretary of Defense Frye was there as well, and that Frye did not look happy. The team rose from their chairs when the president rushed in. He waved a distracted hand in the air: "Please. Sit. Too early. Just bring me up to speed."

An aide brought him a mug of coffee, black, no sugar. President Cross saw Jane Rhys shoot a quick glance at Secretary Frye—she got no response—then lean forward. "Mr. President, as you know from last night's briefing, at approximately ten p.m., local time, a United Airlines 777 made an emergency landing at Pyongyang International Airport. The captain sent out a distress call. He said he had an engine fire and requested clearance to land. His request was denied—the North Korean air traffic controller told him to continue on to Seoul—but the captain landed in Pyongyang anyway. Safely. The plane was evacuated. After that point, our new information gets sketchy. We believe the crew and passengers have been taken into custody and are currently being interrogated."

"Can the North Koreans do that? Interrogate our airline passengers?" Cross asked.

"Unfortunately, they can do anything they like on their own soil. And it appears they have some reason for doing it. The distress call and landing were suspicious. Why the captain chose Pyongyang is a mystery. Also, the passenger manifest lists a certain number of government and military employees. Using aliases."

President Cross took another sip of coffee and rubbed his eyes wearily. Before he could ask a question, his national security advisor continued. "Approximately twenty minutes later, we monitored a massive shutdown of Chinese servers that provide that country with a censorship wall around their Internet access. They call it the Golden Shield. We suspect a potent virus, but we are not sure. The shutdown was unprecedented in scope and speed."

"These two things are connected?" Cross asked.

Ms. Rhys grimaced and cocked her head slightly to one side. "There's more," she said. "At about the same time, videos began to show up on YouTube, purportedly posted from cities around China, showing massive street protests. Young people battling police. Police shooting tear gas. Rocks being thrown. Cars set on fire."

"Good Lord," Cross said. "Are they real?"

"We've called a number of contacts in those cities, and while none of them saw any fighting, they said people are now gathering in the streets. They may have gone initially out of curiosity, but now they've begun protests of their own. It's as if the videos of the protests prompted actual protests. It doesn't seem to matter anymore whether the videos are real or not."

"Are we behind all this?" Cross asked.

Jane Rhys bit her lip hesitantly, then looked over to the secretary of defense.

"Sir, you of course remember the Ascendant program?" Frye said.

"With that kid? I thought he'd been arrested?"

"Garrett Reilly. He was, sir. But he escaped."

"Escaped? Why wasn't I told?"

"We expected he would be caught. Quickly," Frye said, uneasily.

"But he wasn't?"

"No sir, he was not."

President Cross leaned back in his chair. He smiled, adjusting the glasses on his nose. "And you think this is him? Behind all this? It's a counterattack, aimed at China? He's doing what we told him to do? Strike at them without firing a bullet."

"He may be, sir," Frye said. "But we can't be sure. And if he is doing it, he is acting entirely without our authorization. In fact, there is a very distinct possibility that Reilly is operating under an entirely different set of orders. That he has a goal that is not the one you stated to him. That in fact he is trying to achieve something else."

"And what would that something else be, Duke?"

"The subversion of the United States military."

President Cross stared at his secretary of defense. "How would any of what's happened lead to that?"

"By maneuvering us into a place where we are forced to act in a manner that is highly advantageous to the Chinese. And not to us. By putting American hostages in the hands of the North Koreans. By putting the Central Committee of the Communist Party on full alert ahead of our battle plans."

President Cross sipped his coffee again and scanned the faces of the men and women in the Situation Room. He was good at reading faces—it was what had made him such a successful salesman for all those years. And what he saw among his advisors was hesitancy. And confusion.

"But you don't know?" the president asked. "You're not certain of any of this?"

Secretary Frye and Jane Rhys exchanged a brief look.

"Reilly has had contact with an agent of a foreign government. That was why he was detained in the first place. His loyalties are currently unknown."

President Cross stood abruptly. "All right," he said. "The Pacific Fleet stays on high alert. Same with the Eighth Army in Korea. From here on in I want updates every twenty minutes. And for God's sake—find the kid."

83

SOUTHEAST WASHINGTON, D.C., APRIL 19, 6:15 AM

Garrett projected the riot videos onto a white wall in the operations room of Murray's Meats and Cuts. He played them in a continuous loop for fifteen minutes, and everyone got a kick out of the images. They also monitored the page views on each video, and watched them skyrocket. Over half a million views in less than an hour, climbing fast, and it was only just dawn on the East Coast.

Regardless of the videos' effectiveness, Mitty came back from the motel room full of complaints about the video creators. "Total morons," she said.

"But they did a good job," Garrett said.

"Even morons can get lucky," she said.

Ten minutes later she barked from her computer station: the morons had uploaded the next round. Garrett typed in the YouTube URL. The video loaded. It was grainy, like all the others. A vast expanse of blue appeared. The ocean. Writhing, frothy. The camera jittered, but under the jitters was the slow, methodical up-and-down motion of a boat on a rolling sea. The camera panned. The video was being taken from the deck of a ship. An enormous ship—its bow stretching off into the distance, the prow a football field away. Pipes and derricks crisscrossed the deck. It was a tanker. An oceangoing tanker.

Voices were shouting offscreen; nervous, almost panicked voices, their words unintelligible. Then someone said, "There!"

The camera swiveled hard right and suddenly a massive gray warship was visible on the crest of a wave. It was big, but clearly nowhere near as big as the tanker itself. It was steaming right at the tanker, about half a mile away, its forward gun clearly visible above the waves.

"Chinese?" Garrett asked.

Bingo stepped closer to the wall, eyes glued to the projected video. "Type 052, Luhu–class destroyer. Built in 2009, Jiangnan Shipyard, Shanghai," he said.

Garrett smiled. "How do you remember that shit? Just looks like a boat to me."

Bingo lowered his eyes, momentarily hurt. "I don't make fun of your patterns."

Garrett put his hands up, palms forward, in a quick show of apology. "It looks like a very nice boat, Bingo."

On the video, someone could be heard yelling "What flag? What flag?" The camera zoomed in on the destroyer to show the red star standard of the People's Republic of China flying just above the foredeck.

Lefebvre smiled. "Nice touch," he said. "For everyone who's not quite as up to speed as Bingo."

And suddenly, on-screen, the big gun at the front of the Chinese destroyer opened fire, belching red flame. One, two, three, four shots were fired. Someone offscreen yelled and the video camera snapped back to the deck of the tanker. There was a high whistling sound and then a fireball erupted on the deck of the tanker, a huge explosion of red and orange. The video went fuzzy, the camera spinning around and landing on the deck. There were cries of terror. Smoke and flame filled the frame, and then everything went black.

Garrett looked around the room: everyone was nodding in appreciation.

"Yeah, but how did they get the footage on the Web?" Lefebvre asked.

"Uploaded through satellite phone," Bingo said.

Lefebvre gave him a look. "Rather than save themselves?"

"Everyone wants to be on YouTube," Bingo said.

"Not sure people are gonna buy it," Lefebvre said.

Garrett stepped up. "Doesn't matter. Cumulative effect is what counts. Bolts from the blue. Chaos is what we're after." He turned to his small cyber army: "Everyone tweets. Get to it." Then he turned to the Marine lieutenant. "Patmore!"

"Sir?"

"Hit the road."

84

NORTHWEST WASHINGTON, D.C., APRIL 19, 9:07 AM

Timmy Ellis was always up for a good protest. He'd been at Occupy Wall Street in New York, in Boston, and in D.C. He'd tried to make it out to the Oakland port demonstrations, but he couldn't scrape the money together for a plane ticket, which totally bummed his stone. Before that, he'd camped out in Miami to legalize medical marijuana, marched in New Hampshire for gay rights, and handcuffed himself to a chain-link fence in Tacoma, Washington, to end the war in Iraq.

To say that Timmy Ellis believed in the power of the crowd to alter the direction of government was an understatement—it was his reason for living. Of course, he also loved a good party. And every one of those demonstrations—except for the one in Tacoma, where a policeman's truncheon had broken his forearm—had been a good party. He would even categorize some of them as excellent parties. At the OWS camp in Boston, for instance, he'd been high for a week straight and gotten laid twice, which was a personal protest record for him. That had been a really good seven days.

So when Timmy Ellis got the Twitter feed—pushed to his cell phone, as all his protest updates were, so he could respond instantly—about the flash mob at the Chinese embassy, he was on his bike in minutes. He wasn't sure what the issue was with the Chinese, but it didn't really matter—he had nothing else to do until his dentist appointment at noon. He packed a snack, a Red Bull, and a box of Sudecon wipes to counteract pepper spray. Sudecon wipes had become must-haves in every competent protestor's toolbox—pepper spray was nasty shit, and the wipes seemed to decontaminate your skin and face a lot faster than water. Or beer.

It took him twenty minutes to ride to the embassy in Northwest D.C., and by the time he arrived—nine-thirty in the morning—there were at least a thousand people already there, with more pouring in by the minute. They were chanting something about Tibet, and human rights, and also the old standby about how the people, united, would never be divided, so Timmy chained his bike to a railing down the block and joined right in. He saw a few friends up close by the embassy gate, waving rainbow flags and banging on drums, so he snaked his way through the crowd to the front. It was there that he saw the Chinese guards, wearing black suits and looking more than a little unhappy. Timmy Ellis yelled "Peace, brothers" to them, but they didn't respond. A few of them jammed their hands into their suit jackets like they were going to pull out their guns.

Timmy did not like the looks of that.

The embassy building was large, white, and nondescript, with few windows facing the street, and lots of reinforced concrete, as if the architects had been thinking principally about security when they designed the place. There were cameras everywhere, but Timmy didn't care. He'd been filmed at so many protests he figured the FBI had a file on him a foot thick. And good for them, he thought. In for a dime, in for a dollar.

The crowd behind Timmy began to press in on him, shoving him and the other lead protestors up closer to the fence, which gave Timmy pause: he was well enough versed in crowd dynamics to know that things could get out of hand quickly, and you had to be very aware of your exit strategy. The problem was, he was hemmed in now, with a mass of people behind him and a fence in front of him. Plus, beyond the fence, there were even more sullen-looking Chinese guards showing up. A full two dozen of them, as far as Timmy could tell. They were shouting to each other in Chinese, and some of them looked more nervous than angry.

That was more bad news. An experienced protestor wanted experienced police on the other side. That made for a much more peaceful environment.

Overall, Timmy thought, this was turning out to be less of a party than he had expected. It was beginning to feel downright dangerous. He decided to turn around and get back on his bike and go to the dentist. But then he saw a protestor who didn't look much like a protestor. He was the right age—midtwenties—but his hair was buzz-cut like a soldier's, and he wasn't shouting or dancing or banging on a drum. He was watching the Chinese guards and holding something in his right hand, which was hanging loosely by his hip. Timmy thought maybe he was a tourist who'd gotten caught up in the crowd. But that didn't seem right either, because he was moving slowly, steadily, to the front of the embassy gate.

He brought the thing he was holding in his right hand up to his chest and flicked a lighter with his left hand, and now Timmy knew exactly what it was that the serious-looking dude was holding. An M-80. Timmy had used plenty of them when he was younger. Firecrackers. And loud ones. Really loud ones.

Oh shit, Timmy thought. When that thing goes off the Chinese guards are going to freak. Timmy turned fast, ducked his head and started pushing away from the front of the protest. He heard somebody yell—and it wasn't a protest yell, it was a startled yell—then there were more shouts, panicked shouts, and Timmy tried to bull his way further toward the rear of the crowd, but it was no use. People were laid on thick.

Then came the explosion. Loud and sharp and singular, a boom that rang in his ears. Then screams. *And gunshots.*

The crowd surged away from the embassy, like a single living organism, sweeping Timmy up in its force. He knew better than to fight it, so he let himself be carried away from the embassy, and in seconds he was free, the protestors scattering in different directions, most of them sprinting pell-mell down International Place.

Timmy staggered, struggling to catch his balance, when another gunshot rang out, and someone shoved him hard in the shoulder. Timmy fell. A protestor stomped on his hand, and another on his ankle, but that wasn't what really hurt; his shoulder was suddenly throbbing from where he'd been pushed. He reached up to touch the source of the pain and saw that his hand was covered in blood.

Son of a bitch, Timmy thought, as the plaza in front of the embassy emptied out at lightning speed, I've been freaking shot.

85

SOUTHEAST WASHINGTON, D.C., APRIL 19, 10:15 AM

The data flowed: Internet usage in Asia was skyrocketing; phone traffic on transpacific cables had doubled in the last two hours; the U.S. stock indexes, now in the prelunch hours, were becoming volatile, shooting up, then reversing themselves; commodity prices, always a harbinger of trouble, were edging up; the most common searches on Google in the last half hour were "airliner," "captives," "street protests," "Internet censorship," and "China."

"Embassy shooting" was starting to blow up as well.

Garrett's eyes scanned his screens. Numbers and words scrolled across them in an uninterrupted symphony of information: the VIX, up; the Dow, down; Verizon nodes, flooded; Google searches, increasing; Brent Crude prices, zigzagging; Sprint backbone lines, overwhelmed; the dollar was down in late trading, decoupling from the yuan, and the euro was beginning to follow the dollar's lead.

All good, to Garrett. He didn't really care where these data flows led: up, down, it was all the same to him. What he wanted was movement. What he wanted was chaos.

He was getting it.

86

QINGPU, WESTERN SHANGHAI, APRIL 19, 11:57 PM

Celeste Chen couldn't sleep. She'd tried for hours, but her head was buzzing, the same thoughts banging around and around in her brain: she was free to walk away at any time. But should she? Did she want to? She wasn't sure. Everything was jumbled.

She stepped across the tiny, darkened bedroom, and pulled back the yellowing cloth curtain on the window. From the safe-house apartment on the eleventh floor, she gazed out into the night at the Shanghai suburbs below her. Row after row of towering buildings disappeared into the darkness. A few cars raced down the mostly empty streets. It was three minutes before midnight.

Celeste guessed that she was west of downtown Shanghai. Beyond that, she was lost. Hu Mei's compatriots had driven her here from Baoding, stashed in the back of a windowless van, and told her almost nothing. The drive had been long, and boring, and now she wished that she had slept.

So much had happened since she had met Hu Mei twenty-four hours ago. The two of them had hit it off together, like long-lost sisters. That amazed Celeste. They had so little in common, a peasant from northern China and a suburban girl from Palo Alto, but they had clicked. They had sat and talked in that tiny restaurant in Baoding for two hours, asking questions about each other's backgrounds—growing up in China, going to school in America. What did she eat for breakfast, what did they watch on TV, what had happened to Hu Mei's husband, why wasn't Celeste married.

Celeste had told her of Garrett's desire to help the cause, and Hu Mei had said she would take it into consideration. Before she could commit, Celeste would have to prove that the Americans were for real, and that she, Celeste, could be trusted. Hu Mei needed to know she wasn't an agent of the party, out to betray them. Celeste understood completely. There would be a test, and it was coming soon. Probably in the next few hours. It was perfectly reasonable, but it terrified her nonetheless.

Celeste felt that events had overtaken her. She was marching, inexorably, toward a destination that she had not planned for, had never even imagined. Every minute took her farther down the road, plunged her into potential chaos and true, life-threatening danger. And yet . . .

And yet she continued marching. Something about Hu Mei, the rebellion—or maybe it was China itself, the energy and vastness of the place—was drawing her deeper and deeper into the game.

She let the curtains drop, shrouding the room in darkness, and thought back on her life in the States. It had been a good life, steady and middle-class and peaceful, but it had also been lacking. What it lacked was a point. A reason. *A cause.* In the last few days, Celeste had realized that she had been looking for that cause all her life—the absence of it explained her cynicism and her mask of detachment—and perhaps now she had found it. Reform. China. Hu Mei. The rebellion. Could they give Celeste's existence meaning?

Again, she wasn't sure, but it seemed possible. The thought burst into her consciousness that if that were the case—if the rebellion were to become a defining principle of her life—then she might suddenly consider herself, well . . . happy.

With that last idea, she lay back down on the cot in the corner of the room, pulled a blanket up to her shoulders, and waited for the sunrise—and the test that would inevitably follow.

87

THE WHITE HOUSE, APRIL 19, 11:14 AM

ASSOCIATED PRESS TRANSCRIPT OF WHITE HOUSE PRESS BRIEFING, APPROVED FOR GENERAL RELEASE.

LINDSAY TATE, WHITE HOUSE PRESS SECRETARY: Thank you all for coming, I know this is last minute, but the White House doesn't control the timing of events, and events have been unfolding quickly, so we wanted to jump out ahead of this. First off, let me just say that the situation in North Korea is still fluid. What we know right now is that the United 777 has landed safely at Sunan International Airport, and the latest word—and this is not from the North Korean government, mind you, they have said nothing publicly—is that all the crew and passengers are safe and resting in a government building in downtown Pyongyang. We got this information from a Red Cross worker on the ground in the capital. We do not believe they are being held as prisoners, but we also at this time do not know if they are being allowed to leave the building. The White House and State Department have made repeated attempts to contact the North Korean government, but those attempts have so far been met with silence. Obviously, you all know that the United States and North Korea do not have formal diplomatic ties, so we have turned to our contacts in the Chinese government to facilitate talks between ourselves and Pyongyang. The Chinese Foreign Ministry has said that they would work on this, but that there were a number of issues that made immediate contact with North Korea difficult.

ALFRED BONNER, NEW YORK TIMES: Lindsay, did the Chinese Foreign Ministry say what those issues were? That were making it hard to contact the North Koreans?

LINDSAY TATE: No, Alfred, they did not.

BONNER: Do you have information that might shed light on that? We've heard reports that there have been disturbances in northern Chinese cities. Riots and protests.

LINDSAY TATE: I've seen the YouTube videos, as I'm sure you have. We can't, as of yet, verify that those videos are real. However, we are taking those reports seriously.

BONNER: If they are real, what does that say about the stability of the current Chinese government?

LINDSAY TATE: That's outside my area of expertise, Alfred.

ANGELA HIRSHBAUM, LOS ANGELES TIMES: Have you heard anything about the Chinese censorship wall? The Golden Shield? My sources are saying that it's down. That anyone in China can view those YouTube videos or any other previously blocked website.

LINDSAY TATE: Don't have any specific information on that, Angela. That's obviously a highly technical matter. You'll have to get comment elsewhere.

HIRSHBAUM: What about the *(UNINTELLIGIBLE)* protests at the Chinese embassy this morning? A flash mob that got out of control. Early reports are that two people were wounded. By Chinese guards.

LINDSAY TATE: What I know is what you know on that one. The Metro PD are on the scene and handling the investigation. We don't know the severity of the injuries those protestors sustained, or why the protests were called. All the president can say about this incident is that he is praying for the good health of those injured, and that he supports the right of all free people to peaceably assemble in public, which is what we believe those protestors were doing. If anyone was seriously hurt, we will hold the Chinese government responsible.

HIRSHBAUM: We've heard reports that ambulances were called to the embassy before the shooting even started. That's a little odd, isn't it? Makes you think someone planned the whole thing. Like they didn't want anyone seriously hurt?

LINDSAY TATE: You'll have to draw your own conclusions on that one, Angela. The White House isn't going to speculate.

MIKE HAN, KOREA TIMES: Lindsay! Lindsay! My paper is getting information that American warships are on high alert in the South China Sea. And that they are being followed by Chinese vessels. Are we on the verge of a war with China?

LINDSAY TATE: There's obviously a lot of rumors swirling around. First of all, let me say, unconditionally, that the president of the United States does not seek a hostile relationship with China. The Chinese are our allies and number-one trading partner. We have very open communications with the Chinese leadership. Secondly, the president is a firm believer in the power of diplomacy to solve any and all problems that arise between nations.

HELEN JOHNSON, FOX NEWS: But you haven't answered the question. Are we at war with China?

LINDSAY TATE: I think we'd all know it if there was a war between two nations, don't you?

JOHNSON: We wouldn't be asking if we knew, would we?

LINDSAY TATE: It's a little early in the day for this, isn't it, Helen?

BONNER: Lindsay! We're hearing rumors that a certain amount of what's been happening can be traced back to a group of people who had been employed at the Pentagon but then went underground. A lot of press calls have originated from anonymous sources in the District. There's rumors of ties to hacking groups. Something called Project Ascending?

LINDSAY TATE: That's ridiculous, Al. Why would the Pentagon have anything to do with nonmilitary-related events?

BONNER: Cyber war? Psychological war? We've even heard that there's a single source for all of this. One person at the center of events.

LINDSAY TATE: You have this person's name?

BONNER: I don't.

LINDSAY TATE: Come to me with a name and I'll look into it. Otherwise it's all speculative nonsense, Al. Don't believe it. No single, unnamed person has the power to change the course of world events like this. Nobody. Just not possible.

BONNER: Lindsay . . .

LINDSAY TATE: Thank you all for coming. I'll be back in a few hours if I have any updates. Thank you.

END OF PRESS CONFERENCE TRANSCRIPT.

88

SOUTHEAST WASHINGTON, D.C., APRIL 19, 2:15 PM

Agent Paul Stoddard stared at the oscillating, concentric lime-green circles on the tracking program on his laptop computer. They pulsed, emanating outward from spots on a grid map of Southeast Washington, D.C. Each circle—and there were nearly a hundred of them—was a node of Internet traffic, IP addresses scattered around the neighborhood. Each new pulse of green was a percentage increase in the data flow to that node. Only the biggest users of information would register on the program. And one of those nodes, he was quite sure, was Garrett Reilly.

But which one?

Agent Stoddard felt at the raw gash that was stitched up along his left ear. The pain was still there, throbbing in time with the circles on his computer program, as was the ringing in his ears. Ever since Reilly had brought that chair down on the side of his head, Stoddard had heard a shrill, piercing screech in his ears. The ER doctor said it was a form of post-traumatic stress—a wound to the brain as much as a wound to the body. Whatever it was, it bugged the crap out of Stoddard, and he had vowed to make Reilly pay for it.

The Dodge Econoline van eased slowly down the side streets of Southeast D.C. Agent Cannel drove, pulling over every hundred feet or so to get a new Internet usage reading. Stoddard checked the laptop, let the program do its magic, then waited to see if they got a noticeable spike. So far the best they'd been able to do was narrow it down to about a twenty-block radius. But even that comprised nearly a thousand residences, far too many to raid all in the next few hours, even with the dozen other Homeland Security teams that were scouring the district alongside Stoddard and Cannel.

No, they would have to get a big hit, a pulse that made it very clear there was hacking work going on. Then they would kick in doors. Then they would deal with Reilly . . . and Stoddard could get his seriously endangered career back.

"Try the cell monitor," Cannel yelled from the front of the van.

Stoddard booted up a second computer—they had five in the back of the van, along with listening devices, microphones, telescopes, binoculars, not to mention a host of firearms, battering rams, flash-bang grenades, and a sniper rifle—and started the cell phone triangulator. It wasn't nearly as accurate or powerful as the ones they had at Homeland Security headquarters, but it would let them know when a mass of wireless traffic was being handled by a specific cell tower, and it used overlapping signals from neighboring towers to narrow the search. It also had a setting to flag calls that came in from other countries. So far this had proved only partially useful; it seemed like everyone in Southeast D.C. was talking to someone in El Salvador, Mexico, or Ethiopia. Stoddard wanted someplace very different.

The NSA knew Reilly had sent an analyst to China. And they hoped the analyst would be checking in with him. Soon. When she did—and they knew it was a woman—well, that would be very helpful.

In fact, it might be all they needed.

89

SOUTHEAST WASHINGTON, D.C., APRIL 19, 4:56 PM

Someone knocked at the bathroom door.

"Yeah?" Garrett said, trying not to sound as weak as he felt.

"Yo. Garrett. It's Mitty. You okay in there? You, like, passing a bowling ball or something?"

Garrett slid his feet more or less underneath himself and sat upright. His head was spinning; he'd been lying there, head down, for fifteen minutes. He'd stumbled in when the black amoebas had taken over his vision entirely, rendering him effectively blind.

"Yeah," he said, grabbing the edge of the sink and pulling himself off the floor. "I'm fine."

He blinked into the mirror: his vision had begun to come back in bits and pieces. From what he could see, he was white as a sheet, his cheeks sunken, hair matted down on his forehead, flecks of vomit caked around his lips. His whole world smelled of barf—his fingers, his shirt, his chin, his lips. It was acrid and horrible, lingering in the air every time he took in a lungful of breath. And it wasn't like the bathroom at Murray's Meats and Cuts smelled so wonderful to begin with—no one on his team had been overly concerned with hygiene lately. Garrett wished they had at least wiped the place down.

The pain in his head had become so sharp, like an ice pick jammed under his skull and rooting around in his brain, that his body seemed to be trying to expel it by way of throwing up. But vomiting had had little effect. Now his throat burned, his nostrils were filled with stink, and his head still felt like it was going to explode. He splashed cold water on his face, then tried to wipe away the exhaustion with an old towel, but it was no go. His body was collapsing in on itself. He was falling apart.

He opened the door, and Mitty gave him a surprised look. She sniffed at the air wafting out of the bathroom. "Damn. You blow chunks?"

Garrett nodded. "I saved some for you."

"You can still talk shit," she said. "So you must be feeling okay."

Garrett walked slowly down the hall toward their operations room. He ran his finger along the wall, casually, as if just to touch it, but really because he was afraid he would fall over.

Mitty put a gentle hand on his shoulder. "I gotcha, boss," she said. Normally, Garrett would have swatted her hand away, but now he let her help him. He was glad she was with him. More than glad—grateful. No one looked up when he entered the computer room, and Garrett took his seat at the main bank of monitors. The screens surrounding him were lit up with activity. Garrett tried to speed-read the information, but his eye sockets ached. He couldn't do it.

"What's the news saying?" he asked Mitty quietly. "I'm having trouble seeing."

It was Bingo who answered: "Just about what we expected. North Korea leading, China censorship wall next, then protest at the embassy, then riots over there. But they're busy, can't keep up with the flow."

"Good," Garrett said, opening his online trading account. "Let's make 'em even busier."

90

HIGH-SPEED-TRADING DATA CENTER, NEW YORK CITY, APRIL 19, 6:01 PM

It used to be—two hundred, a hundred, even fifty years ago—that the shares of a company were traded on the company's local stock exchange, often manually, by traders working regular hours and selling blocks of shares to each other, for clients who had instructed them to do so in person, or more recently, by phone. Trading volume was steady, slow, and, compared to today's numbers, minuscule. Big players could move the market with a relatively small amount of capital, and sometimes they could even corner the market.

Panics still raced through the markets—runs and bubbles and crashes have been a feature of capitalism since humans first started trading products for money—but they took longer to build, longer to play out, and often longer to recover from. The notorious Tulip Bubble of the 1630s, when Dutch tulip prices soared to a hundred times their normal market value, led to widespread deflation in Holland for more than a decade. The bubble in the South Sea Corporation stock burst in the 1720s, wiping out thousands of British speculators for a lifetime. The Great Depression held sway over the American economy for more than ten years, lasting until the start of World War Two.

Today, with the growth of instant global communications, and the appearance of massive tranches of free-flowing capital, the stock market is global, and instantaneous. It is also a twenty-four-hour-a-day proposition. And it's incomplete to call it a "stock market"; there is a global market in equities, but also in bonds, insurance, debt, mortgages, currency, commodities, and almost anything else that someone, somewhere, can affix a price to and then turn around and sell to somebody else. Money of all types, from every country, sloshes around the globe, constantly seeking out higher returns. If two percent on U.S. Treasuries won't do, money sprints across the ocean to German corporate debt at three percent; if three percent is considered anemic, then that same money slides out of Europe and splashes into African commodities at five percent; if Africa convulses in corruption or revolution, then it races right back to the relative safety of U.S. Treasuries. All this in the blink of an eye.

A modern trader can make thousands of transactions, all in less time than it took a stock broker on the New York Exchange in 1929 to yell "Buy!" or "Sell!" or "I'm going down in flames!"

And not all of the transactions on the global marketplace are visible to all onlookers. Vast swaths of the deals being done are brokered and consummated in so-called black pools, nontransparent, off-the-record negotiations and sales conducted by third parties and anonymous brokers. The market for debt—government and corporate bonds—is particularly opaque, with no governing body making sure that prices are known to all the players. It is a murky pit of "buyer beware" action, an instant economy where fortunes can be made or lost in the blink of an eye, and nobody is any the wiser. At least not right away.

But word eventually does get out. Huge sums of money are not made or lost without some steely-eyed observers taking note, either to seethe in envy or revel in coldhearted gloating. And therein lies the other difference between today's market and that of a century ago. Information flow can travel almost as fast as the money itself. News of a stumbling stock, a faulty product, a debt ceiling, or an impending bankruptcy flashes around the globe with lightning speed. Often rumors travel across borders faster than real data: a stock can rise or crash on the most hastily formed opinions. And those opinions are not always based on fact. And the result can be devastating.

And that was exactly what Garrett was counting on.

It was the rumors that started first, at 11:00 p.m., East Coast time, a day earlier. They were very real-sounding bits of information concerning the solvency of a handful of Chinese companies, all of them traded on American exchanges. They came in the form of postings on financial blogs and stock-trading bulletin boards; official-looking analyst reports from Moody's and Standard & Poor's were suddenly ping-ponging across the Web. But since both of those companies were closed for the night, no one was around to authenticate the reports, and plenty of investors decided to take them at face value.

Then a trading house in lower Manhattan—and people suspected it was Jenkins & Altshuler—sold off a big chunk of Chinese holdings, and they did it in not particularly discreet blocks of selling: thirty million dollars of Star Hong Kong Holdings; twenty-five million dollars of Han Le Manufacturing; fifty million of Ace Software. People noticed. People in every corner of the globe.

By one in the morning, the rumors were ricocheting, growing more extravagant with each retelling: the Chinese companies were actually shell accounting entities, with no factories or real product. The stories morphed: the firms had product, but they were dangerously faulty and were under investigation by the U.S. government. A new PDF appeared at 2:00 a.m., this one bearing the seal of the attorney general's office of the Southern District of New York, verifying the rumor: those Chinese companies were indeed coming under investigation, and in fact the AG was pushing to have them delisted from the New York Stock Exchange altogether.

The tipping point was reached at 4:30 a.m., when Alvin Montague's *Value Trade* newsletter sent out a "sell all China" blast on its first Twitter feed of the morning. *Value Trade* had more than two million subscribers; when Alvin Montague said sell, people sold. And sell they did. They dumped Chinese equities listed on American and European exchanges.

The problem was, Alvin Montague never tweeted any such words.

His account had been hacked. So had the account of the AG of lower Manhattan. As had Moody's. By whom, no one could say. And it didn't matter: the damage had been done; the companies' stocks started to crater. First in after-hours trading in the U.S. and Europe, then in live trading on the Asian exchanges. These rumors, along with the mounting international crisis involving an American jetliner in North Korea, and the growing speculation that the Chinese government had lost control of its country, started a run on the Shanghai Stock Exchange. By ten in the morning, Beijing time, all the on-air reporters for CNBC had gathered in their New Jersey studios to narrate the course of these extraordinary events. They jabbered and screamed about the panic—they also replayed the YouTube videos of Chinese rioters throwing rocks at policemen in a dozen different cities. It was clear to anyone watching—or trading stocks—that the great global slosh of capital had become a tidal wave, rushing away from China, and looking to land someplace else. Anywhere else.

By the time the talking heads on CNBC paused to catch their collective breath, the value of the Shanghai Stock Exchange had dropped by seventeen percent. By noon the drop was twenty-seven percent.

By three in the afternoon the Chinese government pulled the plug and shut the stock exchange down. But the global marketplace no longer sleeps. Or pauses. By the closing bell on Wall Street, every Chinese equity, anywhere in the world, on a multitude of exchanges, had been scorched. The trading day had been a disaster.

And it was all built on lies.

91

SOUTHEAST WASHINGTON, D.C., APRIL 19, 8:02 PM

Garrett watched the run on the Chinese markets with undisguised glee. It wasn't that he liked to see other people suffer—although he didn't mind that terribly—it was more that he loved the concept of global mischief, and he loved that it was *his* mischief. A grand hoax had been perpetrated on the Powers That Be, in all the corners of the globe, and it had all come from his twisted brain: his planning, his feints, his misdirects, lies, and forgeries. As Mitty Rodriguez said as she watched the circuit breakers kick the Shanghai exchange off-line: "Garrett Reilly is *fucking legend*."

It made his head hurt a little less, but only a little.

He didn't even regret that he was leaving money on the table, which normally would have chafed him to no end. He could have shorted every one of those Chinese companies that had tanked. But, he reminded himself, profiting off a stock plunge that he had created—with lies and forgery—was indisputably stock fraud, and you could go to jail for a long time for that shit. He was better than that.

Garrett let his eyes trace over the cascade of tumbling numbers on the French CAC 40 and the German DAX, the Hang Seng in Hong Kong and the JSE in Johannesburg. Panic was in the air; panic on a global scale. Panic about Chinese companies, panic about war, and panic about China itself. Some of it was real, some imaginary; it really didn't matter. What mattered was the confusion. The bolts from the blue. If you kept people off balance, if you kept them guessing, then they didn't have much of a chance to strike at you. Sooner or later they would have to start circling their wagons.

News outlets from around the globe were all in a frenzy; some still led with the plane down in North Korea, others with the Chinese riots, a few with the crash of the Golden Shield, but in the past few hours the stock sell-off had crept into most lead positions. Analysts were coming on the air to weigh in on why it had happened, and whether this was a fundamental slide for China or merely a whiff of momentary panic.

Again, Garrett didn't care how they spun it—the job was getting done.

92

NEW YORK CITY, APRIL 19, 9:12 PM

Avery Bernstein watched the sell-off in Chinese stocks with a mixture of horror and admiration: horror that the supposedly "smart" money in the markets could be so easily misled, and admiration since he knew that Garrett Reilly had planned it, and then pulled it off. Perhaps Garrett's genius was being put to a good cause. What that cause was, Avery wasn't exactly sure.

But Avery knew Garrett had orchestrated it. He was like a conductor leading a symphony, moving bits of digital information here and there, melding it all into a weird, almost magical piece of music. Hacker music. That music seemed to be having a devastating effect on people and countries. But to what end?

He replayed in his mind the conversation he'd had with Garrett over the phone two days earlier. Garrett had promised that if Avery agreed to participate, any losses at Jenkins & Altshuler would be made whole by the U.S. Treasury. That seemed a tall order, but Avery guessed that Garrett was now playing in a world that he, Avery, barely recognized. Which brought him to another thought, one that had been bouncing around in his head for the past few days now—how safe was it for Avery to be playing *in that world*?

Garrett might have promised the full backing of the federal government, but could he come through on that promise? And, still more important, were there other forces out there, like that Metternich character, who might not be so happy with Garrett's antics? If people found out that Avery had been helping Garrett, would they come down hard on him?

It had made him paranoid. So much so that three days ago he'd had his office swept for listening devices by an electronic security company. Then he replaced all the old servers at Jenkins & Altshuler with brand-new ones—at quite a cost—and had those new servers jam-packed with security software. He changed the locks on his town house, and even toyed with the idea of getting a dog, even though Avery hated dogs.

Okay, the dog idea was probably a bit much.

Avery shut down his computer, turned off the office television, said good night to his secretary, Liz, and waved to a few lingering employees. It had actually turned out to be a profitable day for Jenkins & Altshuler: by selling Chinese equities early he had been ahead of the curve, and had avoided panic losses. But the Securities and Exchange Commission would come knocking after all the detritus had been sorted through, and they would want to know what he knew, and when he knew it. At that point, lawyers would be called in, and the shitstorm would commence. He hoped Garrett would be good as his word then, because it would take more than just money to keep him, and his company, in the clear.

He rode the elevator down, and said good night to the doorman at 315 John Street, then stepped out of the front door and looked up and down the street. The sidewalks were mostly empty, and a thick darkness was settling on lower Manhattan. It was a forty-block walk back to his West Village apartment, and it used to be that Avery took the trip on foot, every morning and evening, partially to make sure he got some exercise, but also because the beauty of living in New York City was walking the streets. But since the whole business with Metternich and his trip down to D.C., walking out in the open had seemed less inspiring. In fact, it scared him. He had started taking car services, both ways, jogging from his front door to the car, and then sprinting from the car to his office lobby.

He regretted everything about his involvement with Hans Metternich. On the same day that he'd called a security company to sweep his offices, Avery had hired a private detective to track the mysterious Metternich down. The detective had found one match—he was seventy-eight and lived outside of Munich—and nothing else. The man who had approached Avery on a lower Manhattan street corner was a ghost.

Avery tapped his foot impatiently as he stood on the sidewalk. He'd called the car service a little late, and would probably have to wait for them to show up. The night was warm, and the streets looked less intimidating than they had for the past few days. Avery wasn't sure why, but for a moment his paranoia subsided; whatever Garrett was doing was Garrett's own affair. Avery was a minor player in this drama—all the juicy stuff was happening far above his pay grade.

That thought gave him confidence. He decided to skip the car service. He called the company on his cell phone, canceled the ride, and started off west down John Street. The sun had dipped below the horizon, and Avery breathed deep of the spring air. It was good to be alive. He waited at the traffic light, then turned north and crossed the street on Broadway.

He heard an engine being gunned, and thought for a moment that it was a cabbie racing to get a fare, but then a woman yelled behind him. Avery thought she was saying "Luka!" like in that song from the eighties, but as he turned and saw the car racing toward him down John Street he realized she had said "Look out!"

The car was aiming for him.

The last thought Avery had, as the front end of the Chrysler hit him, full speed, in the midsection, was that he hoped they hadn't gotten to Garrett as well.

He hoped Garrett would be okay.

Then blackness overtook Avery Bernstein.

93

SHANGHAI, APRIL 20, 10:00 AM

Standing in the back of the crowded train station on the outskirts of Shanghai, Celeste could tell that the engineer was having second thoughts. His name was Li Chan; he was a small, balding man with sad eyes and fidgety hands. He was a cousin of Hu Mei—she seemed to have thousands of cousins, scattered across the country—and had been, at first, eager to hand over information. But not now.

"How do I know you are not the police?" Li Chan asked in Mandarin.

"If I were the police, I would have had you arrested already," Celeste said.

Li Chan nodded. That seemed to make sense to him. Around them, travelers hurried from one train platform to another, or out the door to waiting buses that would whisk them away to the center of Shanghai. Noise was everywhere; a thousand voices, chatter, official announcements about trains leaving and arriving, the grind of engines and the metal-to-metal squeal of wheels on tracks. The two of them were standing in the back of the cavernous station, unnoticed by passengers and workers alike, two locals in the middle of an intense discussion.

"They will kill me if they find out," Li Chan said, rubbing his hands together. Celeste thought he looked like he was trying to start a fire with his fingers.

"They will not find out," Celeste countered quickly, quietly. "We are very careful." She knew time was running out. She had been monitoring the Internet all day, stunned at first that she could access any content, uncensored, then alarmed as reports of chaos and political tension raced across news sites and blogs. Garrett was spinning his storm of chaos, but they needed Li Chan. They needed him right away.

This was the test that Celeste had known was coming.

"Master Li," Celeste said, trying to get the older man to look her in the eye. "This is a moment of extreme importance. You have a part to play in history. Isn't that important to you?"

"What do you know of history?" Li Chan said. "You are American. Americans have no history. A hundred years. Two hundred years. Nothing." He swung his hand out in a grand, sweeping motion. "Chinese people know history. Thousands of years. Whatever you Americans are planning, it means nothing. I am done with this. I am leaving."

Li Chan started away from Celeste, his fear clearly overwhelming him, but she jumped to block his path. "No, you are wrong. It means something very important. And not just to Americans. To Chinese people. Isn't what Hu Mei is doing important? Doesn't she understand history?"

Celeste could hear the pitch of her own voice rising, the tension straining her vocal chords. She knew she had to calm herself.

"You cannot force me!" Li Chan said. "I can turn you in to the police right now. You know that? You are a conspirator. An enemy of the state. They will take you to jail. Interrogate you. Beat you. Then put you against a wall and shoot you. I can go to that soldier right there and turn you in. I can!"

Li Chan pointed to a young soldier in a green uniform rolling his own cigarette and lazily eyeing the commuters. He didn't seem dangerous, but Celeste knew that he could summon backup in mere seconds, and then everything Li Chan had predicted they would do to her would absolutely come to pass. Because she was no longer an American student looking to research a social movement in central China. She was a member of that very movement. She was a budding revolutionary. She closed her eyes and breathed deep. If she had learned anything from watching Hu Mei in their brief time together, it was the power of humility. This was a test, and she needed to pass it.

Celeste bowed her head, stepping out of Li Chan's way, allowing him a free path to the soldier, who was now smoking his cigarette. "Of course," she said. "You are right. And you must do what you must do. I was wrong to try to stop you. I have been overbearing and foolish. So American of me. Please forgive me."

Again she bowed, eyes directed only at the floor. Celeste could not see if the engineer was standing in front of her, or if he had stalked off to inform the soldier, but it did not matter to her. Humility was not something to be faked, and acceptance of one's fate had to be real, and fully understood.

And Celeste was glad for it. She would take what came. She took a last calming breath, then looked up. To her surprise, Li Chan was still standing there, only now he had a scrap of paper in his hand.

"There," Li Chan said, thrusting the paper into her fingers, "now you have it."

He turned and walked quickly into the crowd. Celeste watched him go, then looked at the paper: on it was written a username and a password.

Celeste smiled, not with relief or triumph, but with fulfillment.

94

SOUTHEAST WASHINGTON, D.C., APRIL 19, 10:15 PM

Garrett read the text message on his phone three times, then wrote the Pinyin—phonetic Mandarin—onto a legal pad. He turned off the cell phone and dislodged its battery. His team gathered around him.

"Know what it means?" Lefebvre asked.

"Doesn't matter," Garrett said, swiveling his chair to face his computer monitor. "As long as it gets us in."

"But won't the control panel user interface be in Chinese too?" Bingo asked.

"It's from a Finnish company. They make all the cell tower master controller programs. It'll be in English," Garrett said. He paused for a second. "I hope."

He typed a URL into his browser. A black page loaded with a query for a username and password. Garrett carefully typed in the Pinyin he had copied from the cell phone and pressed enter.

The team waited, holding their collective breath. A page began to load. It read: Welcome Li Chan China Mobile Tibet Region Administrator.

Garrett beamed. "We're in."

95

SOUTHEAST WASHINGTON, D.C., APRIL 19, 10:16 PM

"We got a hit," Agent Stoddard said as he watched the software program on his laptop triangulate the distances between local cell phone towers. "A text message. Definitely from China. To a local number."

"Can you give me more?" Agent Cannel asked from the driver's seat.

"Working on it." Stoddard watched the map roll slightly east, then north, as it tried to pin down the recipient of the text. He knew the software was calculating the distance between cell towers, then trying to estimate the position of the receiving device, in this case a cell phone with a local area code prefix.

"Can we read it?"

"Encrypted. It would take hours." Agent Stoddard mumbled his encouragement to the software, whispering, "Come on, come on, come on," under his breath. The map settled, and a large red dot blinked on and off. "Looks like Sixteenth and C."

Agent Cannel threw the van into drive and tore down the tiny side street. Sixteenth and C was only five minutes away. "Any clearer?" he asked.

The red dot blinked one last time, then disappeared.

"Turned off his cell phone," Stoddard said. "Probably yanked the battery. But it looked like two buildings. Maybe three. We can raid two buildings at the same time. Three might be a bit much."

Cannel steered the van down Massachusetts Avenue. Night had settled upon the capital, the streets were flooded in orange halogen light.

Stoddard checked the safety on his Heckler & Koch 9mm pistol. Cannel steered the van right on Sixteenth and slowed as C Street appeared down the block. There were small, two-story row houses up and down the block, most in need of repair and a new coat of paint. On the corner sat an abandoned storefront and warehouse; a faded sign hung over the boarded-up windows.

"Murray's Meats and Cuts," Cannel read slowly, squinting in the darkness. "That can't be the place, can it?"

Stoddard crawled to the front of the van and peered through the windshield. He stared at the sign, the boarded-up front door, the warehouse that stretched out behind the building and fronted the alley.

"Call back up," Stoddard said, "and let's find out."

96

BEIJING, APRIL 20, 11:17 AM

The chairman of the Central Military Commission laced his fingers together. "It is the considered opinion of my department that war with the United States is now inevitable. The events of the last twenty-four hours have made this very clear to us."

The six other members of the Politburo Standing Committee of the Communist Party of China reacted with visible agitation to this statement. They were the seven most powerful people in China. They were all male, over fifty years old, cautious and conservative, and, right now, extremely unhappy. The general secretary—*the single most powerful man in China*—removed his glasses, wiped them clean with a handkerchief laid on the table for just that purpose, then replaced them gently on the bridge of his nose.

"You propose that we strike first?" the general secretary asked.

"If we are to win this war, then yes, striking first would be most advantageous," the military commissioner said. "If we wait for our enemies to land the first blow, then we allow them to choose the place and time of the battle. But if we strike first, then they must fight on our terms, and that is to our benefit." His voice rang out in the deadening silence of the bland conference room in the bowels of a government building near the Great Hall in Tiananmen Square. The vice secretary of the Communist Party sipped his water, while the deputy director of the Central Guidance Commission for the Building of Spiritual Civilization shook his head in disgust.

"This is the exact opposite of what we had planned for, is it not?" the deputy director for the building of spiritual civilization said. He glanced quickly across the table, where Xu Jin, the director for state security, sat silently in shame. All eyes in the room turned to him. "They were supposed to strike at us, no?"

It had been a disastrous twenty-four hours for Director Xu. First the breaching of the Golden Shield, then the faked videos of riots in ten cities across China, and finally the devastation of the nation's businesses on the world stock markets. Everyone on the Standing Committee blamed Xu Jin for these calamities; this much was very clear to him. It was he who had first proposed the stealth attacks on American infrastructure. He had laid out the timing, the severity, even the methods. And the attacks had worked excellently. They had pushed the Americans to the brink of war, which was exactly what the Politburo had wanted. Let them shoot first, Xu Jin had said, and let us be the aggrieved victim. The Tiger's rebellion will pale in comparison, and then we will have stability once again.

It was Director Xu Jin's shining moment. He was brilliant, a visionary planner. There was talk that in four more years *he* would be party chairman.

And then the last twenty-four hours happened. The Americans had struck back with their own form of deviousness. How it had caught his people off guard he could not say—all these things technological were beyond him. All he knew was that they had been fast and effective, and that his time on the Politburo might be coming to a crashing end. Xu Jin was about to be stripped of everything and sent to live in a wretched apartment building in Mongolia. The shame of it made him sweat through the stiff collar of his white shirt.

And yet, he thought, all was not yet lost. He could still fight his way back into the good graces of the committee. He simply had to find someone else to be more wrong.

"Comrade General Secretary," Xu Jin said, straining to keep his voice muted. "We at the Ministry of State Security believe this would be a rash proposition. We believe the chairman of the Military Commission is moving too quickly. We believe the situation is now under control."

"Director Xu," the general secretary said. "How did you come to this opinion?"

"Our teams are minutes away from restoring the Golden Shield," Xu Jin said, bluffing—but it was all he had. "The stock markets will right themselves when we produce accurate information, which we have at the ready. And our security teams have flooded the cities where the riots—real or imagined—took place. No one is allowed on the streets there. At any time. We have achieved stability. A harmonious society."

"And you are secure in these opinions, Director Xu? We have seen the worst of it?"

"We at the Ministry of State Security acknowledge that the Americans have inflicted some damage, but there will be no more." Xu Jin fixed each of the other members of the Standing Committee with a quick look. He was gaining traction with them. He could feel it. "They do not have a long-term strategy. These are random attacks. Haphazard and not well thought out. They do not understand the larger situation. They remain unaware of the Tiger, of the uprising, and of our efforts to combat her. We have monitored no news of this in their press, no word of it from their diplomats or conversations. If we hold steady to our course we will get what we want. The Americans are undisciplined and lazy. Like children, soon they will lash out foolishly with real force and we will have what we need."

He cleared his throat and shot a quick, superior glance at the chairman of the Central Military Commission. "The original plan is still a valid one. And it will succeed."

The main door to the Politburo meeting room opened and a thin young man in a dark suit hurried in. He walked to where the general secretary sat, bowed, and handed him a sheet of paper. The general secretary read the message, then handed the paper back to the young man, who quickly left the room.

A shot of anxiety raced through Director Xu Jin's blood.

"I have been informed," the general secretary said, looking directly at Director Xu, "that we have lost all communications with the Autonomous Province of Tibet. All cellular phone service and Internet traffic has been disrupted. We can no longer communicate with our garrison there. We must expect that rioting will develop next."

He turned his withering gaze to the chairman of the Military Commission. "Chairman, proceed with your preparations for a first strike."

Director Xu's heart sank. Well, that was it, then—war and his disgrace. He only hoped Mongolia had decent restaurants.

97

USS *DECATUR*, SOUTH CHINA SEA, APRIL 20, 12:03 PM

Ensign Hallowell stared wearily at his radar screen. The green glow pulsed in the darkness of the radar room, deep in the bowels of the USS *Decatur*. The soft murmur of the other radar operators and fire-control officers whispering into their microphones was a presence in the air. He clenched and unclenched his fists to keep the blood flowing, to keep his eyelids from drooping. He was eleven hours into a twelve-hour shift, and he'd spent every second of those eleven hours tracking the Chinese frigates that were running parallel to the American 11th Carrier Strike Group.

They had been consistent, the Chinese, dodging within range of the Americans' fastest ship-to-ship missiles, then quickly steaming out of range again. It was a game of long-distance chicken, a game both sides knew how to play, and they were pulling it off to perfection. The game had a monotonous rhythm, and the repeated in-out, in-out sequence was putting Ensign Hallowell to sleep.

Forty minutes ago the four Chinese warships had tacked hard to starboard, coming right at the Americans. It was their fifteenth approach in the last two days. Hallowell knew the drill by heart. They would cross the 124-kilometer missile exclusion zone, steam in a straight line for the American fleet, then, ten kilometers inside the zone, they'd tack to port and cruise out of range once again. Like clockwork.

Hallowell watched the Chinese ships reach the 114-kilometer point. He waited for them to turn off and start the process all over again.

"Three, two, one, okay. Go to it, boys," Hallowell muttered to himself.

He watched the screen patiently. But the Chinese ships didn't turn. Hallowell checked the plotting computer. Was there a mistake? Were they farther off than he had thought? No, the computer checked out.

The Chinese were within range and still coming.

Hallowell held his breath. He would give them another sixty seconds. He watched as the four green dots on his screen continued to come straight at the Americans. At the *Decatur*. *At him.*

And then another radar officer cried out from his monitor: "Bogies lifting off from Guangzhou Shadi Air Base. Fighters, heading 220 degrees, our vector!"

Hallowell's stomach lurched. He pressed the red comm button at his elbow, and the executive officer on watch answered immediately.

"Sir," Hallowell said, "we have a situation."

98

THE WHITE HOUSE, APRIL 20, 1:04 AM

Alexis Truffant had only been back at work for six hours—after reappearing from her stint at Murray's Meats and Cuts—when they came for her. Two Secret Service agents, large and unsmiling, pulled her out of her DIA office, patting her down and confiscating her cell phone, then drove her to an old redbrick building on the Nebraska Avenue Homeland Security complex, where they put her in a holding room in the basement. It was very clear from the moment that they showed up that she had no choice but to come with them. She didn't bother asking any questions of the Secret Service agents—she knew they wouldn't answer. After what she guessed was about four hours—she had no watch or cell phone—a different pair of agents took her out of the basement room to a waiting SUV, and drove her directly to the White House.

Night had fallen. The city was empty and dark. Alexis felt a deep, despairing sense of loneliness. No one said a word the entire ride, but Alexis did manage to glimpse a digital clock on a bank building. It was almost one in the morning.

At the White House she was led to a windowless room below the West Wing and body-searched by a female Secret Service agent. She waited another twenty minutes in the windowless room, then was escorted upstairs, by the same two male agents, to the Oval Office.

There were three other people in the room: The president stood behind his desk, hands under his chin, staring out the window into the blackness; National Security Advisor Jane Rhys sat on the sofa, sipping a coffee, while Secretary of Defense Frye stood in a corner, arms folded. He was the only one in the room looking at Alexis, and she thought he might start screaming at her at any moment. All three looked tense and exhausted.

"Where is Garrett Reilly?" the secretary asked.

Alexis started to answer, then held off, turning instead to the president. "Mr. President, sir, I do know where Garrett Reilly is, and I will absolutely tell you, but—"

The secretary cut her off. "You are an officer in the United States Army, Captain Truffant, and you are standing in front of your commander in chief. I asked you a direct question and you are instructed to answer it immediately."

The president turned away from the window to face Alexis. He nodded at her, as if to give her permission. "Where is the boy?"

Alexis hesitated. This was the moment she knew would come, and it was the moment she most dreaded. She gathered up her entire reserve of courage. "Mr. President, sir. Don't fire at the Chinese first."

"The president did not summon you here to give advice, Captain," Secretary Frye said. "He brought you here to discover the whereabouts of a man who is disrupting vital American operations in Asia, and putting millions of lives at risk. He is a threat to national security, and if you are refusing to reveal his whereabouts, then you are one as well."

Alexis grimaced and forged ahead. "Sir, it is my considered opinion that you need to hold off on military action against the Chinese. Reilly has put them under considerable stress. We believe that stress will force them to pull back their military from an attack."

"What Reilly is doing is cashing in on the turmoil he's created," Secretary Frye said. "He's probably shorting the market as we speak, making millions. Captain Truffant, do you or don't you know where Reilly is? Because if you do, and you do not reveal his whereabouts, I will have you detained and then court-martialed."

"He's thinking about war and the Chinese in a different way. In a way that nobody can predict. Not us. Not them. Isn't that what we hired him to do?"

Frye's face turned blank with an icy cold fury. "You are crossing a line, Captain. One from which you cannot cross back." He opened the door to the Oval Office and barked at the president's secretary. "Natalie, have agents Norris and Silliker come in here, please. Right away."

He held the door open and looked at Alexis. "Last chance, Captain. Where is Reilly?"

Before she could get a word out of her mouth, the two black-suited Secret Service agents rushed into the room. Frye pointed to Alexis. "Arrest her."

Alexis put her hands out, offering no resistance, but took one last look at the president. "Sir," she said. "Trust in the Ascendant program. It will work. Trust in Reilly. The Chinese will be forced to back down."

One agent put his hand on Alexis's shoulder, while the other grabbed her wrist and twisted. They had started to lead her away, when Jane Rhys got up off the couch. She had said nothing for the entire time Alexis had been in the room.

"Why, Captain? Why do you believe the Chinese will pull back?" she asked.

The Secret Service agents halted their march toward the door. Alexis craned her neck around to look at the national security advisor, even as one agent dug his fingers hard into her shoulder blade.

"I believe events are going to explode in China. They are at a tipping point. I believe this is what Garrett—Mr. Reilly—is aiming for." She turned her head a few inches more so she could see the president. "That's the point of his war, isn't it? An underground war. Just like you ordered, Mr. President. To blow up their system from the inside."

The Secret Service agents tugged her toward the door. This time Alexis dug her heels in slightly, to give her one last moment in the room. She grimaced in pain, then said, "Isn't that better than killing people?"

99

SOUTHEAST WASHINGTON, D.C., APRIL 20, 1:32 AM

Garrett picked up a new cell phone and slotted in a battery. It had been sitting, idly, on his desk, next to his bank of monitors, for twenty-four hours. Unused. Untouched. But now it was time.

Jimmy Lefebvre watched him. "What do you think?"

Garrett nodded, a barely perceptible movement of his head.

"They'll know," Lefebvre added, a tension in his voice. "Cell call to China. They'll track it to right here."

"Surprised they haven't already," Garrett said, barely above a whisper. The monitors in front of him were alive with activity, in stark contrast to the stillness of the darkened room. Garrett took a last look at the far wall. The television sets crackled with voices and video. News. Opinions. Fear. Greed. A panoply of human emotions, all on display, naked to the world. Humanity at its most vulnerable. About to reach a tipping point.

It made him slightly queasy, that sense of manipulation, of bad faith pushed out onto the unknowing, innocent world. Well, some of them were innocent, Garrett thought. Many of them were not. He was one of the less innocent, that was for sure, and perhaps now he was joining the truly damned. It didn't matter. He was going to do it anyway.

He dialed the number. Heads turned from around the room. On the fourth ring, Celeste Chen answered.

"Garrett?"

"It's your turn," he said. And hung up. He popped the battery out of the phone again, exhaled, then listened. There was a noise. Something indistinct. Something that was growing louder, coming at him, and then . . .

The plywood boards covering Murray's front windows exploded. Slats of wood flew everywhere, shattering, as flashlight beams poured into the darkness, followed by canisters of tear gas. There were screams as across the room a door was battered into debris.

Mitty ran, as did Bingo. Garrett couldn't see anybody else in the sudden flash of light. It didn't matter. He knew what was coming. They were finally here, and there was nothing he could do about it. There was nowhere to run, and he was too exhausted and too sick to fight any longer.

He raised his hands in surrender.

100

SHANGHAI, APRIL 21, 1:35 PM

Any form of entrepreneurial endeavor can be found in Shanghai, at any hour of the day, at any level of cost or quality. It is the newest of the new world, fueled by a hunger for wealth unmatched in any country, the United States included. No one works harder than the Chinese, and no one works longer or more persistently than the Chinese of Shanghai. From the grand colonial promenade of the Bund to the astonishing comic-book-themed towers of Pudong, from the packed-in streets of the old Chenghuangmiao Market to the throngs on commercial Nanjing Road, Shanghai bustles. It is a nonstop city, modern, competitive, proud, relentless, cutthroat.

So much like an American city, thought Celeste Chen as she rode the Number One Line bus from the Shanghai West Railway Station into downtown. Only more crowded. More thriving. We have so much to learn from the Chinese, she thought. They are a far older civilization and yet, somehow, newer as well. An odd contradiction.

Celeste felt part of the contradiction that was both Shanghai and China; half Western, half Eastern, new and old simultaneously, ambitious and yet settled. Not entirely of one place or of the other, but of both. Her loyalties—and even her nationality—had been turned upside down.

Hu Mei prodded Celeste gently in the arm with her elbow. "This is our stop," she whispered with a smile.

"Sorry," Celeste answered, the butterflies rising in her stomach. "I was daydreaming."

"Daydreaming. Some of my favorite moments of the day. Did your daydreams make you ready?"

"I think I'm ready."

"Good. If you think you are, then you are." Hu Mei rose from her seat, then shoved and snaked her way to the front of the crowded bus. Celeste followed close behind, wondering how many of the people standing beside her were followers of the Tiger. She didn't know. But she would soon. Soon, the unregulated flow of people in and out of the city would become a living thing, organized according to a new principle. Soon, the chaos would become structured. Soon was about to become now.

Celeste stepped out of the bus and into the warm Shanghai afternoon. Around her were thousands of other travelers, commuters, workers, and tourists. Hu Mei plucked her own cell phone from her pocket and punched out a text message. She winked at Celeste—a charming, playful, exceedingly confident wink—and hit send.

And then an amazing thing happened: Celeste watched as nearly half the people in her view reached for their phones simultaneously and checked their text messages. Good Lord, Celeste thought—the Tiger has hundreds of followers right here on this street. Probably thousands within the sound of her voice. Maybe millions in greater Shanghai. More? Ten million? Twenty?

Then she remembered what Garrett had said to her, back in the Pentagon, as he tried to convince her to go to China: she, Celeste, he said, was going to help change the world.

Son of a bitch, Celeste thought. *He was right again.* And with that, Celeste Chen understood the path her life was taking—she was about to become a true and devoted follower of the Tiger.

101

SOUTHEAST WASHINGTON, D.C., APRIL 20, 1:40 AM

It was madness. Dark, streaked with light, blinding, choking gas, and black figures pouring in from the doorway, screaming as they came.

"Down! Federal agents! Everyone down!"

Garrett tried to duck under the tunnels of yellow flashlight beams as they crisscrossed the room. He caught a glimpse of Sarah Finley, the CIA rep, and Mitty diving to the floor, hands over their heads. He knew he couldn't escape, so he wasn't trying, but keeping whoever had raided the operations center at bay for a few more minutes wouldn't hurt. He needed all the time he could get. He scrambled toward the freezer in back.

A hand grabbed his forearm. It was Lefebvre. "Follow me. Use the side door!"

"They'll be waiting," Garrett said.

"Garrett Reilly!" someone screamed. "Where is Garrett Reilly!"

The tear gas seared the inside of Garrett's nose and mouth, burning them with a raw, acrid taste. Lefebvre tugged hard on Garrett's arm. "They want you dead!"

"Reilly!"

Garrett and Lefebvre stumbled toward the side door. Garrett had to squeeze his eyes three-quarters shut from the gas and the flood of halogen streetlight that was now pouring through the broken front windows.

"Garrett Reilly!"

They came up short as the side door burst open, a federal agent filling the doorway like a creature from a horror film, face swathed in a gas mask, semiautomatic rifle swiveling back and forth, looking for prey. Lefebvre turned on his heels and tried to tug Garrett with him. They scrambled away from the SWAT commando and back into the heart of the raid.

Garrett slowed. He knew there was no place to run. He was done, and he knew it. He yanked his arm free from Lefebvre's grip and put his hands up in the air.

"Here! Garrett Reilly! I'm right here!" he yelled.

Flashlight beams snapped toward his voice, bathing him in yellow light. He squinted, as much from the gas as the illumination. Through the haze, he could see half a dozen more commandos ringing the edge of the room, their boots planted on the backs of his team, their rifles cocked and ready, hitched up into their shoulders. A large man in a suit and a bulletproof vest raised a pistol and aimed it at Garrett.

"Reilly?" the man said.

Garrett recognized him, even in the darkness; he recognized his voice and his girth. Agent Paul Stoddard, from Homeland Security. His torturer.

"*Reilly?*" Agent Stoddard barked.

"You know it's me, asshole," Garrett said.

Stoddard trained his gun on Garrett's chest, and Garrett braced himself for the impact of the bullet that would surely end his life. There was no time for him to run or jump, or even move. This was it. The end.

Stoddard pulled the trigger. There was a flash, and the thunderous report of a pistol, at the same time as a blur raced in front of Garrett and someone yelled, "No!"

Something thudded into Garrett, slamming him backwards, and he crashed to the ground, a great weight landing on top of him. Garrett twisted as he fell, trying to break the fall. The weight settled onto Garrett's midsection, as Garrett pulled himself to a sitting position. He looked down.

Jimmy Lefebvre was in his arms, blood was pumping from his chest.

"Damn it," Lefebvre said, groaning once. "Damn it all."

Everyone in the room started to yell again, and Garrett could see some of his team members rise off the ground, shouting "Jimmy!" and "Goddamn it!"

"I think I'm dying," Lefebvre gurgled, looking up at Garrett.

"Ambulance! Call an ambulance!" Garrett yelled.

"No. You don't understand. I'm dying."

"Jimmy—no you're not." But Garrett could see that he was. His eyes fluttered and then lost focus. His breathing rattled. Garrett could feel the life draining out of him. And just like that, Garrett knew he was dead.

Jimmy Lefebvre was dead.

Garrett's mouth went dry. He had never held a dying man before. He wanted to bring Jimmy back to life; he felt it should be possible, and yet . . . he knew it was not. He struggled to breathe.

"You next," a voice growled.

Garrett looked up, stunned. Agent Stoddard was standing over him, his pistol trained on Garrett's head, five feet away.

Garrett shook his head, the energy drained out of him, his eyes dripping tears from the gas and the shock. "You wanna shoot me? Go ahead, do it. But you're being filmed. Every second of this is being uploaded to a website."

Agent Stoddard blinked in surprise. He swiveled his head, looking from wall to wall, from corner to corner. The gun wavered in his hand.

"Webcams," Garrett said. "In every room. Every corner. So go ahead. Shoot me, Agent Stoddard. Pull the fucking trigger. But just know that the world is watching."

Stoddard gritted his teeth. Every eye in the room was on him. His hands began to shake. And then a voice cracked the silence.

"Garrett!" Mitty pushed free of the commando restraining her. "The Shanghai webcam!"

She pointed to a monitor hung on the far wall. Through the smoke, in grainy stop-motion video, a great mass of humanity was visible, marching, in step, down Nanjing Road in central Shanghai. The transmission was splotchy, but there were clearly thousands—if not tens of thousands—of people, walking together, arms swaying in unison, mouths open, yelling something, maybe singing, filling the entire width of the street, and trailing off into the distance. And they kept coming. More and more joining in the march, filing in from side streets and stepping off the buses and out of office buildings. It seemed like there was a limitless supply of people. An infinite multitude. And maybe there was.

Garrett held Lefebvre tightly in his arms and whispered, as much to Lefebvre's still body as to everybody else.

"It's happening," he said. "We did it."

102

BEIJING, APRIL 21, 2:15 PM

Half a world away, the general secretary of the Chinese Communist Party watched the same crowds, in a cramped technical observation room, from closed-circuit surveillance feeds, and he watched them with the same stunned expression as Garrett.

"How many people?" the general secretary asked.

"We cannot be sure yet, sir," the computer programmer said, toggling the view on the monitor from one Shanghai street to another. In every shot, from every angle, the crowds just kept growing larger. They seemed impossibly large, as if all of rural China had emptied out into one city, for one day. "They do not seem to be done arriving."

"Millions," the general secretary said.

"Where are they going?" asked the chairman of the Central Military Commission. "Do we know that, at least?"

The general secretary's face went from tense to relaxed, as if struck by divine revelation. A hint of a smile crept onto his lips. "They are going where they are going."

The general secretary wiped his glasses clean, his old habit, then replaced them on the bridge of his nose and turned to the chairman of the Central Military Commission. "Call back our forces. We need every available patriot on the streets."

"But the Americans?"

"We cannot fight the Americans and our own people at the same time. We have been defeated. Now we must retreat."

103

USS *DECATUR*, SOUTH CHINA SEA, APRIL 21, 2:42 PM

Ensign Hallowell white-knuckle-gripped the arms of his swivel chair. His entire body was tense in anticipation of the launch of the first Chinese missiles. The People's Navy frigates were forty kilometers due west of the *Decatur*. A ship-to-ship weapon fired at that distance would splash the *Decatur* in thirty seconds. The radar operators called it the Blink Zone. Blink and you were dead.

Hallowell's eyes followed the green blips of the Chinese warships, as well as the swift streaks of the J-15 Shenyang fighter jets that were tracing long, looping circles just beyond the frigates. It was a full complement of Chinese naval and air power, and they seemed a hairsbreadth away from pulling the trigger.

The radar room XO craned his head over Hallowell's shoulder, staring down at the ensign's screen.

What were the Chinese waiting for? Hallowell thought. For us to shoot first?

Hallowell knew that his side might do just that. They had two squadrons of F-18 Hornets tracking the Chinese jets. All the antiship missiles on board the *Decatur* were locked on to their Chinese counterparts. The fire-control officers sitting on either side of Hallowell had their fingers hovering over their launch buttons.

At the first sign of a Chinese strike, they would counterlaunch. And then it was every ship and plane for itself. It would be a bloodbath.

Ensign Hallowell's heart thudded loudly in his chest, distorting the sharp beep of the radar ping in his headphones. They had trained him to move beyond his own anxiety at the navigation/radar school, but it wasn't easy. Fear was pulsing through his veins.

"Thirty-five kilometers," he said out loud, even though he knew every other operator in the room had the Chinese on screen now. Everyone was watching. Everyone was listening. "Missile impact would be twenty-five seconds."

Hallowell thought he heard a collective intake of breath, but then realized it was his own gasping. A voice crackled through the shipboard intercom. It was the captain: "Launch missiles on my mark. Five . . ."

Hallowell narrowed his eyes, as if expecting a punch, tightening the muscles in his entire body.

"Four, three . . ."

And then Hallowell saw it. The faintest trace of a course correction in the lead Chinese frigate. Were they peeling off?

"Two . . ."

The radar chirp line swept another circle around Hallowell's screen. Yes, the lead frigate was definitely veering off.

Hallowell barked: "They're bleeding off! Enemy targets changing course!"

"One . . . Mark . . . Fire."

The radar room XO yelled: "Hold fire! Repeat. *Do not fire!*"

The XO ducked his head to look at Hallowell's screen. The two fire-control operators on either side of him leaned in to watch as well. All four Chinese frigates were coming about now, steaming north, parallel to the American fleet. The lead frigate was even beginning to turn farther, heading back west toward mainland China.

"He's going home," Hallowell whispered. And then, louder: "They're going home!"

The radar room let out a spontaneous cheer as the captain barked over the intercom: "XO, where are those missiles?"

The radar room XO grabbed the intercom as Hallowell and his fellow radar operators slapped each other high fives. Hallowell let out a laugh. There would be no war. Not yet, at least. Not here. And not now. He might make it back to Dallas after all.

EPILOGUE

ALEXANDRIA, VIRGINIA, APRIL 23, 3:39 PM

Garrett listened to the footsteps. He'd been listening to them for the last two days. They had been from guards, mostly, with food trays, a slow, uncaring shuffle. Then came the occasional observer, hesitant, watching, footsteps that came, stopped, started again. A doctor had walked in once to take his blood pressure and check his eyes: his footsteps were those of someone who had been lost, passing his cell, then coming back. Then the damn guards again, with another tray of food. The slop that passed for meals at the Virginia federal detention center had been awful, but Garrett didn't care.

He couldn't move his thoughts off of Jimmy Lefebvre's dying face. The blood that had soaked his hands. That last strangled breath.

He had died saving Garrett's life, intentionally putting himself in the way of Stoddard's bullet. But for Lefebvre, Garrett would be dead now. It was an astonishing thought, and it haunted Garrett, a life-for-life trade that could never be undone.

It weighed him down with grief. And confusion.

Why had Lefebvre done it? In that split second of decision-making, as the trigger was pulled, what had he been thinking? Garrett could only guess, and guess he had, constantly for the past forty-eight hours. Had Lefebvre wanted to see combat so badly, and wanted it for so long, that he had jumped at the chance for self-sacrifice? Was it simply instinct, the desire to save lives? Or had he decided that the world needed Garrett alive more than it needed Jimmy Lefebvre?

That last thought terrified Garrett; if it were true, that was a responsibility he would not be able to bear—not if he hoped to keep his sanity.

The problem was that he had little else to think about. He'd been cut off from all news since he'd been arrested; the data flow that he had been immersed in for the last few days was gone, completely and totally. He had gone from digital master of the universe to shut-in. For all he knew, World War Three was raging just outside the detention-center walls.

Garrett didn't think so, though.

Maybe it was the demeanor of the guards, their relaxed shuffle, the detached look in their eyes as they scanned his cell for signs of disturbance or suicide attempts. They didn't seem like people worried about the coming apocalypse. Or maybe he was simply projecting his hopes onto the last bit of news he'd received: a million people flooding Shanghai, putting the fear of God into the Chinese Communist Party.

But maybe he was wrong. Maybe the world *was* burning up.

The steps he heard now were different. They were fast, clipped, direct. They stopped in front of his door with a purpose. Garrett looked up from his single bunk. The door swung open.

Homeland Security Agent Cannel stood there, his face angular and drawn, the corners of his lips turned down slightly, as if he had a bad taste in his mouth. He held an electronic clipboard in his arms. Behind Cannel were two detention-center guards in full uniform.

"Reilly, Garrett?" Agent Cannel asked.

"You're kidding me, right?" Garrett said, laughing dryly.

"Reilly, Garrett?" Cannel asked again, in exactly the same tone of voice—flat, lifeless, fighting to withhold all emotion.

"Yeah, that's me," Garrett said, already tired of the joke. "Reilly, Garrett."

"You are being released from federal custody. All charges against you have been dropped, by order of the U.S. Attorney's office, District of Columbia. You can pick up your belongings from the watch supervisor on the main floor. You will be given twenty-two dollars for transportation from this facility to your home or temporary place of residence."

Garrett let out a surprised grunt. Agent Cannel shoved the electronic clipboard at Garrett. "By signing here, and here, you will be allowed to collect all personal items taken from you at the initiation of your custody. By signing here you release the government from any and all compensation for your time spent in this detention center. Read and sign."

Garrett scanned the clipboard, giving the dense paragraphs of legalese a cursory glance, then signed in all three places. Cannel snatched back the clipboard and walked out of the cell. He waited in the hallway.

Garrett took his time gathering himself, his mind racing to sort through what was going on. And then he realized. He walked into the hallway as Agent Cannel strode ahead of him, leading the way. The two detention-center guards trailed behind them.

"They made you do it, didn't they?" Garrett said to Cannel's back. "They made you release me yourself. As punishment. To humiliate you. And it pisses you off beyond all belief."

Garrett could see the agent's shoulders twitch beneath his suit.

"But you've got it easy, don't you?" Garrett continued as they passed through a set of electronic doors. "Your partner, Stoddard, he's totally fucked. He's sitting in a federal jail, just like this one. Facing murder charges." Garrett smiled, but he knew no one was watching. "I wonder if he's getting ass-raped right now."

Cannel stopped abruptly and spun around to face Garrett. He stuck his face up next to Garrett's, and Garrett could smell the tobacco on his breath.

"This is not over, fuckface. Not by a long way. You step wrong, just once, and I'll take down your whole goddamn family."

Garrett waited until the last of Cannel's rage seemed to have been expelled, then said, "Actually, it is over for me. Completely, totally over."

Garrett said these words without bitterness. They were simply fact. He was done with the government, with secrets, with the Ascendant project. For good.

Cannel wheeled around and stomped off down the hall, no longer interested in keeping up a façade of bureaucratic reserve. Garrett signed for his belongings and the $22 in cash with the watch supervisor on the main floor, then stepped out of the William G. Truesdale Adult Detention Center and into a sunny Alexandria afternoon. He let the warm Virginia sunshine wash over him; the Capital Beltway was humming above him, lousy with cars. He crossed the street and read the thirty-six-point headline of the *Washington Post* in a newspaper box:

Massive Protests Continue Across China
Rioters Clash with Police in Beijing
Most Coastal Cities Under Curfew

The body of the story was hidden beneath the fold, and he had no change to buy the paper. The paper box didn't accept dollar bills. It didn't matter; there was nothing Garrett could do about it anyway. He was officially powerless, one man without even an Internet connection. And he was sick and tired. Of everything. He needed a rest. He needed his own bed in New York City.

He started walking north, to find a bus, to get him there.

The first week back went by in a haze. Mostly, Garrett slept: in his own bed, in movie theaters, sometimes in the park, in the sun, by himself, on a bench. His exhaustion was bone deep, but he healed considerably in that time. The headaches still came daily, but their severity lessened, as did their duration. The neurologist at Roosevelt Hospital said they might never go away entirely, but the downward trend was encouraging. He also told Garrett to stop doing whatever the hell he'd been doing to himself since his original skull fracture. "Because whatever it is, eventually it'll kill you."

Garrett thanked him for the advice and said he'd try his best to comply.

He checked his e-mail every once in a while, but didn't go to news websites; he kept away from newspapers and the TV. He knew the protests were continuing in China, because everyone, everywhere was talking about it: on the subway, in stores, restaurants. It was news you simply couldn't avoid.

Garrett tried not to think about it. He waited for word from Celeste Chen, but it never came. He tried calling her, but the number was no longer in service, and his e-mails bounced back. One of the pieces of news he'd picked up was that the government had regained control of the Golden Shield, and they were clamping down hard, shutting off all incoming and outgoing e-mails. All social media in the country had been banned. Garrett wondered if he would ever see Celeste Chen again. He hoped that he hadn't sent her to prison. Or worse. He lay awake at night fretting about her.

At the end of the week he called Jenkins & Altshuler to ask Avery for his old job back, only to have his call transferred to an on-staff psychologist. A throaty-sounding woman carefully sussed out Garrett's relationship to Avery, and then informed him, with well-practiced compassion, that Avery was dead. He had died in a tragic auto accident two weeks earlier.

Garrett practically fell out of his chair.

"What happened to him?"

"He was hit by a car. As he was walking home from work."

Garrett's mind reeled. "Did they catch who did it?"

"Not yet. The police have a number of leads. They're saying it is a very active investigation."

Garrett thanked her and hung up. He spent the rest of the day staring at the wall, unbelieving. When he got up the next morning he searched the Web for obituaries and found a few dozen. There was a large one in the *New York Times*, calling Avery a much-loved Yale mathematics professor, financial entrepreneur, and presidential advisor. They called his death an unsolved tragedy. The *Daily News* ran a gory crime piece, full of details of Avery's last moments, the rush to the hospital, the frantic search for the driver. And then a follow-up a few days later saying the crime remained unsolved.

And then nothing else.

It was as if Avery had never lived. Nobody seemed to care. Garrett called the Sixth Police Precinct five separate times. Each time, the watch commander transferred him to a detective on the case, and each time Garrett was sent to voice mail. Garrett left messages, but the detective never called back. Garrett even went to the scene of the accident, a block from the Jenkins & Altshuler offices, but there was no marker on the street, no flowers resting on the curb; nothing to remember Avery or what had happened to him.

As he stood at the scene, a wrenching thought occurred to Garrett through his grief: Who would watch over him now that Avery was gone?

No one. He was alone.

Fifteen minutes later, Garrett found himself standing in the lobby of Jenkins & Altshuler. He hadn't even realized he'd walked there. He decided to visit his offices, and the moment he showed up on the twenty-second floor he was surrounded by his old coworkers. They asked where he'd been, how he was feeling, what he was going to do now. Garrett deflected most of the questions, and no one seemed to have any inkling of what he had been doing during the last two months. Everyone expressed their condolences about Avery; they knew he and Garrett had been close.

Then a manager came down from the twenty-third floor and offered Garrett his old job back. The manager—her name was Thomason—said they needed Garrett's quant skills on the bond-trading desk. The firm had been on a losing streak since he left, and could he start the next day.

Garrett came in early the following morning, but in his first hour back at

Jenkins & Altshuler he knew it was no longer his white-hot, burning center of the universe. It was just a place to make money. The pointlessness was palpable to him, as if he'd taken off blinders and could see the bond-trading room for what it truly was—a collection of entitled boys shouting into their phones. The day left him restless and agitated, and after the exchanges closed down he went for a walk along the river, crushing empty soda cans with his shoes, then kicking them into the darkness. The sun had long ago set, and the Hudson seemed thick and slow-moving in the night air. He felt empty.

He called Mitty and they met for a beer in the back of McSorley's later that night. They rehashed all that had happened; how she had been briefly detained, and then, like Garrett, released without further comment; how she had searched for notice of Jimmy Lefebvre's funeral, but there was no mention of one anywhere. She gossiped about Bingo and Patmore: they'd been jailed too, and then released. Patmore had disappeared back into the Corps.

"And Bingo, we spoke once, but then he never called me back," Mitty growled between shots of Jack Daniels. "After what happened. What a little bitch."

Garrett gave her a curious look. "*After what happened?* What did happen?"

Mitty made a rasping sound, halfway between a grunt and a spit. "Maah, nothing special. I hate him."

Garrett thought he saw genuine hurt in her eyes, so he let the subject drop. Later, Mitty tried to egg Garrett into a fight with a drunken derivatives trader, but Garrett wasn't interested—he was taking the doctor's warning seriously—so Mitty got to call him a pussy.

He didn't mind. It actually cheered him up.

He couldn't sleep that night. He obsessed about Avery, and how he had died—his final moments, if he'd seen it coming, was it murder? It seemed too convenient to have been an accident, especially given the bombing a block away the month before. The later he stayed up, and the longer he thought about it, the more he was convinced that the mysterious Hans Metternich was connected to both events. Garrett knew nothing about Metternich, and the only person in his life who did was gone. He typed out an e-mail to the warbyothermeans address. *Where are you? What happened to Avery?* He encrypted it, sent it, then stayed up two more hours , waiting for a reply, but none came.

The next morning, walking to work, Garrett thought he glimpsed someone following him: a middle-aged man, wrapped in a navy pea coat, half a block behind him. When Garrett turned to face him, the man reversed course and walked down a side street. Garrett ran after him, but by the time he reached the side street the man was gone. Garrett felt, instinctively, that it had been Metternich—the timing made sense—but he had no proof. Garrett had never even seen Metternich's face.

When he returned home from work that evening there was a package sitting on his kitchen table. The package was wrapped in a brown paper grocery bag. "FOR GARRETT" was written in neat black Magic Marker on the front.

Garrett's blood froze. His door had been locked, and no one else—not even the building manager—had the key to his apartment. He circled the bag without touching it, then checked the windows, which were also locked, and the other rooms and closets, which were empty. He knocked on his neighbors' doors, but they hadn't seen or heard anything. He returned to his kitchen with his heart pounding and willed himself to open the package.

Inside was a paperback book: *On War* by Carl von Clausewitz. Slotted between the pages was a drugstore condolence card, with a pair of sad-eyed bears hugging each other on the cover, and "Deepest Sympathy" printed inside. The card had been placed at the first page of book one, chapter III. The chapter heading read: "The Genius For War."

Garrett scanned the first two sentences: *"EVERY special calling in life, if it is to be followed with success, requires peculiar qualifications of understanding and soul. Where these are of a high order, and manifest themselves by extraordinary achievements, the mind to which they belong is termed GENIUS."*

He tore the chapter out of the book, ripped the card into pieces, then threw the whole thing in the trash. He paced his apartment, enraged, jamming a baseball bat in the window by the fire escape, and a chair against the front door. He locked himself in the bathroom and tried to calm his breathing. His head throbbed. He thought about calling the police, but he knew that would be a dead end. What could he possibly tell them? That someone had given him a book and that it spooked him? At that moment it became clear to Garrett that he was boxed in. He was trapped in this new life, whether he wanted to be or not. He pounded the tiled wall in frustration. He vowed that one day, when he had his strength back, he would track Metternich down. Garrett didn't care how dangerous or all-knowing he was, or that he could seemingly break into Garrett's apartment at will. If Metternich turned out to be responsible for Avery's death, Garrett would kill him. Without hesitation.

• • •

Three weeks and a day after he had been released from federal detention, Garrett was again at the Greek diner on Tenth and Avenue C, sipping coffee at one in the morning, picking at a plate of scrambled eggs, when Alexis Truffant walked into the restaurant in her full Army service blues and sat down opposite him at his table. Her hair was pulled back in a tight ponytail; she wore a touch of makeup and light-red lipstick. Garrett smelled a whiff of perfume.

He was surprised at how natural it seemed for Alexis to simply show up in his life unannounced and take a seat at his table. It couldn't have been more normal.

"Hello, Garrett," she said.

"Long time no see."

"How's your head?" A waitress poured her a coffee.

"Better. Not perfect."

"I'm sorry about Avery Bernstein."

Garrett nodded. "Yeah. Thanks."

"He was hit by a car?"

Garrett studied her face. "Hit-and-run driver. That's what they say. But you don't believe that, do you?"

Alexis glanced around the diner. The place was mostly empty.

"I don't know," she said. "Maybe I do believe it."

They sat in silence for a while.

"They arrested me as well," she said.

"Why?"

"Because I wouldn't lead them to you."

Garrett thought about that. "I owe you thanks, then."

"No," she said, shaking her head. "You don't."

"They let you go."

"After they dropped the charges against you it didn't make much sense to keep me in confinement."

He gazed at her stripes. "And then they made you a colonel for it?"

She nodded. "Lieutenant colonel. It's all hands on deck at the DIA now. People are predicting a civil war in China. So all is forgiven." She seemed to think about this for a moment, then added, "Or maybe they did it to keep me quiet."

"About me?"

"About everything."

Garrett pushed away his plate of eggs, then stared at her eyes, her hair, her lips; he remembered how they felt against his. "What are you doing here, Alexis?"

She pulled an envelope from her jacket and slid it across the table. "Your salary. For one month's work. Plus a first set of disability payments. For the skull fracture. It got reclassified as a work-related injury."

Garrett opened the envelope. There were two checks inside, both made out to him. One was for $4,840.35. It already had taxes taken out of it. The other was for $370. It was from the Social Security Administration.

Garrett smiled. "Finally, I can retire."

"No one ever said serving your country was lucrative."

"Is that what I did? Serve my country?"

Alexis drew herself up, sitting ever so slightly more erect in her chair. She gave the faintest nod of her head. "Yes. That's exactly what you did. And you did it honorably. With distinction. You should be proud."

Garrett didn't know what to say. He certainly wasn't proud. He folded up the checks and slipped them into his pocket. "That's it? You came to give me my money?"

"Do you like being back at work, Garrett?"

"I'm easing into it."

"But you're awake at one in the morning, drinking coffee in a diner."

Garrett shrugged. "I've had trouble sleeping."

She leaned forward, elbows resting on the tabletop. "People know what you did. People who matter. They were impressed. Blown away, actually. And they are going to want you to do it again."

This time Garrett let out a loud laugh. "They can go fuck themselves."

"The standard Garrett Reilly response."

"Yeah, well, some things never change," he said.

"I think you changed. A lot. And I'm guessing you don't fit back into your old life anymore. Shuffling money around. Buy and sell orders. Doesn't it all kind of pale in comparison? To saving the world?"

Garrett said nothing. He toyed with his fork, moving it back and forth on the paper table liner.

"Ascendant still exists. Dormant, but waiting for you."

Garrett tensed. He could feel the old anger welling up inside of him, the rage that so often consumed him.

"They arrested me twice. They tortured me, put me in isolation. They shot and killed one of our team. *Our team*, Lieutenant Colonel Truffant. And who knows what they did to Avery."

Alexis lowered her voice to a whisper. "It's war, Garrett. In war people die."

"You're not supposed to kill the people on your own side."

"The guilty will be punished."

Garrett frowned. He shook his head from side to side. "Not the guilty at the very top. Not them. They're never punished."

"You're right," she said. "Life's not fair."

Alexis turned her palms upward, as if to say, What can any of us do about it? Garrett felt his rage subside. He realized he had needed to tell Alexis those things; they had been festering in him, and she was the only person with whom he could find relief.

"I know you may not want to hear this, but you saw the war before anyone else did. You studied it, then you fought it. And you brought it to a close. Against all odds. You saved lives. Many, many lives. What you did was astonishing." She fixed her eyes on his. "The president wants you back. He asked for you himself."

Garrett looked away, taking in her words. Then he pulled out his wallet and dropped a twenty on the table. "I think about you all the time," he said, fingering the worn leather of his wallet. "I think about us."

"And?" she asked.

Garrett smiled at her. It made him feel open and vulnerable, that smile, accepting of his true nature, as if the very act of it had expanded his heart and allowed him to say what he'd meant to say for a while now.

"*And?*" he said, grinning stupidly at her. "And I still love you."

Silence enveloped the table. Garrett thought he saw Alexis's cheeks color slightly. She opened her mouth to respond, but no words came. After a few more moments, Garrett pushed back from the table and stood up. "It's okay," he said. "You don't have to say anything."

He pulled a zip-up sweatshirt around his shoulders. "It was nice seeing you, Alexis. Really nice." He started toward the door.

He was halfway to the exit when Alexis called after him. "They will ask for you. In the night, when the next crisis hits. And that crisis is right around the corner. Think about your answer, Garrett. I hope you make the right choice."

Garrett cocked his head slightly to one side, nodded wearily, and walked out into the warm New York night.

ACKNOWLEDGMENTS

I could not have written this book without the expert advice of the following people. My thanks to: Danny Goodwin, for his knowledge of stocks, flash crashes, and black pools of money; Nathan Wright, for helping with military jargon and attitudes; Carrie Pederson, for her brilliance on all things China; Stanley Florek, for explaining message encryption; E. J. Gong, for laying out LLCs and real estate speculation; Peter Loop, for demystifying data centers; John Krause, for updates on Internet security and the power grid; Ting Wang and Matthew Van Osdol, for making sure the Mandarin was up to snuff; Marsi Doran, for unraveling the intricacies of bond trading; and Jack Timmons, for his computer programming genius and rabid enthusiasm.

Also invaluable in the process were Markus Hoffmann at Regal Literary in New York, and my team in LA—Matt Leipzig and Jordan Bayer at Original Artists, Dan Brecher at Rothman Brecher, and my manager, Ragna Nervik.

On the publishing side, a special thanks to Emily Graff and to the insightful Rowland White at Penguin UK. And finally, my heartfelt gratitude to my editor at Simon & Schuster, the incomparable Marysue Rucci.

ABOUT THE AUTHOR

Drew Chapman has written on numerous studio movies. He also directed the indie film *Standoff*. Currently, he creates and writes TV shows for network television, most recently having written and executive-produced an ABC miniseries about the hunt for CIA mole Aldrich Ames. Married with two children, Chapman divides his time between Los Angeles and Seattle. *The Pattern of Fear* is his first book.